KURINJI MALAR

Na. Parthasarathy was born in 1932 in a small village in Ramanathapuram district of southern Tamil Nadu. After a brilliant academic career leading to an MA in Tamil Literature from the University of Madras, his first job was as a teacher of Tamil in Sethupathy High School in Madurai. This was the same school where the celebrated poet Subramania Bharati had once taught. Parthasarathy, a prolific writer, then moved into the area of magazine editing. He was Assistant Editor at *Kalki* before taking up the reins of chief editorship of the respected Tamil monthly *Deepam*, and later of *Dinamani Kathir* of the Indian Express group of publications.

His style of writing, meshing the literary with the popular, won him a large reader base and multiple awards. He was honoured with the Sahitya Akademi Award for his novel *Samudhaya Veedhi*. Many of his works have been translated into English and several Indian regional languages. He passed away in 1987 with his autobiography still incomplete. At the time, his Ph.D thesis submitted to the University of Madras was still under evaluation but was later adjudged to be 'brilliant'.

Malini Seshadri is a freelance writer, editor and translator. She has co-authored the textbook series *Living in Harmony* (2004) for schools, as well as *Reading and Reality* and *A Window to Your World* for undergraduate courses. Her translations from Tamil to English include *Vanmam* and *Just One Word* by Bama and contributions to short story anthologies: *The Oxford India Anthology of Tamil Dalit Writing* (2012), *Katha Vilasam* (2022), *In Defiance* (2022), and *The Greatest Tamil Stories Ever Told* (2021).

MISSION STATEMENT

This is an initiative of the Tamil Nadu Textbook and Educational Services Corporation (TNTB & ESC) under the aegis of one of the announcements for the year 2023–24 by the Honourable Minister for School Education Thiru Anbil Mahesh Poyyamozhi, titled the Translation of Rare and Nationalized Literary Tamil Works into English. These ventures are to be undertaken as either independent or joint publications with collaborating English language publishers.

Members, Academic Advisory Committee (Translation)

1. Dr. R. Balakrishnan, IAS, Researcher and Writer
2. Thiru. S. Ramakrishnan, Writer
3. Thiru. S. Madasamy, Educationist

Project Execution Team

1. Thiru. Dindigul I. Leoni, Chairperson, TNTB & ESC
2. Dr. P. Sankar, IAS, Managing Director, TNTB & ESC
3. Dr. M. Kuppusamy, Member Secretary, TNTB & ESC
4. Dr. T.S. Saravanan, Joint Director (Translations), TNTB & ESC
5. Dr. P. Saravanan, Assistant Director (Publications), TNTB & ESC
6. Thiru. M. Appanasamy, Consultant, TNTB & ESC
7. Tmt. Mini Krishnan, Co-ordinating Editor, TNTB & ESC

The publisher has no objection to this English translation being used to facilitate transfers into other languages.

KURINJI MALAR

NA. PARTHASARATHY

TRANSLATED BY
MALINI SESHADRI

First published in Tamil in 1960 by Tamil Puthakalayam

This translation first published in India in 2024 by Hachette India
(Registered name: Hachette Book Publishing India Pvt. Ltd)
An Hachette UK company
www.hachetteindia.com

1

Paperback ISBN 978-93-5731-568-5
Hardback ISBN 978-93-5731-486-2
eBook ISBN 978-93-5731-547-0

Hachette Book Publishing India Pvt. Ltd
4th & 5th Floors, Corporate Centre,
Plot No. 94, Sector 44, Gurugram 122003, India

Typeset in Dante MT Std 11/14
by R. Ajith Kumar, New Delhi

Printed and bound in India
by Manipal Technologies Limited

CONTENTS

TRANSLATOR'S NOTE

The *kurinji* flower blooms only once in twelve years, covering the hills of the Western Ghats in a carpet of violet-blue splendour. Na. Parthasarathy's novel with that eponymous title is forever in bloom, his protagonists as rare and unforgettable as this mountain flower.

It has been a privilege to bring this celebrated novel to the English-reading public. A privilege, but also a challenge in equal measure! For instance, the author's style is expansive, poetic, sometimes verging on the florid. It was a tightrope walk to retain the essence of these attributes while presenting this period novel to contemporary English-language readers, accustomed to a rather more terse and less stately style.

The book also features excerpts from ancient Tamil poetic texts that act as curtain-raisers for each chapter. I have attempted, with some help along the way, to blend poetry, substance and, hopefully, some echoes from centuries long past, in translating the 'teaser' verses. In this task, I received valuable guidance from Sujatha Vijayaraghavan, well-known writer and music scholar.

In the mid-twentieth century, several successful and popular novels by various writers were serialized in Tamil magazines. This story too originally appeared as weekly chapters in the Tamil magazine *Kalki*, and was a sensational success. A story written as a serial in a magazine tends to evolve as it unfolds, generally enjoying the luxury of lingering over descriptions of people and events. It is much like a bicycle ride through the countryside with plenty of stopovers to smell the flowers, rather than a quick motoring along a highway.

My approach, therefore, was to read it in instalments as the original readers would have done, and to translate as I went along, so as to relive the original reader's experience to the extent possible. This plan has worked for me even with novels that were not serialized. Here, I think it has worked even better. I believe it has helped to retain the immediacy, the here-and-now, of each week's offering. In this novel, for instance, we get to read the diary of the protagonist, Aravindan, and listen in on the soliloquies of the other main character, Poorani. We go into the homes of the dramatis personae, live their lives and dream their dreams.

The novel is set in the middle of the previous century, not very long after Independence, in and around Madurai, an ancient town in the southern Tamil land. The society was largely patriarchal, with girls being groomed from early life to become homemakers and mothers. Scholars and academics were highly respected, though often poor. Patriotism for the Tamil land took the form of championing the Tamil language and working for the upliftment of the poor.

Poorani, the eldest child of a doting scholar-professor-author, has grown up among books and uplifting discussions with her father. She is ahead of her times in her aspirations and goals; at the same time she is very much a creature of the ambient norms of society. Aravindan has had a difficult childhood and is a self-taught savant who writes poetry and champions non-violence. They are both conflicted because of the disconnect between their dreams and the harsh realities.

The tone of the novel is idealistic, and its protagonists, Poorani and Aravindan, are almost other-worldly in their commitment to the betterment of society; and yet they walk on this earth and feel life's pains and pleasures. The other characters are also well fleshed out and relatable.

I hope this translation has managed to convey the tones of love and loss, righteousness and deceit, loyalty and greed, that are the hallmarks of the plot of the story. I also hope that the characters that the author has created and animated on the pages of his novel live on in the pages of this translation.

I am grateful to the Tamil Nadu Textbook and Education Services Corporation (TNTB & ESC) for having given me this challenging but joyful opportunity. I am also very thankful to Meera Parthasarathy, the author's daughter, who read the drafts with great care and offered inputs.

As the author says: Long live Poorani and Aravindan!

Malini Seshadri

INTRODUCTION

Among all the days in my life that mark the beginning of important undertakings, the day I plunged into the writing of *Kurinji Malar* holds a very special place. The period in my life during which the idea for this novel sprouted and grew was a golden period for my inner self. I am a writer who wants every one of his works to send out a loud and clear message – 'This story was born out of the Tamil soil; it propagates Tamil tradition and culture; it celebrates the sweet essence of the Tamil language.' Accordingly, in each of my stories, I want to stress the greatness of this language, this land, its history and its rich culture. One could even say, this wish of mine is the hallmark of my writing.

I am one of those who earnestly believe that this Tamil land of ours, steeped in a glorious tradition, marked by its rich culture and language, should be strengthened by literature that raises the awareness of the people. I take pride in writing for this noble cause.

Many Tamil writers choose to set their stories only in Chennai or neighbouring areas. As a result of this trend, the incredible variety of shades and patterns in the lifestyles of the people in the South remain unnoticed. Keeping this in mind, I selected Madurai and the neighbouring regions of the South as the focal point of my novel *Kurinji Malar*. I wanted it to be a novel steeped in the Tamil essence, the special Tamil aroma, from the first page to the last. I believe that I have succeeded in achieving that goal.

When I started writing this novel as a serial in the weekly Tamil magazine *Kalki*, I wrote under the pen name 'Manivannan'. I thought, 'Whatever the name in which it is done, a good deed is always a good deed.' Yes, I considered this a 'good deed' that I was doing. My readers decided it was a 'very, very good deed' indeed! They were filled with enthusiasm and eager anticipation.

The *marikkozhundu* (marjoram) plant is aromatic right from its root to the very tip of each leaf. Whichever part of it you pinch and smell, it is scented. I wrote this novel intending to make every part of it resound with the message that honesty and righteousness are essential hallmarks of an ethical society. Readers confirmed that my writing achieved this. 'I have done a valuable service,' I told myself in satisfaction. I also wanted to remind readers that the young boys and girls of today, in schools and colleges, are the seedlings that will grow to be the new crop of Tamil people. In this task too, I have been successful, judging from the feedback I received from readers.

The marriage of Thilakavathy (the elder sister of Thirunavukkarasar, a celebrated sage of the Saiva sect) with Kalippagaiyar was never consummated. If one keeps in mind Thilakavathy's story or those of similar couples, one can understand some aspects of my story better and appreciate the resonances of history within them.

In this story, I have presented Poorani and Aravindan as attractive characters. They are exemplars of ideal Tamil womanhood and manhood. Here and there, I have also touched upon the government's impact on the lives of the common people. By the time the story ended, many readers wrote to the author 'Manivannan' to seek his blessings for their sons, whom they had named 'Aravindan', or their daughters, whom they had named 'Poorani'. It was clear that the readers had developed a deep affinity with the story and its characters.

In order to spread awareness of Tamil literary heritage, I appended a verse ahead of every chapter as it was being serialized. Some of these were my own creations, and it gave me immense satisfaction to know that the readers had welcomed and appreciated these embellishments to the novel.

I planned the novel such that it started in the Kurinji land of Thirupparankundram and ended in the *kurinji* fields of Kodaikanal. In the novel, the first time the *kurinji* is in bloom, the mind of the heroine, Poorani, blossoms through her dialogues with Aravindan. On the other hand, the second time she visits the hill in the *kurinji* season, it is the end of the story. She is alone and grieving. In this novel, Poorani is a rare flower among women. She is like the *kurinji* flower that blooms in high places. Death cannot touch her. Poorani will live forever.

It is the author Manivannan's earnest prayer that every young Tamil man should be an Aravindan, with simple tastes and high thinking, wedded to the principle of service to society. and that many *kurinji* flowers like Poorani should blossom among the women of this Tamil land.

Within a few days after the novel was completed, my first daughter was born. She is a ray of sunshine in my home. I dedicate this story in book form to my daughter, whom I see as an incarnation of Poorani.

Na. Parthasarathy

CHAPTER 1

That which was true, in the fullness of time, emerged as
Falsehood, myth, mere imagination.

– Mella Ponadhuve

Another new day. Nature is blossoming anew. The Margazhi season is at the door, peeping in, waiting to enter. The world is a bower of roses, petals glistening with fresh dew, bathing the air in a cool aroma. In harmony with the cool fragrance of blossoms wafts the warm smell of damp earth, as though woven into the same tapestry. It is the cusp of daybreak. The night has ended, and the day is awaited. On the eastern horizon, dawn has not yet applied the turmeric paste for her morning bath…

Poorani stirred, rubbed her eyes and sat up in bed. Through the window of her room, the *kolam* at the entrance of the house across the street appeared pale at that early hour. It was a large white one, embellished with pumpkin flowers here and there. Against the white of the *kolam* design, the flowers glowed like burnished gold, freshly melted and poured out from the furnace. As Poorani gazed at that *kolam*, painful memories assailed her senses. Her heart felt heavy. Her eyes turned moist with unshed tears.

A whole year would have to go by before she could draw a *kolam* like that outside her front door. It was not as though she couldn't get pumpkin flowers. There were cartloads of them in her own backyard. But who would pluck them? And where would they be placed? (This was a land that had regulated even the acceptable rituals of grief and laid down rules for the observance of associated dos and don'ts. The banyan tree that is Tamil life and culture continued to be propped up by these aerial roots of ancient and outmoded traditions.)

Poorani dried her eyes, got out of bed and turned on the light. 'If Appa were still alive, would the house be dark and silent at this hour?' she thought. 'He would have been up at four thirty for his early morning cold water bath followed by recitations of *Thiruvachagam* and *Thiruvembavai*. Every Margazhi morning the house would be redolent with the swirling smoke from the burning incense powder. Appa's *sloka* recitations and the sheer beauty of the Tamil language would add to the fragrance.'

Where now are those fragrant Tamil words that came off his tongue? Where is that towering mountain of knowledge? The thousands of students he nurtured with love and commitment, the years of respect and renown... Alas, that mortal body has turned to dust. The tall, wide bookshelf of his... Was that the only inheritance he left to his daughter? That and inconsolable grief? No, he left behind a great responsibility, one that those young, twenty-one-year-old shoulders would have to bear.

Poorani walked over to where her younger brothers and sister were lying asleep, curled up like millipedes against the cold. They all lay on the floor, with sheets and pillows scattered all over the place. As she looked at her siblings sleeping peacefully, Poorani grew conscious of a great responsibility. She was young and unmarried, true, but she would have to be a mother to these children.

She straightened their sleeping forms, put pillows under their heads and covered them warmly. As she rose, her gaze fell upon a large picture of her father on the wall. He was smiling at her. She stood unmoving, looking at the picture. Was he looking at her, telling her something?

Her father had been a handsome man. His intellect and deep learning had enhanced his good looks. His eyes were very attractive, as though made to order for the man he was. They were eloquent eyes. Embracing everything and everyone in benevolence, they spoke of love, compassion and gentleness. His nose was proportionate, with the nostrils flared just right. His lips seemed to wear the beginnings of a smile even when he was not smiling. That face had endeared him to all his students over the years. Even later, irrespective of their high status in life, however tall the pinnacles of success they had attained, those who had once been his students took pride in recalling that they had had the good fortune to learn from Tamil professor Azhagiya Sittrambalam. That was the real measure of her father's achievements.

Poorani heaved a sigh. She turned off the light and sat on her bed in the darkness. She wanted to let her mind dwell on her father's death. She wanted to sob, weep and wail. Were not tears supposed to melt grief? Was not weeping a means to lighten the burden of loss?

She rose once more, moved towards her father's picture on the wall and stood close to it. Like a devout worshipper standing in front of a favourite deity in the sanctum sanctorum of a temple, Poorani felt goosebumps as she stood and examined her father's face. Tears blurred her vision. Once again, she was lost in her thoughts. 'Those subtle signs of ageing had started appearing on Appa's face only after Amma died. But even when Amma was dying, Appa never broke down or wept. We children refused to eat and were sobbing for three whole days. Maybe his deep learning and wide experience had built a barrier for his emotions.

'I remember how he embraced me and spoke tenderly to me as he stroked my hair. "Poorani! If you break down and sob like a little child, who will comfort your younger brothers and your baby sister? Learn to put aside your own sorrow. From now on, for these children, you are more than a big sister. You have to take on the responsibilities of a mother and raise them. I think of you as a level-headed, sensible girl. If you wallow in grief and carry on like this, what would I do? How can I bring comfort to others if you do not help me?"'

Not only did Appa rise above grief and sorrow but he also did not dwell much upon happy events or joyous moments. His life had centred around the college classrooms and his bookshelf at home. Everything else receded from his attention. Just as fruits ripen over time and are eventually shed from the tree, his intellect had banished from his mind the lesser considerations. His was a life of absolute discipline and unwavering focus.

'Appa is no more.'

That wide ocean of Tamil knowledge, that exemplar of duty, commitment and self-discipline was reduced to dust – soon to become a mere memory or myth. It was difficult for the mind to grasp the reality. It is always difficult to accept the death of loved ones. There was a poem that her father often repeated to illustrate the uncertainties of life: 'He existed, he stood, he fell. He departed, leaving his loved ones bereft.' Appa's life could be summed up similarly. He lived to teach. He stood near his bookshelf, and one day, just like that, he died, leaving his family in the depths of grief.

How easily he attained death! No fuss, no pain, no suffering, no hassles; he did not go like someone who was dying. He went like someone getting ready for a secret meeting. Poorani replayed the scene in her mind. 'That evening, when he returned from the temple, he seemed unusually tired. In a break from his normal routine, he went to bed. I was confused. "What's the matter, Appa? You seem very tired today," I asked. He answered with a smile, "It's nothing, Poorani. Just a slight pain in my chest. Bring me some hot water with crushed, dried ginger, and I will be fine."

'I went to fetch the hot water. The older of my two brothers, Thirunavukkarasu, was doing his homework in the hall. My younger brother, Sambandan, and my baby sister, Mangaiyarkarasi, were playing in the street just outside the front door. As I was crushing the ginger, Appa called out, "If Thirunavukkarasu is there, please ask him to come to me."

'Thirunavukkarasu heard Appa and ran towards the hall, "I'm coming, Appa." From the kitchen, I heard Appa asking my brother to bring the *Thiruvachagam*, sit next to him and start reading aloud. I hurried back with the hot water. Appa was clutching his chest with both hands. Pain was etched on his face. My brother was reading from the *Thiruvandam* section:

Like the fragrance in flowers His fame spreads everywhere, praise be upon Him
The resplendent Lord came to me today with compassion
Bestowed His grace upon me and removed all my future births, praise

be upon Him.

'His young voice rang sweet and clear. "Appa, you seem to be in a lot of pain," I said anxiously. "Shall I go and call the doctor?" Appa smiled weakly but did not speak. Without waiting for his permission, I hurried to get the doctor. As I re-entered the front door with the doctor, my brother's loud wailing, "Oh Appa!" fell on my ears. My last glimpse of Appa alive was that wordless smile as I had turned to leave.

'Appa was gone. He had left me alone to bear the loss, the grief and the great responsibility of caring for my siblings. The whole town mourned him. Hundreds of his admirers, his students from the past and present and colleagues from his college accompanied his funeral procession. All the local colleges declared a holiday as a sign of respect for him. Letters and telegrams are still arriving from all over the world, from his old students, his acquaintances, his admirers.'

Fifteen days since Appa died. Fifteen days had gone by in a haze. Each day brought more letters of condolences. Many visitors dropped in to offer their sympathy. All those emotions, expressions of sympathy and efforts to console wallowed in Poorani's all-encompassing ocean of grief.

The sound of the cowbell at the front door was followed by the milkman's call. Poorani wiped her tear-swollen eyes and stepped out to buy milk. As he was leaving, the milkman said, 'Amma, every morning when *Periyavar* came out to buy milk, with the sacred ash on his forehead and the verses of the *Thiruvachagam* on his lips, it was like receiving the Lord's *darshan* right here.'

His words stirred her sorrow afresh. Appa was always the

first to rise in the morning, and he was the one who brought in the milk. From the milkman to the woman who came to sweep the street outside the front door, everyone had a special affection and respect for her father. Everyone addressed him as *Periyavar*. They all referred to him only that way. She had hardly ever heard anyone address him differently. Only a couple of his fellow teachers, his intellectual peers, addressed him by name.

'In every sense, Appa was a *Periyavar*, a great man. He had won the gratitude and admiration of generations of students, not only because he was such a fine teacher but also because he helped needy students with his own money. Although he was generous with financial help to others, his self-respect would not let him accept help from others. His right hand would often reach out to give but never seek to receive. His mind was incapable of low thoughts. Never by word or deed had Appa ever crossed the boundaries that he had set for himself.

'On one occasion, a few learned Tamil scholars asked Appa for suggestions about starting a movement to prevent the incorrect usage of spoken and written Tamil. Appa told them with a smile, "Why talk only about how the language is spoken and written – from Vengadam in the north to Kanyakumari in the south, if the people of this whole Tamil land could live their lives correctly, ethically, with discipline, how wonderful it would be." I remember how calmly he spoke those words of wisdom, and I remember the goosebumps they gave me. Honour, duty, discipline were Appa's watchwords all his life.'

It was now broad daylight. Discordant noises rose from the street, like an ill-tuned radio set, intruding into Poorani's thoughts. Like the low voice of conscience that speaks from the depths of the human heart, drumbeats echoed faintly from the temple in the distance. Poorani stood and walked towards the well in the backyard to take her bath.

From the highway close by, the busy traffic to and from Thirupparankundram and Thirunagar added its share of noise. Thirupparankundram, situated quite close to the town, has retained its village charm despite its fame as a major spiritual centre. Even though it lacks the grandeur and majesty of Madurai, it has its own modest beauty. The child god Murugan, forever young, always ready to bless his devotees, resides in his temple abode atop a hillock, bringing fame and renown to the village. Maybe centuries ago, the hillock would have been covered with lush vegetation. Today it is a smooth, bare rock, like a bald man's head. To the north, at the foot of the hillock, there is a small dome, a beautiful *gopuram*. The main temple is accessed through many rock-cut steps. From the temple entrance, the town is laid out for view below, as though it was created for the sole purpose of paying obeisance to the deity. To the west of the hillock is a small railway station. Next to it is a row of identical houses, the living quarters for mill workers. Further west is Thirunagar.

As though designed to showcase the beauty of Thirupparankundram, two lakes brimming with water lie to the north and south. The village itself lies among farmlands, coconut groves, sugarcane fields and banana orchards. The beauty of the setting suggests that it has been centuries in the making. It has somehow retained the flavour of thousands of years of Tamil life and culture. Despite the fact that the college where he was teaching was in Madurai – and most of his colleagues and friends lived in Madurai city, which had many more facilities and comforts – Professor Azhagiya

Sittrambalam had chosen to live in Thirupparankundram. The intangible cultural richness of the village must have been the cause of his decision. Additionally, the pure air for good health, greenery all around to please the eye and the Murugan Temple to satisfy the soul.

From the day he was appointed as a professor in the college at Madurai, he decided to settle in Thirupparankundram. That is where his wife later joined him, where Poorani and her brothers were born and where her mother died soon after giving birth to little Mangayarkarasi. Now, he himself had completed his life's journey in that very house.

Like a great artist who has had to leave his masterpiece unfinished, he had departed the world, leaving a young family behind. He had been focused on seeking honour, discipline, righteousness all his life. If only he had also given some thought to the financial security of his family! But no, he did not. Living in very modest circumstances himself yet possessing a generous heart, he had saved no money.

What had he left behind to help his young family? Who was there to support them? All he could leave them were his scholarship of Tamil and the wide renown he had won… and Poorani as the keeper of that legacy. He went when Poorani was yet to attain the stature and maturity that comes with adulthood. Yet he had bestowed some strengths upon her – self-confidence based on knowledge and reasoning, a strong value system born of close association with her father and the resilience to withstand adversity. The arms that wore bangles would henceforth have to wrestle with life.

Poorani had been born to her parents when they were still young. Appa had been researching material for a book on heroic female figures of the past, who were mentioned in Tamil literature. The day his book was released was also the day his first child, a baby daughter, was born. The Tamil poetry he had been exploring had resonated with him as pure beauty, and he saw that same perfect beauty, *pooranam*, in his daughter's face. Thus, he named her Poorani, the name rolling lovingly off his tongue.

Eight to nine months after his book was released, the university acknowledged the excellence of his work and honoured him with an honorary doctorate. He now had the title 'Doctor'. But what gave him far more pleasure was the title awarded by his little daughter when she first lisped the word 'Appa'.

As Poorani grew, her beauty and intelligence continued to be a credit to the name her father had chosen for her. She had inherited the sharp intelligence of Appa and the beauty of Amma. She grew tall and slender, like a graceful creeper. Her complexion, pale gold like the laburnum flower, seemed to have been created specifically to grace her beauty. Her face was like a lovingly created work of art, the masterpiece of a superbly gifted painter who had wielded his brush to express the romantic longings and dreams that crowded his young mind. Her expressive eyes complemented the beauty of her face. Long and narrow at times, wide as a blossoming flower at others, those beautiful eyes seemed to hold a hint of longing, as though on a quest for some lofty goal. Her wide forehead told the story of thousands of years of Tamil womanhood before her. Her expression gave a hint of the mental list she had drawn up of all the responsibilities that awaited her in this lifetime.

Only Poorani can look like Poorani – that was how people

described her uniqueness. Her father had stopped Poorani's education after high school. He had taught her grammar and literature from an early age at home whenever he had the time. Although progressive in his thinking in many ways, he had some fixed ideas about the education of girls. He firmly believed that like exposure to air causes camphor to evaporate, college education and wider exposure to society for girls would destroy their femininity. They would be turned into creatures with women's bodies and men's brains. This was why he did not send Poorani to college. Instead, he imparted knowledge and learning at home itself, which was four-fold of what any university could have done. Just as he had made the Tamil language grow and flourish through his teaching and writing, he had enriched Poorani's mind.

It was nine thirty in the morning. The two boys finished their meal and picked up their school bags to set off for school. At the doorway, they hesitated and stopped. Poorani was bringing little Mangayarkarasi to the front door to get her hands washed. When she saw her brothers in the doorway, Poorani asked, '*Enda*, why are you both still here? Isn't it getting late for school?' The older boy started saying something in reply but mumbled and stopped. Poorani instantly understood.

'Oh, is it the last day to pay the school fees? Wait, let me see.' She washed the little girl's hands, went back inside and opened a box. She counted the money, seven-and-a-half rupees. She checked the bank passbook; nothing left to draw. She called Thirunavukkarasu, gave him seven rupees and said, 'Pay the fees today.' The boys said goodbye and left. As she laid the half-rupee coin, the only money the family now possessed, carefully in the box, Poorani laughed to herself. It was a wry laugh born of despair. How was she to run the household?

The postman came to the door. Mangaiyarkarasi jumped up from where she had been looking at the cartoons in an *Ambulimama* magazine. The little girl grabbed the letters from the postman's hand and came running towards her elder sister, like a pretty rose that has grown arms and legs. The endearing sight of her little sister skipping towards her brought a momentary lift to Poorani's spirits.

As expected, most of the letters were those expressing condolences. A couple of them were from abroad – one from Lanka and one from Malaya. Despite having left their native land long ago, these former students had come to know about their beloved professor's death through newspaper reports and wished to express their sentiments. She felt proud to be the daughter of a man who was so widely respected, even after his passing.

There were still two letters left to open. She opened the first one and grimaced in distaste. It was from a rich merchant who had come to their home to take one-on-one tuition in Tamil from her father. Her father had taken him on as a student but had a poor opinion of his character because his dealings were not straightforward and he dodged his dues to the government. Her father had refused to accept any tuition fee from this merchant because he considered it to be tainted money. But he taught him Tamil well and sent him away.

'He is a bloodsucker who preys upon the poor, Poorani,' Appa used to remark often. 'There is no wealth in his mind, but he has accumulated wealth in his hands. Yet I feel it would be a sin on my part to deny anyone who comes to me with a desire to learn Tamil. That is the only reason I am putting up with this fellow.' However high a person's status might be, wherever in the world he lived, if he were lacking in honesty and ethical behaviour, Appa would not hesitate to call him low and unworthy. His respect was reserved only for those who lived honourably, never for those who only had wealth.

All that accumulated disgust and revulsion against the writer of the letter passed through Poorani's mind even before she commenced reading it.

> *I have enclosed a cheque. I have signed it and left the amount blank. Please fill in whatever amount you want. After the passing away of your father, I can imagine the difficult situation you must be facing. Please do not reject my offer.*

Poorani's deepening frown showed the extent of her disgust. She looked at the thick, coloured slip of paper behind the letter. Was that red lettering printed with the blood of all the poor families he had cheated? To Poorani's mind, what she held in her hand stood for utter degradation, worthy of the utmost revulsion. She threw the letter and the cheque aside contemptuously and raised her head. From the wall in front of her, the picture of her father smiled at her approvingly. It was his usual smile, but now she read a meaning into it. He was happy with her response to the letter.

Poorani went and fetched a pen. She picked up the fallen cheque from the floor and wrote on the back of it:

> *Yes, my father is dead. But his self-respect is still alive in his family. It will never die. Thank you for your offer. Please help some needy people instead. Your cheque is returned herewith.*

She put the cheque into an envelope, found some old unused

stamps, stuck them on and wrote the address. Without further delay, she set off to the postbox at the end of the street and slid the letter through the slot. She felt as if she had washed dirt off her hands. A sense of peace pervaded her mind.

When she got home, the little child was again engrossed in the *Ambulimama* magazine. Poorani spotted the unopened envelope from that morning's bunch of letters. She opened the envelope, expecting to see yet another condolence letter. But this letter from Madurai was from the landlord who had rented the house to them.

> *I intend to sell the house next month. Before that, please pay the rent for the past six months that is still owed to me and make arrangements to move out.*

The letter slipped out of her hand and fluttered to the floor next to the *Ambulimama* magazine. Her little sister picked it up and came up to Poorani. 'Akka,' she said in her babyish lisp, 'Here… take it…'

Poorani stood as though transfixed, staring into the eyes of her dead father's photograph.

> *My dear daughter! Life's first challenge, the first arrow of ill fortune is speeding towards you. This is the first adversity you are facing after I died. Don't lose heart. Life is all about striving to overcome adversity.*

She imagined that her father was communicating with her.

Wasn't there a special glow in those eyes? Wasn't he somehow transferring his strength to her? Gradually, she felt a spark of confidence coming alight in her mind.

CHAPTER 2

In the flame you are the heat, in the flower you are the scent,
Inside the rock you are the diamond, in words you are the truth.
In dharma you are love, in valour you are strength,
You are everything, you are inherent in everything.

– *Paripadal*

The child, Mangaiyarkarasi, had fallen asleep on the floor while looking at the magazine. Poorani sat stunned, the letter from the landlord clutched in her hand. If only she could somehow become a little girl like her sister, how wonderful that would be! The thought brought a pang of longing to her heart. Could anyone be as miserly as the Almighty? Those years of early childhood, the time when you could just live in the moment and had no concept of fortune or misfortune. Every event was to be experienced and just left behind. Those years were so fleeting – gone, before you knew it, never to return. Knowledge, experience, maturity – all these seem mere tools to deal with the sorrows of life.

Poorani sighed deeply. The street outside was empty. In that morning hour, a kind of peace appeared to have descended upon it. Someone somewhere had broken that massive machine called Time and walked away, leaving the emptiness still lingering over the street. At noon, the temple doors would close. So, Thirupparankundram Sannadhi Street was empty without the temple-goers.

Poorani walked towards the front door and latched the grille gate. From somewhere down the street, maybe from the flower stall at the temple entrance, the scent of cuscus grass wafted in the air. It was a scent that was unique to that village. The streets on all four sides of the temple were always redolent with cuscus. She was reminded of what Appa used to say: 'Like the aura of Lord Murugan's grace, this scent too is a special attribute of our town.'

She had to find money to settle the six months of rent that was owed to the landlord. Then, she would have to find another house at an affordable rent to move into. Even more urgent was the need to find a job. Even if ease and comfort were not possible, a respectable livelihood was a must. Though her father had passed away, his renown still glowed around the neighbourhood. Praise and fame can fill the mind with happiness, true. But it would not put food in the belly. It would not sustain the family. Her father's lingering fame would not help her raise her young siblings or pay their school fees.

It would be impractical to hope that those who showered praise so readily would open their purses too. Even if some offer of financial help came, it could be from the kind of unworthy man whose cheque she had spurned just that morning. It would be far better to work honestly and live modestly than to receive help from dishonourable sources and live in comfort. Even a life of poverty was acceptable as long as one lived righteously. That was the kind of life her father had wanted.

In her mind, Poorani could hear the words her father had often spoken to her. 'Poorani, instead of a life of wealth and ease built on secrets and deceit, it is more noble to work honestly, even if one has to live in poverty.' Appa had been a strict follower of the prescribed religious practices. He had strong faith in god. 'Love is the core of dharma. In that love, god resides. At the same time, he also stands in the strength born of valour, prepared to order its destruction. Everything, and everything that is within everything, is merely the *maya* of the lord.'

Appa always quoted this *Paripadal* in all his discourses. In fact, it was his belief in this that had taken him to great heights in his profession. 'The heat of the flame, the scent of the flower, the diamond in the rock, the truth in the spoken word, love in righteousness, the strength in adversity, everything is YOU!' These words from the *Paripadal*, written in bold letters and framed, hung above a bookcase in Appa's study.

Poorani felt a strong urge to hurry to Appa's study, just to stand near his bookcase. She went into the room. Shelves filled with books ran along all four walls. There were glass-fronted cabinets and also cupboards built into the walls. The *Paripadal* verse that had always been close to Appa's heart hung over the bookcase on the wall opposite the entrance to the room, where it would instantly catch the eye of anyone who entered the room. The moment she saw the verse on the wall, Poorani felt a burst of energy, as if she had been dipped and lifted out from a cleansing mineral spring.

Appa's salary had been spent largely on books. Even though he had not left behind thousands of rupees in savings, he had left a huge collection of books. The study was dusty; no one had entered it for the past fifteen days.

It was from that armchair that he used to conduct his Tamil

classes. That black pen on the table was the one that put his thoughts into written words. Under the desk stood the incense holder; the ashes of the last stick he had lit still stained the floor. Just as incense lives only to spread its aroma and then dies, Appa too had lived to spread his knowledge.

Each and every object in that room invoked a pang in Poorani's heart. She felt that if she lingered there any longer in the presence of those memories of Appa, her heart would break. She tried to overcome the wave of grief that threatened to sweep her away. How long can resolve stand firm against the overwhelming sorrow of such a great loss?

If the family had to move into a house at a more affordable rent, what would happen to all these books? It was a dilemma. However, even thinking about an affordable house was out of the question before settling the back rent for this one – fifty rupees a month for six months amounts to a full three hundred rupees. She could expect some amount from Appa's provident fund. But that would take time. The house they would move into would have to be smaller and at a lower rent.

Poorani was preparing to start this new chapter of her life with an eight-anna piece as savings, and the determination to find herself a job. Her brothers were in classes five and three. She was the one who would have to support them at least till they finished college. Mangaiyarkarasi also had to be admitted to school soon – by the next auspicious month of *Thai*, she would be six. There was a primary school close to home.

Poorani made a mental list of all the responsibilities that had fallen on her shoulders after the death of Appa. Some plan had to be put in place soon. What was the point of shutting oneself off when difficulties were already knocking on the door? It was time for her to take a bold step. She could no longer hesitate to get her feet dirty, as long as she always kept her mind clean.

Thirunavukkarasu and Sambandan attended a school in Pasumalai. The two of them walked to school and back. This meant that they could not come home during the lunch break. Poorani would pack something for them to take along and eat at school during the break. They got home only after four thirty in the evening.

It was not possible for Poorani to stay at home till that hour. She would have to leave by at least three o'clock in order to finish all her errands in Madurai and get back. She planned to meet the principal of Appa's college to see if the provident fund matter could be hurried along. The landlord would have to be given the money owed to him and be reassured that she and her siblings would vacate the house soon. One of the publishers who brought out Appa's books lived in Pudu Mandapam. Nothing could be gained by meeting him as he was a miserly man who would sing his usual tale of hard times. Yet she had to meet him and be firm with him. He owed a substantial amount of royalty to her father. She would also have to meet a few people about finding a job for herself.

As for finding a house, maybe she could explore the possibility of living with four or five other families, in some kind of community housing in Madurai itself. But then, even a two-bedroom house in Madurai would be as expensive as their entire house in Thirupparankundram. It would also involve pulling her brothers out of their school at Pasumalai in the middle of the school year and getting them admitted to a school in Madurai. When she thought of all that it would entail, Poorani abandoned the idea of moving to Madurai. How could she ever afford the high house rent in the city?

The house rents in Madurai were as high as its temple towers. Housing around the four majestic temple towers would not come cheap and was hard to find. Only beggars and cycle rickshaws were plentiful. Just like a husband with two wives is saddled with doubled expenses and no peace of mind, Madurai too was suffering because it was the capital of two districts simultaneously. This legacy of British rule was still lingering.

It was two thirty in the afternoon. Poorani went to the well and washed her face. After changing her sari, she was standing in front of the mirror to draw a tilak on her forehead when her little sister woke up from her nap and sleepily walked over to her.

Poorani's face, with its freshly-bathed-in-sandalwood-soap complexion, glowed like a lotus in bloom. Stray locks of jet-black hair, like brush strokes by a careless portrait painter, curled near the sides of her ears. Above the bridge of her shapely nose, at the spot between her eyebrows, Poorani wore a large kumkum *pottu* with a smaller black one above it. Even though her father had been unable to leave much money, he had still left a few gold ornaments for her. Among them was a pair of bangles. Yet she preferred to wear a set of black bangles. Like a black silk thread woven around gold, the contrast of the black bangles on her golden arms was especially attractive.

Poorani opened the jewellery case, took out the pair of gold bangles and put them into a cardboard box to carry with her. If the publisher continued to avoid paying the royalties owed to Appa, she might have to resort to pawning or even selling the jewellery. How else could she meet the debt obligation to the landlord? She would also need enough money to run the household till she could find a job.

'Akka,' said Mangaiyarkarasi smilingly, 'this *pottu* suits you so well. You should wear this every day.'

In the days following the death of their father, Poorani did not have the mind to groom herself in any way. A daily bath was all. The child had noticed, with delight, that her Akka had adorned herself.

'All right, my dear one, I will wear a *pottu* like this every day. Now I want you to listen to me carefully. I need to go to Madurai for some urgent work. I am going to leave you at Odhuvar *thatha*'s home and give him our house key. You must stay there like a good girl till your brothers get home from school. No misbehaving, no tantrums!'

Odhuvar *thatha* was an elderly temple priest and a family friend.

'Akka, let me come with you to Madurai,' pleaded the little girl, her wide eyes fixed yearningly on Poorani.

'No, *Kannu*, you won't be able to walk around so much. I will come back quickly. *Thatha* will tell you lots of interesting stories; stay at their home and listen.' The child seemed to accept the decision and didn't raise any more objections. Poorani had no time to even plait her own hair. She hastily applied some oil to her hair, combed and tied it up in a bun. She had very long hair, reaching down to her knees. Kamakshi, the young woman who lived in the house across the street, had to use two switches of false hair at the same time. Even then, her plait was not any thicker than a dog's tail. She was very envious of Poorani's long, thick hair. Kamakshi was Odhuvar *thatha*'s granddaughter. She was two or three years younger than Poorani. They had been friends since early childhood. There was a bond between the families, born of living in the same town on opposite sides of the same street.

Poorani took Mangaiyarkarasi out through the front door. She turned and locked the door, before leading the child across the street to *Thatha*'s house. The old man was seated on the *thinnai*, sacred ash smeared on his bare chest, reading a book on the *Thevaram*. Even at his advanced age, he did not need reading glasses. Appa had always held this old man in high esteem.

'Oh, Poorani... welcome, Amma! It looks like you are off somewhere? To Madurai, is it?'

The old man's voice was resonant and clear like the sound of a bronze bell.

'Yes, *Thatha*. Please look after the child for me. When the boys return, please give them this key.' Poorani placed the house key next to the old man on the *thinnai*. Of her own accord, with the comfort born of familiarity, the child clambered onto the old man's lap and started nagging him right away. 'Today you must tell me lots of new stories, *Thatha*,' she ordered him. 'Don't disappoint me with any of those old *Ammaiyar Patti* tales or stories about the crow and the sparrow.' Kamakshi and her grandmother were sitting in the hall facing the front door.

'Poorani! Why don't you step in here for a moment?' Kamakshi called.

'Later, Kamu, I'm in a hurry right now. I have to go.'

'What's so urgent, Amma?' asked *Thatha*.

Poorani decided it was acceptable to unburden herself to this old man who had always been a father figure to her. She considered revealing the fact that her landlord had asked for past rental dues to be paid and that the family was in a very tight financial crisis. But somehow, her tongue refused to frame the words. In that moment of conflict between thought and word, the sense of propriety that she had inherited from her father, and which ran strongly in her veins, won the day. Second thoughts prevailed. No, said her mind, it would not be right to describe her problems of debt and poverty to another whose problems were even worse. There was no need for this family, eking out an existence on a limited income and higher expenses than her own, to hear of her money troubles. Appa had always said that managing one's problems by oneself is the most noble path.

Further, he absolutely opposed evoking sympathy in others by narrating one's woes to them. Poorani was her father's daughter in this regard. It was that same determination and sense of conviction that coursed through her. So now, she merely said, 'Oh, it's nothing, *Thatha*. I'm just going to meet Appa's college principal about his provident fund. That's all.' She left the more troubling tasks unsaid.

Poorani stepped out on the street and started walking. Many eyes watched in admiration. It was like watching a bright, beautiful red lotus atop a tall, slender stem moving gracefully in a gentle breeze. She walked north along Sannadhi Street, past the Mayil Mandapam, and waited at the police station bus stop. A group of washermen, working at the irrigation tank to the south, had hung out garments of multiple colours. They fluttered in the breeze along the high mud bank. Beyond the expanse of water in the tank, off to the northwest, fields of paddy, sugarcane and betel, punctuated with tall coconut trees, painted a beautiful picture. At that point of time, Poorani happened to be the only person waiting at the bus stop.

From the south, Bus No. 5 bound for Central Thirupparankundram drew up to the stop. Poorani boarded the bus. The bus conductor greeted her with a broad smile. 'Welcome, Amma!' he called out. He had been one of Appa's several students. Having seen her accompanying her father over the years, many in the town knew Poorani. She parted with her last eight-anna coin, bought a ticket to the college bus stop and accepted the change. The conductor came over and told her how sad he felt about her father's passing. She responded suitably.

The college principal welcomed Poorani warmly and responded favourably to her request. He assured her that he would try to ensure that the amount due from her father's provident fund would be released as early as possible. From there she walked to the Pudu Mandapam. Passers-by stared openly at her. What a variety of stares people had! If she had travelled in a rickshaw or any other vehicle, she could have avoided this attention. But then, which rickshaw man would agree to ply for free? All she had in hand added up to just five annas. She would need three annas for the bus charge back home. It was fine to accept and acknowledge her poverty. Putting on false appearances would be wrong.

And so Poorani walked past all those lecherous glances, through the streets of old Madurai, her tender bare feet blistering and bruising on the hot tar.

At the crowded Pudu Mandapam, Poorani stepped aside to avoid the men who jostled and pushed, whether by accident or design. Soon, she was face to face with her father's publisher.

'Welcome, sister,' he greeted her. 'If you had just sent word, I would have come to you and saved you this trouble.' Perhaps he was pointing out that his age entitled him to some privileges.

Poorani was silent. She stood there like a pillar of flame and just looked fixedly at him. With those remarkable eyes, sharp and clear, confronting him, the man was lost for a response.

He tried to lighten the moment. 'Oh, it looks like you are angry with me, sister,' he remarked with a smile.

'I don't want your fake smiles or false promises,' said Poorani bitingly. 'You are trying to hide your dishonesty behind these pleasantries. You owe three years' worth of royalty payments for my father's books. You conveniently claim that they have not been selling well – that is not true. If you refuse to be straight with me, I will be forced to take legal measures.'

Although he must have been terribly embarrassed to be berated like this by a young woman loudly in public, the man kept his composure. 'By the end of this month, I will go through the accounts and try to help you, Amma,' he said, bringing the palms of his hands together in a farewell gesture. The gesture conveyed the message, 'Don't stand around talking any longer; get going.'

Poorani moved away. Her father himself had given up in frustration, remarking, 'I don't care whether he pays me or not. It is outrageous that someone who is trading in books that are meant to spread knowledge would deliberately cheat the author of those books and keep the money for himself.'

Opposite the Pudu Mandapam, the south *gopuram* of the Meenakshi Temple stood tall. It was a testament to pure truth, untouched by the filth of dishonesty and dwarfing mere humans in its magnificence. On either side, the shops of locksmiths and umbrella repairers jostled for space. This place always took on a special bustling ambience as evening approached. Appa had told Poorani that the street had earlier been known as the Evening Market Street.

Poorani walked past the *gopuram* of the massive temple, into the bustle and bouquet of aromas that swirled near the entrance to the *sannadhi* of Goddess Meenakshi Amman. She thought to herself that even after a passage of a thousand years, even if there were a thousand man-made changes, the unique religious and historical attributes of Madurai city would endure.

Here she was in the midst of the hubbub at the entryway to Amman's shrine. The aroma bursting from flower stalls, the tinkle of bangles and the shouts of the bangle sellers, the pervading scent of sandalwood, the crowds surging back and forth like souls through the gates of Creation.

Poorani skirted the temple tank with its golden-hued lotuses, offered her prayers at the shrine of Amman and returned through the south *gopuram*, past the tank and into the street. She looked around to make sure she was unobserved before quickly entering a jewellery store.

Gold bangles that weighed as much as four sovereigns! The jeweller was prepared to take them at the old gold rates for about three hundred rupees. She quietly accepted the money that the shopkeeper counted out and left to meet the landlord. She handed him the six months of back rent and obtained a receipt. 'I will vacate the house before the end of the month,' she assured him as she left. From the sale of her bangles, she was now left with seven rupees plus five annas of change from the old eight-anna coin with which she had set out.

In the neighbouring street was the house of a good friend and well-wisher of her father. He was an eminent citizen of the town and was widely respected by everyone. He had the reputation of being scrupulously honest. Poorani thought that if she met him and explained her circumstances, he would help her find a job. But when she went to his home, she was told he was away, in another city, and would be back only after two days. So she turned back, deciding to try her luck again after he returned.

By the time she caught a bus at Central and reached Thirupparankundram, it was getting dark. From near the mosque that stood at the hilltop, a blue light glowed. The street was crowded with people on their way to offer worship at the temple. When she came near her house, she saw a group of school students assembled on the street with their bags and books. There was a horse cart standing nearby, and she spotted Odhuvar *thatha*.

The moment *Thatha* saw Poorani, he hurried forward, his face expressing deep worry and concern. 'As if you didn't have enough to deal with already, your younger brother Sambandan climbed a tree at school, fell and broke his arm. They have brought him home…' he told her.

Poorani pushed her way through the throng of schoolboys and ran into the house.

CHAPTER 3

The Sun keeps running
The days sprint in his wake
They die away day after day…
What shall we do hereafter
If the fierce Yama is roused to anger…

– *Natrinai Vilakkam*

Whenever she encountered any problems or misfortunes, a calm voice spoke deep in Poorani's heart. 'Never accept defeat,' it told her. 'You are born to win in life, to be triumphant! The problems you are facing will make you even stronger. The more you encounter the petty harassment and small-mindedness of others, the more will the eyes of your mind widen and grow in wisdom. Just as a flowering plant flourishes in the dirt, draws sustenance from waste matter and manure and produces beautiful blossoms for the scented garlands that adorn the shoulders of the deities, so too will the poverty and hardships that you face serve to nourish you and help you to blossom as a person. You are not one of those millions of women who are swept away in the tide of whatever life throws at them. You are unique among womankind. You are a special creation. You are destined to swim against the currents that try to drag you down. You are destined to win.'

At every close encounter with misfortune, this inner voice of Poorani spoke up.

Whose voice was it? Why did it speak? Those were mysteries, questions with no answers. Maybe it was a carry-over from a past life, part of her identity, her soul. Maybe it would grow stronger as life went on. Yet, does one have to wait for a *davana* plant or a tulsi shrub to grow to full maturity before one can enjoy the aroma? No, even as the plant takes root and begins its life, it is already infused with all its qualities of beauty and fragrance. Similarly, some people are endowed with attractive innate qualities from the moment they are born.

Poorani was like the tulsi plant, sweet-scented in personality even from a tender age. She was pure inside and out, spiritual in outlook, and totally steeped in the traditional Tamil way of life. She had the inner strength to face any hardship and come out victorious.

When Poorani ran into the house, she saw her brother Sambandan laid out on a mat in the hall. A throng of schoolboys milled around. The older brother, Thirunavukkarasu, stood nearby, staring blankly, at a loss about what to do. Sambandan, meanwhile, was heaving and sobbing, like someone who was reaping the consequences of committing a serious crime.

Poorani sat on the floor next to her injured brother. The boy's wails became even louder when he saw his sister. She picked up his right arm and held it upright to test if it could support itself. It could not. Like a tender plantain leaf that had been twisted in the middle and exposed to the sun, the boy's arm wilted.

Odhuvar *thatha* came over and stood behind Poorani. 'He's a young boy, Amma,' he said. 'If his arm is bandaged with a splint, the bone will heal soon. There is a *vaidhyar*, a nature-cure physician, just four houses away. You should send for him.' Poorani turned her head and signalled to Thirunavukkarasu. The boy got the message at once and ran to fetch the *vaidhyar*.

'Akka, it wasn't my fault. There is a rough fellow called Balu, who is our classmate. He grabbed my maths notebook and flung it from the upper floor. Just underneath, there is a big mango tree. My book landed in the branches of that tree and got stuck there. I climbed the tree only to get my book, but as I was climbing, my leg slipped and I fell.'

Poorani instantly understood her brother's burning desire to explain himself to her. Thirunavukkarasu returned with the *vaidhyar*. Poorani stood up and moved away a little. The *vaidhyar* sat next to Sambandan and checked the boy's elbow by gently pressing it. Odhuvar *thatha* stood by.

The *vaidhyar* declared that there was nothing to worry about and that the fracture would heal soon. He placed bamboo strips along the boy's arm and bandaged it tightly with a cloth soaked in beaten raw eggs. 'Don't move or shake the arm, *Thambi*,' he said to Sambandan affectionately. 'In a few days, it will be as good as new.' As the *vaidhyar* rose to leave, *Thatha* whispered something in Poorani's ear. She ran and fetched a plate with an offering of four rupees and held it out respectfully to the *vaidhyar*.

The *vaidhyar* smiled and declined her offer of payment. 'I cannot accept this from you, Amma. I owe so much to your father Azhagiya Sittrambalam. Keep the money with you. Once the boy has recovered, I will ask for something if I need it.'

Poorani was well aware that her late father's reputation lived on in that house. Although he had not amassed material wealth to leave to his family, he had built relationships with people everywhere, who would be happy to help and support them. The *vaidhyar* who had declined Poorani's offer of money, the elderly priest who considered himself part of Appa's family and had always shared in all the family's joys and sorrows, all those from near and far who awaited an opportunity to lend a helping hand... weren't these a sign that the memory of Appa's reputation was still strong?

The crowd of schoolboys still hung around, showing no signs of dispersing. Finally, Odhuvar *thatha* shouted sternly, 'Is this some kind of entertainment for all of you? He is lying there with a broken arm. Don't crowd around, go home.' Gradually, the group of onlookers thinned out.

Young Mangaiyarkarasi, unaware of the details of what had occurred, had nevertheless gathered that something really bad had happened to her brother. Otherwise, why would he be lying on a mat like that, and why would the *vaidhyar* come and tie a bandage on him? Why would so many people collect around? In her distress, the child cried inconsolably. Odhuvar *thatha* took his leave to go back to his home across the street. As he left, he told Poorani, 'Look after your brother. If you need anything at all, call me. I will be resting on my front *thinnai*. Don't let your mind be troubled by anything. Just the phrase "so-and-so's daughter" will have people scrambling and competing to come and help you. There is no reason for you to be sorrowful.'

Poorani thought to herself, 'Everyone tells me this! As if Appa's reputation is some kind of insurance, bequeathed to me in his will, which I can trade upon! Surely a righteous man's honour and reputation should be preserved and treasured for their own worth. What is the need for me to waste that precious reputation by using it up just to get some comfort? I can work and make a living for myself. I can provide for my brothers and sister. I can raise the status of the family. I refuse to spend my father's reputation as a currency for some petty desires. I will never let my father's legacy of honour be soiled by grime and filth of any kind.' She raised her head. Her face and eyes glowed with determination.

'Akka! Will *Anna* be unable to straighten his arm again?' The little girl was stuttering in the midst of her sobs. Her tender lips were like tiny segments of an orange, quivering in distress. Her wide eyes, full of the innocence of childhood, now spoke of fear and worry.

'No, my darling! *Anna*'s arm will be fine very soon,' said Poorani soothingly, picking up her little sister and hugging her. The child's body was as though created with the softness of flower petals and the scent of rosewater. Just one touch from that little child, one smile on her lips, one look into those sparkling eyes would be enough to reassure anyone that there was still room for all that was true and good in this world.

If Appa had been alive, he would be on his way back from the temple around now. Every evening, he would take a long walk along Thirumangalam Salai to the south, stop by the Murugan Temple to offer prayers and return home around seven or seven thirty. He did not like to eat a heavy meal of rice at night. He used to say that eating rice would make him sleepy very quickly. He preferred to eat a light meal of idlis or wheat *dosais*. He would stay awake and read late into the night. Appa's preferences had passed on to the rest of the family as well.

Poorani lit the kitchen fire and put the idli pot on it. Everywhere in the house, in every thought, in every object, in every action, in every corner lived the memory of Appa, unforgotten and unhidden. Can one easily set aside memories that have been built over the years, ingrained by habit, which are now a part of one's very identity? A person dies in an instant, but do memories of that person die fast as well? If that were so, is there anything worthwhile left in this world?

Yet will not time erase everything sooner or later? The sun is in constant motion, with the days chasing after him. One after the other, relentlessly – eroding or being eroded?

Poorani placed a few idlis on a plate and took it to where Sambandan lay resting. She propped him up to a sitting posture so that he could eat. She called Thirunavukkarasu and Mangaiyarkarasi into the kitchen, seated them on the floor near her and served them idlis. How had this young woman, at such a young age, instinctively imbibed a mother's sensibilities? It is said that parent fish keep a close watch on their offspring and keep them safe till they grow up. Poorani was raising her brothers and sister with immense care and attention. She tried to keep them away from the hardships and problems that beset her and their house as much as possible. Thirunavukkarasu was old enough to understand the situation, but she did not wish to share her anxieties with him.

She had promised the landlord that she would vacate the house by the end of the month. She would have to stick to that deadline. Thirupparankundram was neither entirely a village nor a city. It was like a composite of village tranquillity and city facilities. Since there were mills, factories, schools and hospitals in the vicinity, housing was crowded. It was a place in which middle-class families, who could not afford the higher rentals in Madurai city, labourers and those who sought the mental and spiritual joy of living in the shadow of the benevolent God Murugan all lived in proximity. The new engineering college that was coming up in the east of the city, near the red-stone hillock, seemed to give a suddenly expanded appearance to the town.

Poorani decided to set off there and then to go around a few streets, looking for a house they could potentially move into. It was late in the evening but not yet dark. There was still a lot of bustle on the streets. Maybe if she could alert a few acquaintances here and there that she was on the lookout for a house, she would then get to hear about it if one fell vacant. It is as difficult in these times to find a suitable house for rent as it is for a poor family to find a groom for their daughter!

Poorani set out after giving some instructions to her brother. 'Arasu, look after the house. If Mangai feels sleepy, roll out her bedding and let her sleep. I need to go out for a while. I will be back around nine or nine thirty. Don't bolt the door. Go to bed.'

In that hour of approaching dusk, with a mist beginning to settle in amidst the faint glow of moonlight, Sannadhi Street was inexpressibly beautiful. Lined with houses on both sides, lights in the windows, the mixed aromas of many flowers, the fragrance of sandalwood and incense, human voices, sounds from radios, friends chatting, cowbells tinkling – it was like opening the first page of the endless book called the Universe. From where the street began, one could see the tall *gopuram* on its hillock, bathed in moonlight, with the Murugan Temple next to it. In front of the temple, the wide platform with the *yali* statues, poised as though to leap out at any moment to drag the platform away; the horse sculptures, above and below, like creepers branching out and spreading, the chariot streets along which the temple processions would pass.

Higher than the temple's dome, at an inaccessible spot on the hill, the word 'OM' in large letters blazed out a blue light. The sign, fixed atop a building on the hill, shone out in the darkness as though suspended magically in the sky, visible from all around. Poorani's eyes were fixed on the 'OM' above her as she walked along Sannadhi Street. She never tired of the sight of that blue-lit 'OM'. It seemed, to Poorani's mind, that the sign was free of all attachment to anything or anyone above or below. It was timeless. It bloomed like a beautiful flower made of light, spreading its special fragrance throughout Thirupparankundram.

She would often drink in the sight of its splendour from the terrace of her home.

Among the chariot streets, in places such as Velliangiri Lane and Thirukulam Lane, there might be some cooperative society tenements available at an affordable rent. Alongside the Saravana Lake Bund and on Giri Street to the southeast of the railway station, there were a few large cooperative apartments.

There was a special reason why Poorani had chosen to set out so late in the day. She wanted to avoid the attention of familiar people. She felt somewhat guilty about walking around like this, when not even a month had passed since her father's death. If they came to know that she was vacating the big house so soon and moving to a cooperative housing tenement, they would ask probing questions. That was why she had decided that the late evening hour was the best time to make her enquiries without running into people who knew her.

Around where the temple chariot was parked, and at the

shops at the entrance to the temple, there was still the hustle and bustle of crowds. Poorani stopped briefly at the entrance to the *sannadhi* to offer a quick prayer before turning into the wide street to the east, which was the path of the chariot. Here, the bustle persisted even up to three in the morning. The touring cinema that was set up at the far end of the street was attracting crowds well into the small hours.

While large numbers of devotees from near and far, even from abroad, were circling the shrine in prayer, the locals were busy circling the tent of the touring cinema. Poorani remembered that her school friend Kamala's house was on the first lane off Thirukulam. In fact, it was the very first house after turning into the lane.

Kamala was sitting on the *thinnai* outside the house, chatting casually with her mother and another old lady. Poorani was in two minds, wondering whether to go up and meet her. She walked forward with some hesitation and stopped near the front door. 'Kamala,' she called softly, to attract her friend's attention. There was a special quality to Poorani's voice that made it stand out amidst a hundred others. Kamala recognized that voice instantly. 'Poorani?' she said in surprise, rising and coming forward. Then she added playfully, 'Oh, so this was the only time of the day you could spare, Amma? Were you afraid that I would capture you if you came in the daytime to have a chat with me?'

'That's not why I'm here, Kamala. Just come closer; I want to tell you something.' Poorani whispered in Kamala's ear about the purpose of her visit.

'You live on Sannadhi Street with all its facilities. Why would you want to move to a narrow lane like this? There, on Sannadhi

Street, you can get on to a Madurai-bound bus any time easily. If you move here, you would have to walk all that way for a bus. Your brothers would have to walk further to get to their school. Please think carefully before you do anything.'

'Only those who have something can aspire for more, Kamala,' remarked Poorani sombrely. 'For those who have nothing, even what is seen as a lack of facilities will appear to be desirable.' Kamala was lost for suitable words to comfort her friend.

She said, 'There's no way I can win an argument with you, Amma. That time when you defeated me in the debate competition at school is enough for me! You are a wizard with words, with the Tamil language. And me? Am I the daughter of a Tamil scholar? No, just an ordinary farmer's daughter. So let me not try to persuade you any longer. There's a housing complex on the lake bund. Let's go there right now and take a look. It will be an opportunity to take a stroll together by moonlight. We haven't had any occasion to walk together since we were in school.'

'I am ready for it,' replied Poorani. 'But I have my doubts about whether your mother will send you with me at this late hour.'

'Sure, she will. These days, it is totally safe in this area even at a late hour. After the cinema arrived, and the engineering college too, the town itself seems to have grown bigger. Hold on, just a moment. I'll tell my mother and come.'

Kamala was three or four years younger than Poorani. They had been friends in school for many years. Their friendship endured even afterwards, and that was entirely due to the kind of person Poorani was. Anyone who had ever interacted with her, even fleetingly, never forgot her face, her gaze, or her voice... such was the special quality of her personality. If this was the case with people who had met her only fleetingly, no wonder Kamala, after all those years of close friendship with Poorani in school, felt a special bond between them.

Kamala joined Poorani, and they walked eastward. As they approached the turning at the end of the street, Kamala's mother came out of the house and called, 'Come back soon, child.' The houses were fewer, and the street widened as they progressed towards the east. Gardens, fields, the wide expanse of water in the Saravana Lake with lotus leaves and tender buds floating on the surface – the vista extended up to the base of the hill. To the north, the red sand mound, called Koodaithatti Hillock, seemed to proudly flaunt the few green shoots that had emerged here and there on its otherwise bare sides after the recent rain.

The two young women came to a stop in front of a building that was constructed as a series of separate units. Kamala explained, 'This is the cooperative housing building I was talking about earlier. It is far outside the town. No electricity supply. It may come sometime in the future. The landlord has been trying hard to get it connected. Many of the units are still vacant and the rent is very low. There is one small hall, a kitchen and a front veranda. The rent is just twelve rupees!'

'Yes, the rent is indeed low, but it is so far from the town,' thought Poorani. It was past the cinema tent by a good distance. Here, at this evening hour in these surroundings, the sounds of the town were stilled. Only cicadas chirped, and peace reigned. A man who had been sitting and smoking a beedi under a neem tree at the front of the building now got up and came forward of his own accord. He started giving them some information in a friendly manner.

'Amma, Chettiyar *ayya* has managed to get the electricity connection. In a week from now, there will be lights. I heard you remarking that four or five units are still free. That's not the case any longer. People have already come and paid advance rent for all the units, except one. In fact, Chettiyar *ayya* and I were talking about it just a little while ago. Then a man came pleading for that last unit. He was ready to pay the advance. He and *Ayya* are walking along the lake bund right now, to discuss it. Maybe if you hurry and get there before he accepts the advance, he may decide to rent the unit to you instead, out of sympathy because you are a woman.' If this frail man, with his grey moustache and light-coloured eyes, had not volunteered this information, the women would have decided to go home and come back the next day to meet the landlord.

Poorani spoke quietly in Kamala's ear. 'Considering my present situation, it would be a blessing to get a house on a rent of just twelve rupees, Kamala! I think I will settle for this. It's true that my brothers and I will have to walk longer distances if we move here, but I can't go by that consideration.' Kamala nodded as she understood Poorani's desperate situation very well.

Kamala turned to the old man, 'Sir, I know the landlord, Chettiyar, very well. He won't say no to me. He is a good friend of my father. If you will show us the way to go to find him, we will be very grateful to you.'

'Show you the way? No, no. I will come with you. They will probably be sitting and talking under the jamun tree at the edge of the lake. If you just mention your interest in renting the unit, he won't rent it to anyone else then. You can rely on his promise.' The old man was very confident about it.

They set out in single file, the old man leading the way, followed by Kamala, with Poorani bringing up the rear. Only the sound of gushing water, frogs croaking in the fields and the *sarrrr* of the wind swirling around the hilltop intruded into the serene silence of that place. Sounds from the cinema in the distance reached their ears very faintly. Scattered among the shadows of the trees on the red earth, the moonlight made pale patches that shifted and moved, making beautiful patterns. Poorani gazed at the ground as she walked, unable to look away from the sheer beauty of those shifting patterns.

Suddenly Kamala screamed, '*Ayyo*! He has snatched my necklace!'

Poorani was startled. She heard the thud-thud of running footsteps. The old man had turned out to be a chain snatcher! He was fleeing ahead of them. Kamala stood frozen in shock.

At that moment, some unknown source bestowed strength on Poorani. She set off after the old man. Picking up a big pebble, she aimed it at the back of the thief's neck. The missile found its mark, and the fellow was sprawling on the ground. Yet he picked himself up and started running again. But Poorani caught up with him. As one would use a chain to restrain a dog, she used the man's own dirty towel to try and tie his arms together firmly.

CHAPTER 4

No action of mine is of my own doing, O Lord
I have realized that all action arises from You.
No sins have I committed since I took on this mortal form,
Maybe the ones committed earlier have been consumed in the flames.

Driven by a reckless determination born of anger at having been duped, Poorani was trying to keep the thief tied up with his own towel. Kamala ran and picked up her stolen chain from the ground. It had broken into three pieces during the struggle. Hearing the commotion, a few village priests, who had been resting in the *chathram* at the border of the lake, came running towards the scene of capture.

The old thief was exhausted and in pain, not just from the exertion but also from the stone that Poorani had thrown on the back of his neck. Yet, when he saw the priests running towards them, he got up and tried to run again. After all, when it comes to showing one's face to people after committing a misdeed, even a thief feels some shame. He struggled to break free, and Poorani's arms were growing tired with the effort of holding him down. The man's cruel eyes, displaying his fear of being trapped, bulged like enormous marbles.

Who knows what went through Poorani's mind at that moment? She subconsciously eased her grip. The old fellow broke free and ran away. 'Maybe,' Poorani thought to herself, 'now that the chain has been recovered nothing can be gained by turning this fellow over to the authorities.'

Kamala had been too nervous to come closer and was standing at some distance. Now, she came up to Poorani. 'What terrible times we are living in! It looks like you can't trust anyone any more. He pretended to be such a good man, and the next moment he reached for my neck to snatch my necklace. It's my good fortune that I had a brave person like you with me. Otherwise, I would have forfeited my chain to the thief and gone home in tears.' Poorani placed her right hand across her friend's mouth to stop her flow of praise.

'Enough, Kamala! Think of it as a bad dream. It was foolish of us to roam around at this time of the evening looking for a house to rent. Come on, let's leave this place before someone comes along to ask what happened.' She took hold of Kamala's hand and led her back the way they had come.

When they turned into Lower Chariot Street, Kamala caught sight of Poorani's arms. Those beautiful arms revealed red scratches from broken bangles and sharp fingernails during the encounter, like random red lines scrawled across a pristine white sheet of paper. Kamala's eyes filled with tears. She glanced at Poorani's face. Poorani was smiling serenely, as though nothing untoward had happened.

'Oh, you silly girl! Is this something to weep about?' chided Poorani. 'Hand me those pieces of your chain. On my street, there is a goldsmith with a workshop. He will repair the chain, and I will give it to you by tomorrow evening. Till then, just make sure that your mother doesn't notice that it is missing from your neck. Don't breathe a word to anybody about what happened.' Poorani took the pieces of the broken chain from Kamala.

'Losing the chain would have been better than having your arms so badly injured, Poorani,' said Kamala sadly.

'We always try to accomplish things without hurting ourselves. But it isn't possible to get through life without injuries – not only to our arms but also to our minds and thoughts.' Having spoken these words that were wise beyond her years, Poorani laughed. She laughed as only she could under such circumstances.

By the time Poorani saw Kamala safely home and turned back towards Sannadhi Street, the place had become much quieter. It was only after she had knocked loudly and repeatedly at her front door that Thirunavukkarasu finally woke up. Poorani locked the front door behind her, went into her father's study and turned on the light. She wrapped the broken pieces of Kamala's chain in a piece of paper and kept it on the table as a reminder that she had to visit the goldsmith the next day. Feeling the urge to read something before turning in for the night, she took out one of her father's books at random.

It was a book of the works of the poet Bharatiyar. The book fell open to a particular page, and the poem that met her eye was one that was particularly comforting to her at that moment.

Struggling for food every day,
Chatting idly of small matters,
Heart aching with the burden of suffering,
Yet continuing to do harm to others,
Greying, ageing, falling prey to cruel utterances, and then dying… like all those jokers
Did you think I too would succumb to that same pathetic fate?

The grief of her father's death, the responsibility of looking after the family, the pressure to vacate the house quickly, a brother who had fractured his arm, her misadventure involving the encounter with a cunning thief while searching for a house to rent – in a mind reeling under these burdens, the Bharatiyar verse aroused a spark of hope.

Except for the intermittent croaking of frogs from the lakeside and the *sarrr* rustling of palm fronds, the night was enveloped in silence. Now and then, the roar of heavy vehicles plying along the highway would rise and subside. The city slept, but sleep eluded Poorani. Her thoughts were churning.

Reading the lines of poetry and immersing her mind in its meaning brought comfort to her. It was like snuggling into a warm blanket in the harsh cold. Indeed, it was Poorani's habit to dwell deeply upon thoughts and ideas. 'Surely there is more to life than merely eating up time and finally being eaten by time? Undergoing hardships oneself and yet causing hardship to others... Was that even a way to live one's life? Gossiping about others and being gossiped about... What a poor kind of existence that is! There is something bigger, nobler which gives meaning to life, gives it a purpose.'

Like a gentle shower of cool water, these thoughts refreshed Poorani's body and mind. Noble ideas have the power to make one's skin tingle, as though being rubbed with ice. Ever since she could remember, Poorani had experienced this feeling many times. Just like when the pink jasmine is in bloom, and a divine fragrance envelops the whole garden, the radiance of the ideas in some people creates a pervasive aura around them, like a fragrance of wisdom.

Poorani's eyelids drooped. A couple of times, the book almost slid out of her hands. She put out the light and went and lay down on her bed. Her whole being felt light like soft cotton; all the burden of anxiety had disappeared. She fell into a deep, restful sleep.

The following morning, the *vaidhyar* paid a visit to inspect Sambandan's arm. It was a Saturday, a school holiday for Thirunavukkarasu. The milkman supplied milk on a monthly basis, so he measured out the milk as usual and went away. Poorani made coffee and then set out for the goldsmith's shop, taking Kamala's broken chain for repair.

The goldsmith was a well-wisher of the family. But of what material use was friendship when both parties were steeped in poverty? It was as impossible for her to request free service as it was for him to offer it. It took two hours to restore the necklace. As the goldsmith wrapped the finished item in paper and handed it over, Poorani asked, 'What do I owe you for this?'

'Give me five rupees, child,' was his reply. Whatever the age of the person he was addressing, he always called them 'child'. Perhaps a bit of a chat and some negotiation may have brought the price down by a rupee or two. But since Poorani had been raised in an atmosphere of total righteousness, her tongue would not deign to bargain. She handed over five rupees without a murmur and took the repaired necklace to Kamala's house. By then, it was already eleven o'clock and very hot. The chariot street, exposed to the radiating heat from the rocks on the hill, was searing hot, like walking on slaked lime.

Fortunately, Kamala was alone at home. She was reading in the front room. The moment she saw Poorani, she sprang up and hurried over in great excitement to convey an amazing piece of information. 'Poorani, did you hear the news? That old thief that you chased and caught got bitten by a snake later and died. This morning, Amma and I went to Saravana Lake for a bath. They had brought his body and laid it under the jamun tree. We heard that his body was found on a field bund nearby. Some farmworkers, who went there to water the fields in the morning, seem to have spotted him and carried him over to the tree. They said there was a snake's nest under where they discovered him. Not only could he not keep what he stole but he also lost his life!'

When she heard this, Poorani started trembling. She felt as if her bones were sliding around and that the joints between them had dissolved. Her eyes flew open, as if in terror. She was aware that her fingers were shaking uncontrollably. 'Have I committed a murder?' her inner self was asking. Her heart was pounding, and sweat beaded her face.

This change in Poorani alarmed Kamala. 'What's the matter, Poorani? Why are you sweating like this? It was that fellow's fate to die at that time. He happened to die of snakebite. Why are you so agitated?'

'Kamala, have you told anyone about what happened to us yesterday?' asked Poorani.

'Would I ever breathe a word about that? No, except you and me, no one knows. A big crowd had collected at the lake near his body. Last night, his fate seems to have been tied to my chain!'

'See what tricks fate plays, Kamala. Unaware that Lord Yama was approaching him from behind to snatch away his very life, that old man came at you from behind to snatch the chain from your neck. When someone steals a material object, he is made to suffer shame and undergo imprisonment. Yet, here is Yama, who steals life itself as if he is entitled to it, and he is worshipped as a god!'

'Though that fellow was a thief, it is sad to think of the manner in which he died, Poorani,' remarked Kamala.

'Death itself has the capacity to shake up the living. When our neighbour's wall is being demolished, the walls of our house vibrate too. Similarly, the way some people live and die affects others. It makes them question their own beliefs about life and death.'

'Let that be, for now. Tell me, what did you decide? Have you found a house somewhere? I heard your brother fell from a tree and broke his arm. You never told me that.'

'It's true that I didn't tell you, Kamala. I have plenty of worries. What's the point of unburdening myself to you and making you worry as well? Just as a thorn bush's protection consists of its thorns, my problems are my armour. Here is your necklace. It's been repaired. I have a lot to do. Please drop by my home this evening if you can. I will leave now.' Poorani gave Kamala the necklace and started on her way back. Near the chariot parking spot, she saw Odhuvar *thatha*.

'Why would a woman walk around like this in the heat of the sun that can darken her face and skin? What was so important that you had to set out like this?'

'It's nothing, *Thatha*. An old friend of mine, Kamala, lives on the next street. I'm just returning after visiting her.' After offering this explanation to *Thatha*, Poorani walked on. She was accosted by the curd seller, who was sitting near the pillared stone structure that graced the middle of the street.

'Amma,' pleaded the woman, 'I don't have any savings to live on. I only have what you give me now and then to buy cattle feed. Even if you can't spare the entire amount you owe me, at least give me something to get by, please.'

Out of the two rupees and two-and-a-half annas that Poorani had with her, she gave one-and-a-half rupees to the curd seller and earned her goodwill. On Sannadhi Street, at that hour close to noon, there was very little activity, hardly any bustle. Even the betel leaf sellers, without any customers, were idling. The street, the hill, the temple dome were all baking comfortably in the noon sun.

At the railway station to the west, the Thoothukudi Express arrived and came to a stop. Of the three express trains that passed that way, this was the only one that had faith in Lord Murugan and stopped at his feet. It would stop for just three seconds or so. Then, with a mighty puff of black smoke spewing from its chimney, it would set off again. The other trains did not display even that minimal devotion to Murugan!

Poorani thought about her brothers and little sister who would be waiting for her at home. After the morning coffee, hours ago, they must be very hungry by now. She went into a wayside hotel and bought some tiffin for eight annas. As she approached her home, Mangaiyarkarasi came running out and clasped Poorani's legs. 'Akka, I'm very hungry,' moaned the child. With the tiredness brought on by hunger, her face was a drooping sunflower. Thirunavukkarasu was sitting tired near his brother, Sambandan. Like a well-silvered mirror that displays images clearly, these young faces displayed hunger so vividly! As one grows older and gets more inured by hardships, one is able to mask such feelings well. In childhood, it is impossible to do so.

Poorani opened the packet of tiffin and laid it out on three separate leaves for the children. 'What about you, Akka?' asked Thirunavukkarasu. He made no move to start eating his share of the tiffin.

'I've already eaten. I visited Kamala. She insisted that I should eat there. She wouldn't take no for an answer. So, I had to eat with them. You go ahead.' The most useful friend in this world is the lie that comes to the rescue when needed most.

'But you don't look like you've eaten, Akka. Your face looks tired.'

'Oh, stop it, don't be impertinent, *da*! Do you want me to stick an "I have eaten" notice across my face to prove it to you?' Poorani laughed as she chided her brother. That laugh made them begin to believe her. They started eating. As the food disappeared from the leaves, Poorani's heart filled with joy, and her face lit up.

'Akka, the postman has brought some letters,' announced Thirunavukkarasu, handing over the mail to Poorani. As usual, they were condolence letters. An eager, emotional youngster had written to suggest that a memorial should be raised in Thirupparankundram to honour the memory of the great Tamil scholar. Poorani chuckled to herself wryly.

She thought bitterly, 'A memorial! Imagine that, a memorial! They forget the man and need a memorial to be built to remind them! If they will bury us in the foundation they dig for the memorial, our problems will be solved. We wouldn't have to live on like this, battling hunger and poverty.'

A wave of intense hunger hit her, as if her lower bowel had turned upon the upper one to swallow it. 'Maybe a bath will refresh me,' she thought. She went to the well to take a bath.

The rope fastened to the bucket at the well was frayed halfway through. At what moment would it finally give way? Another thing to worry about? After all, her life itself was like that frayed rope!

There was no rice left in the pot, no firewood for the kitchen fire – only two-and-a-half annas in hand. She did not want to tell others about her problems or ask for a loan. Poorani wept as she bathed. After all, who can tell if someone is crying when bathwater is flowing? Aren't tears a kind of bath too? Crying means immersing in sorrow, doesn't it? So, Poorani bathed, in water and in her sorrows. Her body had cooled after pouring all those potfuls of water on herself, but her mind still seethed restlessly.

She tried to summon a mental image of her dead mother's divine face. She could imagine her father's face without any trouble. As the outline of her mother's face formed in her mind, it was as if a pillar of hot flame glowed within her. Like the countenance of Goddess Meenakshi Amman, celebrated in Tamil tradition as the embodiment of motherhood, her mother appeared in her mind's eye and seemed to exhort her.

'My daughter, may you live well! May you help others to live well!' Poorani felt energized by the power of her mother's blessing.

After her bath, Poorani got ready to go out again. Her large, beautiful eyes, which expanded further whenever she opened them wide, were now reddened like a carp on whom an artist had wielded a red-dipped brush.

She gave Thirunavukkarasu a series of instructions. 'If the *vaidhyar* comes this evening, let him examine your brother. Make sure the young one doesn't wander outside in the sun. It will be late before I get back.' Picking up her umbrella, Poorani set off. She was filled with a resolve to find herself a job in the big city before returning home. With fierce hunger in her belly, and even fiercer determination in her mind, a glow in her eyes and a ladies' umbrella in hand, she ventured forth. Not used to such exertion, soreness soon assailed those tender feet. Yet she ignored the pain and walked on.

She bought a bus ticket with whatever little money she had left and got off at the last stop that her ticket permitted. She started walking once more. Her resolve lent her feet the energy to move along rapidly. She was going to conquer life.

It is not shameful for a young woman to roam the streets of a city when the purpose is a righteous one. She does not need to feel any embarrassment at all about such a quest. Thousands of years ago, during the days of the Chozha Empire, it was on these streets of Madurai that a young woman walked, a single anklet clutched in her hand, seeking justice.

Around those four mighty towers of the temple, Poorani sought a means of livelihood. Her searching eyes tried to seek out upright people who could offer her a decent job for decent pay and a way out of hunger. However, only the temple towers stood tall. The humans were all small-minded. There were hardly any job vacancies, and even the few that were available were denied to her.

She was a woman, after all. 'Don't be offended, Amma,' said an elderly manager at one of the places where she enquired. 'I'm advising you as though you were my own daughter. A decent young woman like you should not come looking for a job in such a place, where there are all kinds of crooks. I would hate to see the consequences of such a decision.' So, it was wrong to be a crook, and it was equally wrong to be decent and righteous! Too much enthusiasm was a minus point, as was idleness. In a world that does not recognize the right to speak, who was going to debate whom on the topic of justice?

Reeling under her disappointment, on top of her hunger and weariness, Poorani made her way towards the temple entrance across the junction where the Town Hall Road met the road to the temple tower. At that crossroads, a truck from the south, another from the north and cars from the other two directions sped towards the junction simultaneously. In a split second, there was utter chaos. Poorani could not move in any direction. She felt dizzy; a dark curtain clouded her eyes. Right there, in the middle of the street, still clutching her umbrella, Poorani collapsed like a jasmine creeper whose stem had been cut.

Imagine this scenario thousands of years ago, on this same street. If a young woman had staggered and fallen like this, how many poets would have been inspired to create beautiful verses! When a young maiden is in distress, should not a thousand poets' souls be deeply touched? When Shakuntala suffered a misfortune, did not Ilango and Kalidas create verses out of it? So, what now?

Poorani does not belong to the age of poets or poetry. Alas, she lives among mere mortals.

CHAPTER 5

The boundless flood of light leaps and spreads
The world is enveloped in that encompassing glow
Alas, why does this heart alone wilt in darkness and grief?

– Bharati

Waking up from her fainting spell, Poorani could not immediately recollect what had happened. She could not recognize her surroundings either. She only knew she was in some large house, lying on a bed under a ceiling fan. She gazed around wide-eyed, trying to understand what had happened to her. That was when the woman sitting on a sofa nearby rose and approached Poorani's bed. She spoke in a gentle, comforting tone.

'Don't worry about finding yourself in an unfamiliar place, Amma. Think of this as your own home. I had just seen off a relative of mine and was returning from the railway station. As my car turned from Town Hall Road into West Gopuram Road, you suddenly moved across the road and fainted. I brought you back to my house in my car. You are now in my house. Thanks to god's grace you were not injured when you fell. There is no need for you to be worried or apprehensive.'

Poorani was deeply embarrassed at being told that she had fainted on the street. From what the lady described,

Poorani was able to reconstruct a mental picture of what had happened. Hesitating and stumbling over her words, she tried to thank the lady.

'Where can I find the words to thank you for all that you have done for me? You rescued and brought me here and cared for me as if you were my own mother.'

'The thanks can wait. But tell me, young woman, why did you walk like that, so carelessly? You were paying no attention and were walking right in the middle of a busy crossroads, with traffic and people coming from all directions. One can say that you were saved today by some kind fate. You escaped disaster by a hair's breadth.'

'I may have escaped this danger. You may have rescued me. But an even greater disaster still looms. It is one that everyone meets, willingly or not.'

'What do you mean? What danger are you talking about?'

'I'm talking about life. It seems to me that life itself is dangerous.'

The woman smiled. With perfectly aligned, pearly teeth, her smile flashed like white *thumbai* flowers in a perfect string.

'Where did you learn to talk like a hundred-year-old grandmother at such a young age?"

'What is the use of speaking like this? One can't translate it into wisdom that might help in leading one's life. We need to learn other lessons, different ones. In life's classroom, failed students are promoted, while the ones who pass get demoted. Everything is upside down. What other label fits this situation, except to call it a "calamity"?'

The woman appeared stunned. Poorani's words were like a revelation to her. It was as if one was about to cast something aside as worthless brass, only to discover that it was pure gold. So far, she had only been thinking about how she was doing a good deed for a young woman who had fainted on the street. She had intended to help her recover and then send her off safely. But now, her interest in young Poorani was piqued. Professor Azhagiya Sittrambalam had moulded his daughter into a repository of wisdom. Wherever it may be, at whatever time of the day, the *manoranjitham* flower cannot help but spread an aroma; similarly, wherever and whenever Poorani spoke, and whomsoever she addressed, her words possessed the aroma of wisdom. She would have been unable to speak in any other way.

'You speak so wisely and yet so attractively. You seem to be highly educated, Amma. Tell me something about yourself,' said the woman.

Poorani hesitated. Was it necessary to tell this lady about herself and her situation? She noticed the expression of motherly concern on the woman's face. She recalled how, that same morning, she had sobbed uncontrollably while taking a bath at the well, and it was only the image of her mother's face that had calmed her.

The woman who stood in front of Poorani was neither young nor old, perhaps a bit past middle age. Her face was serene. Poorani felt an urge to open up and speak freely to this lady.

'If I'm wrong in asking about you, please forgive me. You can safely confide in me if you wish to do so. You spoke bitterly about your life. I want to see if I can do anything to help you out of the dangers that surround you.'

Poorani gave the woman a brief account of her

circumstances. She neither boasted about her family's renown nor did she wallow in the misery of her present situation. She simply laid out the bare facts in describing herself.

'I've heard a great deal about your father, Amma,' said the woman. 'I've read a couple of his books too. My native town too is Madurai. We lived for many years across the sea in Lanka and returned here only recently. We had large tea estates there. After my husband passed away, I couldn't manage the estates on my own. I sold everything and returned to my home town. I have two daughters. One is in the eighth grade at school, and the elder one is in college. All is going well with god's grace.'

'May I know your name, Amma?' asked Poorani.

'I am Mangaleswari. Don't you see, Poorani, how I live up to my name by being *mangalam*?' The woman spoke light-heartedly, and Poorani could sense the earnestness beneath the seemingly casual remark.

There are two kinds of smiles. One is just for the sake of smiling because one is expected to do so, the other masks the depths of sorrow or despair. Mangaleswari's smile was the latter kind, the one that tries to hide an inner sorrow. In her mind, Poorani compared Mangaleswari's two kinds of smiles – the genuine smile in response to Poorani's description of life itself being a danger and this other smile that spoke of hidden unhappiness.

Poorani slowly sat up in bed. Through the open window, she could see part of the street. She recognized it as Thanappa Mudali Street. In order to check whether she was right, she asked, 'This is Thanappa Mudali Street, isn't it?'

'Yes,' came the reply. The house was large and luxurious. Marble tiles on the floor, large pictures on the walls, full-length mirrors all around, sofas upholstered in silk, a large variety of tables – the room spoke of prosperity. The woman of the house was the embodiment of compassion. The surroundings reflected not just their owner's tenderness but also her righteousness. Perhaps they also reflected her weariness at the end of a whirlwind existence, the realization that life's journey was drawing to a close. Slender lines of sacred ash, as though drawn with a child's little finger dipped in milk, graced her broad forehead. She approached Poorani's bed.

'Why do you seem surprised by all this, Amma? When we first came here, the house was in shambles, like a dilapidated mansion. Encrusted walls, bandicoot nests under the floors... In just three months, I have brought it to this condition by spending lavishly. I myself am sick of all this, Amma. But it's difficult to say no when children we have raised indulgently want something.'

'In which college does your elder daughter study?'

'I've admitted her to American College. Poorani, one of the drawbacks of this city is that the colleges are scattered in all four directions. She leaves for Tallakulam in the morning and gets back only at five in the evening. We have a car and a driver. But she claims that she is embarrassed to be seen coming in a big car. So, she wants a smaller new car! She insists that until then, she will travel back and forth only by bus. She has stubbornly been following that decision of hers. I've arranged to buy a small car. But even if one has the money ready, it isn't easy to get a car quickly, is it?'

'When there are two women's colleges in this city, why did you decide to admit her to a co-educational college?' asked Poorani. The moment the question escaped her lips, Poorani glanced at the woman's face and wished she had not asked it.

'I am rather progressive in my way of thinking, Poorani. Women's relationships stay in a tight circle all their lives. Whether before marriage or after marriage, there is no opportunity for women to experience a variety of environments or situations. I am of the view that a girl should experience different environments, at least when she is still studying. It will hold her in good stead later in life.'

Poorani smiled gently. When confronted with views contrary to their own, most people look irritated or grow red in the face. That was not the case with Poorani. Whenever she heard sentiments that were opposed to her own, a fleeting smile would flash across those beautiful lips. She had learnt this from her father. Mangaleswari noticed that smile.

Poorani said, 'A circle has no corners; that is what mathematics says. Isn't a woman still a woman even if she is in a different environment? The rules for living, for a woman, are distinct. They are attractive, the way a circle is attractive. It's a big mistake for us to believe that we must somehow also fit into a square.'

'But it is sharpness and capability that are most needed in life. In fact, a little while ago, you yourself expressed this sentiment in a different context, Poorani.'

'In a circle, there is a regularity; there is no danger of going astray. Whereas in a square, there is sharpness and cleverness. But it also holds the risk of errors. It was my father's opinion that it is perfectly acceptable for a woman's life to be set in the form of a smooth circle.'

Mangaleswari was even more taken aback. At such a young age, this woman was able to voice her thoughts clearly, like driving a pin into a pincushion. As she voiced her thoughts, Poorani's face and eyes lit up, glowing like the flame of a lamp might leap and dance. Where did this girl's unique ability emanate from, wondered Mangaleswari.

Poorani could not refuse Mangaleswari's earnest request to stay and have a meal with her. In the presence of that serene face, Poorani's stubborn, independent streak melted away. She was like a child in the presence of her mother.

'Until yesterday, I had only two daughters. Today, you have entered my life like a third daughter. Come, let's sit and eat together.' In response to this heartfelt invitation from the older woman, Poorani got up from the bed and followed her willingly.

In the dining room, plantain leaves were laid out on the table for them to sit facing each other. The cook waited to serve the meal. The table top was smooth, slippery glass. Poorani hesitated. Noticing her discomfort, Mangaleswari asked, 'Are you not used to eating at a table?'

'No.'

'See? This is why it is said that one has to adapt to various kinds of situations,' remarked Mangaleswari, smiling teasingly.

Poorani spoke frankly. 'Forgive me, Amma! I am unable to understand you. With sacred ash on your forehead and the purity of your appearance, you seem to be traditional. Yet when you speak, you come across as modern. In some matters, you praise the traditional ways. In others, you prefer the modern usages. Is it a sign of adjusting to one's circumstances to throw away generations of traditional practices to embrace a modern one? I am used to sitting on the floor and eating off a leaf. That is my practice. It was my father's practice. So was it the practice of his father and father's father and many generations before that. Why should I abandon an age-old practice in the name of modernity? One may choose to change a practice out of love or consideration but never out of fear of being teased for it. I don't know how to eat at a table. If this is something with which you want to tease me, I will move my leaf to the floor and eat there. If you also move to the floor to keep me company, I will have to tease you!'

'My goodness! What a mischievous girl you are! It seems one can't get away even if one says something light-heartedly.'

Poorani bowed her head and laughed.

'If your father had been alive, I would've arranged a felicitation meeting for him to celebrate his choice of a name for you.'

At the mention of her father, the smile disappeared from Poorani's lips. She sighed deeply. Her expression became sorrowful. No one spoke. There was silence.

After lunch and a brief chat, Poorani rose to take her leave.

'My brothers and little sister will be waiting for me at home. I have to get back and cook a meal for them. Allow me to take leave of you.'

'Wait a while. How can you cook anything in this midday heat? You can cook once and for all in the evening. Around five to five thirty in the evening, both my daughters will get home. You can meet them. Then I will have the driver drop you back home.' Mangaleswari spoke affectionately and persuasively. Poorani found herself unable to be firm in turning down the suggestion of her hostess who had not only rescued her but also looked after her so caringly. Her tongue, which had been more than willing to challenge the woman's opinions, was reluctant to defy her wishes. Poorani sat again.

When she cast her mind back to the happenings of the day, she was struck with a sense of wonder. First, the news that the old thief who had snatched her friend's necklace the previous evening and tried to flee had died of a snakebite; then her fruitless wandering around the streets of the city in search of a job, with hunger in her belly and frustration building up in her mind; then the episode of fainting on the street and being rescued by Mangaleswari, their argumentative exchanges… everything seemed to be the stuff of fanciful fiction. Yet isn't fiction based on real life? Turning the pages of life was like turning the pages of a book, one with unexpected events on each page. Poorani enjoyed approaching life this way.

In order to keep Poorani entertained while they waited, Mangaleswari led her guest on a guided tour of the house, upstairs and downstairs. Millions had been spent lavishly to make it look beautiful. There was a large clock in one of the rooms upstairs.

Mangaleswari took Poorani's hand and led her near the clock. She said, 'When this clock chimes, it produces sweet music. I brought it from Lanka. Hold on a while. It's almost four thirty. It will chime once now. You will be amazed when you hear the sound.'

The clock chimed once. It was a long, sweet sound like a piano chord. It echoed and subsided gently, like a wave of honey gushing forth in a flood only to dry up and disappear. Poorani remarked with a smile, 'A clock marks the passage of time. A person's lifespan is measured by it. It would be more appropriate to hear a sob from the clock every time it chimes. More sensible too.'

'Oh, you silly girl! You don't know how to savour life. It's one thing if I were to talk in such a weary tone at my age, but from you it sounds inappropriate.'

'Appropriate or not, I only said what I thought.'

'Your thoughts are like no one else's.'

'I have never been exposed to different situations or environments. So, I continue to think the way I have always thought. It could be that I am wrong in my opinions.'

'There you go again, baiting me with your remarks!'

Poorani found it a pleasure to interact with Mangaleswari, who was an amalgam of the traditional and the modern. The older woman also took delight in provoking Poorani, like a fond mother playfully teasing her child. She too enjoyed their back-and-forth.

At five o'clock, the elder daughter returned from college. 'Ever since they decided to increase the working days in college, they have made Saturdays full days too, Amma,' said the girl fretfully as she entered the house. Poorani was taken aback by the clothes worn by this girl, a college student. A Punjabi-style pyjama and kurta that seemed designed to attract and charm viewers. A flimsy dupatta that looked as though woven from bits of cloud. Poorani's eyes, used only to seeing traditional Tamil attire, smarted as they took in this new sight.

Poorani thought to herself, 'A girl may be a beauty; that is no fault of hers. But to deliberately make oneself look beautiful for others' eyes… that is a big sin!'

But to whom could she express such an opinion? No one, obviously. Poorani stayed silent.

Mangaleswari introduced her daughter to Poorani. The girl appeared to be insincere in her behaviour. She spoke animatedly in a mixture of Tamil and English, punctuated by loud laughter. Poorani learnt that the girl's name was Vasantha. After spending a few minutes in conversation, merely for the sake of appearances, Vasantha disappeared upstairs, her twin plaits swirling behind her.

As soon as she was out of earshot, Mangaleswari smiled and remarked, 'She tends to be a bit too pompous.' It was as if she had read Poorani's thoughts and noticed her reaction when she met Vasantha. Poorani merely smiled slightly in response.

'Today is a school holiday for my younger daughter, but she had to attend a special class. I wonder why she is not back yet.' Hardly were the words out of her mouth than the girl walked in. She was soberly clad, in a wide-bordered full-length skirt and half-sari, traditional like her mother.

'Chellam, I want to introduce you to this Akka. Come over here!' called Mangaleswari. The girl came over obediently and folded her palms together in greeting. Poorani liked the girl straight away. She seemed like someone with good family values.

'It's not only her name that is Chellam but she is also my *chellam*, my pet,' said her mother fondly.

Poorani spoke with no hesitation at all. 'It is in this girl that I see you,' she told Mangaleswari. At that moment, the elder daughter, Vasantha, was coming downstairs. Could she have heard what I said, wondered Poorani. But even if so, she told herself, she had not said anything wrong.

'It's not enough to merely say thank you to me for saving you today. You must keep visiting often, and I will also visit you. I will soon find a way to help you to solve the problems you told me about. You may leave for your home now.' With these parting words, Mangaleswari sent Poorani home in her car.

The car turned from Thanappa Mudali Street into West Gopuram Road. Dusk was just setting in, and the street lamps spread their glow. Crowds milled around, constantly coming together, only to part before going in different directions, like droplets scattering off a sheet of glass. As the car drove on, Poorani noticed the queue that stood at the entrance to the cinema theatre, the crowds at the shops and the blue and red neon advertisements.

It was the peak shopping hour, and the shops were crowded. From the store run by a north Indian, the rich aroma of chapatis being fried in ghee wafted across the street. The street was a flood of light. The lights burnt bright with claims of honesty, wholesale and retail.

As the car sped on, Poorani watched the street scenes rushing by, as though unreeled from a rapidly unwinding film spool. A deep weariness overtook her. Her mind was filled with anxious thoughts about the siblings she had left behind at home, who had gone without a meal the whole day. The car twisted and turned in and out of streets as it took her homeward.

'I asked Kamala to drop by this evening. She must also be waiting at home for me. It would be such an embarrassment if she talked to Mangaiyarkarasi and found out about my circumstances. Oh god, why have you put poverty and propriety alongside each other in this world? Why do you partner hunger with righteousness?'

As these thoughts were swirling through Poorani's mind, the car came to a stop. A railway crossing gate was closed. There are three such gates along the road between Madurai and Thirupparankundram. They are a source of regular annoyance to travellers on that route. The gate near Andalpuram was the one where they had now stopped. The express train was due to pass through from the south.

The train went by. The gates were lifted. The car started and sped on. Poorani did not want to alight from the car at her doorstep in full view of everyone. She asked to be dropped off at the end of the street near the Mayil Mandapam. The driver reminded her, 'Amma wanted me to find out where your house is.' Poorani pointed out her house to the driver and walked on. The car drove away. As she approached the front door, Poorani noticed that it was locked. She was stunned.

CHAPTER 6

A face that has
Captured the moon, wiped clean its tiny blemishes,
And embedded a smile upon it.
Eyes that mirror
Awareness that reflect the thought waves of the mind,
Eyes with beauty sprinkled upon them.

So far, we had assumed that when Poorani, overtaken by hunger and thirst, fainted and fell at the busy crossroads in Madurai city, only Mangaleswari and the readers of this story felt sympathy for her. But on that day, the tender mind of a poet also throbbed with compassion. Are these truly the times when a poet's feelings could be deeply stirred at the sight of a fellow human's misfortune? Is it not the century of news reporting? 'A girl fainted and fell on the street' could be a headline. But whose was the mind that yearned to write a poem about it? Are you not eager to find out about him? Come, let us meet this extraordinary young man.

Very close to the crossroads, can you see that doorway facing east? It is a small printing shop. Let us go in to see what is going on there!

A large advertising board hangs outside the premises. 'Meenakshi Printing House. All kinds of printing works accepted. Prompt service, fair price.' It is high noon. The front room is situated such that it is clearly visible from the street. In fact, the street too is clearly visible from the room. A small car stops outside the shop. An elderly man, who seems like he could be the proprietor of the shop, gets out of the car and walks briskly into the building. He enters the front office and searches for something on the table. A diary as large as a notebook lies open on the table. The man puts on his glasses, picks up the book and starts reading it. As he reads, expressions of irritation and then anger spread over his face.

'Where is the hope for this society of ours? Can it ever improve? In the heat of midday, due to circumstances unknown, a young woman fell unconscious on the street. Cars and lorries, crowds of people – all mere spectators. Is it right that a heartbreakingly beautiful woman should fall and lie like that in the dust of the street? And when the woman falls in the dust, all the traditional decency and rightful conduct as laid down in our culture also seems to fall into the dust! Oh god! My mind is seething with anger! These streets of Madurai were renowned for holding aloft the sceptre of Tamil culture. Prosperity and abundance were the hallmarks of Tamil pride. Such pride belongs only to the past now. There is nothing left of it in the present day.

'What is it that meets my gaze on these streets these days? I see frustrated people milling around. I see souls struggling with their burdens of hunger and poverty. I see ragged women, children in tow – goddesses reduced to begging on the streets. My heart cannot bear this! How could a young woman, so beautiful, educated, refined, fall thus in the street? What led to this? Who was responsible for it? *De*, Aravinda! You are a poet. Is your spirit blind to this? Go on, compose something. Let your storm of feelings take over. Let it roar. Were you destined to be a mere proofreader in a printing shop? Not at all. Never. You were born with a poet's sensibility. Your destiny is to reform society and bring it onto a righteous path.'

As the elderly man read on, his fury was stoked further. His rage expressed itself in the violence with which he rang the bell that stood on the table. After the man had pounded on the bell a couple more times, a small boy scurried in and stood respectfully.

'If that donkey Aravindan is present, send him to me at once. That boy's madness is growing worse by the day.'

The small boy ran into the shop to carry out the errand. Amidst several types of printing machines, all whirring noisily, a handsome young man stood talking to a group of typesetters. He was fair in complexion and tall in stature. He had a long face, with a well-shaped nose. It combined beauty with a mischievous, attractive charm, like God Krishna in a Krishna–Radha calendar picture. He was simply clad in a dhoti and a khadi *jibba*.

'Sir, the boss has come. He is asking for you,' said the messenger boy. 'He seems to have read something that was lying on the table and is very angry.'

With the small boy trailing behind him, the young man strode towards the office room. His stride was self-confident and majestic.

The moment the young man appeared in the doorway, the proprietor launched into an angry tirade. 'Aravinda! What nonsense are you spouting here? I have employed you to do proof correction, not to reform society.'

When Aravindan spotted the notebook that his boss was holding, he bit his lip and lowered his head shyly.

'*Enna da*, I'm asking you a question and you're standing there like a *kalladi mangan*. Is this the work you are putting in from ten in the morning to five in the evening every day?'

'No, sir! This afternoon, just opposite the shop, in the middle of the street, a young woman fainted and fell. I was watching it, and various feelings and thoughts went through my mind, and I just wanted to—'

'Oh, so you transformed all your thoughts into poetry, did you?'

'No, no, sir. It's just my habit to put down my thoughts in this diary…'

'Aha! Of course, how can such precious thoughts be left unwritten! Would they not be lost to the world? What a disastrous loss that would be! You donkey! Instead of earning a good name for yourself by diligently correcting the work that comes to the printing shop, you want to write poetry. Poetry! Ha! Useless fellow!'

After this outburst, the proprietor, Meenakshisundaram Pillai, flung the notebook at Aravindan's face. Aravindan grabbed the flying book with both hands before it could fall to the floor. After all, that book was as precious as life to him. What a treasure trove of lofty thoughts and emotions. What valuable snippets of verse, as they unfolded in his mind, were preserved within its covers. How could his boss even guess that book's value!

Having flung the book at Aravindan and glaring angrily at him once more, the proprietor got up and went towards the printing room. Hoping to revel, once more, in the pleasure of reading his own creative effort before the boss got back, Aravindan hastily turned the pages. Stopping at a poem titled 'Holding the Moon', he read the first two lines silently to himself and then began to read the rest of the lines aloud.

Her lips are twin corals set with pearls,
Her tresses, spun from clouds, flow as ringlets near her ears
Churned from nectar, enhanced with delicate flavours,
She is Beauty created by the love god Madan
For his adoration.

As he read his own poem, Aravindan tried to bring the girl's image before his mind's eye. Her graceful gait as she walked along, umbrella in hand, her sudden fall – all these were etched in his memory. Like one who chews slowly to enjoy a flavour longer, he recited his own verse again and again. 'I have written this very well. What a rhythmic flow! What a beautiful sentiment!' he said to himself proudly. Just then, the stern voice of the boss called out to him. Aravindan hurriedly hid the book and ran back into the printing room.

'Aravinda, about that novel we accepted for proofreading, *The Scoundrel's Story of Azhagappan's Secrets…*'

'Sir! No, sir! That's not correct. It is Azhagappan's book titled *A Scoundrel's Secrets*.'

'Oh, all right, whatever! How many chapters of that book have been completed?'

'Ten chapters are done.'

'Ten? Well, hurry up and get the rest of it done quickly. I'm telling you this because I am personally planning to take up a large project. For that, you will have to visit a particular place today. If you finish your current assignment of that novel soon, you will have more time to devote to my project.'

'Oh, don't worry, sir. We will get it done in the next two days.'

The proprietor's calm tone suggested that his earlier rage against Aravindan had died down. This was his usual pattern of behaviour. One moment he would fly off into a fit of anger at someone, and the next moment he would be talking to the same person calmly, with an arm around his shoulder. He forgot his own angry outbursts quickly.

Even when he shouted at Aravindan and spoke more harshly than the circumstances warranted, he was basically very fond of him and held him in high regard. As for Aravindan, this printing shop was his home away from home. He worked diligently, at all hours, without watching the clock, then spread a few old newspapers on the floor and went to sleep right there.

Indeed, he was all in all for Meenakshi Printing House, the most prestigious printing house in Madurai. He was the manager, proofreader and accountant and, at times, even the bill collector. He had mastered the art of allocating time to these various tasks very efficiently. Not only was he attractive in appearance but also pleasing in his behaviour. The ability to be quick and brisk in executing tasks is a big asset, and Aravindan had this skill in abundance. He was incapable of sitting idle even for a moment. Every second had to be occupied well. Such was the sharpness and intensity of his mind.

He was totally obsessed with making diary entries. His diary was a compendium of two or three large notebooks bound together. In one of them, he would inscribe proverbs and wise sayings. In another, he would scribble his thoughts as and when they occurred to him. The third book would be for accounting records and reminders related to the work of the press shop.

The need to write poetry had gripped him. It had become an important part of his life. Lines of poetry would flash into his mind without warning, anywhere and everywhere. He would grab the nearest scrap of paper and write furiously till the fire of creativity in his mind raged. Just as the ripe castor pod cannot help but burst open to scatter its seeds, so also did the newborn poem in Aravindan's mind threaten to burst, unless it was rapidly written down. It was a beautiful race between thought and the written word.

Often, when the proprietor was away, Aravindan would occupy his chair and scribble his thoughts. Sometimes, he would absent-mindedly leave his diary on the table in the office, and the boss would return unexpectedly and start reading it, sending him into a fit of rage. After a lot of shouting and a severe reprimand, the matter would be forgotten – till the next time. In his own mind, the proprietor acknowledged, 'This fellow will succeed in life. He has a sharp mind. Even when he is scribbling something, it is a scribble with meaning and beauty to it!' The thought gave the elderly man satisfaction and pride.

Meenakshisundaram Pillai was busy inspecting the machines inside the shop. Meanwhile, the young woman with the umbrella, the one who had fallen in a faint on the street, was walking back and forth in Aravindan's mind with a smile on her face. Aravindan carefully slipped away to where he had hidden his diary. He retrieved it and, with not just great speed but with considerable agitation of mind, he penned these lines under the ones he had written earlier:

A hand that held an umbrella,
A face that spoke of the mind's turmoil,
A gait that faltered from great hunger

'Aravinda! Where did you disappear to?'

Aravindan ran.

'The Govinda Theatre man wanted some wall posters printed. Have you ordered the paper?'

'No, sir. He came this morning. He wanted us to buy the paper at our cost and said he would settle the total bill later. I put some fear into him. I told him, "That won't work in your case. Come back this evening with the paper. Otherwise, you yourself are smooth and white, like art paper. I can put you through the machine and print you."'

'Oh, very clever! There seems to be no end to your cheekiness.'

Aravindan smiled to himself. The foreman, typesetters and two treadle men, who had been listening in, also enjoyed the exchange. There actually was no limit to the mischief Aravindan was capable of. He would reveal anyone's error or mistake openly with no hesitation. Being incapable of deceit or dishonour himself, he had no fear of the opinions of others. This made others fearful of him. They were wary about saying or doing anything wrong in his presence. Anything bad or evil was in fear of Aravindan.

Once a typesetter had made a habit of stealing a few of the letters made of lead and taking them away in his lunch box. This matter came to Aravindan's notice. The next day, when the typesetter came to his table, he found the following message composed in typescript for him to read:

> *In just four days you took away 150 'ka' type pieces, 200 'aa' pieces and 70 'lye' pieces in your tiffin box. You thief! You will return all of them by three in the afternoon today. Otherwise, you will have to 'compose' yourself!*
>
> Aravindan

The typesetter read the message with extreme embarrassment. He rushed home, brought back all the stolen pieces, gave them to Aravindan and sought his pardon.

In another case of a customer who had a lot of unpaid bills owed to the printing shop, Aravindan devised another strategy. The customer was a cinema theatre owner who had ordered wall posters to advertise a movie. Aravindan arranged for the following message to be printed in small letters at the corner of each poster where the printer's name usually appears:

> *Your dues have risen and spread like poison. I am tired of sending you bills and reminders. Please pay what you owe immediately. I am left with no other way than to compose this message to you, at your expense, on your paper.*

It was followed by the name of the printing shop. When the posters went up all over the town, and people everywhere noticed the message, the theatre owner became a laughing stock. The very next day, the man hurried in and settled all his dues.

At a mere twenty-eight years of age, Aravindan was the main pillar of support for Meenakshi Printing House. His attributes were a composite portrait of handsomeness, intelligence, competence and a tendency to be impish and mischievous.

When Aravindan was speaking, it was hard for anyone to look away from his handsome face. His red lips seemed always ready to break into a teasing smile. He hated wearing shirts with collars and draping fussy long dhotis. He preferred simplicity in everything. In fact, he would often assert that Tamil culture was one that laid emphasis on simplicity.

'This is a nation of poor people. Here, not only must every person learn to live within limited means but also must be willing to help others,' he would declare with a smile. He had great admiration for Gandhian principles and was fond of praising them at every opportunity. At all times, a tiny, palm-sized book, containing verses from the *Thirukkural,* resided in his shirt pocket.

'Aravinda, come with me. I need to talk to you in private,' said Meenakshisundaram Pillai, leading the young man into his office. Once they were seated, he started explaining the details of the plan he had in mind. Although Aravindan came across as a playful fellow, the older man had deep faith in his abilities. He undertook no venture without discussing it with Aravindan. The plan he described that day won Aravindan's wholehearted support.

'Yes, this plan of action will certainly benefit us… and the nation. It is necessary to publish and popularize the books of eminent Tamil authors and make them available at affordable prices. If we carry out the plan smartly, we will not face any problems.'

Handing Aravindan a slip of paper with an address on it, the proprietor ordered, 'Right! So, go to this address and meet the people concerned to discuss the steps to be taken. I'm going to stay here till seven thirty. So, you can use my car for this trip, Aravinda.'

Aravindan secretly took along his diary. 'Remember, the place you are going to has to be the first source for our new project,' warned the proprietor. 'So, do well and come back with a win.' He accompanied Aravindan to the door and saw him get into the car.

As the car sped along, in the fading light of the approaching evening, Aravindan's poet eyes took in the beauty of the streets of Madurai. After turning west at the Dindigul Road crossing, the driver asked, 'Where do you want to go?' Aravindan gave him the address. Thoughts raced and tumbled through his mind. His feelings floated on ripples of joy. In a voice soaked in honey, his lips sang the words:

Eyes that mirror awareness,
Eyes that reflect the thought waves of the mind,
Eyes with beauty sprinkled upon them.

His mind summoned the image of that face, and an impish smile instantly curved his lips.

You may remember that when Poorani was sent home in Mangaleswari's car, she arrived to find the house locked. At that very moment, another small car arrived at the house.

'Isn't this Professor Azhagiya Sittrambalam's house?'

Poorani, who had been staring dumbstruck at the locked door of her home, turned at the sound of this new voice. The moment he saw her face, Aravindan was stunned by sheer amazement.

That same face! That same beauty! A face that had captured

the moon, wiped clean its tiny blemishes and embedded a smile upon it! The same young woman who had fainted in the midday sun and fallen on the street opposite the printing shop – and had fallen into his heart at the same moment! The beauty that had inspired poetry in him, the face that he had been seeing all day in his waking dreams The elegance and grace that had filled his thoughts – that very creature stood on the doorstep in front of him.

'Who are you? What do you want?' demanded Poorani rather irritably.

'I'm from Meenakshi Printing House. My name is Aravindan. I need to speak to the professor's daughter about publishing his books.'

Aravindan walked over with a smile to the front *thinnai* of the house and sat without waiting for an invitation.

Poorani was in a foul mood. It was a time when angry thoughts filled her mind, such as 'The world is full of scoundrels, cheats and selfish people who will not lift a finger to help others.' Her annoyance at the attitude of the Pudu Mandapam publisher she had met earlier that day spilt over to all publishers everywhere. She was unimpressed by Aravindan suddenly turning up like this, smiling the way he did and deciding to sit on her *thinnai* without being asked to do so. With lips quivering with anger, she confronted Aravindan.

'Hah! Books! You're talking about books! What nonsense! Cattle-feed traders become book publishers overnight. No one can be trusted these days. At first, they smile and make all kinds of promises like honest Harishchandrans. And then, they—'

Aravindan interrupted her before she could finish. The earlier smile had disappeared. 'Stop. It seems you are not in a good frame of mind right now. I will come back another time. Just because you fainted and fell on the road, you don't have to hold the whole world responsible for your troubles and turn your fury upon them.'

He got up from the *thinnai*, walked briskly towards the car, got in and slammed the door. The car sped off in a cloud of dust. Poorani, who had been about to spill more angry words, swallowed them whole. A big question that arose in her mind was, 'How did that young man know that I fell on the street?' Her eye fell upon a book lying on the *thinnai* next to where Aravindan had been sitting. In his agitation, he had obviously left it behind.

She grabbed it and ran out into the street. 'Mr Aravindan!' she called out. But the car was already far away, out of reach of her soft voice. It was only then that she gave a passing thought to his handsome appearance, the smiling confidence with which he had walked up and seated himself on the *thinnai* and his majestic gait as he strode back to the car. It was only a passing thought as more pressing matters claimed her attention. The locked house, the missing brothers and sister… the anxiety of it all was a heavy weight on her mind.

CHAPTER 7

I have never found anyone with my qualities of womanly beauty
and modesty,
And the intelligence to think and reason
You whose feet walk the hot dusty earth,
Are you a thief who can steal in through
A woman's eyes?

– Kamban

Poorani stood on the street in front of her locked house. In her hand was the notebook Aravindan had left behind. Odhuvar *thatha*'s granddaughter, Kamu, spotted Poorani from her house across the street. She came over and informed Poorani, 'Kamala came this evening and waited for your return. But you didn't show up. Just before it grew dark, she sent for a horse cart and left, taking your brothers and sister with her. She told me to let you know that she wants you to come to her home.'

'I understand that she had to leave. But why did she lock up my house and take my brothers and sister along with her?'

'I don't know about that. I only know that she sent for the horse cart, took the children and left.'

'Kamala is always like this. Does strange things without any reason,' Poorani thought in irritation as she hurried to

Kamala's house. Near the road junction, a number of glittering new vehicles of varied sizes were parked.

It was a common practice for those who had bought new cars or trucks to park the vehicles in front of the Murugan Temple sanctum, apply sandal paste and kumkum and drape flower garlands on them before taking them on the first 'official' drive. All four tyres of each new vehicle would crush lime fruits, placed on the street in front of them, as they drove off, thereby avoiding the evil eye. This was a sight that had always given pleasure to Poorani.

As she turned at the entrance to the Murugan Temple and headed for Kamala's home, a large white car, with a swan-like splendour, went by. Its tyres were running over the lime offerings. Poorani glanced at the proud owner of the splendid machine as he sat behind the wheel and hurriedly moved into the shadows so as to avoid being noticed by him.

Why? Who was this man, and why did Poorani want to avoid being seen by him? He was none other than the hypocrite who had sent the cheque that she had promptly returned along with the declaration that her father's sense of honour was still very much alive.

Today, his new car's wheels were crushing limes. How many poor people's lives had he crushed underfoot earlier, Poorani wondered bitterly as she walked along.

Near the entrance to the temple *sannadhi*, a large group of beggars swarmed around the new car. Poorani watched as the owner snarled, flung abuses at them and chased them away. She remembered, with a sharp sting of bitterness, how she herself had been wandering the streets of Madurai like a beggar, hoping to find a job.

The moment Kamala saw Poorani, she burst out angrily, 'More and more these days, you are behaving like some great lady or something! All right, so you have a lot of self-respect. You know how to hide all your problems even from those who are near and dear to you. But once we have come to know what the situation is, how can you expect us to be silent, Amma? You have a strong spirit. You can grit your teeth and endure anything without saying a word. But we possess soft hearts. We believe that giving and taking help are signs of love and affection. You have been on an empty stomach all day. Yes, I know about it, Poorani. You lied to your brothers that you had eaten at my home. Earlier this evening, I saw the situation at your house. What satisfaction do you get from misleading us like this?'

Lost for a response, Poorani merely bowed her head. Little Mangai came running from inside the house.

'Akka, you left us alone without saying anything. Kamala Akka brought us here this evening and gave us dinner.'

After all, how can a child be expected to keep up the falsehoods that adults indulge in for the sake of pride? It was only truth that emerged from the little one's lips. Alongside the embarrassment of having her plight revealed to her friend, Poorani also felt a great sense of gratitude towards her.

Kamala went on with her explanation of the events of the evening. 'Poorani, please don't be angry with me for bringing the children home and feeding them. I felt I had the right to do that as your friend. These children are every bit your equal when it comes to sticking to principles. The moment I invited them to come with me, they refused. "Not without checking with Akka," they said. But I thought, "Akka or no Akka, this is no way for children to be starving all day." So, I said, "I will explain to your Akka. Just come with me now." I locked your house and brought them away with me.'

In an effort to change the topic, Poorani asked Kamala, 'Where are your parents? I don't see them here.'

'Appa and Amma are on a trip. They will be away for two or three days.'

'Oh? For what?'

Kamala did not reply. Her face reddened; she smiled slightly and bent her head. The toes of her rosy feet drew squiggles on the floor.

Poorani understood. As she watched the play of shyness and flowering charm on her friend's face, she remarked, 'Aha! So that's what it is! The auspicious month of Thai is around the corner. Your parents must be on a mission to find a suitable bridegroom for their daughter.'

Like a flower that smiles wider and wider as it blossoms, Kamala's face flushed. Poorani gazed at her friend's face, suffused with blushing beauty, and thought, 'It's true what they say – when a young woman's face blossoms like this, the minds of poets are moved to compose poetry.'

Thirunavukkarasu and Sambandan had been afraid to look Poorani in the face lest she be angry with them for leaving their home and coming with Kamala.

'All right, I will take the children and leave now,' said Poorani, making preparations to turn and go back. Kamala flew into a fit of rage.

'Going back home? What do you mean! What have you got at home? I know for a fact, Poorani, that right now, there is nothing in your home except stacks of books. Don't go on trying to deceive me. Books can satisfy one's hunger for knowledge, but they cannot satisfy the hunger in one's stomach. It's only after thinking things through that I brought the children here. Appa and Amma are away. In fact, they suggested that I ask you to come and stay here and keep me company till they return. I too would be safer if I'm not alone. You and the children must stay here, at my house, for the next few days. If you are planning to sneak back and starve yourself and the children too, I will not allow that.'

'You need not allow it, Kamala. But may I ask you a question?'

'Sure, ask me. What is it?'

'Tell me, how long do you think you can protect and look after me and the children like this?' Poorani laughed as she posed the question. Yet there was more than a tinge of bitterness in that laughter.

'Is that what you mean? Well, you can stay until you find a job. People exist only to help each other in times of need. What is it that we can hoard and carry away with us finally?'

'Well, that's what you say, Kamala, and I can't find the willpower to protest. In today's fast pace of life, one can't find such selfless love and generosity in anyone. All we see is a mad rush. It is as if we are all wearing blinkers like a cart horse, unable to see on either side, unable to tell where we are headed.'

After the children had gone to sleep, Poorani and Kamala went up to the terrace and chatted for a while. In the warm intimacy of their relationship, Poorani overcame her natural inhibitions and narrated all the incidents of that morning when she had roamed the streets of Madurai in search of a job. She even mentioned her encounter with Mangaleswari but without telling her about the fainting fit that had led to that encounter. Instead, she spun the tale differently to bring the lady into the story.

From the terrace of Kamala's house, the temple dome was not far. In the darkness, the electric lamps, strung like jasmine gardens on the dome, pointed their light downwards. From the crest of the dome that stood shrouded in darkness, the letters 'OM', spelt in neon, smiled at her. The water in the lakes around the city gleamed in the fading light, like slivers of polished mirrors that had shattered when they fell to earth from the skies. Watching these and the tiny light points of the city buildings, Poorani lost track of time as she unburdened her heart. She spoke about what lay in her future and the problems that cried for her attention.

As Poorani talked, Kamala, overcome with tiredness, had leaned back against the wall and fallen asleep. Poorani woke her up, and they both went downstairs to go to bed. Kamala was fast asleep the moment she lay down. But Poorani, with all her problems continuing to trouble her, could not get to sleep right away. 'Every day there is a new dawn for the world. When will my family and I get a new dawn? Hey, mighty Muruga! Please open a door for me! My father did not simply entrust me to humans when he departed this world. In your town, in front of your sacred temple, he has entrusted me and my siblings to your care. Muruga, save me. Please don't abandon me. Show me a way to earn a livelihood.'

Poorani lay on the bed with her eyes closed, praying earnestly. In her mind's eye, she pictured Lord Muruga as a boy, with lowered brows and red lips. His face effulgent in grace, holding his spear in one lotus-like hand, like a young Sun God.

With no reason or connection, before her mind's eye there

rose another vision – the face of the young man who had visited her home earlier that evening. Like a child who secretly savours candy, she whispered the name 'Aravindan' softly to herself. It gave her a kind of forbidden thrill, a dizzy joy. It was a joy that could not be described in words and needed no words. Why was she recalling his face at that moment? She had no answer to her own question. Even if one with no knowledge of music, or without any intention behind the act, were to pluck the string of a veena, would it not sing its sweet music? It was in just such a way that Aravindan's face slipped into Poorani's mind.

Without disturbing the sleeping Kamala, Poorani turned on the table lamp and opened the notebook that Aravindan had forgotten on her *thinnai*. Amidst the low hum of crickets and the tick-tock of the clock, the *koodam* of the house was in darkness. The light from the table lamp shed a blue-white glow, like spilt flour.

Till about two thirty in the morning, that table lamp remained turned on.

The more Poorani read of Aravindan's writings, the more intrigued she became. This precocious youngster had used a whole palette of vivid descriptions to chronicle his experiences. The commentaries on things he had seen or heard, punctuated by poems, were composed in a tone always appropriate to their context. Just like one would indulge oneself by secretly opening and enjoying a hidden treasure, Poorani revelled in Aravindan's words. It was only when she came across his description of the fainting incident, and the poem that it had inspired, that Poorani understood why he had retorted in that manner to her the previous evening, 'Just because you fainted and fell on the street, there is no need to blame the whole world and lash out.'

Poorani continued to flip through the pages of the diary at random.

On one of the pages was a passage that had obviously been written when Aravindan's mind was seething with fury.

In today's Tamil land, there is no poetry. There is only hunger. There are only problems, disappointments and worries. In a tangled and knotted ball of thread, can one find a beginning or an end? From where did these dilemmas arise? How can they be resolved? Nothing is clear. At one time, there were problems in life, but now life itself is being lived inside problems. At one time, there were occasions that involved dishonesty and raised doubts. Now, life is being lived amidst all-pervading dishonesty and doubt. Nowadays, there are hardly any humans with warm hearts. Only metal and plastic are found everywhere. People lie unattended on the roadside as if they were mere garbage. How can this be changed? It is all very well for the poet to declare, 'If even one man goes hungry, we will destroy the world.' But the reality is far removed from that. Desperate people are even consuming bug poison to escape life and are being consigned to dust, like worms and insects.

These passages from Aravindan's notebook gave Poorani a good understanding of his mind. A man who lived close by shared her strong feelings about the problems in the lives of this Tamil land's people. She felt attracted to his charm, intelligence, nature and character. She chided herself for having spoken to such a worthy man so rudely. She felt distressed, as though she had stepped upon a beautiful scented flower and crushed it in the dust. The noble aspects of Aravindan's character stood tall in Poorani's mind, like the temple *gopurams* of Madurai or the great pillars of the Thirumalai Naickan Palace.

Poorani lifted the notebook reverentially to her forehead, and then placed it on the table and turned off the lamp. Sleep took over her tired body while Aravindan took up residence in her heart. It was as if, in discovering Aravindan, she had at last grasped what she had been groping for endlessly in the darkness of her mind.

She smiled in her sleep. She was dreaming a sweet dream. Aravindan takes her hand and leads her somewhere. The two of them climb the Thirupparankundram Hill. A gentle breeze is blowing. Up in the sky, the full moon is like a lake of molten silver. As if having spent aeons in severe austerities, just for the privilege of seeing a pair of lovers like these, the stars gaze down on them with playful mischief in their eyes. Around a patch of sky illumined by the moon, a few wispy white clouds appear, like muslin cloths that have slipped unnoticed off the Gandharva women's bodies as they hurry to meet their lovers.

'Poorani, in this sky, in this moon, in this cool breeze, poetry resides, beauty lives. All these are made for you and me,' whispers Aravindan in her ear, with a smile. That smile conveys volumes.

Poorani disagrees with him. She says, 'No, Aravindan, what you say is not true. There is no poetry in the world, only hunger. There is no joy, only grief.'

'You are speaking about the mud beneath your feet. We are up on a hill. When you are up here, do not let your mind descend to the depths.'

'Yes, beauty may reside at the top. But life has to be lived down below, Aravindan.'

The conversation goes on between the two of them. As they continue to climb, Poorani's legs begin to hurt. She rests her hand on his strong shoulder and climbs steadily without losing her footing.

'Look there, up ahead of us. Do you see that sprinkling of lights like scattered diamonds? That is Madurai city,' says Aravindan. She lifts her head and turns to see, but her big toe stubs against a rock on the hill. Blood streams all over the toe; it looks like a pomegranate flower. Aravindan bends and touches her toe. His hand is red with blood. He tears a piece of cloth, wets it in a nearby stream and ties a bandage around Poorani's toe.

'Your hands are covered with blood. Please wash it off,' Poorani urges him.

'Why should I wash it off?' he retorts with a smile. 'No, Poorani. With this blood, I shall write a poem about the miseries faced by womankind.'

Poorani woke from her dream. Her big toe was indeed painful. It felt wet, as if it had been wiped with water. She got up and turned on the light to take a look. An *arival manai*, a vegetable cutting blade, had been kept near the corner of the room. Her toe must have grazed the sharp knife as she moved in her sleep. The light had disturbed Kamala's sleep. She woke up and asked, 'What happened, Poorani?'

'I seem to have cut my toe on the knife when I moved in my sleep.'

Kamala hurried towards her. 'You silly girl!" she scolded. 'Couldn't you have taken more care to sleep a little further away from that knife? If you hadn't woken up and discovered it, you might have lost your toe altogether.' She smeared some slaked lime paste on the cut and tied a cloth around it. Poorani went back to bed, yearning to somehow resurrect that old dream.

The next morning, Poorani and Kamala set off to Saravana Pond for a bath. On the way, they stopped by at two or three community housing complexes, and Kamala made enquiries in an effort to find a house for Poorani. On Rath Street, they managed to find an independent house with three rooms and a well, with the entrance facing south. The rent quoted was eighteen rupees a month. Kamala paid an advance for the house rent from her own money. Poorani was relieved to have found this place. It was small no doubt, but it was private. So much better than having to live in a community housing of ten to twenty units. Also, it was close to Kamala's house.

The two young women had their baths and returned with wet saris wrapped around them. Odhuvar *thatha* was seated on the *thinnai* outside Kamala's front door, awaiting their return. Poorani noticed a young man sitting next to *Thatha*. He was none other than Aravindan! Poorani bent her head, stepped to the other side and hurried indoors.

Thatha called out, 'Poorani, this young man came to your house looking for you. He wants to meet you. Kamu told me that you and the children came here. So, I brought him here.'

'Please ask him to wait, *Thatha*. I will come out soon,' Poorani called back. She continued to hurry into the house.

Aravindan rose to his feet and called out, 'When I dropped by yesterday, I left my notebook on the *thinnai* of your house due to oversight. I thought I'd just come and take it back...' Even as Poorani was moving away, his words reached her ears. She recalled last night's dream and a tingling feeling of pleasure ran through her. She changed into a fresh sari, picked up the notebook and stepped out of the house.

By the time she emerged, Odhuvar *thatha* had left for the

temple. It was the hour when he was scheduled to recite the *thevaram* at the temple. Aravindan was sitting by himself on the *thinnai*. The moment Poorani emerged, notebook in hand, the young man rose and stretched out his hand to take it. Poorani handed him the book and said, 'Please sit down. I need to speak to you. I hope you are not in a hurry.'

Aravindan had been wondering whether this young woman had opened the book and read his writings. The thought embarrassed him. Now, hearing her invitation to stay, his embarrassment became even more acute. He thought, 'She must have read what I wrote about her fainting on the street. She is going to ask me about that.'

Hesitantly, shyly, he sat. From the corner of his eye, he glanced at her. He noticed her freshly bathed face, like a pink lotus still damp with dew. This face was the inspiration for his poem. It was to this face that the idealistic fervour and poetic passion of his mind had paid homage. What indeed could be so special about her face?

Poorani started speaking. 'Yesterday, I spoke very rudely to you. First of all, I seek your forgiveness for that.' When Aravindan heard the gentleness in her voice, he felt easier in his mind and more confident. He lifted his head and looked directly at Poorani. She was already looking at him. Her eyes feasted upon the face of the handsome thief who had stolen her heart with his written words and entered her dreams. As though they had yearned through untold millennia for this moment of shared glances, those two pairs of eyes spoke of their mutual love.

'I read your notebook. I seek your forgiveness for that as well.'

'It doesn't matter. That was no great crime. It's just some random scribblings about whatever occurs to my mind.'

'They are all beautiful. I stayed awake to read them well into the night.'

'Is that so? I had scribbled something about you in the book too…'

'I saw that.'

'If it was wrong of me, then I, too, should seek your pardon,' remarked Aravindan with an impish smile, still looking into her eyes. His smile was always infectious. It made the people around him smile as well. Now Poorani smiled and she said, 'You may publish my father's books. I have come to this decision after going through your notebook. I trust you. Please leave your office address with me. I will come there tomorrow.'

'I'm very grateful for your favourable decision,' said Aravindan, handing her his business card.

As he left, did he by any chance leave his heart behind with her? And did he take her heart with him?

Poorani decided to make the move to the newly rented house, the very same day. At about three o'clock, she arranged for a vehicle and went home, along with Kamala and Thirunavukkarasu.

But things did not work out the way she had planned. Midway through clearing up the house and packing the things, Mangaleswari arrived in her car. She declared that an urgent matter had come up and it could not wait. She rushed Poorani away with her in the car to Madurai.

CHAPTER 8

You are like none other.
In minds that think of you, you are the origin of all thoughts.
You are gold and precious gems, and you the enjoyment that they bring.
You are worthy, above all others to be extolled on this earth.
Except to marvel at the sublime you,
What else can a poor soul like me do?

– Thevaram

'It's something very important. Don't waste time asking questions. Just come with me immediately…' Mangaleswari spoke with a sense of urgency, and Poorani found herself unable to refuse her request. Before leaving with the older lady, she entrusted Kamala, Thirunavukkarasu and Odhuvar *thatha* with the task of clearing out their present house and moving the things to the newly rented place.

Earlier that day, she had enthusiastically gone house-hunting with Kamala. Later, she cheerfully went to have a bath in the Saravana Pond. She had been determined to find a new house and vacate the other before the time limit set by the landlord. Her body had efficiently gone through the motions of everything that had to be done to accomplish that goal. Her lips had worn a smile, yet anxiety ruled her mind. There was no joy within her, only seething frustration. No peace, only unease; no enthusiasm, only weariness.

The worries that she had wanted to keep to herself had now become known to others. Her problems were no longer secret worries. The world now knew about the poverty, hunger and deprivation in her home. The world? Who comprised that world? Well, Kamala knew about it. It was this kind of pity that her mind had been determined to avoid. But in practice, that could not be accomplished. Her closest friend had come forward to help her. How could she, in all conscience, spurn her friend's offer and stubbornly remain hungry and needy at home?

In her mind, raging with a seething flame that burnt thoughts to ashes like a fire in a sandalwood forest, there was only one island of peace – the thought of Aravindan. Her dream about him soothed her mind. Her thoughts about him were the seeds that put forth new shoots of fresh ideas.

A medley of such thoughts tumbled through Poorani's mind as they drove along in Mangaleswari's car. Poorani did not initiate a conversation. She sat silently next to the older woman, who was immersed in her own world. The car went past sand mounds on the west and lush green fields on the east and turned into the busy Moolakarai Street. To the north, rows of similar cement houses, the quarters for mill workers, appeared briefly and then were lost to view. They entered the environs of Pasumalai, with its abundant greenery, and sped towards Madurai. Neither of them spoke for a while. A Sunday lethargy ruled the streets, with shuttered shops gratefully revelling in some well-earned repose after a week of toil.

It was Mangaleswari who started the conversation.

'Do you know where I am taking you now?'

'How can I know unless you tell me?'

'I'm about to save you from the disaster that is looming in your life. I'm about to get you a good job.'

Poorani looked at Mangaleswari, a new hope dawning in her eyes. The car drove along Avani Street and halted next to a large building bearing the sign 'Madurai Women's Sangam'. There were a few other cars parked outside. 'Come, let us go in,' said Mangaleswari, leading the way into the building.

Inside, five or six ladies who seemed to belong to rich families, like Mangaleswari, were seated. They were, obviously, from the influential families of Madurai. Poorani had seen many of them on various occasions and knew who they were. But there was no reason for them to know Poorani. If wealthy folks were expected to remember every poor person or anyone with no social status, what would it do to their pride and prestige?

Mangaleswari came up close to Poorani and whispered, 'Poorani, these ladies are the office-bearers of this women's organization. Do your *namaskarams* to them, please.'

Hesitantly, Poorani folded her palms in greeting to the whole group collectively.

Mangaleswari addressed the women. 'This is the young woman I was telling you about. She is the daughter of the late Azhagiya Sittrambalam. She is well-versed in Tamil grammar and literature. She also has an adequate knowledge of English. I think we can appoint her as a teacher for the new class that we are planning to start in the month of Thai.' With these words, Mangaleswari introduced Poorani to the group and informed Poorani about the nature of the job.

'We have no objection. But she seems rather too young…'

said one of the ladies. Mangaleswari had a crisp, ready response to this doubt. 'What is the importance of age? Just have a brief conversation with this girl, and you will be convinced. This young girl has the wisdom, the knowledge and the deep understanding that neither you nor I have attained, even at our age. Her father named her "Poorani". She has lived up to that name in intelligence, education and wisdom.'

'If you say so, we are satisfied. These classes are not merely for entertainment or a pastime. We are keen to help girls develop their skills and grow through our Sangam.'

As Mangaleswari and the ladies were involved in these exchanges, Poorani sat by in polite silence. She studied the faces of each of those women and tried to read their nature and look into their minds. To Poorani's exploring eyes, each face was a whole world. Each had its own distinctive flavour, history, story and beauty. Each was a book that she would read, analyse and store away in her mind.

Opposite the entrance to the Women's Sangam hung a large portrait of Her Holiness Sarada Devi. It was as though the quality of purity had blossomed and embodied itself in the form of a portrait of the Holy Mother. Elsewhere on the walls hung portraits of Swami Vivekananda, Ramakrishna Paramahamsa, Thiruvalluvar and other such eminent personalities. On the floor on either side of Sarada Devi's portrait, the flames from a pair of *kuthuvilakku* oil lamps glowed gold. The whole building was suffused with the scent of sandalwood incense. The jasmine flowers that adorned the hair of some of the women added their own perfume to the air. The whole ambience – the portrait of Her Holiness Sarada Devi and the divine fragrant air all around – moved Poorani deeply. Sarada Devi's face in the picture contained what can be called the essence of womanhood, and it seemed to convey something to Poorani. As red-hot iron sizzles in water, Poorani's inner self took in certain qualities from the portrait. It was as though her mind had discovered a great truth and was thirsting to attain something.

'Are you married, Amma?' When she heard the question addressed to her by one of the ladies, Poorani dragged her attention away from Sarada Devi's face and turned to respond.

'No.'

'Really? You look old enough to have been married by now.'

More such questions continued. What is the limit to the kind of irrelevant things that women from privileged families want to talk about? Poorani answered each of their questions patiently. Mangaleswari intervened every now and then to answer some of the questions on Poorani's behalf. After listening to everything, the lady who had started the interrogation remarked, 'How can we appoint someone who doesn't have a BA degree in Tamil or English? Even college girls will enrol in our evening classes. How will this young woman manage?'

Mangaleswari had a scathing response. 'A college degree is something handed out by humans. All those who go around for five or six years carrying four or five heavy textbooks in their hands or in their minds alternately will emerge with a degree. But wisdom is inborn. It cannot be bestowed by one human on another. Such wisdom exists in abundance in this young woman. If you find her agreeable, employ her, otherwise just say no. There is no need to humiliate her by indulging in such petty remarks, right in her presence.' Mangaleswari's sharp words put an end to the questions at last. Poorani was silently grateful to her.

Gazing at Sarada Devi's face in the portrait, Poorani made a firm resolve. She was seized with the desire to get this job. Only then would she be able to thumb her nose at the 'educated' ones who had doubted her abilities. She wanted to have the last laugh on those who had doubted her by proving them wrong and managing her classes well.

Mangaleswari's influence prevailed. No one wished to go against her wishes. Poorani was given the job. It was decided that, from the first day of the month of Thai, she would conduct classes from six to eight in the evening and would be paid a salary of one hundred rupees a month. Poorani took leave of the women and left with Mangaleswari. She felt the divine presence of Sarada Devi as she walked out to where the car was parked.

On their return, they stopped for a while at Mangaleswari's home.

'Poorani, I have done my best and got you this job. All those ladies you met are gossip-mongers. It is up to you now to do a good job of teaching and earn a fine name for yourself.'

'You need not mention it, Amma. I will not let you down,' promised Poorani.

The sounds of a piano drifted down from upstairs, where the elder daughter, Vasantha, was practising her music. Poorani was able to meet only the younger daughter, Chellam.

'Poorani Akka, it would be so good if you could come by every day for a chat. Looking at you is like looking at a Ravi Varma painting of Saraswathi. Just talking to you cleanses the mind,' said the girl, speaking frankly with a smile.

'Yes, Chellam, don't let this young woman escape! From the first of next month, she is going to teach Tamil every evening at the Women's Sangam. You should also attend those classes without fail,' said her mother with a laugh.

'If this Akka is going to teach me, I'm prepared to be at the Women's Sangam twenty-four hours a day, Amma,' declared Chellam, frisking like a young deer as she ran and laced her fingers with Poorani's.

It was getting late. Poorani prepared to leave. 'I will ask the driver to fetch the car. You can get dropped at Thirupparankundram and send the car back,' suggested Mangaleswari. But Poorani declined her offer.

'Let me walk back, Amma. Please don't overwhelm me with a whole lot of privileges. There is life on these Madurai streets. It is a life that throbs with joys and sorrows, poverty and plenty. Life writes its story on the pages of an open book. My eyes will take in the pulsating life of the streets and make it part of my experience so that I can turn it over in my mind as I walk along. I like to do that. I will walk to the bus stop and take a bus. I don't need a car.'

Poorani walked along briskly. Like a widow's face devoid of a tilak, the shopping streets on a holiday had no liveliness, no vivacity. As she walked, she noticed a signboard that startled her. She halted and stared at it. Her face blossomed with joy. She mouthed the words silently, 'Meenakshi Printing House. On time. Low prices.'

The day being a Sunday, the front door was shut. Yet, the office light was on. From the street, she could see Aravindan sitting inside. She realized that she was not far from where she had fainted the previous day. 'If I had not happened to collapse on the street at this particular spot, Aravindan would not have composed that poem about me,' she thought to herself as a sharp thrill of joy went through her mind. When she had taken his visiting card earlier, she had told him that she would meet him the following day. But so what? There was no rule about not meeting him sooner, was there?

Poorani moved closer to the window and looked inside. As she was about to call out to him, Aravindan turned his head and spotted Poorani.

'Oh, is that you… Why are you here at this hour? Didn't you say you would come tomorrow?' asked Aravindan, rising to open the door. Poorani was having second thoughts. 'It is already so late, I should have just gone home instead of disturbing him,' she said to herself. Overcome with awkwardness and shyness, she stood hesitating.

'Please come in. Why are you standing in the doorway?' invited Aravindan, holding the door open. The magical smile that played upon his lips had the power to seed beautiful dreams in the viewer's mind. Poorani entered the office and sat down. On the table lay a few peanuts, a single banana and a glass of milk. Poorani noticed them and asked, 'What are these for?'

Aravindan was still on his feet, a little away from where Poorani sat. 'That's my dinner!' he said.

'How will this small banana, a few peanuts and milk be enough of a meal for you?'

Aravindan laughed.

'If we leave it to our stomachs to decide whether a meal is enough or not, it will always say it is not. Instead, I have left the decision-making to my mind, which boldly says, "Enough!" Ours is a country of poor people. Those who can afford to eat three rice meals a day, and a fourth meal of tiffin, should think about the common folk. Millions in our country cannot get even a single filling meal a day! Shouldn't at least one in a hundred people spare a thought for those starving stomachs? Should they not show concern?'

'But that doesn't mean you have to deny yourself food and stay semi-starved.'

'You are wrong. I am not starving myself. I eat at midday to satisfy my body's hunger. The rest of the time, I eat only what my mind dictates, not to fill my belly. I spend exactly three annas for this meal. What I save from this, I distribute to those starving women, sometimes carrying children, begging on the street with outstretched hands. Women are an exalted form of creation, signifying motherhood. What a disgrace it is for a nation to have its women walk the dusty streets begging for food! Women are traditionally those who distribute charity at the doorsteps of their homes, offering food to those who come begging at their door. How degrading it is to have women themselves become beggars and go door to door seeking alms!' Aravindan spoke with passion. His face flushed, and his lips trembled with emotion.

'What you say is true,' said Poorani in agreement. 'These days, women beggars have increased in Madurai.'

Aravindan continued to express his distress. 'You see only the beautiful Madurai with its temple towers, bustling shops, large bungalows and cinema theatres. I see the other side too. As you come out from the railway station, you can see so many homeless families under the trees on the roadside. They live amidst slush and dirt, at the mercy of the sun and the rain. Does anyone think about them? Does anyone care?'

Poorani watched Aravindan's face mirror the passion of his words. She realized that his noble ideals were too exalted for the normal mind to grasp easily.

Aravindan went to a shop next door and bought another glass of milk and a couple of bananas. 'Please take these,' he said, offering them to Poorani. She accepted. As she went over Aravindan's words, a verse from the *Thevaram* came to her mind: 'You are so noble in character that there cannot be another like you. You fall as the seed in the minds of thinkers and grow into ideas and beliefs.' His mind was boundless in scope. While conversing with him, time slipped by unnoticed. Like his face and smile, his words and thoughts too were attractive.

All of a sudden, it began to rain. It started as a drizzle but soon became heavier. Walking the streets in that rain would mean getting soaked. Poorani glanced at the wall clock. It was almost ten thirty in the evening.

'Uh oh! I lost track of time when we were talking. The buses stop at ten thirty. How will I get back home?' said Poorani, jumping up from her chair.

'It's raining. How will you go? If the last bus leaves before you reach the bus stop, what then?'

'I have to get back home. What can be done?"

Aravindan could sense her agitation. He went into the other room and fetched an umbrella.

Handing it to Poorani, he said, 'Hold on to this. I will accompany you to the bus stop. If the last bus has left, then we will make other plans.' Without giving her a chance to react, Aravindan stepped outside with her, turned and locked the door.

'There's only one umbrella,' pointed out Poorani. 'What about you? There is no need for you to get wet unnecessarily. I will manage. Please don't exert yourself for this.'

She stepped out into the street. Aravindan did not heed her plea and stubbornly set out to accompany her.

'It's no problem for me,' he assured her. 'From the time I was a little boy, I have always loved to get wet in the rain. The sun and the rain are the boons that the sky bestows upon the earth. Why should we shun them and stay away from them?' Aravindan laughed with the delight of a child as he looked at Poorani.

The two of them walked briskly. It was raining heavily. Poorani felt uneasy about staying dry herself under the umbrella while letting Aravindan get wet in the rain. He, on the other hand, walked merrily along in the rain like a playful child without a care in the world. 'I have given him a place in my heart, why should I hesitate to give him space under my umbrella?' thought Poorani. With a jumble of thoughts in her mind, she turned and looked at him in the murky glow of streetlights dimmed by rain.

Aravindan's broad, fair forehead glistened with pearly raindrops, making the wetness glow in the abundant hair that was combed back on his head.

'Please come here, don't get more wet!' Poorani urged, moving closer to him and holding the umbrella over both their heads. As she drew close to him, Aravindan felt a profound feeling of joy. It was as if the golden form of this beautiful woman held the fragrance of jasmine, the coolness of rose water and the sacred aroma of camphor. His heart fluttered, and his body trembled in response to the thrill of joy. The next moment, something seemed to blossom in his mind like a lotus opening its petals. His lips parted in a smile.

Yet, the very next moment, Aravindan was back in the

present moment. 'No, no,' he protested with a smile. 'If both of us go under this small umbrella, we will both get thoroughly wet. Please use it and stay dry.' With these words, Aravindan moved away and continued to walk in the rain. Savouring that one fleeting moment of drowning deep in a flood of love, he continued to walk and get wet in the rain. Poorani glanced at the young man with eyes that spoke of love and sympathy; she walked with a tender smile on her face.

By the time they arrived at the bus stop, the last bus for the day had already left. Poorani was hesitant to travel home alone at that late hour in a rickshaw or horse cart. 'I can escort you if you like. We can take a horse cart,' offered Aravindan. But Poorani did not agree to that solution. So, there they stood at the bus stop, the two of them, getting drenched in the rain.

'If you prefer, we can walk back all the way. I will come with you,' suggested Aravindan.

'What? You want to walk in this pouring rain, all the way to Thirupparankundram?'

'Why only up to Thirupparankundram? I am prepared to walk with you, like this, all the way to Kanyakumari if need be,' remarked Aravindan, and smiled. A car drew up to a stop near them, splashing a wave of rainwater and slush. Aravindan's shirt was spattered with dirt.

Indignantly, he turned to confront the thoughtless driver of the car. It was Meenakshisundaram Pillai himself, the proprietor of Meenakshi Printing House. He got out of the car and walked towards them.

CHAPTER 9

Flower-like eyes, a flower-like smile,
Flower-like fingers, flower-like feet,
Flower-like cheeks, a body lithe as a deer
An endearing lisp that is honey to the ears.

– Sa.Thu.Su.Yogi

That rainy night was an unforgettable one for Poorani. She did not think of Aravindan as merely getting wet in the rain while accompanying her. No, his innermost being was aflame, and his melting heart was bathed in love that welled out from some hidden spring.

It was that night that she had understood the vast breadth of his mind. It was the night she had met the proprietor of Meenakshi Printing House, who had generously offered to drop her home in his car and had taken Aravindan back with him. It was indeed very fortunate for them that Meenakshisundaram Pillai had happened to come by in his car at the very moment when they had been stranded at the bus stop in the rain, wondering how she would get home. Was that perhaps a sign that foretold that the gentleman was going to play a central role in supporting Poorani throughout her life?

In the few weeks thereafter, a lot of changes occurred in Poorani's life and the lives of those around her. She adapted to the confined space in the rented house, after having lived in a spacious, mansion-like house all her life.

It requires no effort at all to live one's life if one has enough money and facilities. But it surely requires considerable effort to adapt to a life of limited means and fewer facilities. The plaster cast on her younger brother's arm had been removed. The broken bone had healed more or less completely. He had started going to school with his elder brother as before. The publisher at Pudu Mandapam who had published her father's books came and gave her an amount less than half of what he actually owed as royalty. His calculations were false, and he justified them with more lies and deceit. As a special gesture, a portion of Appa's provident fund was released by the college. It was money that would ordinarily have taken several months to be credited. It was because of the college principal's commitment and personal intervention that it got done so quickly. Meanwhile, the proprietor of Meenakshi Printing House and Aravindan were preparing to publish Appa's writings.

With household work during the day, and the teaching job in the evenings at the Women's Sangam, Poorani had hardly any time to spare. After churning anxious thoughts in her mind for months about her various problems, she had now found some kind of peace. Just as the blades of an electric fan are a blur when the fan is running and become visible only when it stops, so also life's burdens begin to weigh on the mind only in moments of leisure, between spells of activity. Activity, then, is an excellent medicine. It acts as a balm to the worried mind and heals its wounds. Fatigue and weakness retreat.

Kamala's parents returned home after arranging a good matrimonial match for her. Two days after her parents returned, the boy and his family paid a visit to Kamala's home. On that day, Poorani was also present to help Kamala's mother with hosting the visitors. She combed and decorated Kamala's hair with flowers and presented her as a beautiful bride before the groom's family. Poorani's day went by enjoyably in beautifying and admiring Kamala. The marriage was formally arranged, and a date was set for the month of Thai. All the preparations were underway.

Within a few days of Kamala's engagement, another marriage was rapidly arranged in the household of a family very dear to Poorani. Odhuvar *thatha* did not have the financial status to arrange a marriage for his granddaughter, Kamu, with anyone who had an English-medium education and a good job. Instead, he found an ordinary young man, who recited *thevarams* in the temple, and arranged the marriage. *Thatha* had selected the same auspicious day for the wedding as Kamala's family had done.

Like letter writers who rush to the post office to ensure that their messages reach the recipients quickly, parents of young girls were racing to meet the Thai month deadline to get their daughters married. Poorani was aware of many such families. But who was there to feel that sense of urgency and concern about her? She had only herself to depend on. She attended Kamu's engagement function at *Thatha*'s house. Kamu's *patti* came up to her and asked in a kind of patronizing way, '*Enna di*, how long are you going to live alone like this, going back and forth between Thirupparankundram and Madurai every day for your job? Do you realize that both Kamala and our Kamu are some years younger than you? Are you planning to remain a spinster? You don't have any family. You have to make a decision for yourself.'

Poorani bowed her head and did not respond. She thought to herself, 'This *patti* is asking me about the very subject that puts me at a loss for words. She wants me to talk about that very place, the thought of which sucks the energy from my speech and strikes me dumb. She wants me to talk about the emotion which strips all words of reason or relevance. How can I explain that to her? Where could I even begin?'

Her mind was in distress. That whole day, she turned the incident over in her mind. 'Why does everyone rush to get their daughters married and urge others to join the rush, like dogs scrapping for bones? The repeated cycle of marriage, bangle ceremony, baby, family and again marriage, etc., like some mad race… Is that all there is to life? Have I also been born on this Earth to follow this pattern?' The thought, like a heavy stone, seemed to weigh down her whole being. That night, she cried into her pillow. But she had no idea why she wept.

Although Poorani went to the Women's Sangam and returned home by the same route every evening, she did not find the time to meet Aravindan regularly. Only on a few occasions, on the way home, would she happen to meet and exchange a few words with him. Sometimes, Aravindan visited her at home in the daytime to get signatures on documents for the publication of her father's writings. On other days, Mangaleswari and her younger daughter, Chellam, would drop in at Poorani's home after offering prayers at the Murugan Temple and stay to chat for a while.

In the newly rented house, an entire room was taken up by books. Although the space was very limited, Poorani had somehow managed to cram them all in. There was only enough space left for one person to sit in a chair and read. After giving her brothers their meal and sending them off to school, Poorani would finish her household chores and then enter the 'book room'. Instantly, she would be lost to the world.

She would immerse herself in the ocean of knowledge that her father had left as his legacy. It was only by such study that she could open up new horizons to her students and do justice to her teaching job at the Women's Sangam.

Her little sister, Mangaiyarkarasi, never disturbed Poorani's study time. She played by herself or with the neighbours' children out on the street. Sometimes, Kamala or Kamu used to drop in for a chat. But once they were engaged to be married, both girls left their homes less often. Because of this, Poorani had ample time for herself. In those hours of solitude, her goals became clearer in her mind, and she could widen the ambit of her ambitions.

On the wedding day shared by her friends Kamala and Kamu, Poorani went back and forth between the two houses, assisting the families. In Kamala's house, there were others around to make the necessary arrangements. But the wedding in Odhuvar *thatha*'s home was a very low-key affair because of their limited means. There were far fewer arrangements to make. It was there that Poorani spent most of the day, welcoming guests with sandal paste and offering them *vettrilai pakku*. She moved around briskly, helping to serve the meals.

In both the weddings that day, the guests would have got the impression that Poorani was an important person there. She made a deep impression on all the guests at both functions. Her face was seen here, there and everywhere. It was as if she was doing every single thing that had to be done. Kamala's husband had a job somewhere up north. It would have been difficult for him to make another trip to take his wife back with him. So he left along with Kamala a few days after their wedding. Poorani went to the railway station to see her friend off.

The bridegroom in Odhuvar *thatha*'s family, although he was a relative, lived in another town. He was an *odhuvar* in a small temple in some southern district. He also left with Kamu within a week of the wedding. Poorani was at the railway station on that occasion too. Having said farewell to her two closest friends and seeing them depart, one to the north and the other to the south, Poorani found herself depressed whenever she went back home. It was as if someone had tapped on her shoulder and woken her up in the middle of a beautiful dream. Her mind was not at peace.

Maybe this was just another part of life – to say goodbye to people. When we see someone off to another town, it is a leave-taking. When we say goodbye to a loved one who dies, it is a different kind of parting. For a few days after her friends had gone away, Poorani's thoughts were centred on such matters.

Every evening, when she left home to go to Madurai for her teaching job at the Women's Sangam, her brothers would not yet be back from school. So, Poorani would lock her home and leave the keys and her little sister either at Odhuvar *thatha*'s home or with Kamala's mother. When the brothers arrived, they would collect the keys and take their sister back home. Poorani would return around nine thirty in the evening from Madurai. On some days, the children would have helped themselves to dinner by then. On other days, they would wait for her to reach home.

One evening when she got home, her two brothers had already had their dinner. Mangaiyarkarasi, who was usually asleep by this hour, was still awake. The child's face was swollen as if she had been weeping for a long time. Her eyes were red, and the marks of tears were still on her cheeks. Poorani could see she was feeling hungry. Whenever Poorani returned home from any outing, the child would call out loudly in her adorable lisping voice, 'Akka has come back.' She would frisk like a deer, hurrying to clasp her Akka around the legs. But that day, the child did not stir when Poorani entered the house. Poorani turned and looked enquiringly at Thirunavukkarasu.

'She says she is angry about something. She was very stubborn and refused to eat,' said the boy. Poorani was both amused and astonished by the child's anger. She approached her with the intention of pacifying her and getting her to eat. The child turned her face away as though in disapproval. Gently, with a smile, Poorani held the child's chin and turned her face forward.

'What are you angry about, *di*?'

'Don't talk to me. Go away…' The child lifted her little arms as though to push Poorani away. One deep sob followed by some choking noises – the dam of tears was about to break any moment.

'Whom are you angry with? For what?'

'With you!'

'Why? What did I do to you?'

The child did not reply. Instead, she cried hard, heaving with sobs, so much so that the words she tried to say were broken into bits and washed away. Poorani picked up the crying child and held her close on her way into the kitchen. The child struggled to get away from her embrace, wriggling, flailing her arms and kicking her legs. Poorani soothed the child and seated her in front of a plate on the floor, ready to serve her dinner.

'Did your brother hit you?'

'No.'

'Did you fall while playing on the street?'

'No.'

'Then what is making you cry so much?'

'I was talking to that *patti* at Odhuvar *thatha*'s house. I asked her, "*Patti*, you sent your Kamu away on a train to another city with that fair-skinned man wearing a gold chain and a *rudraksha mala*. Does it mean she won't come back here?"'

'You asked that *patti* such a question?'

'Yes, I did.'

'Hmm, and then?'

'That *patti* started laughing. She said…' At that point, the child's words trailed away, and she burst into fresh tears.

'Come on, dear. Stop crying and tell me all that happened. Be a good girl now.'

'She told me, "Your Poorani Akka will also go away like that one day. Anyone who is born a girl has to go away like this with a man someday. You also will have to do that when you grow up."'

Poorani was amused. She wanted to laugh. But she controlled her laughter because she didn't want the child to think that her Akka was not taking her seriously.

'What did you tell *Patti* when she said this?'

'When she said that, I got very angry. I told her, "Our Poorani Akka is not like that. She will always stay with us. Your Kamu has thin hair, crooked teeth and a fat face; that is why she had to go away on a train. Our Akka is very beautiful. You are lying to me." Then *Patti* said, "You silly girl. What has beauty got to do with it?"'

'And then?'

'Then nothing. I couldn't stop crying. The moment *Anna* came with the house key, I came home with him.'

Poorani was silent for a while.

But the child was not done with the topic. She asked, 'Akka, will you do what Odhuvar *patti* said? Will you go away and leave us?'

Poorani laughed merrily. She picked up the child and kissed her. 'You silly child! You shouldn't believe everything someone says for fun. I will never leave you or go away, Mangai! Now sit and eat.' Poorani gave the little girl her dinner. When Poorani looked at her – those eyes, that smile, those arms, as though made of flowers – it was as if she was looking at a form of the Divine. In a way, she admired the child's innocence that had led her to torture her mind about such a small matter. A child's mind was a pure space, like a heavenly flower, that no dust or dirt could wilt or fade. It was a mirror that could never reflect false images.

That night, Poorani made the child sleep next to her. She told her stories. As though stirred by a new thought, the child asked, 'Akka, Kamu went away on a train. But why did Kamala also go? She has also gone to some other city?'

Poorani thought to herself, 'You ignorant girl! Women have to leave their parents and become parents themselves and produce children who will grow up and become parents, and so on… If all the girls continued to stay in their parents' homes, how can the world go on? Is that so difficult to understand?' But instead, she avoided the topic. 'Stop talking and go to sleep, Mangai,' she said. 'It's very late. Ask me in the morning, and I will tell you.' Somehow, this whole incident with her little sister made a deep impression on Poorani's mind.

One morning, about a week later, an unfortunate event brought sadness into Poorani's home. It was about eleven in the morning. The boys had eaten breakfast and left for school, carrying their lunch with them. Mangai was playing with some other children in the shade of a tree on the street, four or five houses away. Poorani had just finished her chores, eaten her meal and entered the book room. She was not sure when the child would return home, and she did not want to be disturbed while studying to get up and unbolt the front door. So, she left the door unbolted.

That evening, she had to conduct a class at the Women's Sangam about the *Thirukkural*. She did not teach merely by writing the words on a blackboard and then giving their meanings, as in a school classroom. After all, the Sangam was not a school. The class had students ranging in age from twelve to thirty. Poorani's aim was to broaden the understanding of the students and make her classes interesting and lively. Within just a few days, her reputation as a teacher had started to grow. More students joined her classes. To these young women who were used to whiling away their time playing carrom or gossiping, Poorani opened up a new world. She planted in their minds a love of learning. She showed them the way to a world of knowledge. She inspired in them a passion for the Tamil language. With every passing day, she rose in the estimation of the managing board of the Sangam. Those who had assumed that her teaching ability would only be moderate were changing their minds. They were in awe of her capability.

With these joyful thoughts in her mind, she opened the *Thirukkural* book and prepared to study the meanings of the verses.

There came the sound of someone opening the front door and walking in. 'It must be Mangai,' she thought to herself. Who else could it be at this hour? Without lifting her head, she continued to write notes and was startled to hear a rough, uncouth voice. It was the Pudu Mandapam publisher, his face flaming with fury. Poorani welcomed him in. 'Please come,' she said. 'Please sit in that chair.'

'I've not come here to sit,' retorted the man. 'I'm here to express my anger in no uncertain terms.'

'Whom are you angry with?'

'Don't pretend that you don't know anything about it. When I am already struggling to sell an author's books, how can you hand over the publishing rights to some Meenakshi or Kamakshi or something Printing Works? That too without a word to me?'

The man appeared to be older than forty. His moustache twitched, conveying his indignation. Poorani responded calmly, 'Excuse me, sir. I am not an ignorant child. Please speak only the truth to me. I am not willing to listen to your lies.'

'What lies?'

'You claim that you are struggling to sell my father's books and that only half of them have been sold. That is a total lie. You are covering up the sales of many books. Your accounts and your words are deceitful. My father let you get away with it. But it is a matter of livelihood for me.'

The fellow retorted, 'You cannot make an enemy of me and hope to make a livelihood. I am a bad fellow, a crook. If you did not know this already, now you do. Let me see how that Meenakshi Printing will bring out the books.'

A new, strident voice cut in.

'Where's the doubt about that? You will certainly see how they bring them out.'

The man uttering the threats turned to see who had spoken. Poorani too lifted her head. She stared in astonishment. It was Aravindan who had thrown out the verbal challenge. He had come to Poorani's house to hand over corrected proofs of her father's book. He had entered noiselessly and had stood hidden, listening to the conversation. The man glared at Aravindan with rage, as though he would burn him down to ashes.

'Oh, so it's you,' growled the angry publisher. He seemed to know who Aravindan was.

Aravindan walked towards the man, saying, 'In every line of his writing, Professor Azhagiya Sittrambalam stressed the importance of honesty, righteousness, humility and justice. In publishing those very same writings of his, you were dishonest, arrogant and unfair in your dealings. Isn't it enough that you cheated him all these years?'

As Aravindan drew near, the man slapped him hard on the face. Aravindan's nose began to bleed. His strong, young arms would have easily thrown the scoundrel to the floor and beaten him up, but Poorani ran forward and held Aravindan back, preventing him from doing so.

CHAPTER 10

Shaken to the core, melting at the heart,
Tears flowing in an endless stream,
As a needle seeks to join the magnet,
Is the yearning for this relationship,
With mind aflutter, and inner trembling.

– Thaayumaanavar

Nature had bestowed good looks and elegance on Aravindan. His skin had the softness of rose petals and the fair colour of a *champak* flower. Even the slightest pinch anywhere on his body would draw blood. He possessed strength but never resorted to violence. He was handsome but never vain about his appearance. So delicate was his frame that even when he was a student at school, he tended to get a nosebleed whenever the teacher hit him with his knuckles on the top of his head as punishment.

That evening, as Poorani watched Aravindan receive a hard slap on his face from the violent publisher from Pudu Mandapam, she felt as distressed as though she herself had received the blow. Tears spilt over from her eyes, and her heart throbbed in agony. Like a needle that seeks to attach itself to a nearby magnet, her mind sped to share Aravind's pain.

The brutish assailant had not lingered after attacking Aravindan. Still furious, he had stormed out of the house.

Aravindan comforted Poorani. 'Why are you crying? If the fellow had belonged to the lineage of the honest Harishchandran, I may have received a garland for having spoken the truth. But in the kind of society that we are a part of, speaking the truth only attracts similar slaps on the face. It is today's culture to avoid speaking the truth as much as possible and thereby escape the consequences. Gone are the days when uttering the truth was a matter of pride. Nowadays, if truth is spoken, the one that it affects becomes angry.'

After being assaulted, Aravindan had lost his composure only for a moment.

Poorani brought water for him in a jug. Aravindan washed his injured nose and wiped the blood from his face with a wet handkerchief. It was as if in doing so he had also wiped away all his anger and even the memory of the event. Like a line drawn on water, his momentary distress soon disappeared, and Poorani noticed that he had regained his usual animation. He brought up the purpose of his visit with Poorani, finished what needed to be conveyed and got up to leave.

Taking leave of Aravindan filled Poorani's heart with profound sadness. In her mind, she addressed him and conveyed her feelings, 'Aravindan! The other day you got wet in the rain for my sake. Today, again for me, you received a slap on the face from a scoundrel. Who knows what other troubles you may have to face on my account? I feel wretched about putting you through so much hardship.'

That same night, Aravindan made the following entry in his diary:

Because I spoke the truth, a rogue slapped me so hard that my nose bled. Life is an elite footwear store. Tanned leather items that live, breathe, eat and wear clothes are stacked on the shelves. But no one thought of inserting some basic decency and culture into those creatures. Instead, it is vileness that pervades everywhere.

Keen intelligence has the ability to cut through all opposition. Even if the obstacles refuse to budge, the alert mind will find a new path towards its goal. Aravindan was a person with such abilities, both in his attitude and in the way he thought. He had the ability to recognize people's innate qualities. The more Poorani got to know Aravindan, the more she understood the merits of his character. It was like reading the works of a gifted poet again and again and finding new beauty in them every time.

On one occasion, when Poorani went to the printing house to meet Aravindan, he was not there. The staff told her that he had left with the proprietor in his car, and they had said they would be back before long. Should she wait for them to return? Or should she go away and try again the next day? Even as she was debating these alternatives in her mind, a car drew up at the entrance. The two of them had returned. Meenakshisundaram welcomed Poorani warmly, his face glowing with pleasure.

'Welcome, Amma! Have you been waiting long? We left only a short while ago. Nothing important. I just wanted to take this fellow along with me to a clothing shop. Tell me, is it enough just to know how to toil away day and night? Shouldn't one also learn how to look after oneself? Surely at this age, this fellow should know how to take care of his own health! He is coughing away; his lips are cracked and chapped with cold. I discovered that he has been sleeping on the cold floor with no sweater or blanket. How can you do a wall painting if there is no wall? How can a person work hard if his body is not healthy enough? He tried to resist my advice. He said, "No, I won't. Let's deal with this later." I scolded him and took him along with me to the shop. I've bought him two sweaters and a blanket. Shouldn't everyone be aware of their own needs?'

Holding the packet of recent purchases and wearing a smile, Aravindan stood behind Meenakshisundaram. The proprietor took the packet from Aravindan and displayed the sweaters and the blanket proudly for Poorani to admire. Poorani was pleasantly astonished at the affection and regard that the older man felt for Aravindan.

Within ten days or so, that same blanket was draped over an old, homeless beggar lying on the street to the north of the bus stand and Poorani happened to see it. 'Surely I am worried about nothing,' she said to herself. 'It's not as if Aravindan is the only one who has a blanket like this. Someone else may have given this to the beggar.' She tried to convince herself. 'Blankets like this may be owned by lots of people.' But another thought cut in and persisted. 'Not everyone can have that kind of empathy or compassion.' She met Aravindan and asked him directly about it. He bowed his head and smiled but said nothing.

'How long are you going to behave like a playful child? You can do charity for others only if you have enough to spare. Isn't that so?'

'You are concerned only about me, but I am concerned about everyone. When I see the plight of three crore Tamils, when I see how many of them are wallowing in stark poverty, I am deeply moved. There are more than thirty crore people in this country. Does everyone live like royals? No, there are many desperate, homeless wanderers who have nothing but the dust and dirt of the bare earth beneath their feet. Was I not born in the same country as them? Am I not their countryman?'

Poorani spoke spontaneously, moved to wonder by his words. 'Aravindan, you truly are an exceptional being! I cannot win an argument with you. Your thoughts and actions are beyond the understanding of ordinary mortals.' Aravindan looked at her and simply smiled.

On another occasion, on the road leading out of the railway station near Madurai College, she saw Aravindan under the most unusual of circumstances. A group of homeless children, in patched and ragged clothes, had surrounded Aravindan. Their faces were alight with joy as they looked at him. He went up to a banana seller, who was sitting under a nearby tree. He negotiated a price with the woman, bought her whole basket of bananas and distributed them among the children.

Poorani happened to see this as she got off at the bus stand and was hurrying to the station to post an urgent letter before going to the Women's Sangam for the evening class. She watched the whole incident from behind a tree, taking care not to be spotted by Aravindan. After he had finished his affectionate interaction with the children, he set off on his way, and Poorani followed him. Aravindan was unaware of her presence. She sneaked up behind him and said, 'Here is another orphan child. Can you not spare something for her?'

Poorani stood there with a mischievous smile on her face and her hand outstretched to ask for alms. As Aravindan turned, her smile widened. Aravindan was tempted to say, 'You? An orphan child? How can that be the case when I have given you my whole self?' But he could not bring himself to express the thought. He was embarrassed at having encountered her on the street in such an unexpected way. Instead, he just smiled in response to her smile.

Poorani thought, 'That Pudu Mandapam publisher who cheats people out of what is owed to them and keeps it for himself so as to live in comfort inhabits this same world where someone like Aravindan also lives. How did Aravindan develop this passion to help others even when it meant denying himself basic needs?'

Although time gave the illusion of being in slow motion, it was, in reality, racing along as usual. In Madurai, the month of Chithirai is known for its blazing heat and famous temple festivals. The daughters of well-to-do families, who attended Poorani's evening class at the Women's Sangam, had gone to places like Udhagamandalam and Kodaikanal with their families to avoid the Madurai heat. So Poorani had that whole month off. Because of the unrelenting work put in by Aravindan, some of her father's books were also published in the same month. When the books were released, the previous publisher, who was already seething with resentment, was even more infuriated.

Mangaleswari had planned to spend the summer in Kodaikanal with her daughters. She tried to persuade Poorani to join them. But Poorani declined the invitation.

'My father's books are being released one by one. I need to be here at this time, so it is not convenient for me now. I will certainly come with you some other time, Amma,' she told the older woman.

During Poorani's vacation month, Aravindan visited her at Thirupparankundram every Sunday. The two of them went for long strolls and opened their hearts to each other. They walked southwards up to the end of the Koothiyargundu Lake and turned. They climbed Thirupparankundram Hill. There was a tradition associated with the hill. Many of those who climbed it left signs of their presence for posterity by having their names carved on the rocks. There were a few stone carvers who made their living from this tradition. Armed with their chisels, they were ever ready to carve the names of climbers for a fee. When Poorani and Aravindan were climbing the hill and enjoying the view, one such stone carver enthusiastically approached them.

'Do you want your name carved, *Ayya*? Your name?'

Aravindan looked at Poorani enquiringly. Poorani smilingly took out a full eight-anna coin and handed it to the workman.

'Tell me your names, Amma,' urged the man.

Poorani blushed and picked up a scrap of paper from the ground. She wrote 'POORANI' and 'ARAVINDAN' on it in beautiful writing and handed it to the stone carver. The fellow was used to dealing with customers who demanded that he carve twenty or thirty names and would argue about paying a couple of annas more. These two must have seemed so wonderfully different in his eyes! Or was he captivated by how well-matched they looked as a couple? Whatever be the reason, he chose a rock that did not bear any name on it yet. Then, in decorative letters, he carefully carved their two names. When the man had finished, Aravindan said to Poorani, 'Our names have been carved on a tall hill in such a special way. So many people spend several thousands to ensure that their names become known and endure in people's memory. But you, for a mere half a rupee, have ensured that for us!' He looked at her face as he spoke and smiled.

Poorani's beautiful face, with its smiling lips and wide, crescent-shaped eyes, glowed with the warm blush of womanly shyness. She had requested him many times to address her by the plainer term '*nee*' for 'you', rather than the formal '*neenga*'. Yet he continued to address her as *neenga*. She had to remind him every time he addressed her formally; she did it by correcting him, pretending to be offended, pretending to sulk, refusing to talk to him and so on. Until he got so tired of it that he got around to calling her *nee*.

That summer gave Poorani the opportunity to spend time with Aravindan and get to know him well. Sometimes they visited the Thirupparankundram Temple together. On one such day, when they were at the shore of the pond within the temple, Aravindan told her something interesting. At that spot, vendors sold cloth bundles containing small quantities of salt, pepper and sugar mixed together. It was a traditional belief that if people bought those bundles and put them in the water to dissolve, all their diseases and even their sins would disappear. Poorani bought two bundles, put one into the water and held the other out towards Aravindan. But Aravindan declined her offer. He said, 'Poorani, please put in this other one too. My wish is for all of society's diseases and sins to disappear. This small bundle cannot fulfil that wish of mine. To accomplish that, noble ideals must rise like a mighty flood and form a reservoir of righteousness.'

Poorani responded in a mock-angry tone that was belied by the smile on her face. 'Ahh, the same chorus again! Society, problems, poverty… Can you not put these aside for a moment and talk about other things?'

Aravindan stared heavenwards. 'What can be done, Poorani? That's the way I am, that's my fate.'

Through several such instances, Poorani began to understand Aravindan's mind and character. The more time they spent together, the more her mind expanded to properly comprehend the breadth of his vision.

In due course, the vacations came to an end and classes at the Women's Sangam recommenced. Poorani's brothers had been promoted to the next class and had gone back to their usual school routine. Poorani admitted her little sister, Mangaiyarkarasi, at a school too. There were a lot of expenses for school fees, books and so on. Since it was Thirunavukkarasu's final year in school, his fee was higher than before.

Although her salary at the Sangam and what she received as royalty for her father's books came in regularly, it was hardly enough to meet all the expenses. It called for a very tight balancing act between income and expense. On some occasions, she even fell short of small change. The bus charge for her evening trips to and from the Sangam also had to be considered. It was her aim to lead a simple life within their limited means.

However, the ladies who managed the Sangam and even the students who attended classes belonged to rich families from the upper strata of society, so Poorani felt that she had to be reasonably well-groomed when she went there. She didn't want them to find fault with her on that count. Somehow, she managed to meet all the expenses and ensure that the children were never hungry. She began to adopt some of the practices she had seen Aravindan doing. She cut down on the portions of her meals. Aravindan was following that as a principle. In her case, it was more a matter of necessity. Her limited resources also led her to do without some facilities. These days, she never fretted about these matters. She had now learned from Aravindan the secret of finding fulfilment even in times of want.

On Fridays, there was always a special forum at which people gathered to listen to speeches at the Sangam. That Friday, a sizable crowd had gathered. Poorani was scheduled to speak on 'The History of Thilakavathy'.

For many days leading up to that Friday, Poorani's mind had been totally immersed in the details of the topic. From a very early age, she had listened to stories of this kind from her father. Her heart melted, and she was moved to tears whenever she heard the story of Thilakavathy. When she was older, her father introduced her to the poems of Chekkizhar and explained his verses about Thilakavathy.

The very same story she had heard as a child, she read again as an adult in the form of verse, and it evoked in her the identical emotions. Her father had told her, 'Poorani, this is the world's most heartbreaking story. Chekkizhar could not have written this verse right away with a stylus on parchment. He must first have imagined the sorrow in this woman's life. He would have had to erase and rewrite in his own mind several times because he must have been moved to tears. Thilakavathy was a woman who could bear unbearable sorrow and withstand insufferable hardships. Only this Tamil land could have given birth to such a noble woman who, even while dying in body, could still nourish an inner life. The blessedness of this land of ours continues to permeate our lives even today. That is why at least a few good deeds get accomplished here.' Whenever Poorani pictured her father saying these words, she forgot everything else, even the book of verses by Chekkizhar, which lay open in front of her. Tears would stream down her face.

That evening at the Sangam, when Poorani spoke about Thilakavathy, all the distilled emotion and passion from her close association with the story of that noble woman came through clearly in her speech. Among the audience, those with tender emotions were moved to tears.

'This is a story dating back hundreds of years. On one of the beautiful streets of Thiruvarur stood the house of a farmer. In that farmer's house lived a girl, blossoming into womanhood like a beautiful bud about to open out in full bloom. This lovely girl-woman's smile was like flower petals, her face was as resplendent as the full moon, and her bodily frame was as bright as lightning.

'One day she stands in the doorway of the house, holding her younger brother's hand. Her beautiful, jet-black eyes look around, as though in search of poetry to explore. There is eagerness in her gaze, as though she is awaiting the arrival of someone special. The tender-faced little boy whom she holds by the hand would have been unable to guess the reason for his sister's eagerness. Some people arrive on a palanquin and alight in front of the house.

'They go in, talk to the elders of the house and leave. A little later, the father comes out and says, "Thilakavathy, it seems that the army general of the Chozha kingdom wishes to marry you. They came to discuss the marriage. I agreed. You are indeed fortunate, my child. A great army general has himself come forward to ask for your hand in marriage."

'Thilakavathy drops her head shyly and runs into the house. Her little brother is obviously unaware of why his sister's face reddened and why she ran away. Time goes by. The parents pass away. Meanwhile, the preparations for the marriage are going on as agreed. Thilakavathy is floating on clouds of bliss. Her thoughts are dream-like, and her dreams are sheer joy. She has that special glow of a bride-to-be. In her mind's eye, she is admiring the handsome face, the broad shoulders and the manly chest of the brave man who is soon to be her husband. Her imagination is drawing, erasing and redrawing his features on the canvas of her mind, embellishing them with improvements every time. She has even put behind her the grief of her parents' death.

'But fate is sometimes cruel. The handsome groom did not come. Instead came the news that he had been killed in battle. Thilakavathy wept her heart out. She wept for the man whom she had seen only in her mind and dreams and never face to face. She mourned the man who was to marry her but died before it could happen. She thought she would weep till she ran out of breath and died. What was there left to live for? "I am here, Akka," pleaded her little brother. "Please live for me." Unwilling to live but unable to die, Thilakavathy had to withstand the cruel slaps of fate like an inanimate piece of sandalwood.

'In that battered, grieving soul, a new life bloomed. Her own dreams of marriage were shattered. But the new life that emerged in her was one that offered a divine experience to the world. It grew as the ultimate literary gem, as poetry.' Poorani finished narrating the story of Thilakavathy, with all its attendant emotion and pathos.

Afterwards, Mangaleswari's elder daughter, Vasantha, raised a question. 'After all, it was only a marriage agreement between

Thilakavathy and the army general Kalippagayar. Even if he died, why should she not marry someone else?' It was like having one's hands immersed in wastewater just after having rubbed sandal paste on them!

Poorani responded, 'You are speaking from the viewpoint of modern values, Vasantha! But back in those days, a woman born in this land would consider herself married to a man once she had accepted him as a husband in her mind. A woman was like an *anicham* flower (scarlet pimpernel), which is allowed only one experience before it wilts and dies.'

The audience applauded Poorani in appreciation, but Vasantha felt humiliated.

Once the meeting was over, many from the audience surrounded Poorani to express their admiration. It became clear to her that the emotional message in her speech had struck deep roots in their minds. 'Akka, you just churned our emotions with your words,' said Mangaleswari's younger daughter, Chellam, sincerely expressing her feelings. Even as Poorani was gasping in this flood of praise, there came a message. 'The Manager amma is waiting to meet you upstairs,' said one of the helpers at the Sangam. Poorani rose and started walking. Her gait revealed her sense of self-esteem at a task so well done.

As she climbed the stairs, Poorani imagined the dialogue that would follow. The lady would tell her, 'Poorani, I've never heard such a wonderful speech before. I want to congratulate you on behalf of the Sangam.' She felt her self-esteem rising with every step up the stairs.

As Poorani entered the manager's room, the lady did not even acknowledge or welcome her. This immediately struck Poorani as very odd. Her usual smile was missing. Poorani stood in front of her. The lady did not even have the courtesy to ask her to sit. By now, Poorani was confused.

'Here, look at this!' said the manager, handing Poorani a sheet of paper. 'Never before has this Sangam received an anonymous letter saying all sorts of things about anyone for any reason. You only pay lip service to talk of righteousness and good conduct, but your actions are in direct contrast. To make matters worse, the Sangam people are singing your praises. All this is absolutely unacceptable.'

As Poorani began to read the letter, her heart started pounding in her chest. It wailed aloud to god and wept. 'Oh, god! I will never forgive you for creating a world full of such scoundrels. Yet you must forgive me for living in this same world as these monsters that you have created.'

CHAPTER 11

They say all those who till the soil are only poor people after all! If we claim our rights, they shoot arrows into our open wounds and demean us for being Pulayars. Young man, this is all that will fill your eyes from dawn to dusk; but after darkness descends, look up and see how the sky has exploded into blisters of stars.

– Bharathidasan

Poorani had read stories of how hatred and jealousy could drive people to act in very cruel ways. She always considered that kind of behaviour in the stories to be totally undeserved and extreme. But now, a cruelty like this had come to her own doorstep in real life, to humiliate her in the presence of those who held her in esteem. The very people before whom she had stood and spoken for hours about righteousness, modesty and culture were now raising concerns about her character. It was the letter that had raised their suspicions. It was an anonymous letter after all.

Yet those who had employed her were inclined to believe it! The letter portrayed her pure friendship with Aravindan in a false and mischievous light. It demanded that her services at the Sangam be terminated. She had some idea of the possible identity of the letter writer whose hatred had inflicted this cruelty on her. Gone were those warm feelings of satisfaction that she had felt after receiving praise for her speech. She stood speechless, forlorn, head bowed in front of the manager.

'What do you have to say about this?' demanded the lady harshly. 'This is a respectable Sangam run by decent, respectable people. It is where women of all ages, from respectable families, meet. Those who teach here must have an immaculate character, even superior to others. Even a drop of poison ruins a whole jug of milk. How could you behave in a manner that invited such accusations?'

Poorani's eyes were brimming with tears. In a voice choked with emotion, she tried to explain to the lady. 'Forgive me for interrupting you, Amma. Someone, giving no name or address, decided to write all sorts of things to try and smear my reputation. Why should I accept that my good character has been damaged by such accusations? You had no right to summon me and throw such accusations at me simply on the basis of a letter like this.'

'Is there ever smoke without fire? Who is this Aravindan who is mentioned in the letter? What kind of relationship do you have with him? How long have you two been meeting each other?'

'He works at a printing house. My father's books are being published under his supervision. He is a person of good character and high principles. My affection for him is born out of my respect for his noble qualities. I do not consider my actions to be impure. Neither can anyone else.'

'What others think is not something you can control. If you are standing under a toddy tree, even if you are only drinking milk, the world will not believe you.' Poorani did not feel inclined to continue the conversation with the lady. She walked briskly out of the room and went downstairs and then directly to Mangaleswari's home.

'Welcome, Poorani! Just a moment ago, Chellam was telling me that your speech today was superb. I'm not feeling well. That is why I couldn't come. I heard that Vasantha also asked a question. Chellam says you gave a good reply to that question...' Mangaleswari's voice trailed away as she noticed the expression on Poorani's face.

'Something is wrong. Are you unwell? Your face looks...' In her concern for Poorani, Mangaleswari spoke in an agitated manner. Poorani moved closer to the older woman and sat down in silence. After a moment, she started speaking calmly.

'Amma, at your Women's Sangam they ask me to talk about the right way to live, they discuss it and praise me. But in their hearts, they are not willing to accept that there may be purity and righteousness in people other than themselves.'

'Why, what happened? Did someone say something to you?'

Poorani explained all that had happened and then handed the anonymous letter to Mangaleswari. The latter read it and heaved a deep sigh. The expression on her face revealed her indignation and scorn. 'Do you have ill-wishers who would want to harm you like this, Poorani?' she asked gently.

Poorani told her about the Pudu Mandapam publisher and the circumstances that had led him to rant and rave.

'Do you suspect him of writing this letter?'

'There is no one else who could possibly have done this. He must be the one.'

'I warned you earlier, do you remember? The Sangam is full of gossip-mongers. You have attained so much knowledge and received so much praise at such a young age; there must be those who are jealous of you. Even that first day when I recommended you for the job, there were objections such as "she is too young", "she is still unmarried", "she does not have a college degree" and so on. I was able to overcome their objections and get you appointed. Now this letter has arrived as something to chew on for those who were chewing nothing but empty air until now. What a misfortune this is!'

Poorani responded, 'Misfortunes do not arrive on their own. Human beings make them happen. There are many people who are too spineless to display their ill feelings openly. Widespread cowardice is the common currency of this century. As bravery ruled in the past, cowardice rules today. Whatever one wishes to mete out to others, one should do it face to face, openly. One should also tackle one's problems face to face. Neither of these happens in society today.'

'Don't be agitated, Poorani. I will meet and talk to those ladies at the Sangam. Just try to forget this incident. I will tell the manager lady not to blow this issue out of proportion. If I had been in her place, I would never have given importance to this letter. I wouldn't have summoned or interrogated you. I would have torn it up and thrown it into the waste basket at once.'

Chellam offered her tea, 'Here, Akka, take it.'

Noticing the young girl's admiration and affection towards her, Poorani thought, '*Ayyo*! So many young minds today hold me in such esteem. If they came to know about that anonymous letter, if all sorts of lies started to spread, what will happen?' The thought made her cringe in disgust. 'The most precious treasure one can possess in this world is the good opinion and esteem of others. Once lost, that treasure would be difficult to reclaim.'

Just as Poorani finished her tea and put down the cup, Vasantha walked downstairs. She looked dressed to go out.

Poorani said, 'Vasantha, I have no ill feelings towards you. I had to reply that way to the question you asked. Please don't hold it against me.' Her tone was conciliatory, but Vasantha did not respond to Poorani's overture. It was as if she had not heard Poorani's words at all. She turned her face away and walked out. Poorani was left regretting that she had made the friendly gesture towards the girl.

As she prepared to leave, Mangaleswari had some parting advice for her. 'Please ensure that this kind of thing doesn't happen again, Amma! There should be no reason for anyone to point a finger at you. I will tell the manager not to breathe a word about this to anyone.'

As Poorani left Mangaleswari's house, her mind was in turmoil. She did have some prior idea of the Pudu Mandapam publisher's dishonesty and boorishness. Like a spider spinning a web to trap its prey, he was capable of ruining people through careful planning. 'Who knows what else he may be plotting?' She thought about the incidents of the evening, her speech receiving praise and applause, her glow of self-esteem, followed by the blow that destroyed it all. She felt a deep disgust towards people, the world and life itself. There is jealousy in this life. There is hatred. There is selfishness. The only thing that is not there in this life is life!

She recalled something she had read in Aravindan's diary.

At one time there was suspicion and distrust in life. Nowadays, life itself is surrounded by suspicion and distrust.

At that moment, she understood the true meaning behind those words. 'If an anonymous letter from a dishonest idiot could raise doubts in the mind of a lady like the manager, surely we are living our lives in the midst of a sea of mistrust.'

Because the lecture had finished earlier than usual that day, Poorani had time to spare before she needed to get home. She thought of visiting the Meenakshi Amman Temple. Her bruised mind sought the sacred space of the temple. Just outside the west tower of the temple sat vendors selling peeled jackfruit, attempting to drive away their poverty along with the flies that buzzed around the fruit; the guardians of the worshippers' footwear, offering the service for a quarter or half an anna to feed their bellies; the flower-selling women, who could not afford even a few drops of oil or a handful of flowers for their own hair, calling out to passers-by and holding out strings of scented flowers; emaciated, wandering beggars muttering unintelligibly out of sunken mouths amid wild growths of beard like a weaver bird's nest. These were the permanent residents there. The ones who could look up at a lofty tower but had to look down to scrounge for their daily livelihood.

At the entrance of the tower, a gust of air blew hard on the nape of Poorani's neck as though urging her, 'Go on inside!' Poorani tried to block out the personal troubles swirling in her mind as her eyes took in the world's troubles that surrounded her. She prayed at each of the shrines and then went and sat at the edge of the lotus pond. From that point, through the opening above the pond, the sky was visible. As though a screen had been torn aside to display a glimpse of someone's work of art, stars were scattered across the expanse of the inky blue sky. In her current state of mind, the night sky reminded her of lines written by a Tamil poet, 'Having watched the ills of the world all day and been saddened and infuriated by them, the sky explodes into blisters at night; these are what we see as stars.' That recollection brought some solace to Poorani.

'Poorani! What are you sitting and watching here?' The familiar voice reached her ears from the steps behind her. There stood Aravindan, temple kumkum on his forehead and his usual mischievous smile on his lips. Next to him was another young man with a handkerchief tied around his neck, an unruly mop of hair falling across his forehead and lips reddened by chewing betel leaf. The youngster had the physique of a mud wrestler. Poorani was rather taken aback at seeing Aravindan in the company of someone like this. The fact that they were holding hands proved that he had indeed accompanied Aravindan. They came down the steps towards her. Just then, she happened to glance at a pair of women who were sitting on the steps to her right. Holding a plate of offerings of coconuts and bananas, the two were chatting. Poorani was startled. At the same time, they also noticed her.

One of them was the Women's Sangam manager, the other was the assistant manager. Poorani felt like an ant that was trapped between two raging fires with no route of escape. There was Aravindan coming closer, hand in hand with a ruffian-like man, whom he was talking to affectionately. At the same time, nearby sat a pair of women who had sought to accuse her of dishonesty and indecent behaviour. She realized that the fates were conspiring to bring matters to a head. She came to a swift decision.

As though she had not noticed Aravindan and did not recognize him, she got up swiftly and moved further away before climbing the steps. The call of 'Poorani' from behind her, in the voice that contained all the distilled love he felt for her, did not stop her or change her resolve. In that split second, she had steeled her will to resist all emotions. Half walking and half running, she went towards the south tower and out into the street. She clambered into a waiting cycle rickshaw without even negotiating a price for the trip. She asked to be taken straight back to Thirupparankundram.

She was bathed in sweat, out of fear or maybe something else akin to fear. She felt as if she had just done something that was beneath her, which she should never have done. She felt as if she had trampled upon that noble heart to whom she had given her whole being, as if she had given a resounding slap to the face that had made her heart blossom with joy.

Her mind stirred from its frozen state and began to torture her. 'You wretch! What a great wrong you have done to him! Can you forgive your own behaviour? *Endi*, Poorani, is your gentle nature really capable of such cruelty? Just a little while ago, you were complaining to Mangaleswari that deception and dishonesty are rampant everywhere. Just stop and think where that deception, that dishonesty, truly resides. Isn't it within you too? You don't even have the courage to express your love. This man has engraved your image on his heart and has been steadfast in his feelings for you. But you? You are afraid of being seen smiling at him and talking to him in public. What were you afraid of? Why did you flee in fear with your face averted? Wasn't it for the sake of a hundred-rupee salary that the suspicious, narrow-minded manager lady gives you? You did not value the man who has given his whole self to you. You are such a petty creature!'

Poorani's own conscience was punishing her. She clutched her head in both hands. It felt as if it would burst in remorse and regret. The cycle rickshaw was moving along. On all sides of the moving rickshaw, the life of Madurai was ticking along like a wound-up clock as usual.

Poorani paid the rickshaw man and entered her home looking like a zombie. Out on the street, Lord Murugan was riding his peacock in a temple procession. The sound of fireworks rent the air. The drummers and *nadhaswaram* players accompanying the procession added to the decibel level. Her brothers and little sister had hurried to the doorway to watch the procession go by. Poorani sat inside and tried to calm her aching heart. But the pain would not subside. How could it? By hurting him, by making his heart bleed, she had inevitably hurt herself deeply. She wished she could rush back to Madurai that very minute, find Aravindan wherever he was, tell him her whole story and weep her heart out. That whole night, her conscience denied her both sleep and peace of mind.

The next morning, she had a raging fever. Her head felt heavy like a stone. Her eyes were stinging. She was too weak to get up and move around. Kamala's mother came over to see her. 'Poorani, just lie down and rest. You are running a very high fever. I will send a messenger to fetch the doctor. Let the children eat at my house before they go to school. You should not exert yourself when you are in such a condition.' Poorani was beset by physical illness as well as mental turmoil. Tortured by worries that she could not freely reveal to others, she suffered in silence. She felt convinced that she could never be free from the burden of guilt unless she could meet Aravindan in person, apologize to him and seek his forgiveness.

The doctor arrived and gave her medicines. The children ate breakfast at Kamala's house and set off to school. Kamala's mother made barley *kanji* for Poorani and brought it over. She mixed some glucose in water for Poorani to drink. But whatever passed her lips only tasted bitter. Could it be that the bitterness in her mind had spread everywhere in her body? For two days, this state of affairs continued. Her fever rose steadily.

On the third day, Mangaleswari arrived with Chellam. She said, 'Chellam told me you have not been coming to the Sangam to teach the evening class for the past two days. I was upset that by not showing up like this, soon after that incident, you were strengthening the suspicion in their minds. Chellam must have urged me a hundred times during these two days to come and check up on you. Now we find you in this condition, sick in bed. Could you not have sent me a message to let me know?'

'Through whom could I send a message, Amma? My brothers go to school. Ever since that evening when I visited you, I have been very troubled in my mind.'

'See? You are still fretting about that incident! I told you even the other day that you should try to forget it. Because your mind is troubled, your body has fallen ill. Why do you have to worry? I have already had a talk with the manager lady, and everything is now smoothed over,' Mangaleswari assured her.

But Poorani found little comfort in her words. She thought to herself, 'It is not the thought of losing my job or of listening to the manager's harsh words that troubles me now. My heart aches because, when my loved one came towards me smiling and serene, I turned my face away and fled from him. I was afraid of showing my love to the world.' It occurred to Poorani that either the manager or her assistant may have mentioned to Mangaleswari that they had seen her on the steps near the temple pond.

She asked Mangaleswari, 'When you met the manager, did she mention anything else about me?'

'What's there for her to say? She only said, "Even though she is a good girl, it is our duty to caution her. That is why I called her and spoke to her sternly."'

Poorani was rather taken aback by this sudden deflation of all the suspicions she had harboured about the manager. A sudden doubt arose in her mind. Could it be that the women had not noticed her in the temple after all, and it was only her imagination that had summoned up that whole scenario?

Chellam said, 'Akka, without you, the Sangam is boring. People come, and when they realize you are absent, they go away. There's no liveliness there any longer.' Poorani found some comfort in the girl's words. It was the kind of good feeling that comes with the realization that there are people who will miss you or feel the loss of you.

Mangaleswari prepared to leave. 'My child, I will visit you again tomorrow. Look after yourself. There will be no problem for you as far as the Sangam is concerned.' Somehow, the news of her illness spread, and the students of the Sangam started dropping in to visit her later that day and the next morning. Chellam alone would have done a good bit towards spreading the word that Akka was unwell with a fever!

What did it matter who came and went? The one person she yearned to see, the one she wanted to pour her heart out to, did not come. He used to come by at least once a day to get some signatures from her or to drop off proofs of the books. But during those days, when she lay sick in bed, he did not visit even once. Poorani chided herself, 'Aravindan is a man with self-respect. You ignored his greeting and would not look him in the face. You turned your head away and ran. From that very second, he would have begun to forget you.' She waited, hoping against hope that he would come. But it did not happen.

Poorani had reached a breaking point. She felt she could not tolerate the stress any longer. All her learning and reasoning was nothing in the face of her heart's intense longing to see him. That evening, the moment Thirunavukkarasu returned from school, she sent him to Aravindan's printing shop with a message.

But a great disappointment was in store for Poorani. The boy returned after an hour and told her, 'Akka, they say Aravindan is not in the city now. That elderly man was sitting in Aravindan's place.'

'Which elderly man?'

'That same man, the one who dropped you home in his car one evening. He is the owner of the printing house.'

'Did he say where Aravindan has gone?'

'He didn't say anything about that. He asked, "What is the news?" I told him you have a fever. He said, "I will close the shop after a while and come over and visit your sister. Go home and tell her." So, I came back.'

Poorani was devastated. She felt her heart would burst from the intensity of her longing.

She heaved a sigh. What else could she do?

CHAPTER 12

In the loom of the mind, tiny threads of thought twist front to back, as delusions, imaginary visions, ruined daydreams, false hopes of victory... Oh, what a web of thoughts you spin, you poor little mind!

When one is sick in bed, it is as if all energy has been sucked out of time itself, which has gone into hibernation and ceased to function. There is a sense of lethargy all around. Poorani's overwhelming feeling was one of utter weariness. Her longing to see Aravindan remained unfulfilled. Had he started thinking ill of her? Was he trying to forget her? These thoughts magnified her sense of hopelessness. Moreover, the latest news that Thirunavukkarasu had brought from his visit to the printing shop added a layer of anxiety to her weariness.

'Where could Aravindan have gone? Wherever it may be, did it not even occur to him to let me know his plan? Could he be harbouring such a strong dislike for me? Oh god! Why did I behave in such a stupid manner at the lotus pond that evening? Like an elephant that picks up muddy water in its trunk and pours it on its own head, I too have brought this upon myself.' Severe illness, fierce longings, deep regrets, and unnamed fears... Poorani's mind was reeling under an unbearable burden. Her mind had always been prepared to accept poverty of material resources and facilities, but it rebelled at the thought of being consigned to the poverty representing the loss of love.

After locking the printing shop for the day, the proprietor, Meenakshisundaram Pillai, visited Poorani as he had promised. Before she could bring up the subject of Aravindan's whereabouts, he himself said, 'I had ordered a few new printing presses, Amma. The company's representative wrote to say that the machine parts have arrived in Chennai. I have sent Aravindan to check the parts and discuss payment terms. He told me he had seen you at the temple the evening before he left town. I assumed he would have mentioned his travel plans to you during your meeting.'

'When is he due to return?' asked Poorani.

'Any day now. He must have finished the work by now. I expect him back either tomorrow or the day after. He himself won't stay away longer than that. Work is piling up here at the printing shop. Everything is in chaos in his absence.' When Poorani realized that Aravindan's trip out of town was for work and had nothing to do with her behaviour or his possible reaction to it, seeds of hope began to sprout in her mind.

'You are so ill, Amma. Who is there to look after you? Shall I arrange to send a maid to help you? If you need money or any other kind of help, please feel free to ask me without any embarrassment. I will get it done for you.' Meenakshisundaram's concern for her was evident in his voice.

'I don't need anything at the moment. If I do need something, I will let you know. Please ask Aravindan to come and see me after he's back. There's no urgency, but just remind him, that's all.'

Poorani did feel a twinge of embarrassment at summoning Aravindan like that, but it was quickly smothered under her overwhelming need to assuage her heartache. As the smell of fresh camphor pervades all the space around, the very thought of Aravindan filled her mind with a special aroma, even though he was far away physically. That night, she slept more restfully than she had done in a while. Her weariness also seemed somewhat less intense.

The next morning, Poorani felt she was almost back to her old self. That evening, Mangaleswari and Chellam visited her. They had brought the manager lady along as well. Poorani thought to herself, 'The credit should surely go to Mangaleswari amma for changing the manager's attitude and actually convincing her to come on this visit.'

The manager said, 'My assistant and I were at the lotus pond in the temple one evening a few days ago. We saw you there. We had some flowers that had been offered to the goddess. I turned to call you, to come and take the flowers and put them in your hair. But the moment you saw us, you got up in agitation and fled, as if you had seen a ghost! What harm did I do to you? When I occupy the top position in an organization, it is my duty to make enquiries if an anonymous letter arrives. That is all that I did.' Poorani was astonished. She realized that she had misjudged everything and everybody and tortured herself for nothing. She guessed that the manager's change in attitude may not have happened entirely on its own and that Mangaleswari's intervention must have had a lot to do with it.

A few minutes after they had left, the doctor arrived. He examined Poorani and declared, 'Tomorrow you can take a bath.' Poorani saw him off, came back to bed, propped herself up on some pillows and picked up that day's newspaper.

'Akka! I need five rupees.'

Poorani lowered the newspaper. Thirunavukkarasu stood there scratching his head sheepishly.

'Why do you need money now? You paid the school fees last week, didn't you?'

'It's not for the fees, Akka. The exams are approaching. I need to buy some notebooks and a new pen. My pen leaks when I write.'

Poorani looked searchingly at her brother's face. She could detect that he was ill at ease, as if he was trying to cover up something.

'Why is your shirt so dirty, *da*? Did you take a bath or not? Are you going to school with your hair uncombed like a wild forest? All right, your studies may be tough and challenging. But is this the way you should look and behave? You rush away even before nine in the morning and return very late in the evening. I have no clue about where you go and when you will return. You don't seem to touch any of your books at home. Are you studying anything, anywhere at all? What on Earth are you doing?'

The boy bowed his head. His fingers played with a shirt button. His toe drew patterns on the floor.

Poorani spoke sternly to her brother. 'Open the cupboard and take five rupees. This evening, show me the new pen and the notebooks. I want to see them. I am getting more and more unhappy with your behaviour. You are old enough now, but you don't seem to think about family responsibilities at all!' For some time now, the boy's behaviour had become undesirable.

He always returned late in the evening and often asked for money for this and that. He was seldom at home and preferred to roam around elsewhere. The ages between twelve and eighteen are very crucial years in a boy's life. It is a tricky stage of life, akin to carrying an oil-smeared glass bottle across a hard stone floor. If good habits slip and fall at this time, they are shattered forever and are next to impossible to develop afresh. That was why Poorani had begun to feel anxious about her brother Thirunavukkarasu. She had been finding out from their younger brother, Sambandan, about how Thirunavukkarasu was behaving at school.

He had told her, 'At school, *Anna* has started going around with bad boys. They all skip classes and go away somewhere. Even when he comes to the classroom, he doesn't obey the teachers. If I bring up the subject he threatens me, "If you tell Akka anything, I will skin you alive!"'

This was a new thing to worry about. Her brother's behaviour had now been added to the stack of worries that were already burdening her.

After the exchange with Thirunavukkarasu, Poorani lost interest in reading the newspaper. After he left, she went and counted the money in the cupboard to see how much he had taken. The balance was short by ten rupees, not five. She was shocked. 'This boy cannot be allowed to go on this way. He must be forced onto the right path somehow,' she thought to herself as she shut the cupboard door.

Just then, a familiar voice, a voice that was sweet to her ears, called from the entrance, 'May I come in?' It was as if a great thirst in her heart had been quenched. Poorani turned to look at Aravindan.

If he had been alone, she would have run towards him that instant and sobbed out her story. She would have told him everything that had happened and asked for his forgiveness. But he was not alone. He was accompanied by the same ruffian-like companion she had seen him with at the temple. So, she said nothing beyond, 'Please come in.' Aravindan's face, usually very fair in complexion, appeared tanned, probably because of his recent travel. A small pimple had appeared at the tip of his shapely nose. To Poorani's gaze, that pimple lent beauty to him, like the sharp, pointed end of a lotus leaf stem.

He came up close to her and spoke affectionately. 'How are you now? I saw you at the temple the evening before I set out for my trip. I called out to you to tell you about my travel plan. I don't think you heard me. You left without a backward glance.' He spoke as usual, openly and cheerfully. Poorani was stunned. His attitude towards her was in direct contrast to everything that she had imagined. 'Can't your mind understand any situation properly, Aravindan?' she asked him in her mind. 'I thought that it was only when you were moved by people's sufferings that you displayed the simplicity of a child. But in the matter of showing affection too, you are simple and direct.' In that moment, he rose even further in Poorani's esteem.

Her tongue flirted with the words that rose in her mind, 'No, I heard you. I deliberately snubbed you and left.' But there was a stranger present, so she curbed the instinct to confess. Aravindan opened the fruit basket he had brought with him and presented it to Poorani.

'Why did you bring all this?' she protested with a smile.

'I returned from Chennai only this morning, Poorani. The moment I entered the printing shop, *Ayya* told me about your illness. When I heard you were unwell, I was very upset. I came straight here. How are you now?'

'The doctor has told me that I can have a bath tomorrow. I had thought of so many things I wanted to talk to you about and discuss threadbare, but now I can't even remember what they were! Nothing is wrong with me physically. I brought the whole thing upon myself because of my troubled mind.'

Aravindan cut in and said, 'You seem to be hesitating about speaking openly because my friend Muruganandam is here. He is not a stranger. He is a close friend. We have been friends since primary school. Don't judge him by his appearance and assume that he is a ruffian. He is a gem of a man. A bit of a chatterbox. He is a master tailor, and his tailoring shop is on the same street as our printing shop. He went to Bombay for special training and has returned with many awards. The style-conscious youngsters of the city swoon over the perfection of his work.'

This was Aravindan's introduction of his friend Muruganandam to Poorani, half accurate and half teasing. Muruganandam responded to the introduction by greeting Poorani with joined palms. She returned the gesture and was immediately given an opportunity to gauge Muruganandam's nature.

He said, 'Akka, I'm going to ask you a question. You must not misjudge me. I am not capable of hiding my thoughts. I openly express what I feel. Aravindan knows that well. I am quite naïve. Aravindan is my guru, guide and friend, all in one. Were it not for him, I would have ended up in all kinds of trouble in my life. I understood why you pretended not to hear Aravindan at the temple and why you went away hurriedly. When you saw me with Aravindan and noticed my appearance, like a rowdy, with uncombed hair and betel-stained lips, you started having doubts about Aravindan himself. Am I not right? When you saw me holding Aravindan's hand, you looked me up and down, and your expression turned to one of distaste. I know for a fact that the reason you left abruptly that evening was not because you did not notice Aravindan or hear him calling your name; you deliberately got up, turned your face away and left. You obviously told yourself, "Aravindan is standing there with some good-for-nothing type of fellow. There's no need for me to meet him." That's true, isn't it? I told Aravindan that. But because of his overwhelming love for you, he denied that you could ever have done such a thing. But it's true, I know it!' Poorani was shocked. Here was this stranger addressing her as Akka and laying out what he saw as the truth. She hung her head.

'This rough fellow always talks nonsense like this. Don't pay any attention to what he said, Poorani,' urged Aravindan, smiling calmly.

'No, he is not talking nonsense. Everything he said is true. That evening I did see you, and I deliberately pretended not to notice you and went away. Circumstances drove me to do that. I am still torturing myself with the thought of how I behaved towards you that day. That distress brought on my fever and confined me to bed.' As she said this, Poorani's voice was hoarse with emotion. Her eyes brimming with tears, she looked into Aravindan's face. He was calm as usual. She took the anonymous letter from under her pillow and handed it to him.

He read through the letter slowly. Then he handed it to his friend. 'Here, you take a look at this too.' It did not even occur to Poorani to prevent the letter from being read by Aravindan's friend because she no longer considered him an outsider or stranger.

Poorani explained, 'This letter was sent to the manager lady at the Women's Sangam. She sent for me and confronted me with it. That day, I was very upset. I was in extreme mental turmoil when I saw you at the temple. The manager lady was also sitting nearby. At that moment, I foolishly decided that it would be best if I did not talk to you in the presence of that lady. I acted on that stupid plan. For the injury that I have caused you, I don't know whether I deserve forgiveness or not. But, somehow, you must find it in your heart to forgive me.'

Aravindan laughed, and Muruganandam burst out, 'Akka, Aravindan may forgive you. But I can never forgive the treacherous hand that wrote such a letter about you and Aravindan. I must find that hand and wrench off those nasty fingers like one would twist drumsticks off a tree.'

'Patience, my friend!' Aravindan told him, 'You are fuming about the hand that wrote this letter, and I have received a hard slap across the face from that very same hand, those very same fingers. You cannot reform people through anger. It will have the opposite effect; it will make them behave even worse.'

Muruganandam was in no mood to accept this. 'Oh, keep quiet, Aravindan! Gone are the days when one could go through life practising pity and sympathy. We live in times when these values have lost their power due to disuse. Today, those who show patience are defeated; those who slap others on the face prosper. Those who help poor, starving people live miserable lives; those who snatch the livelihood of the poor live in luxury. Every bottle of medicine in a pharmacy carries an expiry date on its label. Once the date is crossed, the shop owner can no longer sell it. He has to dispose of it. The government sends officials to the shops to verify that this is done. In the same way, the medicines called patience, sympathy and honesty have crossed their expiry date in today's society. Otherwise, how can these kinds of things happen?'

'Poorani, Muruganandam always flies off the handle at the smallest thing and gets very emotional. Patience as a virtue is a stranger to him!'

Poorani was very impressed. Still looking at Muruganandam admiringly, she said to Aravindan, 'It's true that he is very emotional, but he speaks so well! He shares your opinions, Aravindan. If all young people could feel this passion and indignation, this Tamil land of ours would have progressed so much further!'

'Akka, I owe everything to Aravindan. If I had not known him, I would be just an ordinary tailor today. But now, I run my own tailoring shop and I'm also the president of two or three labour unions. It's all due to what I learnt from my *anna* here.'

Aravindan smiled and protested, 'Don't take pride in saying such things, *Thambi*. Poorani will start thinking that even all these wrong things you said must be from my tutoring!'

Poorani laughed aloud. She was already familiar with Aravindan's calm nature, his deep knowledge and his sensitive poetry. She was now witnessing his friend Muruganandam's intensity of feeling alongside a passion to defeat evil forces. It was as if his fingers twitched with eagerness to take on his foes. On the one hand, Aravindan was a beautiful hill with lush greenery and natural beauty; on the other, Muruganandam was a volcano spewing lava and ash. Just as love was the centre of Aravindan's character, violent passion was Muruganandam's nature.

Even up to that morning, Poorani had been in bed, still recovering from her illness. How had she suddenly acquired such a burst of energy? She went to the kitchen and made tea for her two guests. Aravindan tried to protest. 'You are not well. Forget about bringing tea for us.' But she rejected his protest. When they got up to leave, it was past eleven thirty. 'I'll see you later, Akka,' said Muruganandam as he left, as if he had known Poorani for a long time.

That afternoon, at about three o'clock, Odhuvar *thatha* came by with a piece of news. It opened Poorani's eyes fully to what her brother, Thirunavukkarasu, had been up to.

'What's happening, Amma? Why have you allowed this fellow to become a good-for-nothing? I happened to pass by Saravana Lake. Just outside the touring cinema your brother was sitting and playing card games for money, with two other useless fellows. He even had a beedi in his mouth. When he spotted me, he got up and fled. Can you not discipline him? He is turning into a loafer so early in life. Obviously, he doesn't attend school at all. He has picked up bad habits and bad friends. I saw it with my own eyes, so I couldn't help telling you about it.' Poorani felt stricken. Her mind cried out in agony, 'Oh, god, is there to be no peace of mind for me? Just when one burden is eased, another comes along. One step forward and two steps back. Why are you heaping hardships upon me? I am a woman, all alone. What can I do by myself? How can I tackle these problems?'

At five, Mangaiyarkarasi returned from school, and Sambandan got back at five thirty, with a message from the headmaster. Thirunavukkarasu had not attended school. Poorani described to Sambandan the location where Odhuvar *thatha* had seen their brother earlier in the day. She sent him to see whether he was still there. The boy returned with the news that his brother was not to be found. Poorani stood at her front door till eleven thirty at night, waiting for her brother to return home. He did not come.

Just as she was torturing herself with the dilemma of where to look and how to find him, Mangaleswari's car came to a stop at the door. Mangaleswari emerged from the car. Her dead-white face and frightened expression filled Poorani's heart with dread.

'Poorani! This wretched daughter of mine, Vasantha, has given me a crushing blow! She left for school this morning and never returned. It seems she never went to school at all. I found that she took a lot of money with her from the house. I don't know where she may have gone. I am a single woman, all alone. Where can I go and search? If this gets out, it will be such a scandal.' Mangaleswari was in a pitiable state, close to tears.

CHAPTER 13

Infancy dies, childhood passes away. Adolescence dies, and the full bloom of youth with its carnal desires also dies in its time. All of them are lost irretrievably and give way to old age. We die, we die, we die so often. Why do we never mourn our many deaths?

– *Kundalakesi*

The street was like the contents of the book of life – orderly and elegant. The highway from Melagopuram to Madurai city railway station did not know day from night. It was full of hustle and bustle at all times. With watches strapped on their wrists and dreams embedded in their hearts, countless people were hurrying somewhere, intent on doing something. The crowds waxed and waned, surged and ebbed, and the pulse of life throbbed ceaselessly. Voices of those who were meeting and greeting, voices of those who were parting and departing; shoppers bargaining, shop owners bickering; the medley of noises from rickshaws, cars, horse carts… It was as if life itself was being broadcast on the airwaves such that even with eyes shut tightly one could see it in the mind.

It was past nine in the evening on this busy road, and the street lamps shed their light from both sides. It was Aravindan's habit to go and stand at the doorway of the printing shop whenever his mind reeled with a multitude of thoughts. There he would switch off the turmoil in his mind and calmly take in the scene in front of him with his poet's eye. That evening, he did not have the luxury of spending much time doing this because a whole heap of tasks awaited him in the office.

He had returned to town from his trip only that morning. By the time he returned, after visiting Poorani at Thirupparankundram, it was almost noon. Later in the day, he had to hold discussions with the proprietor, Meenakshisundaram, about the accounts and the plans to buy new machinery. The drafts that had to be proofread had piled up. He had requested his friend Muruganandam to come and help him with this task of reading and correcting the texts. He had planned that the two of them would stay up for a couple of hours after nine and get the job done. Now, he stood in the doorway, waiting for Muruganandam's arrival.

By the time Muruganandam locked up his tailoring establishment and reached Aravindan's printing shop, twirling the key chain on his finger, the hands of the clock pointed to nine forty-five.

'The job here will take a long time. Have you eaten, Muruganandam?' asked Aravindan.

Muruganandam smiled cheerfully. 'Yes, I stopped at a hotel on the way and had dinner. Otherwise, I knew that I would've had to make do with your offer of a few groundnuts and half a banana. I had the forethought to eat before coming here. But I will stay here overnight. I've sent word home not to expect me tonight.'

Muruganandam's house was in a crowded lane in Ponnagaram. All his family members were labourers. His mother, father and sister worked at the mill. He was the only one who had made a slight change in this trend by setting up a tailoring shop. He had first started with a single machine in a tiny niche of a place. He was the only one in the shop and did all the tasks, from measuring the customers to stitching buttonholes in the garments. Due to his self-belief and hard work, he had gradually built up his business and now employed two tailors to work under him. In every city, there are numerous tradesmen plying numerous trades. Yet only a few of them earn renown for the excellence of their work. In the tailoring profession, Muruganandam was deemed to be one of the best in Madurai.

From his close friendship with Aravindan, Muruganandam had developed a love for the Tamil language and an awareness of Tamil culture. He had evolved into a fiery orator. Ponnagaram, Pittuthoppu, Aarappalayam, Maninagaram and a few other towns are full of people who come to Madurai every day to work. He had won the respect of those labourers, with work-worn hands, for whom poverty was a reality in their homes and thoughts.

The main reason for his popularity, at such a young age, was his easy manner and his ability to get along with everybody. Wherever he saw an opportunity to help, he would step up without a second thought. Whenever he saw injustice done to someone, it was as if he himself had been the victim, such was his passion and indignation. He moved around in many circles and met many kinds of people. Because of his open and empathetic nature, the working-class people who lived in the area around his tailoring shop held him in high regard.

Yet, when it came to his relationship with Aravindan, the equation was entirely different. When he was absorbing ideas and ideals from Aravindan, he was the obedient student learning from the master. When he was the friend, he flung his arm over Aravindan's shoulder and was his equal. When he was asked to come and help, he obliged unquestioningly, like an employee. The two friends expressed their shared values in very divergent ways. Aravindan approached his goals through the path of patience and discipline. Muruganandam, on the contrary, had a tendency to achieve his goals through violence and physical force. He had the physique to match his nature.

During the evenings when Muruganandam came over to help Aravindan with proofreading, they would work late, so he would stay over for the night. Even after winding up their work and lying down, the two would chat about this and that before going to sleep.

That night, it was already close to ten by the time they settled down to work. The street was still bustling with cinemagoers arriving for the late show and others departing after the evening show.

'I was expecting you earlier, Muruganandam. You are very late today. Here, take these and start reading,' said Aravindan, handing his friend some book drafts. 'I will note the corrections. Let us finish as much as we can.'

Muruganandam accepted the papers. He remarked, 'Something unusual happened at the tailoring shop today. I come across a lot of customers who get their clothes tailored first and then ask if they can pay later. There are others who start bargaining about the price after the work is done. This morning, a customer from another town came to collect his tailored clothes. He left his wallet behind in the shop by mistake. I waited for quite a while to see if he would come back to collect it. He was not one of the regular customers. I was concerned that the reputation of my shop should not be damaged. That is why I waited. The man did not return. Finally, I opened the wallet. There was a letter and some photographs. Also two or three hundred-rupee notes. So I waited beyond my usual closing time. Otherwise, I would have reached here by nine.'

'Okay, okay, start reading. Don't launch into another story now and waste more time,' urged Aravindan. Muruganandam started reading. It was the galley proof of the first draft of *Tholkappiyar's Treatise on Righteous Living*, a book written by Poorani's father, Azhagiya Sittrambalam.

'Hold on, Muruganandam! It appears that our typesetter holds some grudge against Tholkappiyar. Wherever his name appears, he has printed it as "Thelkappiyar" (*'thel'* means scorpion). Poor Tholkappiyar must be in agony over having been maimed like this!' Aravindan carefully corrected the name wherever it appeared, restoring the revered saint to his rightful form.

Muruganandam was amused. 'Why is the galley proof riddled with mistakes?' he asked.

'Whenever I read galley proofs, I am reminded of the ills of society in this Tamil land of ours. Galley proofs have plenty of mistakes. Our society too has many ills that need to be set right.' Aravindan's response showed how deeply he felt about society's problems and the need for reforms.

'True. But you cannot correct society's problems with your pen. It needs a total revolution of the kind Bharatiyar wrote about. Our situation today is such that no doctors of morality can diagnose our society's ailment. The illnesses are too many and too diffuse, and they combine into one massive, destructive disease. We stand by and watch while people behave immorally and dishonestly and thrive. We tolerate it. People have become too numb to protest. They lack the will and the passion to push back…'

When Muruganandam joined in the philosophical discourse, Aravindan cut in and reminded him about the work waiting to get done. '*Thambi*! Don't exhaust all your passionate rhetoric here. Save some of it for your orations at Ponnagaram and your public speeches at Pittuthoppu. We need to get work done. I travelled overnight on the train yesterday, and I am exhausted. I need to get to bed at least by midnight.'

Muruganandam started reading the galley proof. Just then, he spotted a youngster hovering near the front door of the shop. 'I see a boy near the front door. Did you ask any of your workers to come here now?' he asked Aravindan. Just then, a voice emerged from the doorway. 'Sir?'

'No, I didn't arrange for anyone to come. Maybe it is the telegraph peon. Go and see.'

Muruganandam went outside and talked to the boy. He came back and told Aravindan, 'He says that he is here to meet you. Go and see what he wants.'

Aravindan stepped outside. He was met by the sight of Poorani's brother, Thirunavukkarasu, with uncombed, unruly hair and wearing dirty clothes.

'*Enna da*? Why are you here at this hour?'

'No, it's nothing… Akka wanted me to come and borrow five rupees from you. It is urgently needed…' The boy was stumbling over his words. From the expression in his eyes, Aravindan could tell he was lying.

'*Enda*, are you telling me that your Akka sent you all the way here past ten to borrow five rupees? I met her this morning and talked to her. If she had mentioned a single word about her need for money, I would have given her whatever money I had on me.'

The boy stood in wide-eyed silence. His uneasy stance, the manner in which he had made his request and his rolling eyes made Aravindan very suspicious. Yet, without revealing his doubts, he produced a five-rupee note from his pocket and handed it to Thirunavukkarasu.

'Here, take this. I will come and meet your Akka in the morning.'

Thirunavukkarasu took the money and slid away without saying anything. Aravindan stood in the doorway for a while, watching the boy's retreating figure. Then he called out to his friend, 'Muruganandam, please come here for a moment. Our work can wait. We will tackle it later. I want you to do something for me. Follow that boy and see where he goes and what he does.'

'Who is that boy?'

'What does that matter now? I will tell you later. Get started.'

Muruganandam set off. Aravindan went back to the work table and started correcting the proofs by himself. His mind, thrown into a state of confusion after the exchange with Poorani's brother, became engrossed in Azhagiya Sittrambalam's writings, brimming with deeply researched philosophical ideas. It would be no exaggeration to say he was drowning in that culturally rich sea of profound truths.

He came across a passage in the book draft:

> *What we usually term as 'death' is what comes on the last day of life. Yet, every stage of life ends in a death, and every new stage begins with a rebirth. The death of infancy is the birth of childhood; the death of childhood is the birth of youth. With the death of youth, comes the birth of adulthood. These births and deaths are inflexion points in a person's life span, when habits and outlooks change. Whatever is lost is dead, whatever emerges as new is a birth. In fact, every day, what we experience and put behind us is dead. But we do not weep over those deaths because we do not understand those hidden secrets.*

Azhagiya Sittrambalam had written these profound ideas and illustrated them by quoting verses from the ancient text *Kundalakesi*.

Immediately, Aravindan was eager to write down the verse and the commentary in his diary. He thought to himself with a tinge of regret, 'If only Sittrambalam sir had been alive and had travelled to the Western world on behalf of our Tamil land, he would have been hailed by the Westerners as another Vivekananda! Given his mastery of both English and Tamil, and his scholarly philosophical ideas, we have hardly utilized his talents.' He heaved a deep sigh.

He recalled something he had said to Poorani when they were getting to know each other. 'Many of the tasks that your father left unfinished can be taken up and accomplished by you. You have what it takes to do that. You are proficient in both Tamil and English. When the opportunity arises, you must be ready to raise your voice and spread the sweet scent of Tamil culture worldwide.' Her response had been modest and dismissive.

'You seem to have very fanciful dreams for my future!' she had said with a laugh.

'Please don't say that,' he had urged her. 'I'm confident you can accomplish that.'

Aravindan thought about those times, the way their mutual affection had blossomed with time and turned into the relationship they now shared. In those early days, he had never envisaged that he would develop such a close relationship with Poorani. He was proud of how it had turned out between them. As he was turning over these thoughts in his mind, he started recording in his diary the philosophical passage and quote that had caught his attention earlier. While he was absorbed in this task, he was interrupted by a noise from the back of the shop. Startled by the unexpected sound, he stopped writing and listened intently. It sounded like someone was clambering up the rear wall.

To the right of the printing shop was a hotel, and between the two buildings ran a narrow alley. At the end of it, and common to the backs of both buildings, was an open compound with an abandoned house and half a dozen coconut trees. That whole area was filthy with the wastewater from the hotel, mixed with scrap paper discards from the printing shop. Except for the cleaner, who came into the alley every morning to clear the rubbish, no one else would want to set foot in that place. The back wall of the shop was not sufficient to ensure security; not only was it very old but it was also not tall enough. Just inside the back door, there was a small strip of grass, with a few jasmine bushes and *jalapa* plants. Further inside was a wide veranda, which was the most spacious area in the shop. It was used for the final processes, such as stitching and binding the books, after they were printed. Books awaiting binding were piled high in the veranda. Further inside was the printing room with its large presses. This area was always left unlocked and unprotected by the proprietor in the belief that the materials would be safe.

On working days of the hotel next door, the sounds of flour-grinding machines and utensils being washed could be commonly heard even past midnight. But since the next day was a weekly holiday for the hotel, there was silence from that building. Aravindan did not waste time hesitating and wondering what to do. He bolted the front door from inside and hurried towards the back of the building. It was a longish building. Aravindan turned on the lights as he moved through the building. He had been alone at night in the shop very often, but never had he faced such a situation. Something like this was happening for the first time.

Just as Aravindan turned on the last of the lights and was about to step out near the small strip of garden where the plants grew, he noticed movement near a jasmine bush. The man who had been lurking behind the bush was taken by surprise when the light came on and someone appeared. He jumped up and ran towards the wall and climbed onto it.

'Who's that?' shouted Aravindan and ran after the intruder. All he achieved was the pain of having a loose brick from the wall fall on his toe. The mysterious intruder had got away.

Aravindan had not had a good enough look at him to be able to identify him. The sound of footsteps running away came from behind the wall and faded into the distance. Near where the man had jumped onto the wall, Aravindan found a small wad of cotton soaked in kerosene and a matchbox lying on the ground. This discovery gave Aravindan a clue as to the reason for the break-in. Arson had been planned. If he had ignored the stealthy sounds or taken his time to investigate their source, he would have been able to see only a pile of ashes where the books had been stocked. This revelation came as a monstrous shock to Aravindan. It was a new and terribly unpleasant experience. Never before had the printing shop or its proprietor, Meenakshisundaram, attracted the ill will or animosity of anyone to the extent that they would want to do such great harm to them. Aravindan felt that, at that time of night, it would not be a good idea for him to try to chase the intruder through the filth that lined the ground in that direction. That fellow had somehow braved all that to sneak into the premises of the press.

Aravindan considered going to the hotel next door and asking someone there to accompany him into the alley to find the man. But he soon rejected the idea. By the time he could lock the front door, walk over next door and explain the situation to someone, the intruder would have long gone. 'I will wait for Muruganandam to return,' he told himself, abandoning the notion of chasing after the man. 'We will both spend the night on the veranda, just in case something happens.' Though he was by no means lacking in courage, a dread gripped him at the thought of what could have happened if that evil fellow had succeeded in his plan. What a tremendous loss it would have meant to the printing shop! Books that had taken weeks and months to prepare for release would have been consumed in flames.

There was a knock on the front door. Without turning off any of the lights, Aravindan opened it. It was Muruganandam, who had returned from the errand on which Aravindan had sent him.

'That boy is a useless fellow. He went to the street behind Mangammal Choultry and joined a card game under the streetlight there. You hadn't told me what to do, so I silently observed and came away. Otherwise, I would have administered a few hard slaps on his back and dragged him back here. There are more and more young people going astray like this at an early age in our land.' Aravindan was stunned to hear this news. 'The learned professor's son has come to such a pass,' he thought sadly. He told his friend, 'Muruganandam, please don't mind the extra effort. Please go back and tell the boy that I want him to come here. Don't beat him or hurt him in any way. He is the brother of the young woman I took you to meet at Thirupparankundram this morning. I was suspicious even when he came and asked for money. That's why I asked you to go and see what he was up to. Go quickly and bring the boy.'

Muruganandam could not refuse Aravindan anything. He went back again to fetch the boy. A few minutes later, Mangaleswari's car arrived and came to a stop at the front door of the printing shop. Poorani and Mangaleswari got out of the car, looking anxious and agitated. Aravindan's mind was already reeling from the incident of the intruder in the backyard, followed by the dismaying revelation of Thirunavukkarasu's bad habits. When he saw the two women alight from the car wearing worried expressions, he became even more alarmed.

Yet he exercised self-control and invited them in politely. Poorani explained to Aravindan that Mangaleswari's daughter had gone missing. She asked him for advice, about how they should proceed to look for her. When Mangaleswari had travelled all the way to Thirupparankundram to ask for Poorani's advice about her missing daughter, Poorani had been so concerned for her, that for the time being, she had set aside the problem of her missing brother. It seemed to her that the burden of realizing that a grown daughter was missing was greater than her own problem.

She told Aravindan, 'Like me, this lady is also looking after children at home, with no man to help her. She has money as well as courage. Yet, when this happened, she did not know what to do. She came to me in despair. What could I do? I thought of bringing her to you. Please do something to help her. She is worn out with anxiety.' Mangaleswari, driven by the worry of a teenage daughter gone missing, suggested, 'Shall we give a report to the police along with her photo? Or is it better to take out a "Missing Person" ad in the newspaper?'

Aravindan spoke calmly, 'Please don't agitate yourself, Amma. You say she is a grown girl. Giving publicity to this matter could give rise to all kinds of rumours that will affect her future. It may turn out that you have made a big deal out of something unimportant. So, let us think calmly and not act hastily.'

He took Poorani aside to another room. 'Do you know about your brother?' he asked and proceeded to tell her all that Thirunavukkarasu had done earlier. He also mentioned that he had sent Muruganandam to fetch him.

'Let that be for now,' said Poorani. 'The fellow has turned into a good-for-nothing. Yet another worry for me,' she said sadly.

Just then, Muruganandam returned alone. 'The boys were playing cards for money; a police van came and took them away because they were gambling. By the time I reached the spot, the boy had already got into the van with the others.'

'All right, we will tackle the matter of the boy in the morning. Right now, we need your ideas on how to deal with another problem. You see this lady here? She has come to us for help because...' Aravindan sat his friend down and told him the details of Mangaleswari's dilemma about her missing daughter.

CHAPTER 14

Even if you choose the best soil and fertilize it with the best manure,
Even if you water that soil with scented water,
A garlic plant will grow only according to its innate nature.
You may think even the most ignorant one can acquire knowledge,
Yet, it is his basic qualities that will decide the outcome.

The streets of Madurai had fallen silent in the darkness of the night. But on one street that was still bustling, in a printing shop in which the lights were turned on, the group sat in the front office, deep in discussion. Book drafts already proofread and those yet to be checked lay in unruly piles on the table. The way the pages were scattered untidily was a reflection of the state of mind of the people in that room.

Muruganandam listened to all the details that Aravindan told him but did not immediately respond. His expression was that of one in deep thought. Mangaleswari appeared like one who has lost everything valuable in life. She looked at Poorani. Poorani looked at Aravindan. Aravindan looked at Muruganandam.

Aravindan burst out, 'Muruganandam, what's the use of just sitting there saying nothing? Poorani and this lady have come here because they trust us to help. Should we not do something? You have seen the condition this lady is in, and yet, you are not offering any solution. The matter of a young boy telling lies to steal money, gambling it away on card games with a good-for-nothing set of fellows, even if these problems are tackled after a month, there's no great harm done. But when a grown, unmarried girl has slipped away from home without telling anyone... What a great disaster that is! Imagine the agony in the mother's mind, Muruganandam!'

'Yes, I get all that, Aravindan. But at this hour, where can we go looking for her? Also, it has to be managed without becoming public knowledge. You say she goes to a college, so she would not have been foolish enough to be lured away by someone. It seems most likely that this was her own conscious decision. In which case, we need to find out with whom she left, and why.

'Without finding out more about the girl's usual habits and lifestyle, we will have no idea of how to begin the search for her. Give me some time to think this through. It is past midnight. Take a copy of the girl's photo from them and send them home. Tell them to stay at home as calmly as possible without agitating themselves unduly. If I can do it, I will somehow find this girl and make sure she reaches her home. I am not at all hesitating to help. I only want to go about it properly. Any hasty move may result in gossip. People will be whispering, "I hear the girl has run away from home." That must be avoided.'

Muruganandam's calm analysis of the situation appeared reasonable to all of them. Poorani asked Mangaleswari for a copy of her daughter Vasantha's photograph. On the back of it, she wrote the girl's name and other details and handed it to Aravindan. He stored it carefully in the table drawer.

Poorani told Mangaleswari, 'Amma, please come with

me, to my home in Thirupparankundram. You are in a very troubled state of mind. I'm very concerned about sending you home alone in this condition.' But Mangaleswari did not take up Poorani's offer.

'Isn't it enough that I dragged you here in the middle of the night on the very day that you left your sick bed? It is my misfortune. If it is my destiny to have a daughter who has lost her good sense, what can all of you do? Should I come to your home and lay my burden on you? Poorani, don't worry about me. I won't do anything crazy because of this stupid girl. I remember what I told you when we first met. I said that times are changing and young girls today should imbibe modern culture. You did not agree with me. You vehemently opposed that idea. Today, I understand how right you were, Poorani.'

'Why are you bringing up all those old matters now, Amma? Let us focus on what needs to be done now. I asked you to come with me because I thought you would find some comfort in company.'

'I can't do that, Poorani. I've left Chellam at home alone. I hope the cook stayed back with her for the night. However late it is, I will drop you at your house and then go home,' insisted Mangaleswari.

Before leaving with Mangaleswari earlier that night, Poorani had taken her brother, Sambandan, and her little sister, Mangaiyarkarasi, to Kamala's house and requested Kamala's mother to have them sleep there since she had to go out urgently. She had locked up her own home before getting into the car with Mangaleswari. If she were to go back to Thirupparankundram at this late hour, she could not go to Kamala's house, wake up the children and take them home.

It would be bad manners to go to someone's house in the middle of the night and disturb them by knocking on the door. Neither would it be sensible for her to go home so late and be alone without the children. Instead of making Mangaleswari drive all the way to Thirupparankundram and back, would it not be better for her to go to Mangaleswari's house instead?

Poorani said, 'Please don't take the trouble of going all the way to drop me, Amma. What am I going to do at my house at this late hour? I will come with you to your home and stay the night.' Mangaleswari was only too happy to accept this suggestion. As they got into the car and prepared to leave, Aravindan and Muruganandam stepped out onto the pavement in front of the printing shop to see them off. Muruganandam stepped up close to the window of the car and told Poorani, 'Poorani Akka, in the morning, Aravindan and I will come to this lady's house. We need to find out more about her daughter. Please ask her not to be agitated. We will do our utmost to find the girl. Most probably, by the time we come to meet you in the morning, we will have also found your brother, and we will bring him along with us. Take heart, don't worry.'

Mangaleswari had overheard Muruganandam. She turned to Poorani and asked, 'What was that about, Poorani? What did he say about your brother? Did Thirunavukkarasu go away somewhere?' There was surprise and concern in her voice. When Mangaleswari had arrived at that late hour at her house and broken the news about her missing daughter, Poorani had not confided in her about her own missing brother. She had decided that when the lady was already struggling under such a great burden of anxiety, she should not add to it by mentioning her own problem. Mangaleswari had been helpful to her in so many ways. Now that the lady needed comfort and a solution to such a serious problem, Poorani had not wanted to seek comfort for herself. Her only thought was to take Mangaleswari to Aravindan and seek his help in finding the missing girl. It was fortunate that Muruganandam had also happened to be there.

From what Mangaleswari had overheard, she had realized that there was some problem involving Poorani's brother. She now wanted to know what it was. How could Poorani avoid responding to a direct question? So, during the time it took for the car to make its way from Thanappa Mudali Street to Mangaleswari's house, Poorani told the lady briefly about her brother Thirunavukkarasu's recent changes in behavioural patterns.

Having seen the women off, Aravindan and Muruganandam went back into the office. Both were silent for a while. It was as if there was nothing worth saying. Aravindan broke the silence first. 'I am going to tell you another piece of news, Muruganandam. If I were to tell you that about an hour ago this shop and all its literary treasures were about to go up in flames and be reduced to ashes, that a plot had been hatched to do that, would you believe me?'

'What do you mean? I don't understand. Explain yourself.'

Aravindan led Muruganandam to the backyard and explained in detail all the happenings from earlier in the night.

'What a rogue! Why did you let the rascal escape? What a pity I wasn't there at the time. I would have caught the fellow and beaten him up. I would have ensured that even in his dreams he would never dare to try such a dirty deed again.'

Aravindan laughed. 'Suppose you beat the fellow to within an inch of his life. Instead of scaring him into good behaviour, you may actually end up making him more evil. What would you do then, Muruganandam? If you are bleeding from a scrape on the arm, would you try to wipe it off with the tip of a knife? A lowly nature is like garlic. You may choose the best soil and fertilizer for the plant, you may pour scented water upon it, but when it grows, it will smell only of garlic. You know the proverb: "Who is greater? The thief or the watchman?" Tomorrow itself, I will tell the proprietor that we must have a gate or a wall to block the alley between our building and the hotel. That is the only thing we can do...'

Muruganandam had a suggestion. 'Someone has deliberately set up this plan and hired this criminal. Aravindan, you say no one enters that alley except the cleaner and some hotel employees. The hotel employees would have had nothing to do with this. It could be that the cleaner was tempted with an offer of money. Anyway, we will conduct investigations in the morning.'

Aravindan had a different point of view. 'I can tell you right now what our investigations will turn up. Listen, the only enemy we have at the moment is that publisher at Pudu Mandapam. For a long time now, there has been tension between him and our printing shop. He detests our proprietor heartily. Now that the publishing rights of the professor's books have been taken away from his greedy grip and given to us, his animosity towards us would have increased multifold. He is the kind of man who will stop at nothing. Let it be so. We will follow the righteous path. One day, there will surely be an opportunity for me to confront him and ask, "Is it right for you to behave this way?"'

Muruganandam was scornful about Aravindan's plan.

'What! Do you really think such a fellow is going to listen to you talking about honesty? You will end up getting another slap from him. This time, you deliver the slap. If you do not have the guts for that, take me along when you go to confront him. I will slap him on your behalf. Righteousness! Honesty! Justice! Today, all these ideas are fit only for talking about. They are not fit for acting upon.' Unwinding the kerchief from around his neck, and wrapping it tightly around his wrist, Muruganandam continued to comment on the incident.

'Aravindan, for saving the professor's book drafts from that rogue, no amount of gratitude expressed to you and your proprietor would be adequate. About ten days ago, a friend of mine bought a book brought out by that Pudu Mandapam publisher. In the book titled *An Anthology of Special Poems*, the word "*thirattu*" (anthology) had been printed everywhere from the first page to the last as "*thiruttu*" (dishonest). This error would be present in the thousands of copies of that book! What a great sin it is to the Tamil language itself!'

Aravindan's response was impish, 'The sin belongs not to Tamil but to that wretched fellow. In a way, it is appropriate that *thiruttu* crept into his publication. It reflects the nature of the person who brought it out. He did not search through his own collection of palm leaf manuscripts to unearth those poems, Muruganandam. A scholar had laboured for years, poring over ancient manuscripts, to assemble this anthology of special poetry. This fellow got his hands on it, copied it wholesale in a month and brought it out as his own. It was supposed to be a "low-price" book. But which was really "lower"? Was it the price, or was it the crime involved in bringing out the book? The mistake in spelling actually reflects the truth!'

The two of them spent that night on the back veranda. By the time they went to bed, it was about one thirty. Although they were physically exhausted, the anxiety in their minds prevented them from falling asleep easily. Muruganandam turned, propped himself up on one elbow and asked, 'What is the relationship between Poorani Akka and that lady? Who is she?'

Aravindan told him the background as he had heard it from Poorani.

Muruganandam was astounded. 'A girl from such a good family doing something so stupid! These days, both boys and girls in schools and colleges are gradually losing all inhibitions that might prevent them from going astray. Do you know why this is happening, Aravindan? A son born to a passionate champion of Tamil culture and brought up under the care of a similarly righteous woman, like Poorani, has turned out to be a loafer! A woman like Mangaleswari, blessed with wealth, resources and a good value system, has a daughter who steals money from her own mother and slips away from her home in secret. At this stage of their lives, when tender leaves are still sprouting, how did they venture into such foolhardiness?'

Aravindan heaved a deep sigh. He was silent for a while, debating how to respond. Then he turned towards his friend. 'I am also unable to see what could have given rise to such reckless behaviour. I even wonder if our schools should stop teaching maths, science or history for some time and teach good values instead. Before we achieved our independence, illiterate people were going astray due to ignorance. But now, educated people, fully aware of the distinction between right and wrong, are deliberately choosing the wrong path. When youngsters from the poverty-stricken families of the southern regions of our land come to the relatively prosperous north to study, they are exposed to the comforts and facilities of their new environment. But when they return home, they are misfits. It is like trying to fit a square lid onto a round tin. Grandiose dreams die a natural death in the midst of poverty.'

Muruganandam always took pleasure in goading Aravindan to explain his philosophical ideas. It was not often that Aravindan would speak with such passion from the depths of his heart as he was even-tempered by nature. But when circumstances like this one did arise, Muruganandam revelled in the experience of diving deep into the philosophical stream of thought enunciated by his friend. Aravindan continued his train of thought. 'Muruganandam, you know the kind of things that appear in the daily newspapers? Young boys and girls running away, stealing money and leaving their families – many such news items. Surely, they cannot all be untrue! It seems that the newspapers themselves give ideas to youngsters about the atrocious things they can do.'

'What you say is very true, Aravindan. Respect for good values is shrinking among the youth. But do you think youngsters are the only ones at fault for this state of affairs?'

Aravindan had a measured, logical reply to this question as well. After another debate along these lines, the two fell silent and went to sleep.

The next morning, Aravindan woke to the sound of Muruganandam shouting at someone in the backyard. When he went to investigate, Aravindan found that his friend was browbeating the garbage collector who came by daily to clean the alley. The poor fellow was cringing and claiming ignorance of all the accusations that Muruganandam was throwing at him. Muruganandam was so worked up that he was very close to physically assaulting the cleaner at any moment. Aravindan arrived just in time to save the fellow from receiving a severe beating.

Aravindan led his friend inside and tried to calm him. 'What do you expect the man to do? Even if he is the culprit, do you expect him to confess it to you? If we increase the height of the wall and put a gate at the entrance to the alley, no one can get in.'

'Aravindan, if you want a peacock feather, will you go up to the bird and plead, "O peacock, grant me one of your feathers?" If I had slapped that fellow around a couple of times, he would have come out with the truth. You came and spoilt the whole thing. Anyway, let that go for the time being. Let us at least start the task of finding that lady's daughter.'

Aravindan opened the drawer of the office desk, took out Vasantha's photo and handed it to Muruganandam. The moment Muruganandam set eyes on it, his face expressed astonishment.

'Oh, wonderful!' he exclaimed. 'Now that's a marvellous coincidence!'

Aravindan was thoroughly confused by his friend's reaction and remarks. 'Do you mean you know the girl in this photo?'

'No, not the girl. But I know the photo well. Look at this...' Muruganandam took out a purse and opened it. Inside were two stamp-sized photos of Vasantha, along with a letter written and signed by her, and three hundred-rupee notes. On the outer part of the purse, in a transparent pocket, was a photo of a man. It was obviously the photo of the owner of the purse. Muruganandam opened the letter and read it aloud to Aravindan.

Dear sir,

Greetings!

I have received the application form and your letter containing detailed terms and conditions. I applaud your efforts to bring new faces to the cinema screen and thereby develop the film industry. Thank you for understanding my keenness to participate in this. In my school days as well as in college fashion competitions, I have won several prizes. I have a deep desire to act in films. After seeing my photograph, you have offered to give me the lead role in my very first film. How can I thank you for this? I am ready to offer the fee that you mentioned in your terms and conditions at any time you wish. When you finalize your visit here, please let me know the date and your place of stay. Please send communications only in sealed envelopes. Please do not send postcards.

I look forward to meeting you.

Yours sincerely,

Vasantha

Aravindan's response was a mocking laugh. 'Nowadays, there is no end to the cinema craze among these half-educated young girls. Every time a girl looks at her face in the mirror, she sees a film star or at least pretends to be one. It is one thing to enjoy watching actresses in films. But their fascination with cinema makes so many young girls jump blindly into the unknown. Where is the antidote for this kind of frenzy born of infatuation with the cinema?'

'The search for an antidote can wait,' remarked Muruganandam. 'First, we have to track down this fellow and have him handcuffed and thrown into prison. He seems to have planned everything well, but he stupidly left his purse in my shop. Last night, just before locking up, I happened to open and look at the contents of the purse. That is when I spotted the girl's photos. My memory was jogged when you showed me the picture of that lady's missing daughter.'

'That's all fine,' interrupted Aravindan, 'but how do you hope to find this man just with his photo and his purse? The letter is not in an envelope with an address. There is no address available for him.'

'Don't worry. The fellow will be going around in the clothes I have tailored for him. Plus, we have the photo and know what he looks like. We will find him.'

Just then, Poorani entered the shop. She was holding a telegram envelope. She took the message out of the cover and handed it to Aravindan. It had been sent at four that morning from Tiruchirapalli.

No money to return home. Am at Tiruchi rail station. Come and fetch me. Details later in person. Vasantha.

It was addressed to Mangaleswari. Aravindan read the telegram and passed it to Muruganandam.

CHAPTER 15

To be born a woman, one has to do penance, Amma
Is it not through the hands of women that virtues can spread in this world?

– Kavimani

Muruganandam also read the telegram that Poorani had brought. He showed her the photos of Vasantha that he had found in the purse that the unknown customer had left behind in his tailoring shop and the letter she had written to that man.

Muruganandam said, 'Who knows how many girls this fellow has duped and robbed of their money with false promises of giving them star roles in his films? Unfortunately for him, he chose to come here to Madurai, selected my shop to have his clothes tailored and forgot to take his purse away with him. This time, he will surely be caught and dumped in prison, to spend his time counting the bars on the cell door. Akka! I won't let this fellow get away with this. I will somehow track him down and see that he goes to jail.' He took out the photo of the offender from inside its transparent pocket and showed it to Poorani as he spoke angrily.

Aravindan smiled and asked Poorani, 'You take great pride in having given a speech at the Women's Sangam about the cultural values and traditions of Tamil women. But do you see how the new generation of women is turning out to be? Like a showy croton plant in a pot, with no space to spread its roots and grow as it should, these girls are content with shallow pleasures. The moment a stranger offers her a role in a film, would a girl set aside family, education, reputation, everything… and be idiotic enough to go away with an unknown man? Would she not feel humiliated to have been hoodwinked, cheated of her money halfway through, left stranded with no way to get home and being forced to send a telegram to her mother to rescue her?'

Poorani joined in, 'There was a time when women did not have to be responsible for their own security. Society's rules and practices took care of that. But even then, they had a sense of modesty. Now, the common rules of society are very different. These are times when women have to take responsibility for their own safety. They should not fall prey to exploitation because of petty ambitions or desires. Yet, this girl allowed herself to be duped just like that. I am beginning to wonder whether my lectures about tradition and culture are lost on listeners and serve no useful purpose at all, Aravindan! Perhaps I have to bring more passion to my mission.' She interpreted Aravindan's words as a message to stoke her own passion for reform in order to influence others with her words.

'All right, let us not get into this discussion now. Mangaleswari amma and I will set off immediately to Tiruchirapalli in her car. She feels it would be good if one of you could accompany us on the journey.'

'Muruganandam, you go to Tiruchirapalli with them. Leave the keys of your tailoring shop with me. I will wait till your workmen arrive and give them the keys.'

'But why do I need to go, Aravindan? The two ladies can go on their own. The driver is available for security.'

'No, no. You must definitely go. If some problem arises, you are the best person to tackle it. Please don't say no. It is a large car. If you travel at fifty miles an hour, you can be back by noon.'

With Aravindan insisting so vehemently, Muruganandam could no longer argue. He handed the tailoring shop keys to Aravindan and set off with Poorani. As she was leaving, Poorani told Aravindan, 'Please do me a favour. Try to find that boy and give him a good scolding. I tried to tell myself that I shouldn't shield him and he has to pay for his own mistakes. But he is my flesh and blood, after all. My heart tells me to worry about him.'

'You're talking about Thirunavukkarasu, right? I will find him. You get along.'

After seeing off Poorani and Muruganandam, Aravindan went back inside and sat. The events that had taken place the previous evening ran through his mind and clouded it with confusion. He thought about Thirunavukkarasu and the dark hole of bad habits he had sunk into, and felt troubled. He thought about how he had narrowly averted an act of arson; it shook him to think that jealousy could lead to such evil; and his sympathy was aroused at the thought of Mangaleswari's mental agony due to the actions of her misguided daughter.

In this troubled state of mind, Aravindan raised his head and looked through the window. Framed by the window and directly to the east, in the early morning light, the temple *gopuram* seemed to have split the ground and emerged to reach for the sky. It was a splendid symbol of eternal truth. A temple elephant walked along majestically, transporting water from the Vaigai River towards the temple of Koodalazhaga Perumal for the *thirumanjanam* ritual. The bell that hung from its neck sent out sonorous peals, resonating through the streets in the calm morning air.

On the upper floor of a house across the street, a young girl was practising her music. The strings of her veena harmonized with the sweetness of her voice, as if to waken all the forces of beauty in the universe with music steeped in deep devotion. Alongside, as a reminder of the real imperfect world, came the clanging of pots around the street tap and voices raised in indignation.

Like seedlings struggling to survive in a difficult environment, a few ideas sprouted in Aravindan's mind. He took out the small book of *Thirukkural* verses that he always carried with him in his shirt pocket. He looked for verses that would mirror his current emotions and be relevant to his current state of mind. Soon, he was absorbed in reading.

He was prone to such urges and would often sit for hours absorbed in what he was reading, losing track of time. Sometimes, his eyes would brim with unshed tears at some deeply felt sentiment. At such times, when his mind was a melting pot of emotions, his poetic creativity would be awakened. Words soaked in shades of meaning would form in his mind and demand to be released. Like an infant demanding to be born, his poetry too created birth pangs in his mind. At such moments, his face mirrored the mixed feelings of emotional turmoil and creative satisfaction. You may remember classical pictures of Vivekananda with his back erect, arms crossed across his chest and a confident gaze. There is something arresting about that face, some quality that makes the viewer pause and look again. Aravindan's face, engaged in poetic thought, shared that quality.

Whenever he was lost in deep thought, Aravindan would break out in a sweat. Yet, when the thought process was complete, a sweet aroma would waft through his inner being, as though from a jasmine bud of the *pithigai* variety that had just blossomed into flower. Aravindan often thought that perhaps the name '*pithigai*' was given to the flower because its scent could make people *pithu*, that is, lose their senses. He did not have to be in proximity to the flower. The very thought of it would summon up its aroma and stir him to joy.

Maybe god anticipated that many foul smells would be created in the world and, therefore, created flowering plants with strong, sweet aromas to counteract the evil odours. That was a thought that had occurred to Aravindan, and he had composed a beautiful poem along these lines.

Poorani had once come across the poem in his notebook and read it. She had asked him, 'Do you know about another unique beauty, Aravindan? When Appa was writing a research paper about the elegance of the Tamil language, he taught me a very interesting fact. Whenever we say the words "*poo*" (flower) or "*malar*" (flower), our lips have to part like the petals of a bud opening out. The sounds "*pa*" and "*ma*" cannot be produced without parting the lips.'

During the course of their many conversations, Aravindan had picked up several such gems of knowledge from Poorani. She was offering him not only the gift of her love but also her knowledge of the treasure house that is the Tamil language.

There were three aspects to the relationship that Aravindan

shared with Poorani. One, that she was the daughter of Azhagiya Sittrambalam, and he was publishing her father's works. This was the aspect that had given rise to the other facets of their relationship. Two, the mutual affection they shared, based on a deep understanding and appreciation of each other's qualities. It was the purely personal aspect of their relationship, involving only their own hearts and minds. In the course of life, men and women meet, are attracted by outward appearances and are aroused by physical desire. The relationship between Poorani and Aravindan was not of this superficial kind. The third aspect of their relationship was the one where Aravindan took on the role of a student imbibing the wisdom that Poorani shared from her vast ocean of knowledge about Tamil language and literature.

Although he was a poet and thinker and a man of refined sensibilities, he nevertheless took great pleasure in burying all conceit and becoming a pupil when she shared her insights. Aravindan realized that his relationship with Muruganandam also mirrored a similar teacher–student aspect. Just as Muruganandam was both friend and student to him, depending on the circumstances, he too enjoyed being a student in the presence of Poorani, especially when she was sharing the literary wisdom that her father had imparted to her.

That morning, with his mind tossing thoughts around like a stormy sea, Aravindan found some tranquillity in recalling the nature of these relationships. He reached for his notebook and started writing.

In ancient times, there is said to have existed a bird known as asunam. *Its ears were accustomed to listening to sweet music. The moment it heard anything the least bit discordant or noisy, it would go into convulsions and die.*

When one witnesses the evil that is rampant in the world, one is tempted to think it would be better to end this existence. Yesterday, in the course of just one day, I came to know of so many bad events! It pains me to think of that boy Thirunavukkarasu, born and brought up in such a righteous family, adopting evil habits. At least he is a young boy, and it is still possible to discipline him and bring him back to the right path. But what about a young woman who has taken the decision to run away from home? Women are precious to society. Like seeds sown in a field, they are the key to ensuring that the next crop of youngsters turns out to be of good quality. If the seed itself is rotten, what will become of the crop? It is a frightening thought. Is it not true that the pride of India is in the purity of its holy rivers like the Ganga and the Kaveri? What will happen if one dirties the pure waters? What will follow if womanhood's purity is sullied? Are we destroying the source of life itself?

The sound of approaching footsteps intruded on Aravindan's thoughts. He lifted his glance from the notebook. The proprietor, Meenakshisundaram Pillai, was entering the room. Aravindan hurriedly shut the notebook, thrust it into the desk drawer and sprang to his feet.

'*Ennada*, Aravinda… last night the children were nagging me so much that I agreed to take them to a late show at the cinema house. Fortunately, it was an English film, and it finished relatively early. As we were going home, we passed this way, and I noticed that a light was still on in the printing shop. What were you doing so late in the night instead of going to bed?' The older man had started with his questions as soon as he stepped in, giving Aravindan no opportunity to tell him anything. He continued to speak. 'Whatever the backlog of work that may have piled up, it is not healthy to forgo sleep at night. In fact, I had half a mind to stop the car and come in to scold you last night. As if staying awake and ruining your eyes is not bad enough, you were also troubling that poor friend of yours, Muruganandam.'

'Please sit, sir. I will tell you everything that happened.' Once the proprietor was seated, Aravindan began relating the events of the previous night. Halfway through the narration, there was an interruption. *'Ayya?'* called a voice from outside. An employee from Muruganandam's tailoring shop had come to fetch the keys. Aravindan brought the keys, handed them to the man and explained, 'Muruganandam has gone to Tiruchirapalli. He will most probably return by this evening. He asked me to tell you to open the shop as usual and get along with the work.'

Aravindan did not tell Meenakshisundaram about the disappearance of Mangaleswari's daughter, nor about the delinquency of Poorani's brother, Thirunavukkarasu. He only described the break-in attempt of the previous night and stressed the urgent need to increase the height of the back wall and add a gate at the entrance to the alley. Meenakshisundaram was stunned to hear about the attempted arson. For a while, he did not respond to Aravindan. His face expressed his alarm.

'I have never done anything to hurt anybody, Appa! I took on this project because I wanted to do a good deed. I wanted to bring out the professor's profound writings at an affordable price. Why would this rouse such hatred and bitterness in anyone?'

He immediately sent for a mason and made arrangements to raise the height of the rear compound wall and install a gate at the alley entrance. Aravindan took permission from his employer to go out for an hour to take care of a personal matter. He went to the police station, bailed out Thirunavukkarasu and brought him back. The police officer told him, 'There will be a court hearing in a few days. At that time, you must bring the boy and settle whatever amount they decide to levy as a penalty.' On the way back from the police station, Aravindan tried to give Thirunavukkarasu some advice in a way that would make an impression on him. However, the boy just walked along silently, with his head bowed.

When Aravindan went back to the printing shop with Thirunavukkarasu, the work of raising the height of the back wall had made good progress. Loads of bricks had been delivered. Cement bags were stacked nearby. Meenakshisundaram himself was supervising the work and instructing the workers. Inside the shop, the employees were going about their duties as usual. Aravindan had a bath and changed into fresh clothes. He took Thirunavukkarasu inside and made him wash his face and comb his hair. He was satisfied only when he had transformed the appearance of the boy from that of a vagabond to that of a schoolboy. He sent for some tiffin and shared it with him.

Aravindan did not want to send Thirunavukkarasu to school unaccompanied. What if the boy decided to cut loose and start roaming around, getting into trouble again? So, despite the tall pile of book drafts awaiting attention on his desk, Aravindan went with Thirunavukkarasu to the boy's school at Pasumalai. Along the way, Aravindan continued to offer advice to the boy. '*Thambi*, right from this moment, abandon all your bad habits. Become the diligent schoolboy that you were before you went astray. March is not far away. If you fail the exam, you will waste a whole year. If you study sincerely, day and night, and pass the exam, you can enter college. I don't have to remind you about your family circumstances. How long can your sister struggle alone to look after all of you? After you, your brother has to go through school and college. Can your sister do everything on her own? Think about it and act in a responsible way, son.'

The school, located amidst the greenery on the southern slope of Pasumalai, was a very pleasing sight. This location, on the outskirts of the city, offered clean air and showcased the pure beauty of nature. The educational institutions here were often praised as being the Madurai versions of Oxford and Cambridge. Thirunavukkarasu's school was run with meticulous care and attention to quality by Christian missionaries.

Aravindan went to the headmaster's office to meet him. As he entered the room with Thirunavukkarasu, the headmaster greeted him and offered him a chair.

'Sir, I've come to meet you to explain this boy's situation. His elder sister could not find the time to come and meet you about this matter. I am a close friend of the family.' The headmaster smiled but seemed sceptical.

Aravindan's glance moved to the holy picture high up on the wall behind the headmaster's chair. It was the captivating form of Jesus on the cross, eyes full of gentle love even as blood poured out of his body.

The headmaster said, 'Is there anything left to say about this boy? In this school, discipline and good behaviour are monitored every minute in the students, and yet this boy has managed to go astray. So what is to be done? There is a rule that every student of the final year has to take the SSLC examination at the end of the term and that they should put in a minimum attendance at school. This boy has not fulfilled even 25 per cent of that requirement. This means that even if he were to attend school every day for the rest of this term, he would not be able to take the SSLC exam this year. Such being the case, it is a waste of money for you to pay the school fees now. Admit him afresh next year.'

'Sir, please don't say that! This boy belongs to the family of an illustrious Tamil scholar. He got drawn into bad company and started behaving like this. We will ensure that he does not go astray hereafter. Could you somehow, just this time...'

The headmaster remained adamant. 'I'm sorry, I cannot do that. I sympathize with you. But this is the rule of the Education Department. I cannot bend the rule for this boy or for you.' He smiled at Aravindan and then picked up an envelope from the table. He opened it to signal that the meeting was over. Aravindan looked up again at the picture of Jesus. It seemed to him that not only was the heart bleeding faster but the eyes in the picture were also brimming with sympathy.

'We will take our leave then,' said Aravindan.

'Please do so,' was the headmaster's response.

When they came out of the room and started walking down the steps towards the gate, Aravindan spoke to the boy earnestly. 'Do you see what has happened? You've been stupid enough to ruin your education, right at the end of the final year. Can your sister afford to pay the fees for you to repeat the whole year again?' Thirunavukkarasu had no response. Like a robot, he walked alongside in silence with his head bowed.

Aravindan thought to himself, 'In any case, this fellow has to be corrected and set on the right path. It may be best if I retain him as a helper in the printing shop for some time so that I can keep an eye on him.'

When they got back to the printing shop, Aravindan led Thirunavukkarasu to the bookbinding section and seated him on the floor near a pile of printed books awaiting binding. He showed the boy how to fold and stack each book and requested the foreman to guide him. Then he told Thirunavukkarasu, 'You are not to leave these premises without informing me. Do your work well.'

A while later, Meenakshisundaram made the rounds of the shop to see how the work was going on. He came back to the front office and asked Aravindan, '*En pa*, what's happening? Azhagiya Sittrambalam's son is sitting on the back veranda, folding books for binding! Isn't he still at school? The foreman tells me that it was you who brought him there and gave him that job.'

Aravindan narrated to the older man the circumstances leading up to his decision. 'Oh, what a pity! That such a great man should have a son like this!' Aravindan explained his plan for the boy and received the proprietor's approval.

Around twelve fifteen in the afternnon, Muruganandam turned up looking hot and bothered. Even before Aravindan could question him, he burst out, 'Things happened just the way I had feared, Aravindan. The cheat who had lured away Vasantha took her to Tiruchirapalli railway station and asked her to stay in the waiting room. He told her he had to meet someone in the city but would return very soon and they would board the express train to Madras. The fellow left and never returned. He had cleverly taken the money from her in advance. When he didn't return till four in the morning, she counted out the change she had with her and managed to send her mother a telegram. It was the same man who left his purse in my shop. I showed her his photo from the purse flap, and she recognized it.'

'But where is everyone now? Did you not come back in the car?'

'That poor girl gave in to the stupid temptation of becoming a film star. Now, she is weeping her heart out. They are at her mother's house now. Poorani is trying to comfort her and urging her to forget the whole nightmare.' Aravindan voiced a fear that had been preying on his mind. Apart from the two thousand rupees that the fellow stole from her, had anything else happened between them? It was only after Muruganandam assured him that nothing of the kind had taken place that Aravindan had some peace of mind. After all, a woman's virtue is far more valuable than all the riches in the world.

'These are evil times, my friend!' remarked Muruganandam. 'You have often quoted Kavimani's verse that one should have performed great penances to have been born a woman. Nowadays, one has to wonder whether it would be better to do penances to avoid being born a woman! Because being a woman involves so much loving, caring and protection.'

Muruganandam left for his tailoring shop, and Aravindan set out to Mangaleswari's house.

Fifteen days or so after these events, Muruganandam was measuring a customer for a coat in his tailoring shop one day when a loud, arrogant voice rang out from the front door.

'Hey, you! You tailor fellow!' Muruganandam turned around. The moment he saw who it was, his blood boiled. Somehow suppressing signs of rage on his reddening face, Muruganandam summoned up an artificial smile. 'Welcome, sir. You have come to recover your purse, haven't you? It is safe. You forgot about three hundred rupees for a whole fifteen days and did nothing! Tsk, tsk! Important people like you shouldn't keep standing in the doorway, sir. Please come in and sit down, sir. I realized only later that you are a famous cinema director.'

Muruganandam turned towards a lad who was sitting and sewing. '*Dei*, you can stitch those buttonholes later. Run now and buy some coffee for sir. He is an important cinema director.'

The visitor turned nervous and felt uneasy at the effusive welcome he was receiving. 'I've no time to waste,' he urged. 'I'm in a hurry. Give me my purse.'

'Why are you in such a hurry all the time, sir! Please be patient for a while. After holding your purse for so many days, would it be fair to return only the money? I will pay you back with interest, sir.' Muruganandam approached the man, and now the pretence was gone. The expression on his face mirrored the fury seething inside him. 'You good-for-nothing rascal!' he shouted, grabbing the man by his shirt, shaking him thoroughly and heaving him to his feet.

CHAPTER 16

The tears shed by the hapless oppressed are weapons
That will destroy the wealth of the oppressor;
But honest wealth, even when lost and mourned
Will return in blessings hereafter.

– *Thirukkural*

Muruganandam unbuckled his belt, took it off and started whipping the startled visitor. A crowd collected in the doorway of the shop. Just then, Aravindan happened to come by to meet Muruganandam about something. Such was the rage that possessed Muruganandam that if Aravindan had not interceded, who knows how it would all have ended!

'There are police, and there is the law. Why are you spending your energy beating him up? Let the law take care of it. Leave it!' urged Aravindan as he grabbed Muruganandam's arm to try and stop him. But the latter was in no mood to relent. He shook off Aravindan's grip and burst out, 'Don't stop me, Aravindan. These sleazy weasels should not be allowed to go free. When we do our tailoring, some rough fabrics need to be first soaked in water and dried out before they can be sewn. Similarly, fellows like this can be set right only after a thorough thrashing.' Muruganandam turned and approached the man again with his arm raised threateningly. '*Enda*, how many girls have you cheated and stolen money from with false promises of getting them leading cinema roles? You could still have made a living and survived on your earnings from the most menial of jobs without cheating others. Why did you become such a scoundrel?'

Others from the crowd also stepped forward to help Aravindan in the task of calming Muruganandam. But it was only after he had dragged the man to the police station and seen him in handcuffs that Muruganandam began to simmer down. At the police station, it had come to light that the fellow had been a wanted criminal for some time and had cheated several others using this approach.

After the incident involving Vasantha, Poorani continued to caution Mangaleswari often about her elder daughter. She told her frankly, 'Vasantha has many weaknesses in her character. I am not confident about her strength of mind. It is one thing for a woman to be frail or weak in body – that is a natural trait of womanhood. But the mind should be always strong in virtue. Our ancestors realized this, and that is why they always stressed virtue as a central attribute in women. I feel that if your daughter is put in a family-life environment, she will change for the better. Try to get her married as soon as possible. Don't hesitate. That would be the only way to straighten her mind. You need have no such worries about your younger daughter, Chellam. Even now, though she is still so young, I can assess her and tell you with the utmost confidence that she will never stray from the right path.'

'I agree with your opinion on this,' said Mangaleswari. 'But marriage isn't something that will happen the moment we decide on it. We need to look around for a good match for her and marry her into a good family.' Mangaleswari had lost her customary air of confidence and enthusiasm. The anxiety and shame brought about by her daughter's escapade had sapped her spirit. Poorani realized all the more that when the mind is troubled, a fine house and a big car mean nothing. All the wealth in the world can never soothe a troubled mind nor restore a wounded spirit.

Vasantha herself, with all her arrogance and flamboyance erased, was like a different person. She stayed upstairs in her room all the time. She stopped attending college. The household that had been humming with joyful activity was now sombre. It was as if someone had switched off the lights in the dark of the night. Every evening, Poorani stopped by Mangaleswari's house on her way to the Women's Sangam to spend a few minutes with her and comfort her.

God has given the human tongue only six tastes that it can detect – sweetness, saltiness and so on. But mankind has found a seventh taste for its tongue. That seventh taste is the one felt when the tongue gossips about others. Some people at the Sangam seemed to have a special fondness for this seventh taste. One evening after the class was over, some of the women in her class raised the topic of Mangaleswari's daughter, Vasantha. Their sly smiles revealed that they had heard rumours, although great efforts had been made to keep the whole thing secret. 'The girl ran away somewhere and returned later.' That story had grown wings and started flying around. Among those who asked Poorani, some were of her age and some were even older, not amenable to being disciplined. Yet Poorani responded to them firmly.

'I am being paid here only to teach Tamil, not to confirm rumours. Please raise only those questions that have relevance to the lesson.'

The rumour-mongers were silenced. There were those who were older or wealthier or more beautiful than Poorani. They were influential enough that, had they set their minds to it, they could have had her dismissed. But there was something so noble about Poorani's demeanour that such a low thought did not even enter their minds. Her face, her eyes, her captivating lectures about Tamil literature had won her a place in their hearts. In fact, even the ladies on the management board, who had been doubtful about her suitability for the job, had been totally won over by her eloquence and depth of knowledge, as well as her virtuous behaviour. They would not even dream of thinking ill of her.

Unfortunately, Mangaleswari, who had played such a pivotal rôle in bringing Poorani to this position of renown and pride, was experiencing the very opposite in her household. She was hesitant to step outside her house into the public gaze.

'Family honour is like a bell cast in the purest bronze. Even the tiniest blemish in a corner of the bell affects the clarity of the note it produces,' said Poorani to herself.

Of late, she had been consciously ensuring that every day of hers was spent productively while keeping to the highest levels of integrity and virtuous conduct. The words that Aravindan had spoken to her when she was leaving for Tiruchirapalli with Mangaleswari were etched in her memory. 'You lecture day in and day out at the Sangam about the proud, honourable traditions of Tamil womanhood. Yet those who choose to go astray still do so.' He had spoken teasingly, no doubt, but his remarks had left a deep impression on her mind. She had taken it as a kind of clarion call to her.

To her sensitive mind, it was as if he had said, 'Do something new and different for society. Think big! Why should you not develop your knowledge and eloquence into a movement for progress?' A sense of purpose took root in her mind, like a tulsi plant in fertile soil. It grew and flourished. The blossoming of her mind was reflected in the radiance of her face.

When she first took up teaching at the Sangam, only a few people in the city knew about her. Today, she was known throughout Madurai. In fact, her reputation had spread even to neighbouring towns. There were three people who were mainly responsible for Poorani winning such wide renown. The first was Aravindan, who had inspired her to challenge herself. The second was Meenakshisundaram, who had come forward to publish her father's works, thereby fetching her enough money to ease her worries about how to run the household. The two of them had, together, reformed her wayward brother, Thirunavukkarasu, and turned him into a useful employee in the printing shop. Whenever Poorani received invitations to give speeches in neighbouring towns, either Meenakshisundaram or Mangaleswari would offer her the use of their cars. The third person who helped Poorani to progress in her bid to reform society was Muruganandam. In the working-class colony where he resided, he arranged frequent public meetings for Poorani to address, so that thousands of poor people developed respect and affection for her.

She was aware that she was rapidly moving towards a turning point in her life. She was determined to do everything within her power to reform society into one where honour, tradition and righteousness were the norms. One particular event, arranged by Aravindan and Muruganandam, made her realize the extent of her renown in the large city of Madurai.

It was the month of Karthigai, and there was torrential rain. In the slum colony to the south of the bus stand, the huts of the poor families were destroyed by the downpour. With nowhere to take shelter, these unfortunate families had to live on the pavements. Aravindan, Muruganandam and a few other socially conscious young men got together and decided to help the slum families. They decided on a plan and went to meet Poorani. The moment she heard their plan, her face showed her delight.

'Yes,' she told them, 'this is an excellent plan, and I am ready to help in any way I can. Here…' She went into another room and opened a cupboard. She took out the couple pieces of gold jewellery she had kept with her when she had sold most of them to make ends meet. 'Take these. I don't wear them any longer. Let them be of use in your noble plan,' she said with a smile, and handed them to Aravindan.

Aravindan smiled and handed the jewels back to Poorani.

'Why won't you take these?' she asked him.

'Because we are expecting a far more valuable contribution from you. Listen to Muruganandam. He will explain.'

Poorani eagerly turned towards Muruganandam. 'Akka,' he told her, 'we have come here in the firm belief that you will agree to our plan. We have hired a theatre from ten in the morning to one o'clock. We will sell tickets in the denominations of rupees ten, five, three, two and one. You must give a speech for about two-and-a-half hours on any important topic of far-reaching significance.'

'Are the two of you joking? Is this some kind of entertainment? A drama? Or cinema? Or a music concert? How can a speech attract an audience? You will fall short of funds even to pay the rent for the theatre. Forget this fanciful idea and think of something else,' scolded Poorani.

'Akka, you are unaware of your own powers. Why do you worry about the money part? Just say yes. We will take care of everything else.'

Poorani was very hesitant. As she looked at Aravindan, the expression on her face revealed the question on her mind. Should she say yes?

'Why are you hesitating?' urged Aravindan. 'As Muruganandam said, it is best that you just simply say yes. We have no alternative plan. We are convinced that this plan will fetch a substantial amount to ease the burden of those homeless people.'

Poorani said yes. What else could she do? Yet, she continued to doubt if people would actually spend money to come and listen to her and whether the whole plan would bring in any reasonable amount.

Aravindan, Muruganandam and their friends took up the task of selling tickets. They arranged for large posters to be printed and pasted on walls all over the city. 'To raise funds for those who lost their homes in the rains, Poorani's special speech', proclaimed the posters in bold letters.

'Am I really so empowered? Do I deserve this much of a build-up through advertisements?' thought Poorani to herself, and the thought made her squirm in embarrassment.

By Thursday evening, most of the tickets had been sold. Muruganandam came and made this announcement with great joy. From the women who worked as labourers in the cotton mills of Madurai to the privileged women who arrived by car for their lessons every evening at the Women's Sangam without encountering the dust of the streets, all had bought tickets willingly, without any urging.

'Another astonishing thing happened, Akka,' revealed Muruganandam. 'I went to Mangaleswari amma's house and gave her three ten-rupee tickets. She took them silently and went inside. She came out and handed me a cheque. When I read it, I was startled. I protested, "But I have given you tickets only for thirty rupees." But she said, "It doesn't matter. Given my resources, I should contribute at least this much. Please accept it. Don't talk about it to anyone. In your donors' list, please don't write my name. List this as 'one thousand rupees from a well-wisher'." Such a noble-hearted lady!'

Poorani felt deeply gratified. She remarked, 'When wealthy people are beset with worries, it gives them some peace of mind if they extend a helping hand to the needy. Even in ancient times, philanthropy was the means by which the wealthy attained inner peace. Nowadays, they seek happiness through entertainment. There are only a few left these days, like Mangaleswari amma, who believe in philanthropy.'

'Akka, we have to announce the topic of your speech in the newspapers,' reminded Muruganandam.

Poorani thought for a while. Then she took a small bit of paper and wrote 'The Womanhood That Poets Did Not See' and handed it to him.

Odhuvar *thatha*'s family had fetched Kamu home. She was pregnant, and the Poochootal and bangle ceremonies were to take place on Friday. The old lady had taken the trouble to come over and invite Poorani personally. 'Don't say you have a speech or meeting or something. You must come at least for some time,' she had said. So, on Friday evening, Poorani went across the street to Odhuvar *thatha*'s house before setting off for her evening class at the Sangam.

Kamu was seated in a chair, weighed down with heaps of flowers in her hair and dozens of jingling bangles on her forearms. Several women were sitting around. With approaching motherhood, Kamu, who was otherwise rather plain in appearance, had a special glow. Like the radiance on the face of a poet in whose mind a poem is being formed and is waiting to enter the world, Kamu's face too had the radiance of one in whom a new human being was being formed and waiting to be born. Her grandmother cut two long lengths of flower strands and placed them in Poorani's hair. In that special moment, Poorani felt a twinge of longing for her dead mother. 'If Amma had been alive, she would have combed my hair every day and decorated it with flowers,' she thought. She was momentarily overcome with emotion.

'*Patti*! Have you forgotten about me? Why are you so partial? You put flowers only in Poorani Akka's hair and you are ignoring me,' teased little Mangaiyarkarasi. The room full of women broke into peals of laughter.

'Oh, so you have graced us! You are such a mischievous imp,' the old woman scolded the child fondly as she tucked some flowers into her hair as well.

In that gathering of women, Poorani was the most knowledgeable, enterprising and well-known. Yet she was uneasy in their presence. As if to justify her unease, an elderly woman, a stranger to her, made an absurd remark. She pointed at Mangaiyarkarasi and addressed Poorani in a loud voice, '*Endi,* Amma, is that your daughter? What a sharp tongue she has! She speaks so rudely at such a young age.'

'That's not her daughter, it's her sister,' someone explained. There was another round of laughter. Poorani realized something important at that moment. Despite her renown, her wide knowledge and righteous conduct, she did not possess something these women did. A sharp twinge of despair about this shortfall struck her like a lightning bolt.

Kamu herself rose from her chair, came forward and took Poorani's hand. 'Don't just take your *vettrilai pakku* and run away, Akka. Please sing a couple of songs.' Unable to refuse her friend's request outright, Poorani sang a Tamil song of Meenakshiammai Pillai and then got up to leave. 'It's getting late for me; I have to go now,' she told her hosts. 'My sister, Mangaiyarkarasi, will stay till the end of the function.'

Poorani went into an inner room to find *Patti* and take leave of her. She was in for a shock. She heard *Patti* talking to someone, and the topic seemed to be Poorani herself. Poorani hesitated outside the entrance to the room.

'Who is that girl? Fully grown like a temple cow and not yet married, you say?'

'She is the daughter of the Tamil professor Azhagiya Sittrambalam. Her name is Poorani. She has two younger brothers and a sister. The elder of the two boys fell into bad ways and is now employed in a printing press. The other two go to school. She has no parents. She is the one who has to raise the children and look after them. Where is the question of marriage? She is giving discourses on the streets. I also went to a couple of those and heard bits and pieces. It doesn't look as if the thought of marriage has ever crossed her mind. She has won name and fame. Her name is on posters on the walls of all the streets. But what does all that matter? Certain things in life have to happen at certain times. Who knows what is on her mind?'

To Poorani, broad-minded and virtuous as she was, *Patti*'s words were like a dagger to the heart. She somehow overcame her agitation and went and took leave of her. For the past couple of days, she had been engaged in the joyful task of weaving ideas and words for her upcoming speech on Sunday, on the topic 'The Womanhood That Poets Did Not See'.

After the experience at Kamu's *vilai kappu,* the joy in her mind had given way to pain and weariness. If she had known that her presence at that function would lead to so much heartache for her, she would have skipped it altogether.

Poorani thought bitterly, 'A woman may achieve renown. She may acquire deep knowledge. She may earn great wealth. Yet, in this commonplace society, in which common people live common lives, if a woman does not achieve the accepted commonplace norms, she is not a woman at all!' She had been indulging in visions of a life lived large, but these women had reminded her of the smaller obligations of life as they knew it.

When she first met and got to know Aravindan, longings for a life of love and togetherness did arise in her heart. Now, Aravindan had been permanently installed as an ideal in her heart. But she was no longer thirsting for the element of romance in their relationship. Neither did Aravindan show any signs of wanting to take their relationship in that direction. They were united by strong mutual affection. Like the small flame of a tiny oil lamp growing into the larger flame of a *kuthuvilakku*, their feelings for each other had been sublimated to the larger ideal of serving society. Their feelings for each other lay locked in their hearts, like unlit incense sticks whose fragrance is not evident to all. After the incident of the anonymous letter received by the Women's Sangam manager, both of them had decided to be circumspect during their meetings. But somehow, this wretched society still has eyes everywhere!

Sunday morning at ten, a large audience of women had filled the whole theatre. Poorani rose to speak. Aravindan handed a beautiful rose garland to Chellam, the younger daughter of Mangaleswari, and asked her to garland Poorani. The audience responded with loud applause accompanied by the jingling of hundreds of bangles. Poorani commenced her speech. The audience was silently attentive.

Poorani started. 'This occasion has been planned as a means to help poor families. It is our duty to aid those who are struggling due to want. Valluvar has written, "The tears of the poor will rise like a flood and destroy the world." Those who bring tears to the eyes of others through oppression will one day weep for their own loss. It gives me great pride and satisfaction that you have all come forward to contribute to this cause.' Having established the context of the event, Poorani took up the topic of her lecture. The honeyed tones of her voice and the clarity of her diction were captivating. She was overtaken by emotion now and then as she expanded on her theme, bringing out nuances of her ideas as a singer would embellish a raga presentation with variations. There was pin-drop silence among the audience.

'The poets of the world created many heroines for their poems. But the women they have created are like perfect lotuses in a painting, never wilting, never fading. In the real world, women face many challenges. Even when the poets wrote of the hardships faced by Kannagi, Shakuntala or Seetha, they explained them away as the burden carried over from their previous births. But today, do we not see women driven to despair to such an extent that they seek to sell their own children on the streets? Women's lives do crumple and fade like real lotuses do. Poets have fooled us by pretending otherwise. We live amidst misery and hardships. We must strive to conquer them...'

Her voice failed. Her eyes went pale. From the depths of her chest, there arose a deep cough, so intense and powerful that it felt as though it would rip out her heart. Instinctively, she raised the palm of her right hand to cover her mouth. When the cough subsided, she removed her hand. On the palm of her hand glistened two drops of fresh blood.

CHAPTER 17

From somewhere you call me,
From somewhere I hear you.
From somewhere you are thinking of me!
From somewhere I am thinking of you!

Poorani's vision blurred and faded. She was losing consciousness. Yet she felt a searing pain from her abdomen to her upper chest, as though a red-hot rod had been driven through her body. 'Amma,' she muttered weakly, and staggered over and collapsed into a cane chair behind where she had been standing and speaking. Like the petals of a lotus that are blown away in the wind, her consciousness was slipping away. That single word 'Amma', muttered in agony, resounded as sympathetic echoes from a hundred throats in the theatre. She lay crumpled in the chair like a discarded garland, her mind and body slowly shutting down. She had retreated into a dream world.

'Amma! Amma!' When the tongue struggles to form words to express unbearable pain, is the first word to emerge always 'Amma'? In grief, do the lips instinctively call to the mother? In times of agony of mind or body, how does the mouth always shape the word 'Amma'? Maybe Poorani's mother herself, when bringing her child into this world, her body racked with labour pains, would have called out to her own amma.

Birth takes place in the midst of pain. The new life, born through the pain of another, hears 'Amma' as the first word. As a life departs from this world, the parting word uttered in grief is again 'Amma'. Maybe, as the human life is dying, it recalls the first word it ever heard as it was being born… the mother moaning 'Amma' and instructing the tongue to say that very word. Whatever the reason, the word 'Amma' is like nectar. It soothes the grieving mind and gives it the resilience to withstand loss. It is a divine word.

In that moment of crisis, Poorani's mind reverts to early childhood. In a swirling *pattu pavadai*, her flower-petal lips part in a smile, she is nestled in her mother's lap like a baby bird. Her mother opens out her hair, oils, combs and plaits it. Her father returns from his college. She looks at him, wide-eyed and eager.

Her father smiles and tells Amma, 'Mark my words, someday you will realize how right I was. Our daughter has extraordinarily beautiful… no, perfect eyes. These eyes of hers will shake and move the world. People who have eyes like these have a touch of divinity to them.'

Amma laughs. 'They say if people cast envious eyes on someone, it will bring that person bad luck. You yourself are doing that right now to our daughter.'

'Nobody's eyes can have the power to do any harm to her. Even a single glance from her will banish all impurity and wrongdoing. So don't worry.' He lifts Poorani off Amma's lap and hugs her tight.

Amma and Appa have faded away from Poorani's dream. It is now taking a different course.

Where is Amma now? Where did that embodiment of love go? Poorani sees a sky shaped like an open umbrella, ash-coloured, with red and blue clouds drawing and erasing and remaking patterns across it. Suddenly, two large shapes emerge from the clouds, like the tusks of an elephant. They are two red arms adorned with bangles. Then, between a gap in the clouds, she sees her mother's face like a resplendent full moon. How large the vision of that face is! It is almost as large as the sky itself.

'Amma, from where are you stretching out your arms and calling me? From where do I hear your call? From where are you thinking of me? From where am I thinking of you? I don't understand; what is going on? Why does my body feel so much lighter? Had I, this creature of flesh and bone, become a festering sore, and has it now turned into a light, fragrant flower soaring upwards towards the outstretched arms and glowing face of Amma in the heavens above? Why am I turning into a flower? *Ayyo*, a heavenly maiden has sprinkled nectar on my face!'

Muruganandam ran forward, but Poorani had already collapsed motionless in the chair. From the open soda bottle in his hand, he sprinkled a few drops gently on her face. A crowd of women had gathered around the dais. Poorani opened her eyes. She was panting for breath, and there was an agonizing pain in her chest. Her eyes fluttered open and closed, again and again. 'What happened? Just a moment ago she was standing there like a golden *kuthuvilakku* and speaking. Which villain has cast his evil eye on her?' an old lady in the audience remarked to her neighbour. Hundreds of eyes gazed in deep concern at the motionless figure in the chair. Poorani was drifting in and out of consciousness. Some snatches of conversation reached her ears.

'I heard that they have collected more than ten thousand

rupees for the homeless people's fund. With just the power of her words, this one woman has been able to raise and donate so much. What a marvellous orator she is! How beautifully she expresses her ideas!'

'Such abilities are not given to everyone. It is said that they have to be inborn. It comes from an inner urge, a hunger to attain knowledge, as though one had fallen short of the ideal in a previous life. Look at the rest of us... content with a life of just kitchen and clothes and an occasional trip to the cinema.'

'May Goddess Meenakshi bless this woman with a long, healthy life and protect her from all harm,' said another voice from the audience.

Words of praise, of encouragement, of good wishes were pouring in from all sides.

Perhaps these words of praise helped soothe the heartache caused by the comments Poorani had overheard about herself at Odhuvar *thatha*'s house a couple of days ago. Gradually, her mind cleared, and she felt some strength returning to her body. She got to her feet a bit unsteadily. Like leading a sleepwalker, they led her slowly to the door, helped her into a car and drove her to the doctor's home.

Aravindan was tormented with anxiety. Neither he nor Muruganandam could breathe easy till the doctor reassured them about Poorani's health. Mangaleswari's younger daughter, Chellam, had been in the audience at the theatre. She ran home and reported the incident to her mother, who rushed at once to the doctor's house. The news spread to the publisher Meenakshisundaram, who also arrived in a hurry. Some of those who had travelled from Thirupparankundram to Madurai, to listen to Poorani, returned to their homes with the news that halfway through her speech, Poorani had fainted and collapsed.

Her brother, Sambandan, and little sister, Mangaiyarkarasi, burst into tears. Odhuvar *thatha* tried to reassure the children. 'It won't be anything serious. Your sister will be home soon,' he told them. Meanwhile, Thirunavukkarasu had rushed to the doctor's house from the printing shop.

In that short period of time, Poorani had unleashed a torrent of emotions among those who loved and cared for her. The doctor told Aravindan, 'As of now, there is nothing to worry about. But if she continues to strain her throat with too many lectures, she may become seriously ill. It is best to prevent that from happening. Please listen to my advice. This young woman needs total rest for at least six months. Please take her to some healthy spot and see that she gets enough rest. She needs nutritious food and a healthy environment. This should be done without delay.'

Aravindan realized that the doctor's advice was absolutely right. For the past year, Poorani had been continuously on the move, lecturing at different places in different towns. She had not been eating properly or on time. She had not been getting enough sleep. Apart from delivering speeches, she had also spent time on other social service activities. In a small village with no rail or car facilities, malaria was spreading, and at least four people were dying of the disease every day. It was in a remote corner of Madurai District. The moment he read this news item, Aravindan made preparations to travel there. But Poorani had beaten him to it!

She had argued, 'If you start taking up every one of these social service tasks, what will happen to my father's book publication project? Let *me* go to this village.' She had set out with a stock of anti-malaria medicines and had spent time in that village helping the patients. Aravindan remembered that and was even more convinced that Poorani needed a period of rest to avoid becoming chronically ill.

Aravindan consulted Mangaleswari about which would be the best place, in terms of clean air and environment, to which they could take Poorani. Mangaleswari did not hesitate. 'Vasantha and Chellam are my daughters, my flesh and blood. Poorani is also my daughter, though not born to me. That is how I have thought of her from the very beginning. There is nothing I would not do for her. I have a bungalow in Kodaikanal. My husband bought it. My children and I visit there occasionally. Right now, it is unoccupied. Once I make the necessary arrangements, Poorani can stay there for six months, or even a year, if needed. It is set in very healthy surroundings, and she will find it very refreshing.'

Aravindan remarked jokingly, 'So you want Poorani to reach great heights! Isn't that so?'

'She deserves a high place always,' was Mangaleswari's response in the same vein.

The question arose about who would be entrusted to look after Poorani's siblings. When Mangaleswari took on that responsibility as well, Aravindan was lost for adequate words to express his gratitude. When these arrangements were conveyed to Poorani, she said apologetically, 'I am giving all of you so much trouble. I have not been able to do much for you, but I am receiving more and more support from all of you... My life has become a burden to others.' Her voice was hoarse due to throat inflammation. In just these two or three days, she had become thin and weak. There were dark circles under her eyes. Every time she tried to speak, a nagging cough took over and drowned out the words.

Aravindan felt deep regret for having done nothing to limit the amount of work she had been undertaking – travelling, giving speeches and doing social service. But he chided her too. 'You have brought this problem on yourself. You should have looked after yourself better. How can you continue to serve others if your body is not well enough?'

It was decided that Poorani would be taken to Kodaikanal on Wednesday. But who would stay with her to assist her while she was recovering in the healthy air of the hill town?

Mangaleswari discussed this with Poorani. 'My elder daughter, Vasantha, feels too embarrassed to leave the house. She is ashamed to be seen in public. She doesn't talk even to me and only cries constantly. She has been refusing to leave the past behind and resume her old lifestyle. I feel confident that she could change if she were to spend time with you. Shall I send her with you to Kodaikanal? I am planning to get her married in the coming Chithirai month anyway. She can stay with you in Kodaikanal till then. I'm sure she has now realized your true worth. She will agree to come with you.'

Muruganandam heard this and made a light-hearted remark. 'Amma, you are planning to send one sick person to keep company with another sick person. Is that a good thing?'

'What is to be done? If anyone can bring her around and get her out of her present state of mind, it is only Poorani. If even Poorani can't do it, then no one else can. I have brought up my daughter badly and ruined her character.'

Mangaleswari made arrangements to send a woman cook

along with Poorani and Vasantha. Meanwhile, Poorani wrote to the manager of the Women's Sangam, seeking a lengthy leave of absence on health grounds. That lady paid a personal visit to meet Poorani. She said, 'Of course, take all the time you need. What a pity that you took on so much of a load and fell ill! Just get well and get back to us soon. That is all we need.'

As Poorani was leaving, little Mangaiyarkarasi held on to her legs and wailed. 'Akka, you are going away and leaving us,' she sobbed. Sambandan stood by, his eyes brimming with tears. Mangaleswari pulled the little girl close to her side and comforted her. 'Don't cry just when your sister is leaving, little one! I will look after you. You can have everything you need in my house.'

Aravindan stepped close and spoke to Poorani. 'Don't be apprehensive about the place being unfamiliar. Just go and concentrate on getting rest and becoming well again. If possible, Muruganandam and I will visit you in the middle of next month. Drop me a postcard once you reach there. Write to us regularly about your health. If you need money, just let us know, and we will send it immediately. Don't feel embarrassed about it. Don't hesitate to ask.'

'Akka, please take care of your health,' said Muruganandam, with a respectful *namaskaram*.

Poorani had a last-minute reminder for Aravindan. 'Start the slum relief work immediately, Aravindan. Don't let greedy people lay their hands on the money that was collected. Don't let the poor families be cheated. You both should see to it personally. I feel very sad that I am leaving at such an important time instead of staying and participating in this important work.'

Aravindan comforted her by saying, 'It's all right if you are not physically here to help with the work. Had it not been for you and your reputation as an excellent orator, we would not have got the money for the project.'

Poorani, Vasantha and the cook began their journey. Mangaleswari had instructed her driver to drop off the women at the Kodaikanal bungalow and return to Madurai. The car sped through Ammaya Nayakanur, Nilakottai, Vathalagundu and other picturesque towns of Madurai District. Before taking the road up the Kodaikanal hill, they stopped for refreshments in a shaded area on a riverbank. Then they set off on the hill road, which curled and coiled like a black serpent.

On either side of the road, unexpected treasures of nature met the eye. On the one side blue slopes with lush greenery plunging to the valley below, on the other, bulging, soaring peaks. What a variety of flowers! What lovely creepers! What huge, majestic trees! The sky seemed within arm's reach, inviting one to reach out and stroke it. At every twist and turn of the road, splendid new sights appeared, as though awaiting their turn to say, 'Here I am! Look at me!'

Orchards of hill banana plants putting forth early fruits, bunches of cashew flowers, gardens with grapevine trellises… a flood of visual beauty met the eye at every turn. 'The splendid handiwork of nature' is how Nakkeerar had described it, and Poorani was reminded of his words.

She also recalled a memorable essay by the Tamil scholar Thiru.vi.ka, describing the captivating beauty of mountain views.

Poorani turned towards the girl sitting silent and listless beside her. 'I did not know Kodaikanal would be so beautiful,

Vasantha! Last summer, your mother invited me to come here with her. Only now I realize what I missed by not accepting her invitation.'

Vasantha replied in a bored and disinterested tone of voice, 'You feel this way because it's the first time you are coming here. I have been seeing all this year in and year out. When we were living in Lanka, Appa would bring all of us here every summer. We would return to Lanka only in July. Amma has retained this bungalow only in memory of Appa.'

'She should never sell it! I will tell her so. Surely, she shares your father's love of nature.'

'Appa was totally obsessed with this bungalow. He laid out a large rose garden in the front. As long as he was alive, we were not allowed to pluck a single flower, however much we were tempted to do so. He was totally against removing flowers from plants.'

In this way, Poorani had managed to draw out Vasantha from surly silence into some degree of animated conversation. The cook was mostly silent.

They reached Senbaganur. Like white silken threads, rain was drizzling from the sky. Nearby, a twisted mountain peak loomed, peering down from a cow-like face. 'This is the tallest peak here. They call it Perumal Peak,' explained Vasantha. The hillside had been turned into multiple rows of garden plots with various varieties of plants. Kodaikanal town appeared from between the hills like a young girl who has drawn back her green muslin veil slightly to peep out and smile shyly.

The car drew up in front of a palatial bungalow on the southern slope adjoining the lake in the centre of the town. In the deepening dusk, at an elevation of more than eight thousand feet, the building was as beautiful as a wedding venue. Poorani took in all the wonderful sights around her, and her heart leapt for joy like that of a child. It was as if she had received an infusion of energy and enthusiasm.

Every day, bit by bit, she explored the beauty of the hill town. The day after they arrived, she sent letters to Aravindan and Mangaleswari. In her letter to Aravindan, she mentioned that she was already feeling much better and that she wanted to read some new books in this setting. She requested him to get them for her from the Madurai Tamil Sangam and send them over. In her letter to Mangaleswari, she described how she was slowly bringing Vasantha out of her shell and getting her to talk animatedly. 'Look for a good match and arrange her wedding in Chithirai,' she wrote.'

After four days, a large parcel of books arrived along with a letter from Aravindan. Vasantha also received a letter the same day. Since Vasantha was away shopping at the time, Poorani collected the letter on her behalf. The address on the envelope did not appear to be in the handwriting of her mother Mangaleswari, nor was it Chellam's. It looked like a man's handwriting. Though doubts did arise in Poorani's mind, she handed the letter to Vasantha when the latter returned home. The doubts, however, remained.

The transformation that came over Vasantha after reading the letter was absolutely astonishing to Poorani. Her lips moved as though she was singing under her breath; she had put roses in her hair; there was a glow in her face and a new spring in her step. She was actually smiling. That evening, she announced, 'Akka, today we must go down to the lake and take a boat ride.'

'What has come over you today, Vasantha? You seem to be bursting with enthusiasm,' enquired Poorani.

CHAPTER 18

After frantically doing this and that,
Day and night, wasting time, when one is finally
Shown the right path, why this hesitation and confusion?
How can such a one be redeemed?

– Kumarakrupar

The evening sun was making orange patterns in the western sky, like needles of gold descending to the earth. How beautiful everything looked... the streets, houses, trees... as though being viewed through yellow-tinted glass. As if a million yellow *nerunji* flowers had been tossed in heaps everywhere to make a golden landscape. How beautiful these golden evenings were!

That Sunday evening, as Aravindan walked along near the market on Tamil Sangam Street with a cloth bag in hand, he was reminded of an apt phrase to describe such evening conditions – '*Marul maalai*'.

It was a market day, and the crowds were milling around on the street, almost as though some festival was going on. The women vendors had spattered the pavements on either side with betel leaf spit. It looked as though some recent Holi celebrations had taken place. Aravindan found it distasteful to wade his way through the filth of the street. He had set out barefoot, fearing that if he were to be caught in a sudden shower, he would have to carry his footwear in addition to his bag. He was always particular about personal cleanliness, including his feet. He had beautiful golden-pink feet, like the ripe leaves of a white *gulmohar* tree. Friends of his own age would often teasingly ask him, 'How do you maintain your feet so well, almost like a woman's?' In fact, whenever Aravindan happened to notice Muruganandam's feet, full of cracks and callouses, he would advise him, 'Take care of your feet, *Thambi*. Like you, they are also becoming rough characters!'

'I never think about my appearance, Aravindan,' Muruganandam would reply. 'It is true that the locality I live in is called Ponnagaram, that is, Golden City. But in reality, the streets are full of dirt, slush and potholes. How else can my feet look?'

Aravindan's errand that Sunday evening was to get the books that Poorani had asked for from the Tamil Sangam. There was a large library on the premises of the Sangam, well-stocked with English and Tamil books. Professor Azhagiya Sittrambalam had been the patron of the library. He was keenly interested in developing it. After three Tamil Sangams had died out in a span of half a century, the royal family of Ramanathapuram, along with the philanthropist Pandithurai Thevar, had started this fourth Sangam.

From an early age, Professor Azhagiya Sittrambalam had formed close friendships with the Sethupathies, the chieftains of Ramanathapuram, who were instrumental in promoting the classical Tamil language. During every Navaratri holiday, he would travel to Ramanathapuram to participate in the Kalaimagal Poets' Meet and always returned with awards. These relationships, built by her father, now came in handy for

Poorani. She was in the habit of borrowing from the Sangam library some rare books that were not available among her father's collection of books at home.

The moment Aravindan produced Poorani's letter and list of books at the Sangam library, the staff swung into action right away. The books were brought quickly, and Aravindan filled his bag with them. He hurried towards the printing shop so that he could pack the books securely to be mailed to Poorani the next morning. The market stalls were beginning to close down. Although it had 'Sunday' attached to its name, the market took place on Thursdays as well. The market ground was named Tilak Square, in honour of the freedom fighter involved in the struggle for Independence. After six thirty in the evening, when the traders had finished selling their vegetables and moved away, the square turned into a political maidan. Public meetings would take place there, with skilled orators 'selling' their ideologies to the public. That evening, as Aravindan was crossing the entrance to that maidan where goods, as well as ideas, were regularly marketed, he ran into Muruganandam unexpectedly.

'What's this, Aravindan! Have you stuffed the entire contents of the Sangam library into that bag?' teased Muruganandam.

'No, no. There were a few books that Poorani particularly wanted to read. She wrote and asked me to borrow them from the library and send them to her. I'm on my way to pack them so that I can send them tomorrow.'

'I received a letter too…' Muruganandam said, smiling jovially. The next moment, like a TV screen that goes blank when the electric supply fails, he abruptly stopped talking and bit his lip. His whole demeanour suggested that he had just blurted out something that he had intended to keep secret. Aravindan looked searchingly into his friend's face. The latter seemed caught between a mood of pleasurable excitement and a feeling of acute embarrassment. Unable to meet Aravindan's eye, Muruganandam turned his head, averting his gaze. But Aravindan could detect all the signs of a new emotion on his friend's face. His eyes, his lips spoke without speaking.

'Who sent you a letter, Muruganandam? In her letter to me, your Poorani Akka had mentioned that she did not have the leisure to write another letter to you as well and that I should convey her wishes to you.'

Faced with this direct question, Muruganandam's embarrassment increased. When he remained silent, Aravindan did not relent. He asked again, '*Ennappa, Thambi*, what's happening? You seem to be feeling uncomfortable about something. You mentioned that you received a letter. But when I ask you who sent it, you just look here and there and try to avoid the subject.'

'Oh, it's nothing, Aravindan. Just…'

'Stop mumbling! Speak up like a man. Tell me.'

'That girl, Vasantha, wrote a letter to me soon after they reached Kodaikanal. That is what I blurted out by mistake.'

'Ah, so you blurted it out! A love story is being born here… How long has this back-and-forth communication been going on, *Thambi*?'

'I swear, Aravindan, I didn't do anything. It was that girl who….'

'*De, de*! Don't bring deep stuff like swearing into this. This matter is only one of romance,' teased Aravindan. Muruganandam smiled and bowed his head.

'So that's the news! Have you written a reply?' Yes, nodded Muruganandam.

Aravindan continued, 'Oh, things are becoming clear to me now. From the moment you returned after rescuing that girl from Tiruchirapalli, you started frequenting Thanappa Mudali Street regularly. You explained it away by saying her mother, Mangaleswari, was giving you some tailoring jobs. So, this is the real story you are stitching, is it?'

'Aravindan, please let this matter go for now. I will come to the printing shop at nine at night and tell you everything from beginning to end. There is a public meeting at Tilak Square at six thirty in the evening. I am due to speak there.' Muruganandam was in a hurry to rush away.

Aravindan was still in a mood to tease his friend. 'From now on, what will be the fate of all your public speeches, social service, uplifting the poor… now that you have got trapped in the net of romance?' Once Muruganandam had left, Aravindan went to the printing shop, still trying to assimilate the astounding news he had just heard. Although he had dealt with the matter in a light-hearted way with his friend and teased him, he was actually quite concerned about it. The more he thought about it, the more apprehensive he felt.

Aravindan mulled it over in his mind. 'What will Mangaleswari think of this relationship? What will Muruganandam's parents say? Isn't the whole thing rather juvenile? Sometimes, after meeting here and there and having a casual conversation or a laugh a few times, people decide, rather foolishly, that they are in love. I must talk to Muruganandam sternly when he comes to the printing shop this evening,' decided Aravindan.

'The girl is arrogant and full of vanity about her wealth. She is given to stupid extravagances and is obsessed with outward appearances.' This was how Poorani had described Vasantha. How did such an arrogant girl turn her attention to someone who was the direct opposite of her in every way... in attitude, in sincerity and in economic circumstances? How did such a relationship blossom and flourish? The more he thought about it, the more of a puzzle the whole thing seemed to be. Aravindan was reminded of a quote from Shakespeare's *Hamlet*: 'Frailty, thy name is woman.' This was among the quotes from famous world writers that he had written down in his diary. Yet, his mind rejected the suggestion that the description would fit all women. 'There are also women like Poorani, who are immersed in acquiring knowledge and in working selflessly for the betterment of society,' he reminded himself.

His train of thought was interrupted by a young boy who approached him and held out his hand. He was sobbing miserably. '*Saar*, I haven't eaten anything for the past seven days. I have no money to get back home. Please help me. I can't bear my hunger any longer. In a few hours from now, I will just collapse on the street and die.'

Aravindan had been walking along briskly. He now paused and took in the appearance of the frail boy who had confronted him. The boy looked weak and thin enough to break and fall to bits at any moment. His face looked like a worn piece of grubby paper that had been written on and erased over and over. His eyes had sunk into the hollows of his eye sockets. He had probably not had a bath for days, and his clothes were sweaty and filthy. That young, unfortunate creature was like a poster boy for the poverty, hunger and unemployment that stalked the land. His face, his outstretched hand, his whole demeanour were such that they would evoke sympathy in the viewer. Aravindan asked him, 'Which town are you from?'

The boy mentioned a town in Ramanathapuram District, known for the extreme poverty and distress of its population.

'Till which class have you studied?'

'SSLC, *saar*! I know typewriting too. I sat for the Service Commission exam, but I didn't get through. I've come to Madurai looking for a job.'

Aravindan felt deep sympathy for the boy. His mind was troubled. He thought to himself, 'This is what is happening these days. Youngsters study and sit for exams; they pass out of school and walk out into the world with high hopes and dreams in their hearts. But many of the youth of this land end up like this boy, desperately seeking a livelihood on the streets of big cities. What do we as a country have to be proud about unless we can protect the dignity and honour of the youth?'

The boy cried out again, '*Saar*, I can't stand this hunger.' He was clutching his abdomen with his left hand; his right hand was outstretched pleadingly. Aravindan reached into his jibba pocket, took out a one-rupee note and offered it to the boy. 'Here, take this and get yourself something to eat,' he said. Without waiting for a response from the boy, Aravindan walked away swiftly. As he went, he imagined himself in the shoes of that youngster. It could well have been so, he realized. Had it not been for his good fortune in finding a generous-hearted man like the proprietor of Meenakshi Printing House, he himself may have been wandering the streets of some big city asking strangers for handouts. That thought added to his distress.

As he entered the premises of the printing shop, the burden

on his mind weighed heavier than the Sangam books that he carried in his hand. The working hours had ended, and the workmen were leaving.

'After you left for the Sangam, *Ayya* came by. He has now gone to Keezhavani Stationery Shop. He left word that if you returned, we should ask you to stay here. He has something important to tell you,' said the peon. At that moment, Aravindan's mind was filled with thoughts of the poor boy he had just met. He collected himself with an effort and said, 'I will stay here. I'm not going anywhere tonight. Please go inside and see if Thirunavukkarasu is there. Tell him I want to see him.'

In a short while, Poorani's brother, Thirunavukkarasu, entered the room.

'*Saar*, you sent for me?'

'Yes. Take these books and wrap them in a neat parcel. They are to be sent to your sister tomorrow morning.'

Thirunavukkarasu picked up the books and went back into the shop. Once again, the image of that unfortunate, starving boy on the street occupied Aravindan's mind. Steeped in deep emotions, he reached for his notebook and started writing.

> *Like the groans of one who has been loaded with a far greater burden than he can bear, the moans of countless such unfortunate souls are being heard everywhere. Just as the thorns of a thorn bush grow bigger and stronger along with the bush, poverty and hardships are growing alongside the country's technological and economic advances. The more you enlarge a flawed photograph, the more glaring the flaws appear. The 'progress' of our country is just like that. The young generation is struggling with poverty, hunger, joblessness and insecurity. They neither find jobs to suit their education, nor fair*

reward for hard work. Have these young people been born just to kill themselves in despair? Throwing themselves in front of approaching trains, hanging themselves from trees, drinking poison...

Aravindan's pen nib scratched and tore the paper. It had run out of ink. His frustration at having the flow of his thoughts cut short by the inadequacies of his pen made Aravindan turn his wrath on that lifeless instrument. He overcame the instinct to twist and break it and cast it away. Truly, there is no greater annoyance to a writer in this world than a pen that runs out of ink. He fumed as he opened the desk drawer and took out a bottle of ink. Like a well that has been exposed to the burning summer sun till all the water has been sucked out and only dry mud remains, the ink bottle was totally empty. Infuriated beyond control, he yelled for the peon, to send him on an errand to buy a bottle of ink. The peon, busy with something inside the building, did not immediately respond. 'All these fellows seem to have turned deaf. There's no other way than to go and buy the ink myself,' he told himself.

He went out, walked to West Temple Street and bought a bottle of ink at a shop near the cinema theatre. They must have been showing a new movie. The queue in front of the theatre ticket counter was very long. As he idly cast his glance at the people in the queue, he was startled at the sight of a familiar face. The shock in his mind was as if some large edifice had crumbled in an earthquake. He frowned as he stared fixedly at that face.

The boy who had spun a tale of extreme hunger and made Aravindan part with one whole rupee just minutes earlier was now standing in the twelve-and-a-half anna queue to watch the new movie. Puffs of smoke emerged from the cigarette he held between his lips. Aravindan felt as if the whole world had somehow turned over and was spinning upside down. If Muruganandam had been in Aravindan's place, he would have marched over, dragged the boy out of the line and given him a good beating. All kinds of thoughts were raging in Aravindan's mind. He thought of going up and having a word with the boy. But in the meantime, the queue had moved, and the boy had entered the building.

'Let him go to hell! There's no hope for such fellows. Unthinkingly, hastily, as though rushing to catch a train, they commit all kinds of mistakes and ruin themselves with not even the slightest thought of reforming their ways. They are like the buffaloes that roam aimlessly outside temples. How can such fellows be rescued from their destructive path? Great saints, mahatmas, have to be born in this land to reform such youngsters. It is a task beyond the ability of any ordinary human.

'One who earns a thousand rupees a month goes to watch the cinema once a week. The labourer who earns a mere thirty rupees a month leaves his wife and children hungry at home and watches the same movie seven times! The arts should not further impoverish the poor and turn them into beggars. The arts, which are meant to enhance the welfare and progress of society, have become the means of dragging them down further into the abyss of poverty. What a tragedy this is! I should not have handed that boy a rupee right away. I should have taken him to a hotel and given him a meal. Let it go now. Let this also be a lesson for me. I will be more alert in future and not be taken in easily like that.' There was no other alternative for him than to console himself with the thought of a lesson well learnt and turn his steps towards the printing shop.

After he got back to the printing shop, Aravindan wrote a letter to Poorani in addition to the parcel of books he was planning to send. The matter of the exchange of letters between Muruganandam and Vasantha came back to trouble his mind. But he did not mention this to Poorani in his letter. His mind was also grappling uneasily with the mystery of why Meenakshisundaram had left a message asking him to stay at the shop and what it was that he needed to discuss so urgently.

Aravindan was still awaiting the arrival of Meenakshisundaram when the Women's Sangam manager dropped in. She said two or three important letters had been received at the Sangam and that she would like to consult with Poorani before replying to them. She asked for Poorani's address in Kodaikanal.

'Are you going to Kodaikanal yourself, Amma?' asked Aravindan with the idea of sending the book parcel with her.

'No, no. I will write and ask for her opinion,' said the lady. Realizing that sending the parcel through her was not going to be possible, Aravindan wrote Poorani's address on a slip of paper and handed it to the lady.

'It looks as if they won't leave her in peace, even when she is trying to recover her health,' he thought to himself. It was growing dark. At about seven forty-five, Meenakshisundaram returned.

'Come in here, Aravindan,' he said. 'What I'm going to say is to remain a secret. Without your help, I cannot fulfil this deep desire of mine. It could lead to a spurt in our business and income. It is a way to get a lot of advantages and facilities easily.' He went on in this manner, skirting around the matter without getting into the details. Aravindan stood in front of his boss's table and said, 'I won't know what you are talking about unless you tell me, sir.'

'First of all, please sit down.'

Aravindan sat in the chair facing Meenakshisundaram. He looked at his boss rather apprehensively.

'I assume Poorani won't oppose anything you suggest, am I right?' asked the older man.

Aravindan was lost for a reply. He had no clue about the context of the question. What was it all about?

CHAPTER 19

With radiant gemstones in both ears,
In his tresses the laburnum flower beloved of bees,
And the moon plucked from the sky. Such is the Lord of this blessed Ekadam
Worship him with folded hands and be rid of all woes.

– Thirugnanasambandar

'If you put your mind to it, you can surely accomplish this task, Aravindan. I have given this a lot of thought before venturing into it, and I know that this is the right time.'

At this point, Meenakshisundaram found that Aravindan was displaying no reaction. He was merely sitting in silence and watching the older man's face. Meenakshisundaram rose from his chair, clasped his hands behind his back and started pacing back and forth across the room. It had always been his habit to walk around when his mind was busy with ideas.

'What's the matter? I'm the only one talking here. There's not been a word out of you.'

'How can I respond unless I get an idea of what you are proposing?'

'I said that right in the beginning. I asked you to confirm whether Poorani will agree to anything you ask of her. I need to know that upfront.'

'Why would she agree only to *my* request? She would agree to yours too, wouldn't she?'

'No, no. This is a matter that only you can put forward to her and explain clearly. Only you can get her to accept it.'

'Get her to agree to what?'

'Be patient. I'm going to explain. Listen carefully.'

Aravindan focused his attention on his boss.

'The general elections are due in another seven to eight months.'

'True, they are due then.'

'You must have noticed that these days those who work for the government, or hold posts in it, live lives of comfort and earn fame and fortune.'

'I know that. But that doesn't mean…'

'The way you are interrupting me and protesting, it sounds as if you have already formed an unfavourable opinion about what I am about to propose.'

'No, no, not at all. Please go on with what you were saying.'

'Don't think I am manipulating you for some ulterior motive. This is an idea that came to me at an opportune moment. Many important people and leaders of society in the city are in favour of this idea. They are of the unanimous opinion that victory is achievable, and they have promised to work together to make it happen. I'm not worried about the financial cost. I can afford it. The circumstances are also favourable.'

'Are you thinking of standing for election?'

'Me? Goodness! Is that all you've understood after listening to me? It's like someone listening to the story of the Ramayana and then asking if Rama was Sita's uncle! If I stand for election,

I'm sure to lose my deposit. I don't have the necessary popularity and name recognition.'

'Then whom are you talking about?'

'You haven't understood yet, Aravindan? My idea is to field Poorani as a candidate for the Madurai North parliamentary seat. If she stands, she will surely win. She has won a lot of respect and goodwill through all her public speeches. There's not a single village that has not heard her speak. She is widely known in practically all the areas of the constituency.'

Aravindan argued energetically against the idea. 'Before Independence, the goal of government was to serve the people. Now, politics is just another profession. You are asking a good woman like Poorani to descend into the filth and mire of politics! The fame and recognition she has earned so far have been because of her oratorical skills, her deep learning and knowledge of Tamil, her selfless service to society and the fact that she is the daughter of the respected scholar Azhagiya Sittrambalam. She could lose all these if she enters politics. Also, in this century, the largest commercial platform that earns the maximum profits is the political arena. It is best for good people to stay away from politics and concentrate on social service. Besides, right now, she is very sick and is away on a rest cure. Do you really think it would be wise to upset her peace of mind by bringing this up with her?'

'There will be very little hardship for her. She just has to come and sign the papers as a candidate. She needs to come here only ten days ahead of the election date and speak in four places, at most. We can look after the rest of the campaigning ourselves. We have you and also your tailor-shop friend. Even if he is asked to address a hundred meetings a day, that fellow will be up to the task. There is no need for any huge publicity blitz. It is enough to highlight the fact that a woman is standing for election. Whatever opposition there is will wither away when confronted by a candidate of Poorani's reputation. What do you say, Aravindan? Why are you still hesitant?'

'What you say is true, but…'

'But, but what? Come right out with it and give me a favourable decision. Surely the government itself can change for the better if someone like Poorani enters it; she has the ability to bring purity into any environment that she enters. So why should we have any second thoughts?'

'Sir, you are convinced of this. But I have my fears about it.'

'Look, Aravindan, don't treat this matter so casually. My honour is invested in this plan. In a meeting with the elders of the city, I have pledged to do this. They agreed unanimously that we could win the district only if Poorani was the candidate. We are meeting next Sunday for further discussions about the elections. I have told them that I will confirm Poorani's candidature at that meeting.' Meenakshisundaram spoke firmly with a hint of insistence.

Nevertheless, Aravindan continued to press his argument, this time with more vigour.

'There are enough potential politicians and government officials in our land for the next hundred years to come. What we do not have in this century are social leaders and philosophers, like Vivekananda and Ramalinga Vallalar, who can move the minds of people and stir their conscience. Allow Poorani to progress along that noble path. Please don't drag her into the mud pit of politics.'

Aravindan had never argued so forcefully with his employer

on any issue. Neither had he contradicted the older man's perspective on anything to this extent. He was his employer and mentor. It was Aravindan's duty to show obedience and gratitude towards him. It was not appropriate to lecture his employer like a wiser person. Yet, in the heat of the moment, he had perhaps said rather more than he should have.

Meenakshisundaram was not put off. He came up to Aravindan, smiled at him and patted him affectionately on the back. He said calmly, 'Aravindan! Stop being a child and imagining all kinds of terrible things. Like you, I too have a deep concern for Poorani's future well-being. I would never dream of bringing harm to her in any way. I am embarking on this path only because I am firmly convinced that victory will be ours. I am planning to sell my farmlands at Thiruvedagam and Melakkal to raise money for the campaign. The lands on the banks of the Vaigai are fetching excellent prices nowadays. Would I do all this if it meant bringing harm to Poorani? You have been like a son to me all these years. Haven't you understood me yet? Anyway, it is your decision to make now.'

Aravindan was lost for a suitable reply. Meenakshisundaram looked fixedly at him, awaiting a response. Just then, Muruganandam arrived, talking loudly even before he had entered the building in the belief that only Aravindan would be there. 'The meeting is just over. I spoke for an hour and a half. It was about workers' rights. I tell you, I didn't pull any punches! My throat is so sore.' From the garland in his hand, many of the flowers had withered and fallen away. When he noticed Meenakshisundaram's presence in the room, Muruganandam was overcome with embarrassment.

'Come, *Thambi*!' the older man welcomed him. 'You

have arrived at just the right moment. May you live to be a hundred! Just a few minutes ago, I was talking to Aravindan about you.' Meenakshisundaram's welcoming words reassured Muruganandam, and he relaxed. In fact, when he spotted the proprietor in the room, Muruganandam had been momentarily apprehensive that Aravindan may have confided in Meenakshisundaram about the matter of the correspondence with Vasantha from Kodaikanal and may have asked him to be present for an interrogation. But Meenakshisundaram's words and manner showed that such was not the case.

Now, Meenakshisundaram turned to Aravindan. 'There's no urgency to tell me right away. Take your time and think about it. Discuss it with your *thambi* here and let me know by tomorrow morning. Then I can send you to Kodaikanal, and you can clear the plan with Poorani herself. It's late now, and I have to get home. We will meet in the morning.' Aravindan and Muruganandam saw Meenakshisundaram to his car and came back indoors.

Aravindan sank into a chair in a pose of intense thought, the palm of one hand supporting his chin and a deep frown on his forehead. Completely unaware of Aravindan's state of mind, Muruganandam asked, '*Ennappa*? Why are you sitting there looking as if you've just heard news of a shipwreck or something? The old man mentioned that you are to discuss something with me and let him know in the morning. What's that about?'

Aravindan had planned earlier that when Muruganandam got there he would confront him and demand details about the when and where of his relationship with Vasantha and would scold him for embarking on such a relationship. But now, that earlier plan had fled from his thoughts altogether. He could now think of nothing but Meenakshisundaram's bombshell – his plan to launch Poorani into the world of politics by asking her to stand for the elections.

With Muruganandam insisting on knowing what the mystery was, Aravindan gave him a brief outline of the proprietor's plan. But Muruganandam did not react with either astonishment or sadness, much to Aravindan's surprise.

'Pooh! Is this why you are looking so worried? It's something to celebrate! If Poorani Akka enters politics, its entire nature will change. Politics itself will become clean and might just earn a good name. Your employer has obviously given this matter serious thought before thinking of such a plan. I like it, I endorse it,' declared Muruganandam vehemently.

Aravindan was angry now. He burst out, 'You are all concerned only about cleaning up politics. I want to see righteousness and honesty restored in society as a whole. It looks as if there is no one in this nation today who can or will take up this second task. I always knew you were politically minded, Muruganandam. I expected this response from you.'

Muruganandam took issue with his friend about his reasoning. 'You see the two tasks as separate. That is why you are confused, Aravindan. If the first task is accomplished, the second one will fall into place automatically. Poorani Akka has the ability to work for both the objectives. I believe this with all my heart.'

'Just because she has the ability, is it fair that her health and peace of mind should be ruined in the process? She has never been one to pay attention to her own welfare ahead of the welfare of others. You saw what happened when she spoke with such passion at the theatre. Yet here are people planning to thrust her onto the election battlefield the moment her six-month rest is over!' Aravindan's voice betrayed raw emotion born of his feelings for Poorani. Only he was capable of this all-encompassing concern for her. They truly were soulmates. It was a special relationship, above and beyond any relationship experienced by anyone else. He had never attempted to display his feelings openly, but his concern for her could not be hidden under such circumstances.

Muruganandam continued to support his own argument forcefully. 'These days, government is no longer some separate entity. It is a part of every aspect of life. Just as the breaking of a single strand of thread affects the whole net, changes in any aspect of the government will have an effect on every aspect of our life. If someone of good character and deep knowledge, like Poorani, becomes part of the government, society itself will benefit.'

Throughout the course of their friendship, Muruganandam had always been the 'student' and Aravindan the 'teacher'. Today, their roles were briefly reversed as Muruganandam continued to press his point of view.

'Look, I've nothing to do with it now. My boss has an idea, and you are also singing his tune. Why don't you both check with Poorani and act according to her wishes?' said Aravindan, sounding weary and indifferent.

The next morning, when Meenakshisundaram asked for his decision, Aravindan replied in the same disinterested manner. But his boss was not willing to overlook Aravindan's attitude. He spoke to him sternly. 'If you are going to act as if this matter is of no interest to you, and that it is up to others to do as they wish, then I will drop the idea here and now. It's no great disaster. I will lose face with a handful of the elders to whom I had suggested this in the first place, but so what? What stake do I have in this that is not shared by you two? If you agree wholeheartedly to go along with the plan and help me to achieve it, go to Kodaikanal within the next two days, meet Poorani and talk to her. Otherwise, tell me right now that you refuse.'

Aravindan agreed, though only half-heartedly, to go to Kodaikanal within the next two days and broach the subject with Poorani. It seemed to him that he was cornered and had no choice but to accept.

Meenakshisundaram's home town was a very pretty place named Thiruvedagam, on the banks of the Vaigai River, close to Madurai. There was an ancient *thevaram* verse that had been composed about the deity of that town. Although Meenakshisundaram now lived in Madurai, he still owned farmlands, orchards and a house in Thiruvedagam. He had converted his house into a school that taught *thevarams*. He sponsored the education of ten students, who were given free board and lodging under that roof and were taught the ancient verses. Previous generations of his ancestors had set aside a parcel of land for a school. The school was started there by Meenakshisundaram's great-grandfather and had been running smoothly for several decades now.

As a routine, Meenakshisundaram made at least two trips to his home town every week, to worship at the temple of the town deity and to oversee the farmlands he owned. Another practice he had followed regularly was to visit that temple whenever there was an important decision to be made or whenever an unexpected obstacle arose in his plans. He would pray, ask the deity for a sign and decide accordingly. He had an unshakeable faith in this process. The day before Aravindan was to leave for Kodaikanal, Meenakshisundaram took him along early in the morning to visit that temple.

In Madurai District, near Chozhavandaan, the north and south banks of the Vaigai are dotted with villages amidst lush greenery. No landscape could possibly rival it for sheer beauty. The poet Ilango, in his classical work *Silappadhikaram*, describes the Vaigai as 'the true flag of the land'. If you want to witness the majesty of her youthful energy, you should watch her in this section of her journey; she drifts as gracefully as a swan and as elegantly as a nubile maiden between dense coconut groves on either flank. Banana plantations like forests of green pillars; acres and acres of farmlands. Every inch of ground was lush with crops of rice and grains and betel leaf gardens bursting with greenery. Along that section of the river, every village on its shores was a beautiful poem, every vista was a splendid dream.

It was Meenakshisundaram's firm opinion that nothing could give one greater pride and honour than to have been born in this land, to belong to this soil. It is said that in the olden times, at the request of the Pandya queen, the poet Thirugnanasambandar had negotiated with the Samanars and won debates. In a final contest with them, it was his *yedu* that had floated intact across the Vaigai and reached the opposite shore safely. The landing point of the manuscript was named *Thiru Yedagam*, subsequently becoming known as Thiruvedagam.

Aravindan had visited Thiruvedagam with his boss a couple of times earlier. Each time, he was captivated afresh by the natural beauty of the surroundings and the *thevaram* school.

Far from the bustle of the city, amid the serene setting of coconut groves, rose a temple tower. As though pouring forth in the very voice of the deity of the temple, the sweet sounds of children offering prayers in song filled the air. The remarkable melodious verse created by Thirugnanasambandar, 'O Lord who wears radiant gems in his ears', reached out to the heavens from those young lips and descended in fine slivers of sound back into the grove, spreading sweetness, permeating the surroundings slowly and creating a surreal experience for the listener. Aravindan always found it exhilarating to soak in this experience and drown in its beauty.

From afar, the village was invisible to the eye. The tower alone, as though standing upon a carpet of greenery, reared tall amidst the coconut palms. Every time he visited, Aravindan would think, 'Yes, these things are the life and pride of our Tamil land – this temple tower, the divine music of *thevarams* and such picturesque little villages. Without these, this will no longer be the Tamil land we know and love. These old sights and sounds should flourish forever, and every Tamilian should take great pride in them.' Life in the cities favoured outward show and shallowness. Instead of developing the mind, the focus was on making money. Obsessed by the mindless rat race of city life, the Tamilian was beginning to ignore, even to forget, the existence of these timeless beauties. Aravindan was pained by the thought of people losing their roots and straying towards the wrong paths.

'If you fold your hands in prayer to Lord Edaganathar, all your troubles and sorrows will vanish,' wrote Thirugnanasambandar. Aravindan could sense the innate power of this place to retain its natural beauty, untouched by the dirt and grime of life. What a feast for the eyes it was to watch River Vaigai as she ran along! Like an innocent young girl playing on her own, frisking and turning and twisting far, far away into the distance, among coconut groves, away from human eyes. Vaigai was not given to displays of power and arrogance. She did not leap over her banks on either side. Instead, she was a coy bride, stepping daintily, swaying from side to side, a symbol of modesty.

After inspecting the *thevaram* school, Meenakshisundaram and Aravindan proceeded to the Edaganathar Temple. They had decided to seek a divine sign at the shrine of the goddess, consort of the Lord, before proceeding with their plan about Poorani. The goddess bore the title 'Elavarkuzhali Amman', which meant 'goddess with fragrant tresses'. It was said that the temple had been built by the Pandya king who ruled at the time of Thirugnanasambandar. Later, Nattukkottai Chettiar families expanded the temple and adorned it. Every stone pillar in every temple in the Tamil land will forever be grateful to them for their generosity.

When they had entered the temple, Meenakshisundaram said, 'Aravindan, you know my practice well. Only after asking for a divine direction from the deity at this temple do I embark on something important. And if the answer is yes, I will go ahead regardless of any obstacles that may arise. Do you agree to go along with this and accept Amman's decision wholeheartedly?'

Aravindan believed in god but not in superstition. Yet now, he did not want to upset the older man. So, he said, 'Yes, I agree.' The two of them went and stood at the entrance to Amman's shrine.

Meenakshisundaram Pillai took some leaves and flowers from a bag. He told Aravindan, 'Here are two flowers; one is a white *nandiyavattai*, and the other is a red *chevvarali*. I will wrap them in two identical leaves, tie them up and throw them at Amman's feet. If the white flower emerges, we will ask Poorani to stand for election. If the red one shows up, we will abandon our plan.' He tied the flowers in the leaves, shuffled the two packets in his hands and cast them on the floor. A little girl in a dirty *pavadai*, wearing a rat-tail hair plait, was standing in the shrine. Meenakshisundaram called the girl and told her, 'Little one, out of these two packets, pick the one you like.' The girl hesitated for a while, unable to decide between the two identical packets. Then she bent and picked up one of them, handed it to Meenakshisundaram and ran away.

'Open the packet and see which flower it is, Aravindan,' said the older man, handing it over. With conflicting emotions, expectation and apprehension battling in his mind, Aravindan opened the packet.

In Aravindan's hand, the *nandiyavattai* flower lay smiling in all its pristine whiteness against its bed of green. It was as if it was laughing at Aravindan for having lost his argument. Meenakshisundaram smiled.

'God is on my side in this, Aravindan,' he declared, his tone revealing the pride and joy he felt at that moment. 'It will all go well. Tomorrow morning, you will leave for Kodaikanal. Take your friend, Muruganandam, with you. Between the two of you, please persuade Poorani to accept the plan. You can do it! I will send a telegram to her this evening and tell her that you both will be there tomorrow.'

Aravindan nodded. They returned to Madurai, and Meenakshisundaram despatched a telegram to Poorani: *I am sending Aravindan to meet you tomorrow to discuss an important matter.*

CHAPTER 20

You breathed life into a cell and created me,
You bestowed a mind upon me; you are all-encompassing;
Without my volition you entered my consciousness
And became my guidepost to tell right from wrong.

In the deepening dusk, under an inky-blue sky full of restless clouds, Kodaikanal displayed a special beauty. The medicinal scent of eucalyptus wafted on the breeze, the cool weather refreshed the body and the greenery everywhere delighted the eye. With the sky overcast, the days too were never hot. With walkers and people waiting for boat rides, there was quite a crowd around the shores of the lake. Men with ponies waited here and there for customers who couldn't do much walking but still wanted to enjoy the outdoors.

Poorani and Vasantha rowed their boat from one end of the lake to the other and then came ashore. They were both wearing woollen coats to protect themselves against the chill air.

'Akka! I would love to take a short ride on one of these ponies. Will you also join me? I will ask for two ponies,' suggested Vasantha. She seemed to be in high spirits. Poorani was astounded by the transformation she saw in Vasantha in the past few days. The sullen girl had become a frisking fawn.

To make the girl blossom like a jasmine flower in the monsoon, to lend a fresh bloom to the face, a new brightness to the eyes, a new swing to the gait – there must be a special reason, thought Poorani. She very much wanted to uncover that secret. Yet, if she were to bring up the matter directly with a girl like Vasantha, it could go badly. So, she hesitated to ask. But she kept revolving these questions within her own mind: 'Who had written that letter addressed to Vasantha? What did it contain that had transformed her outlook so completely?'

Instead, she said, 'You wanted to go for a boat ride on the lake. We have done that. Now you want a pony ride around the lake! Don't mistake me for bringing this up again, but how is it that you are so bouncy and joyful today? Will you share the reason with me, please?'

Vasantha blushed prettily, and a smile hovered on her lips. 'Oh, come on, Akka. I'm talking about something, and you are bringing up something entirely different! Well, I'm going to take a pony ride.' She clapped her hands to attract the attention of a nearby pony man.

'What an idea! Are you and I small children to get on ponies and go around?'

'Not only you and me, Akka; anyone who comes here will become a child again in spirit. Look over there.' Poorani looked in the direction where Vasantha was pointing. An English lady and a man who was probably her husband were riding majestically on sturdy horses. It is true, thought Poorani, people do forget about their age when they are in the mountains or near the sea.

Vasantha alone took a pony ride around the edge of the lake. There was a sloping street towards the top of the hill known as Coaker's Walk. From there, the towns of Madurai District appeared on the plain below as pinpoints of light in the dusk. After taking in that view as well, the two of them returned home.

Although it was only seven thirty in the evening, it had turned very cold, and mist had descended on the hills. Poorani couldn't stand the cold. She had planned to finish dinner early that evening and start reading one of the books that Aravindan had sent. But things did not turn out that way.

On the very day she arrived, Poorani had noticed that the henna plants in the garden were putting out new leaves. From early childhood, she had loved to grind and apply henna on the palms of her hands and rejoice in their bright red glow the next morning. Since her father's death, there had been no opportunity to do this. In fact, with the various worries that were crowding her mind, she had not even thought about this childhood pleasure. Her father used to buy mounds and mounds of henna leaves and bring them home in bagfuls, unmindful of the cost.

'Your henna-reddened palms have a special beauty of their own, my child,' he would tell his daughter. 'Go ahead, grind these and apply them. I want to see your palms red as corals.'

So, when Poorani spotted the henna plants in the garden of the Kodaikanal house, the old yearning returned. She had told the elderly cook, '*Patti*, if you can, please go into the garden one evening and pluck a lot of these henna leaves and grind them to a smooth paste. I will apply it on my hands before I go to sleep.'

It happened that the cook had finally found time for the task that evening. And because of that, it also happened that Poorani's plans to read a book had to be abandoned.

'If the colour is to set in properly, it must be applied quickly, and you should go to sleep early,' said the elderly cook. She made Poorani and Vasantha sit down, and applied henna paste generously on their palms, fingernails and the borders of their feet. 'Now go to sleep without disturbing the henna,' she ordered. In the cold of the late evening, the drying henna on their hands added to the coolness. The two young women lay chatting and fell asleep midway through without even knowing it.

The next morning, Poorani admired her coral-red hands and fingers. She picked up one of the books and sat down to read. As she was reading it, the postman arrived with an envelope marked with the seal of the Women's Sangam. It was a thick cover containing two or three letters that had arrived for Poorani and one that the manager lady had herself written. Those letters spoke of how her fame had spread far and wide and emphasized the high regard in which she was held by all sections of society. They revealed how people, even in distant places, were eagerly waiting to listen to her and learn from her. Poorani felt a sense of fulfilment as she read the letters.

One of the letters, addressed to the manager of the Sangam, asked for Poorani to be sent to deliver a lecture at the Tamil Literary Conference, due to be held in Jaffna in two to three months. Another letter was an invitation for her to participate as the Tamil Nadu representative in the East Asian Women's Conference due to be held in Calcutta in four months. A third letter was an invitation to participate in Pongal celebrations to be conducted by the Tamil community in Kuala Lumpur, Malaya, in the month of Thai. In her covering letter, the manager had written:

I need your acceptance of these invitations so that I can reply to them. Or you can yourself write separately to each of them. We all feel that you should accept these invitations. Don't worry about the state of your health. All of us here are convinced that the stimulation and pleasure you will get from these events will be enough to restore you to health. Besides, even if you accept all these, you will still have two full months of vacation time before they come up. I think that will be sufficient for you. Your participation in these events will be a matter of pride not only for you but also for our Sangam. I have enclosed the application forms for your passport and visas along with this letter. Please fill them in and sign them. Have your photograph taken and enclose two copies with the forms. We will take care of all other arrangements at our end. You should not miss these opportunities. Please think well and decide. I got your Kodaikanal postal address from Meenakshi Printers.

Poorani read all the letters several times. She thought about it. There was no clarity about it in her mind. It was like trying to solve a complicated mathematical problem that does not yield a clear solution. She remembered what Aravindan had told her earlier. 'When the opportunity arises, you should be prepared to spread the pride and beauty of Tamil culture and language across the world.' She had expressed her doubts to him at that time. The memory of their conversation brought a hint of a smile to her pomegranate-bud lips.

Vasantha entered the room.

'What's the news, Akka? Why are you smiling to yourself? Please stretch out your arm. I'm going to measure your forearm to buy bangles. New bangle shops have been set up in the town for the tourist season. I'm going to buy a bunch of bangles for myself. If I measure your arm, I can get them for you, too.' Vasantha approached eagerly and sat next to Poorani, a silk thread held at the ready for measuring. Unwilling to dampen the girl's enthusiasm, Poorani stretched out her arm. The captivating golden hue of Poorani's forearm and the creamy white of the palm of her hand embellished with the coral glow of henna, each separate finger like a fine red jewel, roused a tinge of envy in Vasantha.

'The henna has set well on your hand, Akka!' exclaimed Vasantha. 'Look at my hands. The colour hasn't set at all.' Poorani laughed and remarked, 'Some skins are like that; henna doesn't set on them.'

After Vasantha had set off to buy bangles, Poorani was once again lost in thought. She closed her eyes gently and pictured Aravindan's face. The eyes can see only the things that are in front of them. Only when the eyes are closed can one see what is not there. The ability to see things clearly in the mind, with eyes shut, is a kind of meditation. Not everyone is blessed with this ability. Only one in a thousand may possess this unique capability. Poorani had the ability in abundance. To this day, whenever she closed her eyes and summoned up the face of her mother, it would appear to her, sharp and clear. Similar was the case with her father's face. Like one who can absorb texts on different subjects, store them all in the mind and draw them out as and when needed, Poorani had a storehouse of images in her memory that she could search through and bring out at will.

With her mind's eye, Poorani looked at Aravindan's face – his eyes that were carved out of light, his smiling lips born of humour and his long, straight nose, a tribute to symmetry.

Aravindan's lips and his smile were synonymous with each other, like milk and its whiteness. His mouth was a red bud about to bloom.

'Poorani, you have been put into this world to spread the glory of the Tamil land, in which you were born, far and wide,' Aravindan said in Poorani's mind. 'Do I really have that much influence?' she demurred. 'Your abilities are far greater than you give yourself credit for. After all, can a flower appreciate its own fragrance?' he replied.

It wasn't only Aravindan's smile that captivated her and touched her heart. His way with words, his ability to argue his point of view logically… these too were part of his attractive qualities.

'Aravindan, you must be some kind of prophet! I thought I knew a lot about myself, but you seem to know much more about me! So, the flower is unaware of its own fragrance. Does that mean I'm a flower? In which case, what are you? Goodness, what a bag of mischief you are! Where did you learn the trick of conveying such depth of meaning in so few, seemingly simple words? You are a poet at heart. You don't see the world through ordinary eyes. You do not speak in an ordinary way. And you certainly don't think in an ordinary manner!'

Poorani opened her eyes. On the opposite wall was a large mirror. She saw a beautiful woman. Was this really how she appeared to others?

She had just finished an oil bath, and her long hair flowed loose around her head and down her back, tied in a loose knot at the end, close to the floor. Vasantha had playfully placed a red rose behind one of Poorani's ears, and it glowed against the inky blackness of her hair. She felt a thrill of exultation that she could not explain. 'How did I grow to be this woman, with all her beautiful attributes, that I see in the mirror?' she wondered in genuine amazement. It seemed to her that she had grown up without herself being aware of it. She was aware of all the efforts she had put in to acquire learning and knowledge, but she had never thought of or cared about her body. Yet, even as her intellect grew and blossomed, her physical form seemed to have blossomed as well. 'Even though I have never made any effort to enhance my appearance, I seem to have flourished like a tree on a riverbank,' she thought to herself.

In recent memory, she had never had occasion to view her own image in such a large mirror and that too in privacy and soon after a momentous conversation in her own mind.

She had been taking her body for granted, perhaps imagining herself still as the little girl being rocked on her father's lap. The large mirror was telling her, 'You are not that girl any longer. You have grown into this woman.' She had faced sorrow and hardships. The strings of fate had played every kind of doleful music in her life. But those experiences had not destroyed her. She had not had either the time or the inclination to even think about her body, let alone pamper it. In her preoccupation with other matters, she had forgotten herself. But her body had not forgotten her.

Poorani found it soothing to contemplate her own image in the mirror while turning over important matters in her mind. It was only when the cook came into the room to announce that it was time for Poorani to take her medicine that she was reminded of practical realities. The doctor in Madurai, who had suggested a prolonged rest cure for Poorani in a cool climate, had also prescribed a number of pills and tonics. He had advised her to eat plenty of greens, fruits and vegetables and drink lots of boiled milk. The responsibility for ensuring that these instructions were carried out had been entrusted to Vasantha and the cook.

Poorani took her medicines and then returned to her easy chair. She was in an agony of indecision. Should she accept these invitations to speak, which would involve long journeys and even crossing oceans? She wished she could discuss it with someone. If Aravindan had been available, she could have talked it over with him. She thought she could confidently hand over to him the responsibility for making difficult decisions on her behalf. But the very next moment, she started on a different train of thought.

'What special ability does Aravindan really have? Every time I have a thought, he comes along with it as if he is an equal part of me in both mind and body. In every cell of my body, in every breath, in every thought in my mind, how did you mingle into me and become a part of me? Unknown to my own consciousness, you are there in my mind, directing me to choose right from wrong. Great poets have sung of the exalted emotions that arise from the meeting of minds between man and woman. Is this what Aravindan and me share?' The thought made her skin tingle, and deep in her heart, a lotus of emotion bloomed.

'Maybe in a previous life Aravindan and I were birds who perished without being able to express their love for each other. Maybe a cruel hunter's arrows extinguished our lives – and with them, our dreams and our love.' Poorani was beginning to understand what it meant to yearn desperately for something.

A soft, cool mountain breeze wafted in gently. After the soothing oil bath, leaning back in the comfort of the easy chair, Poorani's eyelids closed in relaxation. In her mind and body, she felt a strange urge. She wished she could run and leap across the mountains and confront Aravindan. She would say, 'You are a thief! Give back what you have stolen from me! Give my heart back to me.'

Poorani was highly educated. Her mind had been strengthened in the fire of various deep anxieties. She had even learnt to segregate her innermost emotions from the routine of her daily life. Yet, what she was feeling at this moment, this deep yearning, she doubted that any woman anywhere could have the power to quell it. The emotions that had lain dormant during her hectic routine of travelling to deliver lectures and perform social service had now surfaced during this calm period of rest. Like fire consuming a parched tree, her emotions raged through her. She realized that the capacity to feel emotions is a hallmark of humans, and it is no easy matter to suppress them.

Vasantha woke Poorani when it was time for lunch. Afterwards, she sat Poorani down and adorned her arms with the bangles she had bought for her. They covered her forearms entirely and tinkled as they moved like a *jalatarangam*.

'Akka, decked out like this, you look like a bride,' remarked Vasantha and smiled. Vasantha's words stoked the flames of Poorani's emotions even further instead of distracting her. She felt so overwhelmed by her own feelings that she felt she would burst. How was she to bear this turmoil? With whom could she share those thoughts?

Poorani hit upon a solution to sublimate her emotional state. She decided that for the next two days, she would not stir out of the house and would just read the Tamil Sangam books from end to end. She immersed herself in Tagore's *Gitanjali*, and the works of Rama Thirthar, Vivekananda's speeches in English and the English philosopher C.E.M. Joad's essays. There were a few books by H.G. Wells, Bernard Shaw and others too.

On the evening of the second day, when she was deeply absorbed in the explanatory notes on the last page of C.E.M. Joad's *The Story of Civilization*, the telegraph peon called out from the front door. Vasantha ran and signed for the telegram. It was the one that Meenakshisundaram had sent: *I am sending Aravindan to meet you tomorrow to discuss an important matter.*

Poorani was stunned. It was almost as if her innermost thoughts had somehow acquired magical abilities! The one whose presence she had yearned for was coming without her calling for him. It was as if the universe was arranging events to fit in with her desires. Her night was filled with pleasant dreams.

The next morning, Poorani rose early, took a bath and seated herself with a book at a spot from which she could see cars approaching the house. Kodaikanal is brimming with beauty, perhaps in honour of Aravindan's arrival, she thought.

That morning, she had paid special attention to her appearance. She had plaited her hair and adorned it with a string of fresh jasmines. 'Am I also following the path of all those empty-headed girls who are obsessed with how they look and want to adorn themselves?' she wondered. The thought made her squirm a little. Yet something had made her overcome her inhibitions that day. She had consciously chosen a sky-blue handloom sari, patterned with white flowers, and draped it so that it flowed gracefully, like the spread-out plumage of a peacock.

At eleven o'clock, Meenakshisundaram's car entered the driveway of the house. Poorani jumped to her feet, bangles tinkling merrily on her arms and her heart brimming with joy. Her eyes widened in anticipation of seeing Aravindan any moment. With a smile on her lips that was specially meant for him, she hurried to the car. Her heart was pounding with excitement. Some mischievous imp had placed a lump of ice somewhere deep inside her and it was spreading a mist.

Meenakshisundaram alighted from the car. Aravindan was missing. He had not come! The flowers of joy in her heart withered and began to fade. Despite her disappointment, she did not want to seem rude, so she politely said, 'Please come,' and attempted to smile welcomingly. 'Are you well recovered now?' asked Meenakshisundaram. Instead of replying to his question, Poorani asked, 'Why didn't Aravindan come? Your telegram yesterday said he would be coming.'

'Yes, he couldn't make it. This morning, something came up, and he had to leave immediately for his native village. Let's go inside. I will tell you all the details.'

CHAPTER 21

As the breeze of thought fans the flames in his heart
He swelters in the red hot smoke from the embers…

– Pugazhendi

According to the original plan, Aravindan and Muruganandam were to have made the trip to Kodaikanal. However, a telegram arrived just before they were due to depart that morning and forced a change of plan.

Aravindan had no property back home in his native village, but he did have relatives there. However, they were relatives in name only. In reality, they were ill-wishers, full of malice and jealousy. They were constantly quarrelling about money and laying claim to ancestral land and wealth. These people respected only money and cared for nothing else in life except making money. Before continuing with this story, it is necessary for the reader to learn something about Aravindan's parents, his early life and his native village.

He had a chronically ill uncle, his father's younger brother, in the village. Aravindan realized only too well that this man had never shown a single gesture of goodwill towards him or his family. Very often, Aravindan had thought back to all the many instances when this *chithappa* had cheated and harmed his family, and the bitter memories inflamed him. It was this resentment that had made him leave his village and come to Madurai to study, find a job and make a life for himself.

Appa had been a generous-hearted man, prone to dispensing charity liberally. *Chithappa,* on the contrary, was a miser who would never part with even a quarter of an anna, unless it was absolutely necessary. If he came across any villager struggling under a mound of debt that he could not repay, he would take the unfortunate fellow's land or house or jewellery as collateral for a loan and charge him outrageous rates of interest. Only after he grew up did Aravindan realize that this was why his father had gradually become impoverished, whereas his *chithappa* had become richer and richer and built himself a two-storey house.

It was this same uncle who had hastened his father's end. In his final years, Aravindan's father had needed a few thousand rupees to continue the cultivation of his land. Though he knew the real nature of his younger brother, he convinced himself that blood was thicker than water. He hoped that his brother would come to his help in this time of need. He did, indeed, part with the money, but that year, the crops failed. Aravindan's father visited his brother's home to plead with him. He said, 'You are my brother, after all. With god's grace, you are well off. You have saved your wealth instead of spending it all away as I have done. I will pay you back in full after the next harvest. Please allow me this extra time; it is only because the crops failed this year.' But Aravindan's uncle was adamant. He was swayed by the advice of *Chithi,* his wife, and spoke harshly to Aravindan's father.

'Repay what you owe me and go. Money has nothing to do with relationships or family.'

Aravindan's father was provoked to anger. '*Enda*, were you

born into money? Were you not born into the same family as I was? Is it right for you to speak to your own brother so disrespectfully on the urging of your wife and be so inflexible in your demands?'

'Why all this unnecessary talk, *Anna*? In money matters, there can be no flexibility.'

So, Appa had to sell the only remaining parcel of land that he still owned to settle the debt he owed his brother. He and his wife had been childless for years, and their only child, Aravindan, was born relatively late in their lives. They had lavished love and attention on him. When his father was forced to sell his last bit of land, Aravindan was ten years old. He was old enough to get a sense of what was happening. He was in class three or four, in elementary school.

After having had to sell his last remaining property, Appa became very depressed and lost the will to live. The memory of the day his father died was etched permanently in Aravindan's mind like a scar. With no explanation at all, he was fetched from school and taken to the barber shop for a tonsure. Later, with the pot of live coals for the funeral pyre hanging heavy in his little hands, he accompanied Appa's body to the cremation ground. He had never forgotten the emotional pain of that experience. The mental image of his young self, weeping and sobbing as he took his father to be cremated, stayed like a raw wound in his heart and brought tears whenever he thought about it.

The next big blow in young Aravindan's life was the death of his mother. He was just twelve and hardly out of elementary school when it happened, and he became an orphan. Like a child who stands on the shore of a mighty ocean, totally unaware of its vastness and depth, and dreams of making and sailing paper boats, Aravindan was totally unequipped to face life. Yet somehow, he wanted to make something of his life. On the other hand, he was ignorant of how to go about it.

The struggles of the young mind remained unknown to the wider world. Probably apprehensive about the criticism of the townspeople, his uncle took Aravindan into his home for some time. His aunt was cruelty personified. 'Why do we have to feed you for nothing? Should you not be doing some work to earn your food here? Go and graze the cattle,' she ordered him. He dropped out of school and became a cowherd instead. Every day, as the animals grazed, young Aravindan would sit and weep his heart out. Many were the days when he would demand of his dead parents, 'Appa! Amma! Why have you left me to such a fate and gone away? Why have you left me here to be beaten by *Chithi* and scolded by *Chithappa*?'

Chithappa and *Chithi* had no children. *Chithi* had brought a girl, the daughter of a relative, into her home and was raising her as a daughter. But Aravindan was not raised like a son. Far from it, the care he received was no better than those of the animals left in the stable. In fact, he had to eat his meals in the stable and not in the house. A corner of the stable floor was where he slept. He would be up early in the morning to take the cattle to the grazing fields.

One day, as the animals grazed, Aravindan became absorbed in a book that he had taken with him. Some of the animals encroached onto a neighbouring farmer's field and began to graze there before he noticed and drove them back. But the farmer immediately went and complained about it to *Chithappa*. When Aravindan returned that evening with the animals, *Chithappa* thrashed him mercilessly while *Chithi* showered him with abuses. That day was a kind of revelation for Aravindan. It was as if his mind and eyes had opened for the first time. 'I cannot stay here any longer. I should not. I have to run away somewhere,' he determined. That night, when the household was asleep, Aravindan collected the few old, torn clothes he possessed, wrapped them in a bundle and started walking along the railway track. In pitch darkness, slipping and stumbling on the metal rails and the sharp stones between the rails, scratching and scraping his shin and knees, he stumbled on.

As it happened, Aravindan had set off on this night journey from a village about eighteen miles east of Madurai on the route to Rameswaram. He had started walking towards Madurai. Not deliberately, not knowingly, but as part of something designed by Fate. This night journey was also a life journey for Aravindan. The years since then, which saw Aravindan grow and study and build a life, were also beset with their own share of problems and worries. Yet, through his staunch self-belief, he weathered all the storms and persevered.

Before ten in the morning and after five in the evening, he worked in a hotel, cleaning tables or serving food, to earn a living wage. In those days, there was a large hotel named Bhima Vilasam, near Madurai railway station. The proprietor of the hotel was a very generous man. He allowed Aravindan to work at his hotel during his free hours and also attend school during the day. Aravindan was enrolled in the sixth class in a high school close to the station, to the west. His classmates were in the habit of visiting the same hotel for snacks after school finished at five o'clock. They would mock Aravindan as he waited to clean the tables, clad in soiled clothes and carrying a cleaning rag. His classmates had given him the nickname 'Table

Cleaner'. Aravindan staunchly bore all these insults. Some mornings, there would be no time to change clothes. He would have to run to school in the same soiled clothes he had worn to do the cleaning at the hotel. Even some of the teachers would mock his appearance. The boys would whistle and shout, 'Hey, Table Cleaner, why don't you clean yourself first!'

The years from the ages of thirteen to twenty were highly significant for him. This was the period when his relentless hard work began to make his life blossom. He had worked as a newspaper boy, distributing the morning papers from door to door to pay school fees; he had folded paper in printing shops; from time to time, when no other job was available, he had become a manual labourer, lifting and transporting heavy sacks. These day jobs had funded the purchase of schoolbooks. It was no easy task for a young teenager to display such focus and undergo such hardships to achieve success. But his tenacity led him there.

These early experiences were the ones that had built strength of character and fostered a wide knowledge about life in Aravindan. In fact, his sense of empathy towards the poor, and his inclination towards social service, could also be attributed to his childhood experiences. At an age when youthful exuberance usually runs high, and youngsters are inclined to seek pleasure and entertainment, he had chosen the path of hard work and dedication after running away from his uncle's home and coming to Madurai. It was only when he had achieved his ambition of completing his school education that his fierce thirst for progress was somewhat satisfied.

When he had passed out of school, one of his Tamil teachers took him along to introduce him to the proprietor of

Meenakshi Printing House, recommending him for a job. There, he proved his worth as a quick learner and an honest, loyal worker, rising from the ranks and earning a position of trust in the office. Often, when he thought about his journey up to that point, Aravindan was astonished by his own achievements. He wondered if Thiruvalluvar had someone like him in mind when he wrote the *Thirukkural* verse, 'If those who set goals for themselves have the strength of will to strive for them, they will achieve success.'

On the morning when Aravindan was due to set off to Kodaikanal to meet Poorani, he received a telegram. It opened the doors to old, painful memories from his childhood years. He could see everything clearly in his mind's eye.

The telegram read, *Your chithappa has died. Come at once.* In these last years of his life, his uncle had been bedridden with severe diabetes. His wife, Aravindan's *chithi,* had planned to arrange matters so that one of her own relatives could inherit her husband's wealth, instead of it slipping out of her hands. But before she could arrange this, she herself passed away, even before her husband.

Here was this telegram announcing that the lonely, bedridden existence of his uncle had now ended. His relatives in the village knew that he was living and working in Madurai. The thought of meeting and interacting again with those small-minded, money-grabbing bunch of relatives was distasteful to Aravindan. He understood why this urgent message had been sent to him.

His uncle had no children of his own. It was Aravindan who would have to conduct the funeral of the cruel man who had beaten and abused him when he was just a tender lad and driven him away. Yet, if his uncle had not driven him away all those years ago, would Aravindan have become the man he was today? It was only because of the ill-treatment he had received from his uncle and aunt that he had acquired the firm resolve to work hard and succeed in life. It was that resolve that had sustained him and led him to his present status.

As he read the telegram again, his thoughts went back to the past.

When he had run away from his *chithappa*'s home as a thirteen-year-old boy, he had sworn never to set foot in that house again. He had reaped the rewards of that decision. As for *Chithappa*, he had cheated many people all over the town. He had turned his back on his own relatives and he had driven many families to poverty and despair in order to amass money and lands for himself. What rewards had he reaped for his actions? Did at least death come easily? Wasn't it the kind of death that came at the end of a long journey of pain and suffering, after being bedridden with diabetes and praying for the end to come? Some people seem to think having money is enough to accomplish anything in life. But money is only a beautiful dream. However wonderful a dream may be, one has to wake up at some point. If not, one will face the same fate that had overtaken *Chithappa*.

In a way, Aravindan felt sorry for the man. It was as if his life's story had been unexpectedly cut short, like a story half-read and then abandoned. When the telegram was delivered to Aravindan, both Meenakshisundaram and Muruganandam were with him. They also read the message. They both thought to themselves, 'Here is a man who has just heard that he has inherited a fortune of a lakh of rupees. How is it that he is displaying no excitement at all? Instead, he just seems dazed.' They thought only about Aravindan having inherited one lakh rupees from his uncle. They did not think of how Aravindan's own father had been a victim of the greed that had led to the accumulation of his uncle's wealth, nor of the circumstances that had led to him running away from his uncle's house. Aravindan's face was now darkening with anger.

'Let anyone put his body on the funeral pyre as if he were some homeless creature with no kith or kin. Who needs his tainted money!' exclaimed Aravindan as he tore up the telegram and threw away the pieces. Meenakshisundaram took him aside and gave him some wise advice.

'*Dei*, don't be an idiot! Death is a very important event. It is not the occasion to bring up old animosities and bitterness. Just listen to my advice. You need not go to Kodaikanal today. Muruganandam and I will go. You go to your village and carry out your *chithappa*'s funeral rites. If not, some distant relative will walk away with the entire inheritance. If that wealth comes to you, you can use it for so many good deeds. Why do you turn away and shut your eyes to such an opportunity?'

'But he has done me so much harm that I cannot bear the thought of setting foot in that house!'

'Let that be so! A good way to take revenge on him is to use his wealth for good causes. Why don't you do that?'

Meenakshisundaram was finally able to make Aravindan see his point of view. A train to Rameswaram was scheduled to start from Madurai station soon. Meenakshisundaram and Muruganandam took Aravindan to the station in the car and saw him onto the train. Still seething with resentment at his uncle, Aravindan set off to his village to conduct the last rites of the dead man. Throughout the journey, his mind was in turmoil. Visions of the past blew like raging storm winds through his mind, fanning the embers of early memories into roaring flames.

Alongside were thoughts of the current scenario. 'Meenakshisundaram and Muruganandam are on their way to Kodaikanal to meet Poorani. Will they be able to convince her to stand for election? Will she agree to it? Would she not want to discuss such a momentous decision with me first? Let me wait and see whether she reaches out to me or decides to accept Meenakshisundaram's logical arguments right away. It would have been ideal if I had been there to help her weigh the pros and cons of the proposal before deciding on a decision. She too would have felt easier in her mind. I was supposed to be there with Muruganandam, according to the telegram that was sent to her. But here I am on my way to perform the last rites of a wretched old man. Poorani must be greatly disappointed that I couldn't come.'

Aravindan felt anger growing in his mind towards Meenakshisundaram for trying to fulfil an agenda of his own by using Poorani. 'What more could I do?' he told himself. 'I tried my best to convince him that it was not a good idea. But it was no good. He was stubborn about it. He even took me to the Thiruvedagam Temple, made me witness his "flower test" in the shrine of the deity and became even more adamant about going ahead with the idea.'

When he reached his village, it was already past nine in the morning. The relatives had been awaiting his arrival. A couple of elderly women came up to him weeping theatrically and offered their condolences. The others merely said, 'Alas,

Chithappa is no more!' or some words to that effect. It was all done for a mere show of sorrow and sympathy rather than out of any genuine sentiment.

During the funeral rites for his *chithappa*, an important truth resonated in Aravindan's mind. 'The end does not justify the means. Just as a correct answer to a mathematical problem will not fetch marks unless the steps are correctly shown, wealth accumulated by false means is not worthy of respect.' No wonder not a single righteous person in the village accompanied *Chithappa*'s body to the cremation ground. He had heard rumours that he himself was being criticized. In fact, he overheard a jealous relative spewing venom. 'After all, money talks, doesn't it? That's why he is here. Is it for this fellow that the old miser accumulated all his wealth?'

Another man remarked, 'You said he has parted ways with his uncle and so he won't come for the funeral. Do you see it now? Money, *Ayya*, money! See how he has come running like a dog.' Aravindan was deeply hurt to find that people here thought of him this way. A couple of relatives had travelled from Madurai to pay their condolences. One of them was an elderly man with many connections in government circles in Madurai. He had vast experience in many areas. After the funeral, on the way back from the cremation ground, he asked Aravindan something that stunned him. The man was casually mentioning in public, in the midst of many people, something that Aravindan had assumed was a secret.

'*Ennappa*, *Thambi*, I hear that your boss is planning to put up that young woman Poorani as a candidate in the coming election. You must have heard the news?'

While a stunned Aravindan was still groping in his mind

for a suitable response, the man went on. An important fact emerged from what he said.

'Meenakshisundaram is very clever at this kind of thing. He would have thought it through. But let me share something I know. Just alert him about it. I hear that the competition in that district is going to be very tough. There is a publisher in Pudu Mandapam. He is a ruffian with no scruples. Rumour has it that he is going to stand for election in that constituency.'

Aravindan interrupted the older man to ask, 'Who exactly is the publisher you are talking about?' His apprehension was justified. Sure enough, it was the same publisher who was now their enemy. Further, he was said to be campaigning vigorously. Aravindan felt a compelling urge to set off to Kodaikanal that very minute to convey this news and sound a warning.

CHAPTER 22

Whenever I saw withered crops
I too withered and grew lean with hunger;
Whenever I saw those who begged from door to door,
And yet grew frail from hunger;
Whenever I saw those who had nothing,
My mind writhed in agony.
When I came across those who had suffered long illnesses and sorrows,
My heart melted in sympathy.
Noble souls will not seek help from others even in the hardest times.
Whenever I saw such noble ones struggling in poverty, I too withered.

– *Thiruvarutpa*

Meenakshisundaram explained to Poorani why Aravindan had been unable to come to Kodaikanal and why he had to go to his native village instead. He was able to sense that Aravindan's non-arrival had disappointed Poorani greatly. Though she tried not to reveal her disappointment, she could not hide it from Meenakshisundaram's keen instincts. Women reveal their inner feelings like mirrors. Whatever her mind thought or felt couldn't stay hidden.

'I hope Mangaleswari amma, Chellam, my brother and sister are doing well in Madurai. Is my brother, Thirunavukkarasu, working properly at the printing shop? You have come away from the office when Aravindan is not there either. What is the urgency?' asked Poorani.

'Yes, it is urgent. Otherwise, would I have come now?' replied Meenakshisundaram. He then went into a detailed description of his proposal, preceded by an elaborate introduction.

Poorani's expression changed. Her forehead was creased in worry. After the old man had finished speaking, she sat silent for a long time, immersed in her thoughts. Her face had that special glow that habitually appeared when she was internally debating a matter calling for deep responsibility and reasoning. The two men were eagerly awaiting her response.

As she continued to remain silent, Meenakshisundaram attempted to forestall any ideas she may have been forming about turning down the proposal.

'It was as if god himself had called to me and said, "You must do this." That's how it felt when this thought first came to my mind, quite by chance. I told Aravindan and this friend of his, Muruganandam, about it. At first, Aravindan raised some objections to the idea, but now, he has come around somewhat. Muruganandam, here, has been all for it, right from the beginning. Please don't give a contrary decision. I expect no less than a yes from you.'

Poorani looked intently at him and then smiled. There was a hint of a question in that smile. Sure enough, she asked, 'When and how did it occur to you to involve me in this dilemma?'

'Where is the dilemma in this, Amma? Are you not eminently suited for such a position? Or is the government not a fit place for you to step into? Isn't this the way to more fame and progress for you?'

His words brought a smile to Poorani's lips once more. Her face bore the sign of her intense internal debate in the form of a beautiful, gentle flush like the skin of a ripening fruit. Her expressive eyes, which always seemed to be seeking some truth from somewhere or somebody, also revealed the intensity of her thoughts. As one is exposed to newer experiences in life, one naturally feels the urge to expand one's horizons. 'I need to go higher. Yes, I need to go higher,' insists an inner voice. That impulsive urge was just the one that Poorani now wanted to resist, to turn away from. Yet here was Meenakshisundaram saying, 'Don't run away, take it.' On the other hand, her instinct was telling her, 'Don't get trapped into this. Run, escape.'

What should she do? Which voice should she listen to?

Muruganandam added his voice to the argument. 'Akka, what is there to be apprehensive about? If you attain success in this, you can be of so much service to the many, many poor and needy people in our country.'

She did not respond to him. She began to think deeply. A memory arose in her mind. It was an incident that had occurred about two years before her father died. Her father had the courage of his convictions. However attractive an opportunity may seem, if it did not appeal to his way of thinking, he had no qualms in rejecting it. The strength of his mind was his greatest wealth. The trader whose cheque she had returned after her father died was one whom her father had looked down upon as dishonest and immoral. In the letter that accompanied the returned cheque, she had told that dishonest trader, 'My father is dead, but the principles by which he lived are still alive.'

It was that same trader who had approached Appa two years earlier to try and persuade him to stand for election for a post in the government. He had promised to take care of all the expenses for the campaign. Her father's reply to the trader still rang in Poorani's ears.

'Just because I am teaching you Tamil, do you think you can advise me about how to live my life? From tomorrow, please come only for the class and not to instruct me about what I should do,' he had said, the smile on his face softening the sternness of the words. The trader tried to explain himself. 'You have misunderstood me. You are so learned and accomplished. Should you not have the comfort and facilities to match your accomplishments? That was my only intention.'

Poorani's father made his stand clear. 'For someone, who has no comfort or facilities, anything would seem to fall in that category. "Those who have nothing know peace," wrote Kamban. *Ayya*, I wish to live my life quietly. I want to live a righteous life. To be successful at what you are proposing, one has to be clever. Merely being a good person is not enough. Please don't raise this subject with me hereafter.'

Like an oak tree that grows ever upwards, discarding small branches and twigs as it grows, Appa had stood tall due to his own principles and ignored temptations along the way. Poorani was aware of a new clarity of mind brought about by the memory of her father. Whether in the college lecture hall or on a public speaking platform, whether at home, in his study room or anywhere else, Appa always carried an aura of uprightness and honesty around him. Like a *manoranjan* flower that spreads its aroma all around it, Appa's character and lifestyle spread their fragrance into the hearts of the people he met.

With the firmness of mind brought about by her recollections of her father, Poorani addressed Meenakshisundaram as he sat in front of her with Muruganandam alongside.

'You are a respected elder with vast experience. I am very grateful to you for your support. Yet, I am unable to see how I can consent to what you are now proposing. I have seen my own father vehemently refuse such worldly paths to earn money and fame. If that was the situation then, things are much worse today! These days, passions rule over wisdom; momentary excitement wins over basic decency; greed rules over compassion; and agitation triumphs over calmness. In such a scenario, you are urging me to enter government and struggle against the tide.'

'I am urging you because I am convinced that you are capable of doing it. Amma, it seems to me that Aravindan and you share the same thought processes. When I brought up this plan to him, his arguments against the idea were very similar to the ones you just expressed. But he listened to my explanations and then agreed to some extent. He also said that he would try to convince you about it. If he had not had to rush away for his uncle's funeral, he would have come in person and tried to persuade you to agree. My work would have been made much simpler. I would not have had to debate with you so extensively. I could just have left it for the two of you to talk it through.'

Meenakshisundaram's attempt at persuading Poorani was like trying to drive a small screw into the hardened trunk of a mature tree. She told him about the invitations she had received from Malaya, Lanka and other places to come and deliver lectures. But she did not give any definitive reply to him.

He persevered. 'I've made all the necessary arrangements to file your nomination as a candidate. I went to the Thiruvedagam Temple as well and carried out a flower test in front of the deity.

It came out positive. Please do not disappoint me, Amma!'

Poorani remained silent.

'By all means, accept those invitations to speak in other countries! It is a matter of pride for us all. Along with that, we are trying to add to your fame in our own way. Please accept it. You will definitely succeed at it. You will rise in stature, and the nation will also benefit.'

Poorani told him, 'Let me see. I'd like some time to think about this. Perhaps you were hoping to come, put the idea to me and immediately return with a yes from me. Please stay for two or three days. Is Kodaikanal not worthy of at least a three-day stay?'

'I have no objection to staying a few days, Amma. If you wish, I will ask Aravindan to come as well. I realize that your hesitation about coming to a decision is precisely because he is not here.'

His words brought a hint of shyness to her face. She bowed her head slightly. Her eyes and lips expressed her inner bliss. Meenakshisundaram watched her intently.

At that moment, he realized that Aravindan had won her heart through some magical attraction that was far greater than any influence or wealth he, Meenakshisundaram, himself possessed. He thought to himself, 'Even in the normal course, a man requires a special capability to win the heart of a woman. Obviously, Aravindan possesses some remarkable gift to be able to capture the affection of a woman such as Poorani. It is surely more than just physical appearance. There is some magic in the whole package – his face, his manner of talking, his behaviour.'

This realization automatically raised Aravindan's stature in Meenakshisundaram's estimation. He thought about his earliest interaction with Aravindan, a waif from nowhere, with not even a spare set of clothes to call his own. He had taken him in and given him a job. The boy had raised himself through hard work and also helped the printing business to grow. In his mind, Meenakshisundaram compared the Aravindan of those days with the Aravindan of today. Like a father being reminded about a son he had lost touch with a long time ago, Meenakshisundaram felt a flood of affection for Aravindan.

'I understand what is in your heart, Poorani. I will send a telegram to Aravindan asking him to come here.'

'He may not be able to leave in the midst of his uncle's funeral ceremonies. What will he think if he sees a telegram like that from you?' wondered Poorani.

'No, no, that's not a problem. If I send a telegram, he can leave tomorrow. The funeral will be over by now. He will have to go to the cremation ground tomorrow morning to collect the ashes and finish the ceremony. Then, he needs to go again only on the sixteenth day for a ritual. I will send a telegram at once.' He turned to see what Muruganandam's reaction was. The latter was missing. His chair was empty.

'Where did the fellow disappear to? I thought I would send him to the post office to despatch that telegram to Aravindan. Never mind, I will take the car and go myself.' Meenakshisundaram rose to leave.

Poorani stopped him. 'No, please don't! Just a short while ago, I noticed him going out to take a look at the garden. I will call him. Let him go to the post office. Why should you trouble yourself?'

She went out into the garden. There was no one there. She went back into the house and went to look for Vasantha in her room. The girl was not there either. Poorani asked the cook about it. The cook told her, 'She was here! She was showing the garden to that young man who came along with the older gentleman. They were sitting and talking in the garden. I saw them there. Take another look outside.'

So, Poorani went out into the garden again and looked everywhere. From a high spot in the garden, one could get a good view of the lake. Poorani climbed there and looked towards the lake. Muruganandam and Vasantha were in a boat on the lake. Poorani smiled inwardly and went back inside.

Seeing Poorani coming back alone, Meenakshisundaram said, 'I will go to the post office, Amma,' and set off in the car. It seemed to Poorani that the relationship between Vasantha and Muruganandam had come to a level of maturity in a very brief span of time. Now that she thought about it again, she realized that the address on the mysterious letter addressed to Vasantha had been in Muruganandam's handwriting.

'How will Mangaleswari amma react to this piece of news?' was the worrying thought that came to Poorani's mind. 'True, Muruganandam is a young man with a heart of gold. Yet, will Vasantha's family, living atop a mountain of wealth, get along with Muruganandam's family, which lives in poverty?' she asked herself, doubts churning in her mind. It was as if a situation that could happen only in novels had come about in real life. She realized, however, that such a meeting of hearts could happen quite by chance and very quickly. She thought of her own deep emotions from the previous evening when she was thinking about Aravindan. 'It's no fault of women that they lose their hearts easily to love. Oh, god, you have deliberately made us women thus,' she thought.

In ten minutes, Meenakshisundaram returned from the post office after sending off the telegram to Aravindan. Poorani wanted to wait for Vasantha and Muruganandam to return so that they could all sit down for lunch together. In a short while, the two of them returned, talking and laughing, in high spirits.

Vasantha said, 'Akka, he says he has never seen Kodaikanal before! I took him around and showed him everything. We have planned to visit Pillar Rocks this evening.'

'Sure, go ahead. But please don't ask me to come along. I have work to do. I have to catch up on my reading,' said Poorani, smiling. She noticed a new gentleness, a subtle change in Muruganandam's face. Perhaps it was the pride and joy of a young man realizing that he had won the heart of a girl. Soon after lunch, Meenakshisundaram announced that he wanted to visit a close friend who owned a coffee estate in Pattiveeranpatti, a village nearby. He set off in his car, promising to be back by about seven o'clock.

Poorani immersed herself in reading a book.

Around three thirty in the afternoon, Muruganandam and Vasantha came to tell her that they were leaving on a sightseeing trip. Never before had Poorani seen Vasantha so prettily turned out. She also noticed the wonder of Muruganandam actually having applied a comb to tame his unruly hair. 'Ah, so love has the power to awaken childlike emotions too,' she thought. 'What a pity it would be if this pure young love is caught in the cross-currents of family issues of rich versus poor.'

As she watched the two of them leaving the house and flitting away like a carefree pair of butterflies, Poorani's heart was full of joy for them. It was brought home to her at that moment that pure love is a powerful force that lends beauty to the world itself. Poorani realized that the kind of carefree love games that she now saw Vasantha and Muruganandam openly enjoying were denied to herself and Aravindan because of their education, their sense of propriety and their being known in society.

Meenakshisundaram's telegram from Kodaikanal reached Aravindan at about ten in the evening in his village. The nearest post office was five kilometres from the village, and a messenger would have had to bring it all the way on a bicycle. No wonder, thought Aravindan, that it was arriving after such a delay.

The telegram read: *It looks as if it will be difficult to get her consent unless you are here. Come at once.* Poorani had not agreed to his employer's request because he, Aravindan, was not present and she could not consult him! The thought brought a surge of joy to his heart. With every fibre of his being, he had wanted her to reach out to him. In fact, he himself had decided, even before the telegram arrived, that he would go back to Madurai the next morning, soon after his uncle's ashes rites were over, and travel from there to Kodaikanal. The very moment he had heard the news that the Pudu Mandapam publisher, who was their enemy, was also going to be a candidate in that very same constituency, he had determined to go to Kodaikanal and reveal the information.

When Aravindan left the next morning after the rites were over, the senior government official who had come from Madurai to condole his uncle's death also travelled back with him. He was the same man who had brought the news about the identity of the potential rival to Poorani in the constituency. Aravindan had a high opinion of this government official. But when they reached Madurai, the official invited Aravindan to his home, and Aravindan received a shock that made him change his mind about the man. Such luxury and wealth on display at the home of a government official? Goodness, what kind of government was this! Aravindan was stunned.

A verse of Ramalinga Vallalar ran through Aravindan's mind.

Whenever I saw withered crops
I too withered and grew lean with hunger;
Whenever I saw those who had nothing,
My mind writhed in agony.
When I came across those who had suffered long illnesses and sorrows,
My heart melted in sympathy.

When reading these lines, Aravindan would tell himself that this would be the ideal model for people in charge of running the country. But this official had tried to buy off Aravindan with an offer of five thousand rupees!

Aravindan had never experienced anything like this!

CHAPTER 23

When all dishonesty and deceit are uprooted,
And this moral paradigm is adopted...
When will such an era dawn?

– Chithar Paadal

Just as a stem of sugarcane may be sweet on one side and salty on the other, every human being has both good and bad tastes, thoughts and feelings. However, there is a kind of sugarcane in which every stem is salty, with no hint of sweetness. They call it *peikarumbu*, that is, 'ghost sugarcane'. It looks like any other sugarcane plant, except that it lacks the sweetness of the latter. Similarly, there are men who pose as respectable people but don't have even the least amount of decency or righteousness. They may appear, at first glance, to be genuine 'sugarcanes' but will turn out to be the 'ghost' variety instead. They are simply cheats or rogues. Such people in society are like pebbles that pollute a bag of rice.

When Aravindan realized the true nature of the government official who had accompanied him on his journey back to Madurai, his blood boiled with indignation. He thought to himself despairingly, 'When will society see through these cheats who pose as righteous people while hiding darkness in their souls? When will the world recognize these kinds of villains for what they truly are? In this century, the knowledge attained only through reading books is not enough. One has to learn about humans and their nature too. It is the most important tool for surviving in society. Why? Because each person is a book full of contradictions and confusion. Reading such a book can be an exhilarating exercise!'

It was about three thirty in the afternoon when Aravindan and his travelling companion, the government official, arrived in Madurai. Aravindan had bought a third-class ticket for the train journey. The government official had bought a first-class ticket. He insisted that Aravindan should also travel first-class.

'Che, che!' he scolded Aravindan, 'why do you want to travel with riff-raff, squeezed in like a sack of tamarind? You won't have even standing space there. Here, hand me your ticket. I will get it exchanged for a first-class ticket. We can travel together and chat on the way.'

'It's no problem for me,' protested Aravindan, 'I'm not used to travelling first-class. You please go ahead and travel first-class. I will travel third-class, and we will meet at Madurai station.' But the other man would not allow Aravindan to have his way. He spoke with a wink and a smile, 'What is all this talk about not being used to first-class travel? You are a rich man now. A lot of wealth has come your way. You shouldn't behave in a manner beneath your status. These days, fame and praise don't come easily. Money is the base that can earn those other things, my young man!'

Those words grated on Aravindan's ears. They were the sentiments of a person of low thinking. 'Such an elderly man with so much experience of life... Is this the way he should think and talk? He has such a poor opinion of the meaning of life.

He should be a role model to others; instead, he is so shallow,' thought Aravindan to himself sadly. Though it was true that these days most people's main goal in life was to make money and use it to gain recognition and status, it was still upsetting to hear this seemingly respectable man preaching this openly. Aravindan's respect for him had severely eroded. Yet the older man was adamant.

He snatched the third-class ticket from Aravindan's hand and went to get it upgraded to first-class. Aravindan continued to protest as vehemently as he could but to no avail. The other man grabbed Aravindan's hand, tugged him to the first-class coach and seated him next to himself. The train started just then, and Aravindan had no alternative but to stay where he was. The train moved between lush green betel leaf groves on either side.

'What can I do, tell me?' said the old man in an attempt at light-hearted conversation. 'There's no one else I can chat with on the journey. It feels strange to travel all alone. Don't be offended with me because I forced this ticket change on you.' Anyone who has witnessed the expression on the face of a tiger – crouching in hiding before leaping on its prey – would have no difficulty in recognizing the expression on the old man's face at this moment. He had the cunning look of one who was plotting something.

Although Aravindan had not interacted with him much in Madurai, he had heard a good deal about him. Aravindan had lost touch with most of his village folk years ago because he had run away at an early age and had never gone back there again. The government official he was now travelling with had also left the village at an early age. In fact, he had left the country itself and gone to Burma. There, he had set up a money-lending business and amassed a lot of wealth. He returned but not to his own village. Instead, he chose the urban facilities offered by Madurai and built a big bungalow for himself there. If one were to mention his real name, very few in Madurai would have heard it. But, as 'Burma Man' he was very well known indeed. He was well past his youth and middle years and was stepping into old age when he returned from Burma. There was something novel about his return itself.

Not only did he return with his acquired wealth and his aging body but also with a young Burmese woman as charming as a pet parrot. When he had left for Burma, he was single. But why should he be expected to remain single forever? As and when circumstances and desires intersect, so many dreams and yearnings fulfil themselves. Many were the occasions when the beauty and grace of young Burmese women had aroused his passions and fuelled many dreams. Finally, just the year before his planned return to his native land, his long-held desire was fulfilled. He married a Burmese woman, who was not even one-third his age. He also obtained permission to bring her back to India with him. He was like a happy child who had been given a new toy. After his arrival in Madurai, with his great wealth and pretty wife, many fortunate events took place in his life. His acquaintances and many social organizations built up his reputation as a prominent citizen. His wealth and renown opened the door to a role in the government. He entered through that door and reaped even more rewards in the form of wealth and fame.

In Madurai, the northern bank of the Vaigai has vibrant residential areas, such as Tallakulam and Chokkikulam. But

Burma Man chose a location far away from those areas and even beyond Pudur, on a street leading to Azhagar Temple, to build his palatial bungalow. It stood amid one-and-a-half acres of mango and coconut trees, densely planted like a forest. Even in the middle of the day, the property was in deep shadow. Along its perimeter, he had built a compound wall resembling that of a centuries-old fortress. The property was an 'estate' by itself, and people referred to it as 'Burma Man's estate'. When he had first appeared in Madurai, as an old man with plenty of money and a foreign wife young enough to be his daughter, people laughed and made fun of him. But his wealth was his strength. It bought him respect and a high position in society. It helped him consolidate his renown even more.

That was all that Aravindan knew about the man. But had he really come to the village to pay his condolences to the family of a relative who had passed away? Or was there an element of 'a rich man seeking to align with a newly rich man' in his actions? Aravindan wondered about the man's real motives. At first, when the man had started a conversation with him on the way back from the cremation ground, Aravindan had attributed genuine sentiments to him. At that time, Burma Man had talked sympathetically about the move to put up Poorani as a candidate for the upcoming election and had also made respectful enquiries about Meenakshisundaram.

Although Aravindan found the man's cheap talk distasteful and was put off by his winks and grins that were totally unsuited to both his age and his position in society, Aravindan had not suspected him of being a person of low character or of hatching any evil plans. His face reminded one of a tiger because of the long, sharp canines. But Aravindan had met many men with teeth like these, who had been good people at heart. So, on reflection, he decided that this feature too was not to be held against the man.

Throughout the train journey, Burma Man's attitude towards Aravindan was that of an affectionate friend. Yet Aravindan was startled by the extent of knowledge that his travelling companion seemed to possess about the details of the Madurai political scene and of Meenakshisundaram's idea to propose Poorani as a candidate for one of the constituencies. Some of the details were news to Aravind. Burma Man made disparaging remarks about everyone he talked about. Talking about Meenakshisundaram, he said, 'Your boss, Meenakshisundaram, has reached some kind of comfortable lifestyle today. But before he set up this printing house, he had bought a large share as an investment in a textile mill called Shanmugam Mills. The business collapsed. Right then, he should have applied for bankruptcy, forfeited everything he had and slunk away. I know all about it.'

Burma Man's topics of conversation were mostly this kind of gutter gossip, perhaps more suitable in a third-class compartment than the first-class.

Aravindan tried to put a positive spin on Burma Man's story of Meenakshisundaram's business problems. He said, 'All rich people have had such experiences, *Ayya*! Sometimes money comes, sometimes it goes.'

'No, no, *Thambi*. What I mean is that these days, every small fellow wants to come up fast. Take the example of this young woman, Poorani. Because she gives speeches about Tamil here and there, and teaches in a Sangam, she has become known to a few people. Her father, Azhagiya Sittrambalam, came to

Madurai with nothing, not even a single rupee to his name. My lawyer friend, Panchanadam Pillai, was the head of the management committee of the college. I'm told he gave him a job as a Tamil teacher on sympathetic grounds. And now, your boss Meenakshisundaram is proposing the name of such a man's daughter as a candidate!'

Aravindan winced inwardly. Here was this man dragging the reputation of respectable men into the mire and doing it all so casually. Aravindan detested people who spoke rashly with no thought of the consequences. He believed that the destruction of a person's reputation and respectability was an even greater crime than the actual murder of the person. Consequently, Burma Man's reputation was steadily falling in Aravindan's estimation as he spoke.

The train steamed into the busy hurly-burly of Madurai station. Burma Man's young wife and daughter had come to the station to receive him. Aravindan was seeing them for the first time. The daughter, of mixed Burmese and Indian lineage, was a pretty girl. With her glowing face and captivating eyes, she was the very picture of a girl belonging to the Tamil land. But her mother, despite having moved to Madurai so many years ago, had retained her Burmese tradition as regards clothing and accessories. Aravindan took in the appearance of mother and daughter with a poet's observant eye. There was not even a hint of any other sentiment in his mind as he looked at them, nor was he capable of any such thought.

Burma Man introduced Aravindan to his family. 'This is a relative of ours. He bears the beautiful name Aravindan. It was this young man's uncle who died recently in the village and whose funeral I went to attend.'

Then he went on to introduce his wife to Aravindan. 'I went to Burma with the goal of making some money. Just before I was due to return, this naughty woman stole my heart. And I, in turn, stole this beautiful woman away from Burma and brought her here as my wife,' he said jovially. The Burmese wife nodded slightly. Her already rosy face became a shade redder as she smiled. So captivatingly beautiful was that smile that one could well wonder whether the elegance and beauty described by all the great poets around the world had come together on those lips.

Aravindan took leave of the family. 'I need to go to Kodaikanal. If I leave right away for the bus stand, I can catch the last bus and get there in four hours.' His distasteful experience with his travelling companion's gossip on the journey had made him eager to get away at the earliest.

'Hey, come on, don't be silly! Having come all this way together, I thought you would at least come home with me now. You can leave for Kodaikanal in the morning. But now I insist that you must come to my home.' His daughter joined in and added her invitation as well. His Burmese wife too, in her chirpy voice and half-baked Tamil, said something along the same lines.

Aravindan thought to himself, 'Here is an old man who respects only money and status. Why is such a man trying to endear himself to me now? Is it because I am the heir to my uncle's fortune? Oh, money! Do you really possess such a sweet aroma? Do you really wield such an influence?' He tried to figure out the hidden agenda behind Burma Man's show of joviality and affection towards him. 'Is his entire behaviour – every gesture, every smile – planned meticulously like an accurate alarm clock?' wondered Aravindan. He determined that he needed to find out what lay behind Burma Man's demeanour and decided that it may be useful to accept the man's invitation. So, Aravindan accepted the family's invitation to visit their home. They all got into a waiting car and left.

'Listen to me, *Thambi*,' said the old man earnestly. 'So far, you may have lived any way you want. But from now on, you need to have a stature. You have become heir to a fortune of one lakh rupees! You have to develop habits and relationships that will suit your new circumstances. I feel you should quit your job at that Meenakshi Press. You now have the capacity to buy four printing presses and set up a business of your own. Why stick to that lowly errand-boy job? What do you say?' Burma Man tried to read the expression on Aravindan's face, but Aravindan kept looking steadfastly out of the window of the car and made no response, as though he had not even heard the suggestion.

The car was traversing Vaigai Bridge. Every time he crossed this bridge, Aravindan would have the same thought. 'This is a bridge that connects North Madurai, filled with wealthy folk and palatial bungalows, to South Madurai, with its crowded and cramped roads where the common people live and work. The bridge connects two parts of the same soil on either side. Yet it does not connect minds across the divide. For this to happen, we need to build a different kind of bridge – a cultural bridge.'

The car sped along past the red-walled American College buildings and the striped compound wall of the Perumal Temple at Tallakulam. In the far distance, where the blue sky met the horizon, the hillocks of the Azhagar Hills appeared like a hazy picture. The car turned into 'Burma Man's estate'. Aravindan was fascinated by what he saw. What a beautiful setting! An extensive garden, a variety of flowers and such a magnificent bungalow! One could house a whole township here – such was the extent of the estate.

Tea and snacks were offered on a lavish scale. After a short while, Aravindan rose to leave.

'Why are you rushing away? After all, you are going to Kodaikanal only tomorrow morning. I want to introduce you to a friend of mine. Just hold on, I will call my friend on the phone and ask him to come over.' He made the call. As he was speaking, Aravindan noticed the man's artificial smile and sly blinking of the eyes. A new doubt arose in Aravindan's mind about the motive behind his actions. To his eyes, the old man's already tiger-like face took on even stronger tiger-like characteristics. His inner voice warned him, 'You are getting yourself into some big trouble here.'

Inside the north tower of the Meenakshi Temple at Madurai, there are some pillars. They are called 'Musical Pillars' because each emits a different musical note when tapped gently. Aravindan thought to himself, 'Like the musical pillars at the temple, one can find out the real resonance of a person's character only from tapping it up close.' He now felt uneasy and apprehensive about being in the presence of Burma Man in his house. Yet he did not lose his courage.

In a short while, the friend, who had been invited over the telephone, arrived. Aravindan was startled when he set eyes on the new visitor. He required no introduction. He was already well known to Aravindan. He was none other than the Pudu Mandapam publisher, the man who had barged into Poorani's house many months ago, got into an altercation with Aravindan and landed a stinging slap on his face. Now, he approached with a sly smile and sat. Thereafter, things proceeded like the storyline of a mystery thriller. Attempts were made to persuade Aravindan, and then came threats.

From whatever the two of them said to him, certain things became clear to Aravindan.

At the funeral in the village, Burma Man had brought up the topic of Poorani being put up as a candidate by Meenakshisundaram. This was obviously a ploy to make Aravindan open up about the whole plan. Burma Man had all along planned to put up the Pudu Mandapam publisher as a candidate in that constituency and had been scheming to sink Poorani's chances. All his cheap talk on the train about Meenakshisundaram, and this latest scheme to prevent Aravindan from going to Kodaikanal and persuading Poorani to accept, now fell into a pattern that Aravindan was able to recognize.

Tiger-face spoke firmly and sternly. '*Thambi*, I am good to those who are good to me; towards those who oppose me, I am a very bad man. Not an ant will stir in this town without my permission. Nothing can happen without my knowledge. Your boss, Meenakshisundaram, belongs to the past. As a sworn enemy, he has started doing everything he can possibly do to harm us. You are our kind of man. Just listen to me and do exactly what I say. I will give you five thousand rupees. Persuade that young woman Poorani to say no to the proposal to make her a candidate. You are capable of achieving that. I have decided to put up this man here for that same post.'

Like Lord Siva opening his third eye in wrath, Aravindan stared at them with rage-reddened eyes. Burma Man held out a wad of fifty crisp new blue currency notes.

Aravindan rose to his feet. 'Throw that money in the gutter! The stench of this money will be even greater than that of the gutter,' he shouted and knocked the notes out of Burma Man's hand. The notes swirled around in the breeze from the fan.

Instead of flying to lay his hands on the money, Aravindan had made the money fly by knocking it out of Burma Man's hand. The two men glared at him in fury. Burma Man's glare was more ferocious than that of the tiger his face resembled. The Pudu Mandapam publisher's eyes were like live coals, seething with fury.

Burma Man called out to someone in the house. '*Va, pa,* Balaram! This young man is creating a scene and wants to leave. Take care of him.' Aravindan, who was already on the front steps on his way out, turned to see what was happening. He saw a burly man emerging from inside. He had a sickle-shaped moustache with sharp, pointed ends. Aravindan knew of such musclemen only from novels and films. But this was real life.

Aravindan had thought that strength of mind was the only necessity for success in life. He now realized that some circumstances require strength of body as well. He rolled up the sleeves of his jibba. His hands, hitherto used only for writing poems and revolutionary articles, were now clenched ready for battle.

CHAPTER 24

The maid of the West holds her child, Moon, on her hip,
Milk drools from his lips as his mother mourns
The death of her husband, Day.

– *Thiruviruṭham*

When a rubber band is being pulled in opposite directions by both hands, its dimensions are no longer its natural ones. It takes on an artificial length to match the arm span of the puller. There are some people who are not righteous by nature but display to society an artificially inflated appearance of virtuousness. Burma Man, for instance, who was cruel by nature, had put on an act to achieve the aura of a gracious gentleman in the city. This was crystal clear to Aravindan, especially after what he had just experienced in that man's house.

Even the gentlest person needs to have some innate capacity for violence in order to feel hatred towards someone or to respond to events with physical force. But those who are loving by nature and are steeped in artistic sensibilities and culture cannot answer violence with violence. Therefore, although Aravindan made some preparations to take on a physical assault by the burly bodyguard, his mind was not seething with fury. Without that fuel of fury, how could his response be effective? The rough and tough bodyguard approached Aravindan menacingly, hand raised to deliver the first mighty blow. If he had succeeded in his attack, Aravindan would have fared very badly indeed in that encounter.

However, a perfect opportunity presented itself to enable Aravindan to avoid the physical encounter and any resulting injuries. It was a common belief that a divine force watches over the good people of the city and ensures that they come to no harm. Now, whether it was divine intervention or just plain coincidence, a miracle occurred. Just as the ruffian was about to land a blow on Aravindan, a large car swept into the compound of the estate and drove rapidly up to the front door of the bungalow. Two or three respectable and wealthy-looking people got out of the car and approached Burma Man, greeting him with folded palms raised in traditional *namaskarams*.

It was as if the scene in a stage drama had been instantly switched. Burma Man and the Pudu Mandapam publisher rushed forward, all smiles, to greet the visitors. 'Welcome! Welcome!' they gushed. Turning to the burly servant, Burma Man ordered, 'Balaram, go inside and tell madam to prepare coffee and snacks,' diverting the fellow from his earlier assignment of assaulting Aravindan. Further, to forestall any urge by Aravindan to denounce him to the visitors and disgrace him, he pretended that nothing unpleasant had happened. He turned and smiled at Aravindan and said, 'Okay, so goodbye for now. Come back tomorrow, *Thambi*. I have no time right now.'

So remarkable was his play-acting that Aravindan found himself admiring the man's skill!

With the recent mix of emotions – astonishment, fear and many others – still swirling in his mind, Aravindan walked out of the compound and onto the street. Soon, a bus came by.

He held out a hand, to request it to stop for him, and climbed in. It was a bus coming into Madurai from another town. He alighted at the end of the Vaigai Bridge, near Yanaimalai. It was past eight in the evening.

Many stalls selling a variety of fruits, including mangoes and jackfruit piled in heaps, filled the area with their aroma. Indeed, the place was known for its special fruity aroma that would often waft into other parts of the town. The street itself, littered with jackfruit segments and other discarded parts of fruits, was itself a kind of fruit map, pointing the way to the stalls.

Aravindan walked along the street. His mind was still processing everything he had experienced in Burma Man's estate. He had heard earlier, that in the run-up to elections, people were sometimes kidnapped and hidden away somewhere or taken to some abandoned place and threatened. He had read reports in newspapers about such crimes close to election time. But he had never imagined that such things could happen in this day and age, in this very city.

The thought that he himself had very nearly been the victim of such a plot today and had escaped only due to good fortune gave him goosebumps. Today, given his own experience, he had to acknowledge the fact that, just like a sweet fruit has a hard seed at its centre, society with its many good and hard-working people harbours evil forces within it too.

Aravindan proceeded westwards from Yanaimalai, where he had alighted from the bus. As he reached the gates of Sokkanadhar Temple and turned south, he heard the sound of clapping. That alone may not have made him turn and look, but along with the clapping came a shout in a familiar voice, 'Look, there is Aravindan mama.' When Aravindan turned to look, he saw Poorani's sister, Mangaiyarkarasi, her brother, Sambandan, Mangaleswari amma and her daughter, Chellam, on the front steps of the temple. The lady's car was waiting on the street nearby. It was Mangaiyarkarasi who had spotted him walking on the opposite pavement and called.

As Aravindan walked over to them, Mangaleswari asked affectionately, 'How are you? I hope you are doing well. Were you away somewhere? After Poorani went to Kodaikanal, I have not set eyes on you. Even today, it was this little one who spotted you, and then I clapped to attract your attention.' The lady's face reflected a mature, refined elegance. Aravindan greeted her with a *namaskaram*. He remembered having read somewhere the line, 'As a woman grows older, the mesmerizing beauty of youth transforms itself into the divine beauty of maturity and motherhood.' The natural maternal grace of Mangaleswari's face masked any signs of advancing age. Aravindan instinctively paid obeisance to that special beauty of the mature woman. He was one who believed that the glory of Tamil womanhood rests in the mature mother figure.

He responded to the lady's queries and told her about his uncle's death and his trip to his village to conduct the funeral. He also told her about his plan to go to Kodaikanal the next morning. He told her that Meenakshisundaram and Muruganandam had gone there a couple of days earlier. Mangaleswari did not ask him why they were all going to Kodaikanal, and neither did Aravindan offer an explanation.

'I'm also thinking of dropping in at Kodaikanal with these children, just to have a look around. Poorani had written to me as soon as she reached there. Afterwards, I have heard nothing from her. I've sent my elder daughter with her. I've been wanting to get her married, and I am looking for a suitable match for her. Nothing has clicked so far. If you are not in a hurry, why don't you come home with me? You can have dinner at my place. I'd like to have a heart-to-heart talk with you.' Aravindan could not refuse her.

As they all travelled home in her car, Aravindan said, 'I don't have a meal at dinner time, only some snacks. If you are willing to join in, we can all go to Kodaikanal together tomorrow morning.'

Mangaleswari said, 'I hear that Poorani has received invitations to deliver lectures in Lanka and Malaya but has not decided on her response yet. The Women's Sangam managers are nagging me, asking me to go and persuade her. I need to go to Kodaikanal and meet Poorani about that too.' It was news to Aravindan that Poorani had received these invitations. But he rejoiced that his prediction about the spread of her renown was coming true.

The streets of the city were flooded with lights and sounds, and their car raced through this flood. It was as if the city had grown thousands of mouths producing a medley of sounds. From one street corner to the next, loudspeakers blared and cinema songs rang out on the evening air. Having just recently spent a day and a half away from this hustle and bustle, out in a parched village in Ramanathapuram District, Aravindan somehow felt that the city had grown bigger and more unfamiliar even during his brief absence. Aravindan felt this tinge of strangeness every time he returned to Madurai from a trip away.

The car came to a stop at the front door of Mangaleswari

amma's home on Thanappa Mudali Street. Aravindan alighted from the car with the others.

'Come in, Aravindan mama,' urged little Mangaiyarkarasi, pulling Aravindan's arm with her delicate hand. Aravindan had always felt a special affection towards this child, not only because she was Poorani's sister and Azhagiya Sittrambalam's youngest child but also because she was a captivating little girl, like a slim-stemmed golden *kuthuvilakku* oil lamp that has come to life. Her face and limbs were all seemingly made out of flowers that radiated their fragrance. Her eyes, expressing wonder and curiosity, were like snow-white lily petals with a black grape rolling gently at the centre of each. As young girls grow older, the expression in their eyes changes from innocent wonder to mischief. But in this child, thought Aravindan, so complete and deep was that special beauty that it would never go away. The charming toddler stage of life has been described by writers as 'the age for exploring everywhere, stretching out tiny hands to touch and feel'. In a sense, Mangaiyarkarasi, though now grown into early childhood, had still retained that special toddler charm. This was what endeared her to Aravindan. Poorani's eyes had this beauty too, but hers spoke of knowledge and wisdom.

Mangaleswari welcomed Aravindan to her home and showered affection on him as if she was meeting a brother again after a long time. He was always struck by the total lack of even the slightest hint of arrogance in this lady, despite her wealth and status. She had the unique ability to draw her friends close to her heart. Poorani had once told him about Mangaleswari's capacity to touch the hearts of people she interacted with. It is said in the Tamil language that love like this is a kind of glue or a string that binds hearts together.

After dinner, the children – Chellam, Sambandan and Mangaiyarkarasi – stayed up reading for a while and then went to bed. Mangaleswari amma talked freely with Aravindan. She shared everything with him as she might have done with a close family member.

'I know I'm pouring out everything to you as if I've gone mad. But I have no one with whom I can feel this close and comfortable. I just have you and Poorani. I consider you both as my close confidantes. There will be many who come and share one's fame and fortune, but we may find none to share our sorrows and hardships. You both are not like others. God has given you golden hearts. You are both able to look upon the world as your family and offer love, sympathy and support to everyone. The way Poorani and I first met was a happy accident. She must have told you about it. From that very day, I started regarding her as my eldest daughter. It is through her that I met you, Aravindan. Please don't stand on any formalities with me. If Poorani is my eldest daughter, you are my eldest son-in-law.

'You and Poorani have equal rights in this house and everything it contains, along with the two daughters born to me, Vasantha and Chellam. I did not have money when I entered this world, nor will I take my money with me when I leave this world. In my childhood, I had not even dreamt of living in such comfort someday. I was a girl from a poor family, and I happened to marry a man who, through sheer hard work and effort in Lanka, became wealthy. I returned from Lanka with what he had left me – wealth, two daughters and deep grief at his death. What is the use of all this money and status? I am unable to find a suitable match for Vasantha.' Mangaleswari sighed in frustration.

Aravindan's heart was deeply touched by the lady's affection and her words. 'In the same world where heartless people like Burma Man live, there are also noble souls like this lady,' he told himself. He realized that this would be the right moment to tell her about the Vasantha–Muruganandam relationship. He was sure that, given her large-heartedness, she would not reject the idea of marriage between those two.

Aravindan asked her, 'Amma, you say you are having difficulties in finding a match for Vasantha. What is the problem?'

'You know what happened. She had this craze about joining the movies, so she ran away from home and was with some stranger for a few days before she returned home. That story has sprouted arms and legs in the form of gossip and lies and has gone around town. We know our daughter well, but the town is suspicious. Every time a possible match is being negotiated, someone comes and spreads the lie, and the family calls it off. I don't know what these mischief-mongers get by behaving like this.' Mangaleswari sounded plaintive.

Aravindan tried to console her. 'Yes, her obsession with cinema made her leave home and go with that crook. Apart from that, there is no stain on your daughter's character. Is it an unforgivable sin to have travelled from Madurai to Tiruchirappalli alone with a man?'

'Exactly! That is why I feel so bitter about it. How they have managed to make a mountain of lies out of nothing and prevented any chance of arranging an alliance for her! How can I, a lone woman, fight this injustice?' Mangaleswari's voice was hoarse with emotion, and tears brimmed in her eyes. Aravindan was deeply moved by the lady's plight and the suffering he could see on her face. The poet in him found a voice and spoke. He was indignant and frustrated.

In the *Uttara Ramayanam*, when Rama agreed to the demand of the people of the kingdom and ordered a test to verify the purity of his wife, Seetha, Mother Earth herself was unable to tolerate the injustice. So, Mother Earth tore a gash in her own self and took her beloved daughter back. How wonderful it would be if Mother Earth would come to the rescue of all the innocent women who are faced with such sorrow. Every innocent woman whom society points the finger at as being fickle in character is a Seetha. 'Embrace me, O Mother Earth!' said Seetha as she sank into the ground. What can women like her do today? What recourse do they have?

'I am going to speak frankly to you, Amma. Please don't mistake me. I believe that you too are progressive in how you think, just like Poorani and me. That is why I feel confident about bringing up this matter with you. Will you accept a young man from a poor family, much lower than yours in wealth and status, as your son-in-law?' He was smiling as he spoke but was also watching her face intently to gauge her reaction.

Mangaleswari also smiled. She said, 'Aravindan! You should never have entertained such a doubt about me. I have never respected people based only on their wealth and status. I grew up in a poor family and was married to a rich husband. Let my daughter, who has grown up in a wealthy family, marry a man who is poor. I don't want to force her into any match that is against her wishes. That is my only consideration in this. I am not concerned about wealth and status. You think only you and Poorani are progressive thinkers. Let me tell you I am even more progressive in my thinking than the two of you. Of course, you have no way of knowing that. But I think Poorani would have realized it to some extent.

'I admitted my daughter to a co-ed college because I wanted her to be able to adjust to different circumstances in life. As for Poorani, her opinion was that girls should not be exposed to unfamiliar environments. You probably think I must be old-fashioned in my views because of my age and this sacred ash smeared on my forehead. I had already decided that if Vasantha met a young man at college whom she liked with all her heart and wished to marry, I would have gladly conducted the wedding. I firmly believe that marriage unions that are based on true love and meeting of hearts promote a beautiful, healthy family lineage and help to bring harmony in society.'

When Mangaleswari expressed this opinion fervently and fluently, Aravindan could not believe his ears. 'Such fresh ideas exist within this woman despite her age!' he thought in astonishment. 'Muruganandam is a really lucky fellow!' His heart filled with joy for his friend's good fortune. He told himself that Muruganandam's accomplishments, as a speaker on various public platforms and in Sangam meetings, paled into insignificance next to his accomplishment of capturing Vasantha's heart without any use of words.

Mangaleswari added, 'Don't hesitate on account of the boy being from a poor family. If you know of any good alliance, please let me know. I am depending completely on you and Poorani in this matter. Any alliance that you indicate even with your little finger is good enough for me to go ahead and fix for my daughter.'

'If that is so, your daughter is as good as married right now, Amma!' announced Aravindan with a smile. Mangaleswari was delighted at hearing this news.

'Tell me the details, Aravindan,' she asked.

'We are all going to Kodaikanal together tomorrow, Amma. Poorani will also be there. We will all sit together and finalize it. Poorani also knows the young man I am talking about,' he told her with a teasing smile. Although she tried her best to get him to reveal the identity of the potential bridegroom, Aravindan would not oblige her. 'That secret will be revealed only tomorrow in Kodaikanal!' he declared.

They had lost track of the time, and by now, it was very late in the night. 'Go and sleep in the upstairs room,' Mangaleswari told Aravindan. 'We can leave from here directly tomorrow morning.'

'No, I will go back to the printing shop to sleep and will come back tomorrow morning. That boy, Thirunavukkarasu, will be alone there. If I go now, I can instruct him about looking after the shop for the next few days when both my boss and I will be away. That would be the most convenient thing to do.'

The next morning, they left for Kodaikanal. It was a cloudy day and not too hot, and they had a pleasant journey. When Poorani saw Aravindan, Mangaleswari amma and the three children arriving together, it was as if Madurai itself had come to Kodaikanal! Meenakshisundaram was away in Pattiveeranpatti and had not yet returned. Therefore, they were not able to make any decision about Poorani's candidacy that day. They preferred to wait for him.

That evening, Mangaleswari, Muruganandam, Vasantha and the children had gone out to take a walk around the lake.

Aravindan and Poorani left for the Kurinji Andavar Temple of Lord Murugan. It was a pleasant climb in the evening air of the hills. It was twilight, the hour when the maid of the west, Dusk, having just lost her husband, Daylight, stands with her son, Crescent Moon, on her hip, milk drooling from his mouth as she mourns her widowhood.

To Aravindan's eyes, Poorani was a shade fairer in complexion and even more beautiful than before. She remarked, 'Have you been travelling a lot? You look darker.'

'Yes,' he agreed with a smile.

'Do you remember how we once climbed the Thirupparankundram Hill together? Whenever we are together, it seems we are always trying to reach some higher place! Isn't that so?'

Aravindan felt a tingling sensation run through him. What a profound observation she had made! Were the two of them indeed born to journey together, ever upwards?

CHAPTER 25

You are golden of hue, with eyes like flowers,
Melodious in voice, elegant in gait,
Made from a lightning flash are your fingers, your hair like dark clouds,
Like the lyric of a beautiful poem
Is your smile… Your smile;
You encompass all the pride of our culture,
In your smile.

– Aravindan

In the whole of Kodaikanal, the environs of the Kurinji Andavar Temple are the most beautiful and serene. From the rear of the temple, one gets a clear view of the Palani Hills and the town itself. Rolling hills, like carelessly strewn green velvet blankets, fill the landscape as far as the eye can reach. Here and there, wildflowers grow on the slopes, as though the hills themselves are laughing aloud through open mouths. In that beautiful setting, Poorani and Aravindan sat talking on a grassy mound.

A pair of parrots nearby were playing a game; they would fly together to a distance and then turn and fly back to the branch of a tree again and again. From somewhere very close by, a *koel* was calling out. It was as if the interval between one call and the next was precisely timed to allow the listener the opportunity to savour its sweet tone. Like little children with red-gold complexions rushing forward and smiling mischievously before being pulled back, large rose bushes flaunted their flowers when the breeze blew, only to pull them away a moment later. The canopy of the sky, the magnificence of the hills, the scenery all around – everything was delightful to the senses. It was as if this whole world had been reborn afresh, rising from the ashes of some apocalypse that destroyed whatever had been there before. It had a special beauty because of being steeped in solitude.

Like someone recalling an old joke and laughing afresh, Aravindan laughed.

'Why are you laughing?' Poorani wanted to know.

'Oh, nothing. I just remembered what you said a while ago, and I felt like laughing. You said, "Every time we go somewhere together, we seem to be climbing." What did you mean?'

'Why do you ask? What did you think I meant?'

'Let me tell you what I think, Poorani. In this race to the top, you are the one who will win. It could be that someday, I will run out of strength and remain behind. You must not grieve over that.' Though he said the words with a light-hearted smile, they arose out of a very serious train of thought. Without his being aware of it, that earnestness was evident when he spoke. Why and how this was happening, he was at a loss to understand. Poorani smiled as she looked into his eyes. He pulled a notebook out of his bag and started writing.

Poorani said playfully, 'Why can't it be this way? In this race to the top, *you* will win. It is I who will someday become too tired and stop my journey.' As she spoke, she reached for his notebook and took it gently out of his hands. Aravindan tried to make a grab for it before she could open it and read what he had just written. He failed. Poorani had leapt up like a gazelle and run away.

A little while ago, she had looked at him and smiled. It was the beauty of that smile that he had tried to capture in a hastily written poem. He was embarrassed at the thought that she might read the words he had written about her.

That was exactly what she did. The poem, which commenced with the line, 'Golden of hue, with eyes like flowers, you smile…' went straight to her heart. Sweet on the tongue like sugar, and sweet to her senses too, were those words, as she recited them to herself again and again.

With a mischievous smile, she turned to Aravindan and remarked, 'You seem to be a dangerous person to be with! If I talk, smile, stand, walk, you write a poem about it!'

'I can't help it,' said Aravindan. 'You are yourself a living, breathing poem, Poorani!'

With a hint of shyness, head slightly tilted and eyes not quite meeting his gaze, she responded, 'Well… But what did you mean when you wrote, "You encompass all the pride of culture in your smile"?'

Aravindan smiled as he told her, 'In your smile and your gaze, I can see great beauty and purity of heart. I was attempting to express this in my poem.'

Poorani came up close to him and held out his notebook. Without taking it from her, Aravindan looked down at her right hand. As he gazed at her coral-red, henna-dyed palm and slender fingers, it was as if he was seeing them for the first time. He smiled.

'What are you staring at?'

'Women's fingers have a special elegance. They are made of lightning,' remarked Aravindan, taking the notebook from her.

'And men's hearts have a special harshness. They are made of cruelty. If not, why would you have promised Meenakshisundaram that you would "make me agree to stand for election" when you had not consulted me or found out what I want to do?'

'Until yesterday, I felt terribly guilty about having made him that promise! But something that happened yesterday evening has made me rethink my stand on it. Now I am totally convinced that you must go ahead and stand as a candidate in this election.'

'Why? What happened yesterday?'

He told her everything that had happened from the time he boarded the train along with Burma Man after his uncle's funeral in the village up to the events in that man's house later. Poorani listened in utter amazement.

Aravindan went on to say, 'People say that poverty is what drives people to crime and bad ways. Why then is this Burma Man living a scheming, dishonest life? What poverty is he suffering? Poorani, I feel that all the problems and hardships that beset our nation are brought about by the rich people in society. Poor people are blameless in this. They hardly have the time to scratch out a living. Where is the time for them to plot and scheme?'

Poorani responded, 'People of low character and impure thoughts will never shed their low traits, however high they may rise in society. There is a beautiful parable by Ramakrishna Paramahamsa about this. Have you read it? Shall I tell you the story?'

'Please tell me! I would love to hear it.'

'One evening, in a town, there was a street market. Some fisherwomen who had brought fish to sell at the market were returning home with their fish baskets. Suddenly, the sky clouded over, and torrential rain poured down. What could those poor women do? They ran towards the hut of a flower merchant nearby. The flower merchant happened to be a good man.

'Seeing the plight of the women, he cleared out one side of his small hut for them to stay. Greatly relieved, they went into the cleared space and found that there was a strong aroma in the air. There were some flower baskets in the corner. They contained flowers that the merchant had planned to distribute to his regular customers the next morning. The fisherwomen had lived their whole lives breathing air steeped in the smell of fish. They could not tolerate the smell of the flowers. They could not sleep. Just as those who are used to nothing but sweet aromas cannot sleep amidst an unpleasant stench, these women who had adapted to nasty odours could not sleep amid the unfamiliar scent of flowers. One of the women, wiser than her companions, came up with a solution.

'"We are unable to sleep because of the smell of the flowers. Nor can we move the flowers elsewhere. Let us splash some water in our fish baskets to dampen them and place them close to us. The odour they give out will mask the smell of the flowers, and we can sleep comfortably." And that is what they did. They reproduced the nasty smell they were used to and had a good night's rest. "The smell one is used to" – that is the key. Think about it, Aravindan! Just think about this story and those two characters, Burma Man and the Pudu Mandapam publisher, and you will see the parallel!'

Aravindan was once more in awe of Poorani's skills. 'What a collection of marvellous ideas she has stored away in her memory! Crowds collect to hear her speeches, as they would to hear a musical concert. It is because of her rich ideas and her way with words.'

'Aravindan, forgive me for talking about myself at length like this, but I want to share something with you. Ever since I was a little girl, I have had this recurring dream. In that dream, I light an oil lamp and walk out into the darkness, where a huge crowd of poor, starving, suffering and sick people have gathered. As the light from my lamp spreads, it banishes hunger and sickness. It lifts away the burden of poverty and suffering. The faces of lakhs of people glow with joy and hope when they see me and my lamp.

'I walk on and on, endlessly. As I walk, the flame of my lamp grows bigger and stronger. In the expanding pool of light, I see even more people. A voice from deep within me says, "You have been put on this Earth to ease the burden of these people, to work for them and to serve them." Like Florence Nightingale, I have always felt a calling towards service to society, a realization that it is my destiny to help lakhs of needy people. Now and then, a life force from deep within me opens its eye momentarily. It is as if it is challenging me. Whenever that happens, it seems to me that whatever I am doing at that moment is trivial and not worthwhile, and the real big tasks still lie ahead. That thought makes me weep in frustration.'

As she uttered these words with the utmost passion, Aravindan saw a kind of divine glow on her face. Tears formed like pearls in her eyes and rolled down. As he gazed at her face, an indefinable feeling of ecstasy gripped Aravindan. 'These were the kinds of thoughts that brought about an awakening and created the saint known as the Buddha. These were the kind of tears of enlightenment he must have shed as he walked away, leaving behind his palace and all its luxuries,' he thought to himself as he gazed at her face, enraptured.

At that moment, he felt that she had already left him way below and risen to heights unattainable to him. Aravindan realized that far greater than the beauty of her face, her eyes and her outward appearance, which had inspired him to write poetry, was the boundless and imperishable beauty that was blossoming inwardly in her. When they were seated together, talking and laughing, only her outward womanly beauty was evident. But every time he caught a glimpse of her incredible inner world, he felt he was somehow in a place very far below where she was. Could it be possible that he was interacting with two different aspects of the same Poorani on the same day?

The beautiful woman, Poorani, with her fine feelings, her affection and her femininity was one person; the woman, who dreamed of walking with a lamp in hand through crowds of poor and hungry people to help and serve them – that was a different Poorani. Which of these two Pooranis was in love with him? Which Poorani he was in love with? Which Poorani was the flower that he, with his mere human hands, could pluck? Or would that flower gradually turn into a fruit as the petals withered and fell? Which of these two Pooranis would attain ultimate fruition?

'I am not afraid!' declared Poorani. 'I am somewhat hesitant. But if you and Meenakshisundaram persuade me, it is possible that I can even overcome my hesitation.'

'I think that is how things will be, Poorani.'

'Let us see.'

The conversation turned to other matters. Poorani told him about the relationship between Vasantha and Muruganandam.

'I knew about this even before you did, Poorani,' said Aravindan. 'In fact, I have even obtained Mangaleswari Amma's acceptance of her daughter's relationship with my friend.' He proceeded to tell her the details of his conversation with Mangaleswari the previous evening.

Poorani said, 'I have faith in that lady's progressive outlook. But I was rather uncertain because of the difference in social and economic status between the two young people. Now that you tell me it is not an issue, let us talk and settle the matter this evening itself, if possible. If we both talk to her about it, I'm sure she will say yes.'

Aravindan sounded confident as he said with a smile, 'The matter is as good as settled. All that remains is to reveal the identity of the groom. The only thing I have not yet told her is, "Muruganandam is the bridegroom."'

The light began to fade, and the sky took on the colour of slate. A milky mist was swirling around. Aravindan and Poorani started walking back from the Kurinji Andavar Temple. They were alone as they walked in the cool evening air redolent with the combined aroma of the varied greenery on the hill slopes.

On the trip back, Poorani became aware of some strong yearnings.

'Yesterday and the day before that, how eager I was to see him again! How I thirsted to be with him! Now he is here, but I am still unable to express my feelings to him. Maybe my learning and education are barriers to free expression of what is in my heart! I had intended to pour out my love to him, but instead, I spouted a philosophical speech. There are so many silly dreams I have been having since childhood. Why did I go and tell him about that dream and send his thoughts in the direction of who is higher or lower? I wonder what he would be thinking about me. He wrote such a beautiful poem about me. I didn't even have the presence of mind to praise his work.

'*Che*! *Che*! Should not my heart know how to express its love? The other day, I was standing in front of the mirror looking at myself – flowers in my hair, bangles on my arms and a thirst in my heart to be with him. I was mad with yearning for him. But today, when I was sitting next to him, talking to him, where did that deep yearning go? The elders have said that arrogance has no place in piety and in love. How true that is! When he said, "In a race to the top, you will certainly win and I will be left behind," was it because he detected some arrogance in me? Or was it merely a joking remark? It was with pure intent and utmost sincerity that I told him the story by Paramahamsa and about my dream. Could this make him hesitate to speak freely to me? He was always so free and animated when we spoke. But today, after I said all those things, he became more guarded in the way he spoke and behaved.'

These thoughts and feelings overwhelmed her. It felt strange to be walking with him in silence like this. She ventured to break the silence between them. 'What's the matter? Why are you so silent? Are you upset with me about something?'

Aravindan laughed. How she wished he would always be cheerful like this! He said, 'What an idea! You seemed to be buried in deep thought, and so I did not want to disturb you. But certainly, it was not my plan to walk in silence all the way!'

Poorani smiled in response. Her smile affirmed the sentiment Aravindan had expressed in his poem: 'You encompass all our culture in your smile.'

'Poorani, did you read all the books I sent you?'

'Yes, I read all of them with utmost enjoyment. I immersed myself in them. This mountain environment is very stimulating for thinking and reading.'

The sky darkened further, and a slight drizzle started. They picked up their pace. As they entered the compound, it was evident that Meenakshisundaram had already returned from his trip to Pattiveeranpatti. His car was parked outside the house. Mangaleswari and the rest of the party had also returned from their walk by the lakeside. That evening and the next day, they all sat together and made some decisions after discussion.

After a fair bit of resistance and counterarguments, Poorani finally agreed to stand as a candidate for election. When Aravindan himself was pleading with her and urging her to accept the proposal, she could not continue to resist. He had explained that if she were to back down, Burma Man would get the impression that they had succumbed to his evil plans and open threats. Thus, an unavoidable series of events combined to trap her into a decision that went against her judgement.

When Aravind brought up the topic of the feelings between the young couple in their midst, Muruganandam attempted to slip away shyly. But Aravindan drew him forward by his arm and told Mangaleswari, 'This is the man who will be your son-in-law, Amma! If you doubt me, ask your daughter.' Vasantha blushed, and her eyes glowed with joy before she hid her face in her hands and ran out of the room. Muruganandam, taken totally by surprise at this drama, squirmed in embarrassment. From the next room, Vasantha eavesdropped on the conversation.

'We can conduct a simple wedding at the Thirupparankundram Temple,' suggested Meenakshisundaram. But Mangaleswari rejected the idea. 'My daughter's wedding must take place at my house. I won't settle for any abbreviated ceremonies. After I returned to Madurai from Lanka, I have not celebrated a single auspicious occasion at home. I insist on conducting this wedding only at my home.'

'*Ennada*, Muruganandam, do you give your consent?' teased Aravindan. Muruganandam's face radiated his happiness.

'Whatever new clothes are planned for Vasantha for the wedding should be given to Muruganandam for tailoring,' remarked Poorani, bringing a wide smile to his already joyful expression. As detailed discussions and plans about the wedding went on, it was as if the atmosphere itself had taken on an auspicious aura.

The next day, Poorani responded to the letter she had received from the Women's Sangam manager. She accepted all the speaking assignments offered to her in Lanka, Malaya and other places. Meanwhile, Aravindan was making preparations to arrange for an international passport for Poorani that would enable her to travel outside the country at any time. That evening, he took Poorani to a photographer's shop in the town to have a passport photo taken. The proprietor of the shop assumed they were a young married couple and addressed them accordingly, giving them both some moments of embarrassment. After the passport picture had been taken, the proprietor insisted on taking another photo of the two of them standing next to each other. Since they made such a good-looking couple, he planned to put the photo on display at the front of his shop.

After the embarrassing misunderstanding by the photographer, both Poorani and Aravindan walked home. In each of their hearts, the incident had stirred tender feelings and fond dreams. As they neared the house, they saw Meenakshisundaram and Mangaleswari awaiting them at the entrance.

Mangaleswari came up to Poorani and said, 'I want to talk about something with you in private. Could you come with me?' The two women moved away to talk. At the same time, Meenakshisundaram made the very same request to Aravindan and drew him aside.

Both Poorani and Aravindan were mystified by this. A medley of questions and doubts arose in each of their minds.

CHAPTER 26

If a cuckoo lays its egg in the nest of a crow,
The crow will raise the chick without a second thought;
So too does the body grow, without conscious thought,
With no will or plan or direction.

– *Thirumandiram*

When Aravindan and Poorani were away at the photographer's studio, Meenakshisundaram and Mangaleswari were talking about them at home. Mangaleswari opened the topic. 'A thought occurs to me. Instead of conducting Vasantha's wedding as a single function, why don't we conduct the wedding of Poorani and Aravindan too, at the same time and at the same venue? After all, how long can the two of them go on like this? Good things in life should happen at the proper time. And Poorani is old enough.' Her suggestion struck Meenakshisundaram as being very timely and appropriate. He agreed at once.

'I agree! We should do that. In fact, I have been having the same thoughts myself. Poorani doesn't have anyone else who can look into the date and time and so on to plan her wedding. Aravindan will agree if I put it to him. He doesn't have anyone else either. It is up to us to nudge them into a commitment and settle the matter. They are both such innocent souls. They share the same values, such as righteousness, honour and so on. Once they return, let us have a word with them and finalize it.'

Mangaleswari suggested, 'I will talk to Poorani and find out what she feels, and you talk to Aravindan. We are their only family. You in the role of his father and I in the role of her mother should ensure that this auspicious event takes place.'

That was why, when Aravindan and Poorani returned from their trip to the studio, they were whisked away in different directions by Meenakshisundaram and Mangaleswari, respectively.

When Mangaleswari brought up the topic, Poorani seemed to turn instantly into a blushing bride. She stood with her head bowed shyly. In the instant when the heart is filled with the joy of true love, there is space only for feelings and thoughts. There is no need for the tongue or the voice. They simply fall silent.

Poorani could not respond in words. She was too shy to raise her head and meet Mangaleswari amma's gaze. She felt shaken by the sheer strength of the emotions coursing through her. Beautiful expressions flitted across her face. Mangaleswari stood looking at Poorani's bent head and was surprised by her lack of response. Here was a young woman who had graced countless platforms and delivered intellectual speeches but was now strangely silent. The instincts and reactions that define femininity are inescapable for any woman, thought Mangaleswari.

'*Enna di*, Poorani! I've been asking you a question, and you are just standing there saying nothing. Why do you need to feel shy to be frank with me? You are not a child, neither is Aravindan. Without putting us through further turmoil, just say yes. If you both agree, we can conduct both the weddings together.'

Poorani was still silent. But her feelings had poured over into her eyes and face. She smiled joyfully. 'Think of me as your mother, Poorani. I am not some stranger. So, tell me.'

After another lengthy silence, Poorani spoke in a soft voice that conveyed the sweetness of her inner feelings. 'Please go ahead with whatever he wishes. If this is what he wants, I am also agreeable to it.'

'When you say "he", whom are you talking about?'

'I mean... He...' Poorani blushed and smiled in confusion. Overcome with shyness, she turned and hurried out of the room. Her heart leapt with joy, and a medley of fond longings, hopes and dreams danced in her mind.

While Mangaleswari was savouring the success of her mission, she was taken aback to see Meenakshisundaram approaching with a dejected expression.

'Successful or not?'

'No. He did not consent.'

'What was his reason?'

'He didn't offer any reason. He just said, "There's no hurry about this now." Then he just left.'

'Why didn't you explain our plan to him in detail?'

'How could I? He was not prepared to listen.'

'Poorani has said that she is willing. What is this fellow's problem! Where is he now? Let me try to talk to him.'

'He went towards the garden. You could try your luck if you like,' said Meenakshisundaram, his tone of voice suggesting that it would be to no avail. Mangaleswari went into the garden in search of Aravindan.

Just then, Muruganandam and Vasantha returned with the children. They had all been out, in Meenakshisundaram's car, for a sightseeing trip of the place. Vasantha helped the children out of the car and took them indoors. Muruganandam went and stood near Meenakshisundaram with a respectful attitude.

'Sit down, *Thambi*,' invited the older man. 'I want to talk to you about something.'

'It's all right, I will stand. Please tell me.'

'After a great deal of effort, we somehow managed to get this young woman to agree to stand for election. From what Aravindan told us yesterday, it appears that the competition is going to be very intense and difficult. We have to work tirelessly day and night to ensure Poorani's victory. I can't do this alone. I ventured into this assuming that you will all support me. The combination of Burma Man and the Pudu Mandapam publisher will be a major complication. That evil pair is capable of burning the city to the ground to get their way.'

'Never fear, *Ayya*! Those fellows will not get the pleasure of reducing Madurai to ashes. About a thousand years ago, a Chozha woman named Kannagi threatened to burn Madurai because of the injustice that had been done to her. But these are people who want to burn down justice itself.' Muruganandam spoke cheerfully with a smile.

'That's what you say, *Thambi*. But who cares for honesty in elections these days? They descend to all kinds of dirty manipulations. Did you hear what Aravindan said yesterday? These are times when people have no compunction at all, even about kidnapping people who are opposed to them and threatening them with bodily harm. That's what happened to Aravindan.'

'That fellow will not get away with what he did to Aravindan! I will see to that, *Ayya*. I too have musclemen, whom I can use against them,' declared Muruganandam heatedly.

'*Che, che*! If a dog comes to bite you, will you also go and bite it? As far as we are concerned, we must always proceed along the right path.'

As these two were talking about the forthcoming election campaign, Aravindan was seated on the lawn outside, deep in thought. Mangaleswari came and sat facing him a little distance away.

'I never expected you to say no,' she told him. 'I have come here hoping to talk to you and make you change your mind.'

Aravindan did not reply. He sat looking expressionlessly at Mangaleswari. She said, 'Meenakshisundaram and I are older than you and have more experience of life. Please trust that we are acting only for your welfare. I would like to see Poorani's wedding take place, along with Vasantha's, at my expense. When you both were away at the photo studio, your boss and I talked about this. He approved of my suggestion readily. He said he would put it to you and get your consent. He says you refused, saying there was no urgency for it.'

'Forgive me, Amma. I can only give you that same decision again. There is no need for such haste as far as our wedding is concerned. We are not children. We are mature, and we understand. Neither of us is in a hurry right now to enter married life.'

'Why not? You are both more than old enough to get married. We should conform to the norms of society. We should not allow idle tongues to wag and spread gossip. Neither you nor Poorani will lose anything by getting married. She can continue with her activities, as usual. I cannot understand why you are holding back...'

Aravindan smiled gently. 'There are so many reasons... We can talk about some of them, but we cannot talk about some others. And there are still other reasons that you cannot grasp even if I tell you.'

'No, no, Aravindan. You are talking in riddles to trick me so that you can avoid the issue.'

Aravindan's smile died away, and his expression reflected his inner feelings. He seemed to be preparing to share some of those feelings. He sighed deeply. He glanced heavenwards briefly, where dark clouds scurried along the sky like shredded bits of a deep-hued silk sari. Whenever he was thinking or speaking of lofty principles or ideas, a special glow would light up Aravindan's face. That same glow was on his face as he turned towards Mangaleswari and spoke.

'Amma! Please permit Poorani and me to live a little longer with just a meeting of minds. I have not even contemplated a physical union between us. I believe that a relationship based on the body is a false dream. A crow that finds a cuckoo's egg in its nest will raise the cuckoo chick as its own, unknowingly, unthinkingly. After the chick is hatched, the crow will feed it and protect it. Only when it starts chirping like a cuckoo and prepares to fly away from the nest will the crow realize its folly. But by then, it is too late. This is why I hesitate. If you hurry us, if you force us to agree with you, I fear we may end up in disappointment, like the crow in the story.'

'You are talking about some story in a book. I've no idea what you mean, neither do I find your example relevant. You both share a love for each other. We are not asking you to do something different now. I am only urging you to take a step that everyone in the world takes. Once you are a married couple in the eyes of the world, you are free to spout any philosophy or belief, and no one will raise an eyebrow.'

'The life of togetherness that you are advocating for us is the one we are already living in our minds. Every person can live two kinds of lives at the same time. Whichever life we are yearning to live, we can do so through the thoughts that dwell in the mind. The life we live in our minds is a superior kind of life. It will not die. I fear that the noble life of the mind cannot be lived on mere mud and earth below. Mud has many impurities and faults. That is why I implore you to let the two of us live a little longer with only a union of our minds, as we presently have.'

'I too can reel out quotations and examples like you are doing, Aravindan. "One can live a good life even in the mud," is what our elders have written. The times were different when our elders wrote that. Things are very different today. Now, those who are living well conspire in their evil minds to prevent others from sharing that same good fortune. There are plenty of people today who will do everything to prevent others, those with talent and resources, from entering their own professions and doing well. They would like to cap the bottle tight and never share it. That is why there is so little of sharing, compromise or give and take in life these days.

'You are straying away from the topic. I asked Poorani this same question about arranging a wedding for the two of you. She indicated her preference quickly in just a few words and seemed to have accepted the suggestion. She merely said, "If he is happy with it, so am I." Now, you are the one who is beating around the bush and refusing to commit yourself.'

'What can I do, Amma? I am not yet able to think of Poorani as just another woman whom I can wed and claim as my own. There is another Poorani within the one you see. In her dreams, she sees herself holding a lamp and walking through a crowd of poor and needy people to help them and be of service to them. If she is the cuckoo who will one day want to leave the crow's nest and fly away, I will be heartbroken, devastated. She will rise to great heights. I will remain below. Right now, we are both on an upward journey. For our journey, there is no need to be tied together in marriage. The meeting of our minds is sufficient. Please don't force me; just let us continue this way for some time.'

Aravindan rose from where he had been sitting on the grass. Mangaleswari understood that this was now a closed topic to him. His arguments and examples appeared silly to Mangaleswari. But he was obstinate about it. She guessed that he had something in his mind that he himself had not quite understood and which he could not describe to others.

Anyway, whatever the reason, the grand plan of Meenakshisundaram and Mangaleswari to conduct the wedding of Poorani and Aravindan was now shattered. That evening and the next morning, Aravindan did not get even a glimpse of Poorani. That morning, a miracle unfolded all along the mountain slopes. The mountains were blanketed in blue as hundreds of *kurinji* flowers bloomed together. For the past few days, a few flowers had been visible here and there. But because of last evening's gentle rain shower, today there were *kurinji* flowers as far as the eye could see. Because the *kurinji* plant blooms only once in twelve years, this marvellous sight was eagerly awaited. This was one such year, and the whole town was agog with excitement. Everyone was talking about it. The *kurinji* flowers had brought a festive atmosphere to the town.

Meenakshisundaram, Muruganandam and Aravindan had originally planned to return to Madurai that day. But in order to enjoy the special *kurinji* beauty on display around them, they put off their departure by a day. Around ten o'clock, Aravindan and Muruganandam went to the photo studio and collected the photographs. The one that the studio proprietor had taken of Aravindan and Poorani standing together had come out very well. Muruganandam was all praise for it. When they entered the house, Poorani and Vasantha were sitting and chatting in the front hall. Aravindan had expected that Poorani would come forward eagerly with a smile to ask him for the photos. He assumed that she had kept herself away last evening and this morning out of disappointment that he had not agreed to the wedding plan. But she would surely be restored to her old spirits once she saw the photographs.

But that did not happen. The moment he entered the room, Poorani sprang up, averted her face and hurried out of the room. Vasantha came forward to take the photographs from Aravindan. She whispered, '*Anna,* Akka is very angry with you. When you and Mangaleswari amma were talking on the lawn yesterday evening, Poorani and I were nearby, on the other side of the fence. Akka heard everything you said. She started crying right there.'

Aravindan smiled. 'Oh, so that's what she is angry about!' he remarked, handing over the photos to Vasantha. With the intention of talking to Poorani and soothing her anger, he tried to enter the room into which she had hurried away. She slammed the door in his face, almost injuring him, and bolted it from inside.

Muruganandam, who had been watching the drama unfold, asked teasingly, 'Aravindan, shall I try to sing a song like Pugazhendi did, to make a door open?' Vasantha shot down the idea. She said with a smile and a meaningful sideways glance at Muruganandam, 'You are *anna*'s close friend. If you start singing, Poorani Akka will use another bolt on the door.'

Vasantha went on to remark, 'Don't you think the photo of *Anna* and Akka together looks like a wedding portrait? Only the garlands are missing.'

'Absolutely true!' agreed Muruganandam, 'And did you notice that they slipped away quietly to take the photos without letting any of us know?'

But Aravindan was in no mood to appreciate their light-hearted teasing. He was saddened by the thought that even Poorani had not understood him properly.

That evening, they had all planned to set out together to enjoy the beautiful view of the *kurinji*-covered mountains.

'I don't want to see anything. I am not coming,' said Poorani stubbornly.

'In that case, neither am I,' responded Aravindan and got out of the car in which he was already seated.

'What's the matter with the two of you today!' scolded Mangaleswari. 'I haven't seen a smile on either of your faces.'

Even after lengthy efforts at persuasion, both Poorani and Aravindan refused to join the others for the sightseeing trip. Finally, the rest of the party drove away, leaving the two of them behind in the house.

They sat in adjoining chairs on the front verandah without exchanging a single word. The cook was busy washing up vessels at the back of the house. The jasmine flowers in the garden that had been left unplucked sent their scent wafting into the air. A group of about ten parrots flew across the sky like wisps of green paper blowing in the breeze. The atmosphere was utterly pleasant in every way. How long could those two sit in stubborn silence, like sworn enemies?

It was Poorani who first broke the silence, pretending to still be angry.

'So what if I didn't want to come? You could have gone ahead,' she said.

'Yes, I could have gone. But the beautiful *kurinji* flower that I'm longing to see is not on those mountains. It is in bloom right here beside me. Or at least it was till yesterday, but today it has furled its petals in anger. It was necessary for me to stay back to ensure that this special *kurinji* blooms again as before.'

Poorani had told herself that she would not melt under his words or show any emotions at all. Yet her face took on a glow that revealed how much she appreciated the sentiment he had expressed.

'Ah! My *kurinji* has blossomed again!' remarked Aravindan and clapped his hands.

CHAPTER 27

People who live their lives with no meaning,
On whom learning and knowledge are wasted,
Who drift along knowing not where they go,
O why are such people born in this unfortunate land?

– Subramania Bharati

Early the next morning, Meenakshisundaram, Aravindan and Muruganandam left for Madurai. Aravindan had a few tasks to complete in Madurai before going back to his village to conduct the sixteenth-day rituals following his uncle's death. He visited the Madurai District Office with documents to seek permission for Poorani to travel for her speaking assignments. He met and talked to the relevant officials to speed things along. Without this kind of intervention, nothing would get done in a government office! He also informed the Women's Sangam management that he was taking care of securing the travel permits for Poorani.

Poorani's speech to raise money for housing for the poor had been successful in bringing in a good amount. Aravindan and Muruganandam had found a very trustworthy mason and given him the contract to build houses for the poor out of the money collected. They now went to meet the mason to check how far along the project had come.

Near the low-lying area south of the Madurai bus stand, there used to be a holy stream known as Krithamala Stream. Now there was nothing the least bit holy about it. It was merely a dirty drain. This waterway would flood its banks during the rains and destroy the huts of the poor folks who lived there. Despite diverting the stream slightly and raising the banks on both sides, flooding continued to take place after heavy rainfall. That is why, this time, they had given clear instructions to the mason to pack the ground firmly with a lot of soil to raise the level before starting building. During their inspection, they were relieved to find that the mason had carried out their instructions correctly. The building work too was more or less finished. The mason came up to Aravindan and asked, '*Ayya*, whom are you going to invite to inaugurate this project? Will you call a minister from the government?'

Aravindan smiled. 'Muruganandam, did you hear what our mason friend is asking? These days, young people like us are keen to see an end to religious intolerance and outdated practices that cause tension between people. But in our attempt to untie some of the knotty problems we face, we are unknowingly creating other kinds of knots. We must have the courage to abandon all practices, traditional or modern, which have no reason or logic to them. Someone to lay the foundation stone using a silver trowel to apply cement; someone else to declare it open; garlands, auspicious limes, loudspeakers – what a lot of empty rituals! The main obstacle to our country's economic advancement is the presence of these useless ceremonies.'

'Well said, Aravindan! Yes, the next thing we know, a boy at school may send for a minister to open his fountain pen whose cap has been screwed on too tight! Mason *ayya*! You are the one who has built these houses with so much care and commitment. It is important to honour those who labour honestly and sincerely. We don't need our government leaders to inaugurate these dwellings. We don't need ministers, who will come in their swanky cars, carefully avoid the slush and mud and delicately cut a silk ribbon to declare the colony open. You are the appropriate person to inaugurate this colony!'

'Are you making fun of me?' asked the mason in genuine puzzlement, scratching his head.

'No, we are not teasing you, Mason *ayya*. Tomorrow you shall declare this colony open,' confirmed Aravindan.

Sure enough, the next day, the inauguration took place exactly as the two of them had planned, with no fuss and ostentation. On the approach path to the colony, the mason lit a small *kuthuvilakku*. There were no garlands, no loudspeakers, no soda bottles handed around. No press reporters. The only ones present were the families that would be moving into those new huts.

The mason was touched by their gesture. '*Ayya*, you have paid me for my work, yes. But I am even more grateful to you for the way you have honoured me today.' Aravindan thought to himself, 'Workers don't feel fulfilled merely by earning money for their work. They want their work to be appreciated. But for many reasons, they hesitate to express these sentiments openly.'

The poor families were waiting to move into their new homes. Elderly men and women, youngsters and children had tears of gratitude in their eyes as they thanked Aravindan with folded hands. 'These tears of joy, these expressions of gratitude, belong rightfully to Poorani. How wonderful it would have been if she were present here today!' thought Aravindan. 'She, who dreams of carrying a light into the darkness of poverty and sickness, would have had her dream fulfilled here.' He was overcome with emotion at the thought.

That evening, Muruganandam insisted that Aravindan should visit his home in Ponnagaram. Aravindan could not, at first, understand why his friend was urging him to make a visit just then. It had been Aravindan's habit to go to Ponnagaram about once a month on some free Sunday and meet with his friends who lived in the area. On such days, he would also drop in at Muruganandam's home and pay his respects to his friend's parents. He had known them since he was a child and felt close to them.

Though they were unrelated to him, they had lived in his village at one time. When they had moved to his village as a needy family, Muruganandam was just a boy, slightly more aware of the ways of the world than Aravindan was. They both attended the same elementary school. A few years later, Muruganandam's family moved to Madurai, where his parents became mill workers. Naturally, Muruganandam left with them. Later, Aravindan's mother had died, leaving him at the mercy of his cruel uncle and aunt from whom he ran away to Madurai. At the high school in Madurai, when Aravindan was mercilessly bullied and mocked by his classmates because he was poor and had to work to survive, Muruganandam stood up for him and supported him against their cruelty.

Once they realized that they had known each other well as children, their friendship grew deeper. Muruganandam looked upon Aravindan as a beloved elder brother. Once he passed out of school, Aravindan landed a job at Meenakshi

Press on the recommendation of his Tamil teacher at school. As for Muruganandam, he had learnt tailoring as a hobby and set up a small shop. He prospered in his profession. Within the next six months, he spent some time in Bombay studying fashion design and came back with a certificate to show for it. His shop was called 'Bombay Tailors'. Through all these successes in his life, Muruganandam remained a loyal friend to Aravindan.

'*Enda*, Muruganandam! Why are you insisting that I should come to your home this evening? What's the urgency?' Muruganandam shifted awkwardly, as though in embarrassment, and hesitated to reply. Aravindan understood.

'Oho! You want me to talk to your parents about your marriage arrangements and get their approval, right? Why were you shy about telling this to me right away? Sure, I will come. We can leave right now if you'd like to.'

However, so much work had piled up at the printing shop in Aravindan's absence that he could not ignore the backlog and leave in the middle of the day. Meenakshisundaram was away most of the time, talking to people and making arrangements for Poorani's election campaign. He was like a man rejuvenated in his old age, working briskly. Aravindan had his hands full with replying to important letters, checking the accounts, reading and correcting the proofs and so on. He had hardly any breathing time at all.

By five thirty in the evening, he had completed the urgent tasks. He freshened up and waited for Muruganandam. The two of them set off walking, chatting as they went. At the level crossing near Madurai Mills, there was a milling crowd. This was the path they usually took to get to Ponnagaram. 'Hold on,

Aravindan,' said Muruganandam. 'I will go and check what is happening there.' He disappeared into the crowd.

After a while, he emerged. 'Come on, let's go,' he said, drawing Aravindan along, making a path through the crowd for them to move forward. 'It appears that some exam results were published in the evening newspaper. A boy who had failed had thrown himself in front of a passing train. His body lay covered with blood, all limbs severed. In his shirt pocket, he had left a note: *No one is responsible for my suicide. My failure in the exam is the only reason.*'

'Oh, what a pity!'

'Where's the question of pity or praise, Aravindan? Do our schools and colleges teach young people how to live? Or do they drive them to suicide like this? An education system that does not teach children how to face life courageously is a disgrace to the country. Should not learning stimulate self-confidence and an enthusiasm for life? What kind of education is this that neither allows you to live nor to die?'

Aravindan spoke with passion in his voice. 'Schools are nothing but boarding and lodging hotels, though they don't carry advertising boards announcing it. Those entering the teaching profession are already weary of life, or they become weary of life after becoming teachers. How can such people, who are themselves tired of living, instil in the children's minds the inspiration to live their lives courageously? Every province should have a university of the calibre of the poet Tagore's Visva Bharati University or of the quality of Santiniketan. That is the only way students can be taught how to live courageous lives.'

'It's not only the teachers who are world-weary and

uninterested, Aravindan. There is no use in blaming them alone. Even after Independence, teachers earn hardly anything to live on. It is as if all of society decided to put one community out of its mind, to ignore it altogether – that is the teaching community. Do you know that about fifteen days ago, at that very same level crossing where that young boy killed himself today, a primary school teacher committed suicide? He had four or five daughters. His suicide note read: *I am taking my own life today because I do not have the means to get my daughters married.* Probably not a day goes by without the wheels of trains that run in this sector getting traces of human blood on them.'

Aravindan joined in with his opinion. 'Unemployed youth and unmarried girls are major problems for our land these days, Muruganandam. These are the two major reasons for most of the suicides that take place. Bharati has written, "When the grass loses its tenderness and hardens, that is when the Goddess Parasakthi will emerge from the earth." If these two problems of our nation become more and more difficult to handle, every citizen will be asking himself in frustration, "Why was I ever born in this land?" As one walks along the street and sees the evidence of poverty, despair, disease and death, enlightenment emerges from somewhere within oneself, like Buddha may have experienced. Then one tells oneself, "This cannot be allowed to go on; we must quickly find a remedy that will remove all these hardships." And yet, why is that moment so short-lived, why does it melt away into indifference again?'

The two of them walked along, sharing their thoughts about society and its ills with great passion. A group of weary women mill workers trudged by after their day's shift, bits of cotton still sticking to their hair and clothes. The racket from the noisy machines in the mill echoed throughout the street.

Muruganandam remarked, 'Aravindan, there are at least four or five cases of suicide a day in this part of the city. To make matters worse, there is this new bedbug poison that is out on the market. It makes things easier for those who are planning to take their own lives.'

Aravindan spoke with bitter irony. 'There is no medicine to ensure that people live. Till that is discovered, people will only be seeking out drugs and poisons as ways to die.'

Aravindan had to spend more than an hour at Muruganandam's house in Ponnagaram. Muruganandam's parents were totally taken aback on hearing that their son's marriage was being planned with a girl from a wealthy family. They had to be told the background and all the details, and this process took time. Finally, he obtained their consent. They had never turned down any request or suggestion from Aravindan. They thought of Aravindan as their own dutiful and responsible son.

When Aravindan was leaving Kodaikanal with the others a couple of days earlier, Mangaleswari had requested him to go and meet Muruganandam's parents, obtain their consent to the marriage alliance and settle on a date if possible. Accordingly, now that he had carried out her wishes, Aravindan hurriedly wrote the news on a postcard, dabbed auspicious turmeric paste on the four corners of the card and sent it off to Kodaikanal from the post office. Muruganandam's family insisted that he should stay and have his evening meal with them.

When Aravindan got back to the printing shop, it was about eight o'clock. A light was still on in the front office. He assumed that Thirunavukkarasu must be entering some expense figures. But when he entered the room, he was surprised to see Meenakshisundaram himself. He was sitting with his cheek resting on one hand, deep in thought. He looked very tired, and his face showed that something was wrong. Aravindan had hardly ever seen his boss in such a condition. It happened very rarely.

'Are you unwell?'

'My body is fine. It is my mind that has a problem.'

The deep hoarseness of his voice made Aravindan hesitate to say anything. He knew that any extreme emotion, whether anger or worry, would send up Meenakshisundaram's blood pressure.

'Every fellow is waiting for his chance to ditch us. They ask you to bend, and then they leap-frog over you and push you over. Do you remember that I was negotiating the sale of my land in Thiruvedagam to fund the election expenses for Poorani?'

'Yes, you were to sign the agreement yesterday.'

'That is what I wanted to do. But the buyer didn't turn up. So I went along to find out what had happened. It turned out that the buyer was now reluctant to go ahead with the deal because Burma Man and the Pudu Mandapam publisher had gone and said all kinds of things to him.'

'That's not the end of the world. So what if this buyer is backing out? There will be a thousand others who are willing to buy the land.'

'That's not true, Aravindan. There won't be anyone else willing to invest this much money in buying land in that location. I am in all kinds of financial difficulties right now. I owe thousands of rupees to the paper supplier. It is only out of consideration for me that they are not pressing me to settle the amount.' Aravindan felt deep empathy for his employer's situation and his state of mind. He wanted to say something comforting to him. But he felt tongue-tied. There was nothing he could say.

Four or five days later, when Aravindan was about to leave for his village for his uncle's death rites, Meenakshisundaram became bedridden with high blood pressure. Aravindan requested Muruganandam to take care of the old man and went to perform his uncle's sixteenth-day rites. Burma Man did not attend the ceremony this time, and that was just what Aravindan had expected. He had already come to realize that even the trip Burma Man had made for the funeral was with the sole purpose of luring Aravindan away from Meenakshisundaram's influence. 'Now that I have escaped his trap, my boss, Poorani and I are all sworn enemies of his, and he will display his evil intentions,' said Aravindan to himself.

The people in his village, naïve, innocent and concerned only with minor matters and shallow thoughts, had built up all kinds of expectations about Aravindan's future plans. Most of them thought he would move to the village and enjoy the wealth and luxury his uncle had left behind. An elderly villager had words of advice for Aravindan. '*Thambi*, now you should come and stay here in the village. What is there in Madurai for you now? Why would you want to work under someone and be answerable to him? You need to look after your property. You could also resume your uncle's pawn business. That is my *advice* to you.' The old man spoke the word 'advice' in English with a grand air, probably the only English word he knew! Aravindan listened to him in silence and smiled inwardly.

The morning after the ceremony, Aravindan went to his uncle's house and took down the stained and rusted sign that read, 'Loans will be given here against pawned jewellery'. He threw the sign into the dustbin. His uncle's accountant tried to prevent him. '*Thambi*, don't throw it away. The pawn business accounts have not been closed yet. Many have not yet come to claim their pledged jewels. Many have not been paying the interest amounts properly for the loans they have taken.'

Aravindan merely smiled in response. He checked the accounts and the pledged jewellery. He found a pile of jewellery, ranging from *thali*s to rings, pledged by poor families. The accountant revealed that those who had pawned their valuables were mostly from that village itself or from adjoining small villages. 'Take your bicycle, go at once and tell all these people to come here,' Aravindan told the accountant. The latter tried his best to protest the idea. 'It's not proper for those who have given the loan to go and invite those who have taken the loan,' he argued.

'Proper? Nonsense! Just go at once and do as I say,' ordered Aravindan sternly. The accountant had no option but to follow the order. By noon, all those who had pledged their jewellery to Aravindan's uncle had gathered in front of the house. When Aravindan noticed how poverty and hunger had made each of them thin and weak, his heart ached with sympathy for them. He realized that the fruits of Independence that had contributed to the development and prosperity of cities had not penetrated into the rural areas of the country, leaving the people here untouched by any progress. He thought to himself sadly, 'It was to help people like these, to improve the condition of those who live dark lives in dark villages, that Gandhi worked so hard. Alas, the benefits of his work had stopped at the cities.'

Aravindan asked all the assembled people to sit. Then he called the accountant out from the house and told him, 'Please go and fetch all the pledged jewellery and the documents for them.' The accountant obviously did not understand what Aravindan was getting at. He said, 'Why do you need the jewellery and the documents, *Thambi*? I have written a separate list of the interest owing from each borrower.'

'I don't need that list,' insisted Aravindan. 'Just bring me the things I asked you to.'

The accountant sensed that Aravindan was determined and could not be persuaded out of his plan. Aravindan distributed the pledged jewellery to the respective owners according to the documents. He told them, 'None of you has to pay any interest that you owe. It is enough if you repay only the loan amount. It is not necessary for you to give it to me here and now. I will give you an address. You can send the loan amount to that address within the next two or three months as and when you are able to, and you will get a receipt.'

The address he gave them was 'Poor Girls Marriage Assistance Sangam, Maninagaram, Madurai'. An elderly woman in the gathering said, 'You are so generous, *Ayya*! God bless you!' Some came forward to try and touch his feet to express their gratitude. He smilingly prevented them from doing so, said goodbye with folded palms and sent them home. The accountant looked shocked and ready to faint. He was holding on to a pillar for support. He began to wonder whether this young man had taken leave of his senses!

Aravindan stayed in the village for another ten days. He was keenly aware of Meenakshisundaram's plight, struggling to meet the expenses of the printing shop and also somehow raise money for Poorani's election campaign. In the neighbouring village, there lived a wealthy landlord who had amassed a lot of money and was always looking to buy more and more property. Aravindan sold all his uncle's properties, except the house, to the landlord for just over fifty-seven thousand rupees.

Aravindan's heart grew lighter at the thought that his uncle's wealth would come in handy at the right time to help Meenakshisundaram. The accountant mentioned that he had to get his daughter married. Aravindan gave him two thousand rupees and told him, 'You can live in this house for now.'

'You are such a gem of a person, *Ayya*,' stammered the accountant.

Aravindan had been imagining that when he returned and put a bundle of notes totalling fifty-five thousand rupees in front of Meenakshisundaram, the old man's blood pressure problem would vanish into thin air. But that evening, just as he was setting out to board the train, he received a telegram that destroyed that dream and reduced him to tears of inconsolable sorrow. He read that telegram and wept aloud like a little child.

CHAPTER 28

After the whole town has gathered and wept,
After the dead man's name becomes 'the body',
After taking him to the cremation ground and turning him to ashes,
They take a bath and forget all about him.

– Thirumoolar

Meenakshisundaram has died. Come at once, was Muruganandam's message on the telegram.

Even when his own father had died, Aravindan had not wept aloud like this. He felt heartbroken and bereft. At the time of his father's death, Aravindan was just a child. Now, he was an adult, with an adult's range and depth of emotions. When he read the news in the telegram, that the beloved father figure who had raised him and set him on a good path in life had passed away, his mind hesitated to accept the reality of it. The one for whose sake he had sold his uncle's properties and converted them to cash in the hope of ending his financial problems was now no more.

He mourned the death of the saintly man just when good news about an end to his money troubles was around the corner. It was as if, at the very moment when the churn was beginning to separate the butter, the pot had broken to bits. He was particularly shocked because it was so unexpected.

'He was good and kind not only to me but to everyone. Oh, why did god take away such a good soul who was doing so much for the whole city?' thought Aravindan. He felt shaken by overpowering emotions.

'He should not have died like this. Those devils drove him to it,' he told himself, boiling with fury. He blamed Burma Man and the Pudu Mandapam publisher for having brought about the circumstances that had caused great stress to Meenakshisundaram and ruined his health. He thought of the many, many occasions when Meenakshisundaram had reached out to help him in different ways. 'You showed tenderness and love towards me, greater even than a mother's love for her child. Now, I can never properly express my gratitude to you,' he mourned.

Just before the train enters Madurai station, where the track curves around a bend, a beautiful vista of Madurai city, adorned with its tall temple towers, appears. Today, that exhilarating sight appeared sombre to Aravindan's eye. The towers and the city laid out beneath them seemed listless and tired. To his numbed senses, the city itself seemed devoid of energy and life.

The moment the train arrived at the station, Aravindan stepped out and hurried to Meenakshisundaram's house. At the front entrance, on the veranda, as well as on the roadsides, people had assembled for the funeral. Muruganandam was at the doorway, taking care of the arrangements. A flower-decorated palanquin was being prepared for the man whom life had abandoned, leaving only a 'body'. The traditional sounds heard at a funeral filled the air – loud wailing, conch shells being blown and gongs being solemnly struck.

Aravindan hurried indoors, shielding his tear-laden eyes

from onlookers. In the front hall, the plank of the swing had been taken out and placed on the floor. On it, they had laid out the body of Meenakshisundaram. The sounds of weeping and wailing from many throats signalled that this was no longer a living person but merely a corpse. Yet his face showed no signs of having died. The calm nobility that it wore in life was still on that face. Aravindan gazed at that beloved face and wept copious tears. He brought his handkerchief to his lips to try to stop himself from wailing aloud. But his grief could not be stilled. When confronting death, a kind of primal fear arises in the mind, as though all life has frozen to a standstill. What had seemed to be signs of hope and success now appeared as mere signs of loss and grief. As Aravindan stood mourning his great loss, eyes welling with tears, it was as if he was suspended in time, seeing nothing, feeling nothing, all his senses sacrificed at the altar of his grief.

Were these the same hands that had many a time patted him affectionately on the back and encouraged him when he was feeling low? Now, they could neither feel nor convey any emotion. Were these the lips that had spoken words of affectionate advice to him time and again, whenever he had appeared red-eyed from lack of sleep. 'Aravinda, have you been staying awake late again? If you don't get enough sleep your health will suffer!' he would say. Now, those lips would never utter those or any other words.

The more he thought about these things, the more his tears flowed. But how long could he just stand and weep? What would be accomplished by that? He wiped his swollen eyes and joined Muruganandam to help with the arrangements. Many people came and offered condolences. Some of them attempted to remind him of events or occasions in the dead man's life. Aravindan went about his work like an automaton, with no thoughts in his empty mind.

Meenakshisundaram's three eldest children were all daughters. The older two were married. The oldest one was married into a family in Tirunelveli and the second into a family in Trichy. The third had finished college and was at home awaiting marriage. The last child was a boy, just over ten years or so in age.

Muruganandam had sent urgent telegrams to the older daughters. Meenakshisundaram's wife did not want her husband's body to be taken away before her daughters arrived. Within a short time after Aravindan had arrived, Poorani, Mangaleswari and the others arrived from Kodaikanal by car. They had also been informed of the sad news through a telegram from Muruganandam.

As more and more women entered the house, the sounds of sobbing and wailing became louder. Near the entrance, the crowd of men was also growing – neighbours, acquaintances, friends and well-wishers. The true test of a man's character is not measured by how many crowd around him in his lifetime but by how many come to bid him goodbye when he dies. The huge crowd there at his house bore testimony to the noble way in which he had led his life. Among them were the sorrowful group of his printing shop employees, all of them in tears. Like an age-old tree that had suddenly twisted and crashed to earth, this man's death had shaken the city. Just before dark, the two daughters arrived with their husbands.

Since the Vaigai was in flood, the funeral party could not go across the bridge. They had to take the long way via Chellur to the Thathaneri cremation ground. It was past eleven in the evening when they returned. As if in some kind of waking dream, Aravindan walked like a zombie to the printing shop. Muruganandam sensed that this was a time when his friend needed him, so he accompanied Aravindan.

As they approached the entrance, Muruganandam told Aravindan, 'This was the place that spelt his doom. After you went to your village, he recovered from his illness after a couple of days and started coming to the office. But then he heard that Burma Man had bought this building next door and that the Pudu Mandapam publisher was going to start his own business from there. That news sent his blood pressure to dangerous levels, and he collapsed.' Aravindan stared with amazement at where Muruganandam was pointing.

On what had been the hotel building next door, the usual board of 'Kumarakrupa Vilas Coffee and Meals Hotel', which had always hung on the blackened wall, was missing. The whole building had been spruced up with paint, and the new shiny enamel board 'Kamakshi Printing Press' glowed in the lamplight from the street. Underneath, in smaller letters, was the proprietor's name, none other than that same Pudu Mandapam publisher! Aravindan was stunned by the radical changes that had taken place in the mere two weeks that he had been away. He could see visions of Burma Man's tiger face snarling at him with an open mouth.

'How many days ago did this happen, Muruganandam?'

'Just four days ago, they conducted a grand ceremony. Burma Man himself came and declared it open.'

'Oh, so we now have a new problem it seems!' remarked Aravindan as he entered the printing shop, with Muruganandam following close behind.

That night, Aravindan did not get a wink of sleep. People with resources, such as Burma Man, could very quickly destroy their enemies if they set their minds to it. But when the poor fought against the poor, it was just an ugly scuffle on the street, each pulling at the tuft of hair on the other's head and slapping each other on the face. The rich could take their revenge against their targets in a civilized way, without soiling their own hands. Aravindan realized that Burma Man was embarking on that kind of plan. He also realized that Meenakshisundaram had not just died but had been driven to his death. By piling insurmountable problems and worries upon him, Burma Man had destroyed his spirit and ruined his health.

That night, as he lay sleepless, contemplating the situation following Meenakshisundaram's death and the way the enemies were closing in, Aravindan arrived at a firm decision. 'I will not take revenge upon these people,' he resolved, 'but I will teach them a lesson.' He decided he would not change any of the decisions they had taken earlier or abandon any of their plans because of Meenakshisundaram's death.

He remembered how he had argued vehemently against the idea when Meenakshisundaram had first proposed that Poorani should stand for election. Now, he had changed his mind. The first step had been taken, and he was determined not to retreat. His determination to persist with the plan was fuelled by Burma Man's sly manipulations.

Aravindan remembered what the man had said when he had lured him to his mansion from the railway station. 'In this city, not even a speck of dust can move without my permission. I have enough manpower and money to reduce you and people like you to nothing.' How could Aravindan forget that arrogant threat? How could he forget the day he had almost received a thrashing from Burma Man's henchman for turning down his offer?

Muruganandam, hot-headed as he was by nature, was liable to go around venting his fury openly. 'Money chests brimming with wealth, minds brimming with evil schemes and personalities brimming with deceit; people like these, who go around like leaders of society, deserve to be exposed. They must have their masks stripped away in front of the whole world,' he would rant. But Aravindan had another approach altogether. His way of thinking was, 'Yes, these are evil people. But I do not wish to destroy them. I wish only to destroy the evil that they do.' It was like putting a red star against them in his mind.

A month after Meenakshisundaram's passing, when all the ceremonies were over and things had somewhat settled down, Aravindan met Meenakshisundaram's wife to discuss the future plans for Meenakshi Press. She said, 'Let everything go on as before. What new idea can I suggest? I am confident that you will do only what is good for my family. Who else but you can take up the job honestly and responsibly? If you will take over the running of the press, I will be happy.' Aravindan already knew her to be a large-hearted, good person like her husband.

With two printing press businesses sitting right next to each other, how can there not be professional competition and motivated claims? Problems cropped up one after the other. One morning, when Aravindan and Muruganandam were in the front office of Meenakshi Press, a man entered and enquired about a printing job. He seemed to be visiting Madurai from some other city. He wanted to know what it would cost to print one thousand wedding invitations using two colours on high-quality paper. Aravindan made a quick calculation on a scrap of paper and gave the man an estimate of the cost.

The man was very angry. He said, 'The press next door has offered to do this job at half the price that you are quoting, sir! You are trying to cheat me!' He got up in a huff and strode out of the office. The next day, the same man turned up again, this time carrying a package. 'Look at these,' he shouted, showing Aravindan a couple of printed invitations. 'These are what I have collected today from the press next door at half the price you quoted. Take a look. Aren't they perfectly fine?' Aravindan took one of the invitations that the man was holding out. He told him calmly, 'Please sit for a moment, sir.' Aravindan started reading through the invitation. Where it should have printed '*manam*' (wedding) it had been printed '*maranam*' (death) instead. In effect, it was an invitation to a funeral.

Aravindan underlined the errors in the invitation in red ink and handed it back to the man. 'Sir, please read the portions that I have underlined,' he said with a smile. 'Here, in our press, we are never so careless as to turn a wedding into a funeral! We do not make errors. We take our responsibility seriously and do a very good job. That is why we charge slightly higher than some others.' The man took a closer look at the underlined portions of the invitation. His expression turned to one of fury. 'Miserable, stupid idiots! What kind of printing job is this? May coals of fire descend on their heads! May their houses fall into ruin!' he fumed as he got up and stormed out, headed for a battle next door.

On another occasion, an organization that was planning to conduct a Bharati festival wanted a programme schedule to be printed. Their representative came and discussed the price with Aravindan but decided to place the order next door at Kamakshi Press because they charged less. The words *'Thol Kottuvom'* (we will rejoice) were to appear as part of the title, taken from a famous poem of Bharati. The printed copies read *'Thel Kottuvom'* ('we will sting like a scorpion'). It was a huge embarrassment. At that same event, Muruganandam was to speak. In the course of his speech, he brought up the matter of the disgraceful misprint, and it soon became public knowledge.

Aravindan chided him afterwards. 'There may be many personal issues we have with them. But why did you announce the mistake during your speech? People may not take it well.' But Muruganandam was unfazed. 'Oh, come on, Aravindan! Why should I be afraid of anyone? When something is obviously wrong, pointing it out is the proper thing to do.'

Aravindan tried to tackle the professional rivalry issues, as well as the jealousy of their neighbour, with as much decency as he could. He avoided unnecessary conflicts. The money he had brought back from the village after the sale of his uncle's properties was used to settle the business debts of the press. The rest he put aside in a fund for Poorani's election campaign expenses. His reputation for sincerity and honesty ensured that Meenakshi Press continued to have loyal customers. The newly opened rival press next door could not make a dent in the continued success of Meenakshi Press.

If they had not succeeded in harming his business, it was not for want of trying! Both directly and indirectly, they were always thinking of ways to ruin Aravindan. But the latter did not spend any time or energy worrying about them or trying to counter their plans. He had enough to do with whatever spare time was available to him. A date had been fixed for the wedding of Muruganandam and Vasantha. As the man who represented both families, Aravindan had a lot of arrangements to make.

After Poorani and the others had come down from Kodaikanal to attend Meenakshisundaram's funeral, they had stayed back in Madurai instead of returning to the hills. For about two or three weeks, Poorani rested at her Thirupparankundram home. In the house opposite, Odhuvar *thatha*'s granddaughter, Kamu, had given birth to a baby boy. Poorani visited her. Her friend, Kamala, had also come to her parents' home for a visit. She was expecting a baby. One evening. Poorani visited her at her home, and they had a long chat. As the day of the wedding drew nearer, Poorani moved to Mangaleswari's house to be of help to her. She accompanied her to sari shops, jewellery stores and all the other errands that needed to be done. Poorani was scheduled to travel to Lanka a week after the wedding for her speaking engagement. The necessary travel permits had come through. She was to speak at the International Tamil Conference in Jaffna, and later at other venues in Lanka.

Vasantha's wedding with Muruganandam was a beautiful ceremony.

It had the whole town talking about it. Whenever she thought back to that day, Poorani felt a thrill of pleasure. Among the families that had come to attend the wedding, there was one perky little girl who was a chatterbox.

In the evening, Aravindan was welcoming a wedding visitor at the front pandal. He was the one who had the storeroom key. Just then, a group of women from the Women's Sangam arrived, and Poorani wanted to give them the traditional *thamboolam* bags. The bags were in the locked storeroom, so she needed the key to the room. She turned to the little girl, who was skipping around merrily in her trailing *pavadai*. 'Do you see that tall, fair, handsome man near the entrance talking to someone? He has the storeroom key. Tell him I sent you and bring me the key.'

That mischievous little girl had made a mental note of Aravindan and Poorani from the very day she arrived. She saw them together often, talking and laughing or going shopping together, so she had assumed they were husband and wife. The little one, the bundle of mischief that she was, hopped and skipped her way to where Aravindan was standing and talking with many people around. 'Mama, Mama!' burst out the little one, 'your wife is calling you. She is very proud that you are tall, fair and handsome. She told me so when she sent me. She asked me to bring the storeroom key. Hand it over quickly. I have to go…' All the people standing nearby, including Muruganandam, in his bridegroom finery, started roaring with laughter.

Aravindan stood bemused. The little girl laced her tiny fingers in the fingers of Aravindan's right hand and pulled him indoors. He struggled to keep pace with her. The child dragged Aravindan right up to where Poorani was standing with a group of women. She stopped in front of Poorani and declared triumphantly, 'Tall, fair, handsome – the husband you described so proudly. I have brought him to you. Now, you can ask him for a key or lock or whatever you want.'

The child clapped her hands in glee and jumped up and down. Her laughter was full of mischief. The sight of that cute child jumping about, and those cute lips laughing, in a face dripping with mischief, set off a wave of laughter in the women gathered around. Aravindan and Poorani lowered their heads in embarrassment. At that wedding venue, bathed in the scents of jasmine and sandalwood, the two of them felt that those sweet scents had entered their hearts and overflowed. They simultaneously experienced a kind of epiphany, as though they had been linked together through several births in an age-old, long-lasting marriage of minds. They stood soaking in the boundless thrill of that revelation.

'*Ayyayyo*! It looks as if the husband and wife are feeling shy!' chirped the mischievous little girl, again giggling and clapping her tiny hands. Aravindan stretched out his hand to grab the little imp, but she was too quick for him. She had flitted away like a butterfly. Vasantha, who had been sitting demurely on the *mandapam* awaiting the rituals, raised her head to take in the happenings nearby.

'Serves you right, *Anna*!' she called out, smiling. Mangaleswari smiled and added, 'A child's words are like god's own words. It's not as if the child said something untrue. It will surely come true one day.'

It took a few moments for the hilarity caused by the little girl's antics to settle down. Aravindan returned to the real world and took out the storeroom key. 'Here, take it,' he said, holding the key out to her. Poorani, who had been standing slightly away with her head bent shyly, now lifted her eyes.

She looked at him through the corners of her captivating eyes, and her petal-like lips smiled tenderly as she reached for the key. At that moment, Aravindan captured the image of that beloved face and etched it in his heart. He remembered his own poem praising that face.

'Capture the moon, wipe away the stains on it, and put a tender smile on it...' Aravindan sensed a heady aroma, as if a blend of scents had been applied to his body, his mind and everywhere else. Yet, the next moment, the illusion was destroyed; now Poorani was walking through the darkness like a forest deity, lamp in hand, seeking to save those in the darkness of poverty. She was no mere woman; she was a holy soul.

The wedding of Vasantha with Muruganandam was a big success. Mangaleswari was so happy and relieved that she decided to accompany Poorani to Lanka. She already had a passport, and Aravindan managed to get the visa for her at short notice. They had planned to take an Air Ceylon flight from Chennai via Tiruchirappalli to Jaffna. Aravindan, Vasantha, Muruganandam and the manager of the Women's Sangam went to the airport to see them off.

Poorani turned to wave to them from the top step of the ladder just before she entered the plane. Aravindan called out to her loudly with a smile, 'Whenever we climbed, you wanted to keep pace with me. Now, you are up there, and you have left me here below.'

Poorani wanted to smile lightly in reply. Instead, her eyes filled with tears.

CHAPTER 29

Reaping the benefits of virtuous deeds
And glowing brightly in the aura of righteousness
The image of him entered through her eyes
And etched itself in her heart.

The plane was cruising high up in the sky. In the seat next to Poorani, Mangaleswari was reading a book. Poorani wiped tears from her eyes. As she departed, Aravindan had called out to her with a smile, 'Whenever we climbed, you wanted to keep pace with me. Now, you are up there, and you have left me here below.' She tried to visualize the expression on his face as he said those words. As the plane took off, Aravindan's form on the tarmac grew smaller and disappeared from view.

But then, she had never had any difficulty in picturing his face clearly in her mind. Even when he disappeared from her physical sight, she could always see him. After all, the picture of him had entered through her eyes and been etched in her heart. She could vividly recollect the image of Aravindan's face as he stood on the tarmac at the foot of the steps of the plane, his smile like a row of pearls shimmering on a red velvet cloth.

'Aravindan! Your smile contains nectar. It is this nectar that has the power to drive progress in life. I gain inspiration from this precious image alone,' she whispered in her mind to his image. 'This image of Aravindan's smiling face empowers me to go out into the world courageously and win renown,' she thought to herself. Whenever she travelled by a rapid means of transport, she always felt a surge of self-confidence; noble ideas and thoughts would fill her mind. Like a child in a new dress, she would feel the urge to go everywhere and do everything here and now. Here she was, travelling in a plane for the very first time. No wonder, therefore, that these feelings were now increased twofold!

About Lanka and Jaffna in particular, Poorani had learnt a lot from her father. What he had told her about the illustrious people who hailed from that land was still fresh in her mind. He had talked to Poorani about Arumuga Navalar, Kumarasamy Pulavar, C.W. Damodaran Pillai, Kadirvel Pillai, Vipulanandar, Panditha Mani Ganesa Iyer and other such luminaries of Lanka who had helped the Tamil language to flourish and the Saivite religion to spread across the land. When she thought of the contributions of these 'uncrowned kings' of the Tamil language, she felt a thrill of awe and admiration. The very thought that she was heading towards a land where Tamil and Saivism were both intact and thriving in their traditional form gave her great joy and satisfaction.

After her mother's death, her father had confided to her several times, 'When I was a young man, I was determined to go and become a disciple of Swami Vipulananda and renounce the world. It was because of your mother that my wish remains unfulfilled.' Her father had a passionate desire to spread the message of Tamil language and culture throughout the world. Those who had not understood his feelings properly labelled his passion as madness. However, his passion had no madness in it. 'Poorani,' he would tell her often, 'the Tamil-speaking population is now a large family whose members are spread throughout the world. Just as a mother who bears many sons raises them and sends them one by one out into the world while she remains at home attaining greater divinity by the day, Mother Tamil too sends her children far and wide, into every corner of the world. Those who live far away from her are even closer to her in tradition and principles, with a better understanding of her greatness and virtue, than those who remain at home near her. In this matter, none other can be greater than Mother Tamil.'

Appa had strong ideas about developing a love for one's motherland and mother tongue. On many occasions, Poorani had heard her father talk with intense fervour about their importance. 'Those who do not feel passionate love for their motherland and language should be made to spend six months with either a native of Jaffna or a native of Bengal. Those without strong feelings of loyalty towards land and language can never be upholders of our great values and traditions.'

Poorani recalled many details about Jaffna, its Tamil-speaking people and their connections with Indian Tamils. The more she thought about it, the more she was reminded of her father's accomplishments and achievements as a Tamil scholar. She felt inspired. She sensed the familiar feeling of inner awakening, one that she felt quite often. The plane flew through the sky, carrying her to her destination. Everything and everyone was peaceful around her, a sense of deep satisfaction pervaded her. Her mind was urging her to strive for greater heights of attainment in thought, speech and action.

Poorani's serene state of mind continued as she flew towards Lanka dreaming big dreams.

Mangaleswari called for the flight attendant and asked her something in English. Poorani, who was deep in contemplation at the time, missed what she had said.

Mangaleswari told her, 'She says we will be landing in Lanka soon, Poorani!'

The plane started losing height gradually. It felt amazing to Poorani that they had covered such a great distance almost in the blink of an eye. 'I knew Jaffna and Tamil Nadu were close in language and culture, but I didn't realize that we are so close in a literal sense too,' she thought to herself.

When they landed, Poorani alighted from the plane, followed by Mangaleswari. She was elated at the thought of setting foot on the soil where Arumuga Navalar had lived and propagated the glory of the Tamil language and culture.

The organizers of the Tamil Literary Conference, who had invited Poorani as a speaker, were present at the airport to welcome her. Poorani was pleasantly surprised by the large number of people, all holding garlands, waiting to greet her on arrival. 'So many people have come!' she whispered. Mangaleswari said, 'Even if a much greater crowd had turned up, I would not have been surprised, Poorani. The people here are well known for their spontaneous warmth, respect and hospitality towards visitors. They could easily set up a school to teach the world these virtues! You just have to spend a day with them to understand what I mean.'

The convenor of the conference, Thiru Rajanaickam, and his wife, Kanakammal, came forward and welcomed them with warm smiles and joined palms in a traditional greeting. Mangaleswari knew this couple well from her life in Lanka earlier. She introduced Poorani to them and them to Poorani.

Kanakammal said affectionately to Mangaleswari, 'We are very happy that you were able to come too.'

It took about half an hour to complete the immigration formalities and exit the airport. Poorani was overwhelmed by the genuine warmth and affection she received from these people. The Rajanaickams and a large group of women had draped multiple garlands around her neck, so much so that she could barely lift her head. She noticed that the faces of the Tamil women of Jaffna had a kind of unforgettable quality, a unique, attractive aura. They crowded around her eagerly, as though they were in the presence of a special daughter of Mother Tamil. Cameramen from some of the Tamil newspapers that were published in Lanka took photographs of Poorani. Wherever her gaze turned, she was met with expressions of affection and admiration and gestures of welcome. Poorani's heart was full of joy.

The Rajanaickam couple took Poorani and Mangaleswari to their own home in their car. The warm welcome that they received at the house confirmed to Poorani the truth of Mangaleswari's earlier remark, that the people of Jaffna were famous for their hospitality.

The Tamil Conference was due to start the following morning and continue for three days. The preparations were every bit as grand as those for an important festival. A respected Tamil poet of Jaffna inaugurated the conference. The proceedings commenced with the lighting of the traditional *kuthuvilakku* on the stage and the chanting of *thevarams*. Poorani was very pleased to see that these traditions were being adhered to meticulously.

The tent at the venue was completely packed with people,

both men and women. Poorani noticed that in Jaffna, the women were equally interested in attending lectures. The poet who inaugurated the conference also introduced Poorani to the audience. He spoke admiringly about her father, Azhagiya Sittrambalam, and his impressive body of work, including publications and research. Poorani's heart swelled with pride at the thought that her father's reputation was so great, even so far away across the sea from his native land.

On the first day, Poorani delivered an excellent lecture on the theme 'Literary Sentiments'. She opened by saying, 'Most people tend to dismiss feelings as mere memories of events. But poets make word paintings out of them. When we experience joy, sorrow or longing in our lives, they remain mere feelings. When they appear in literature, they ascend to a higher level and transform into beautiful sentiments. Day-to-day feelings are like plain boiled milk; in time, they lose their freshness and are tossed away. But literary sentiments are like *thirattu paal*, which retain their sweetness and stand the test of time. Hence, feelings are the most important factor in a poet's profession.' Poorani went on to expand upon this theme. She gave examples; she struck a lighter note now and then with humorous stories; she quoted philosophical writings on the subject. At the end of one-and-a-half hours, the audience was still craving for more. 'Please don't stop!' urged Kanakammal, standing up from her front-row seat. 'Please speak for at least another half an hour.'

Poorani could not refuse such an earnest request.

On the second day of the conference, Poorani addressed the audience on the theme 'Literary Extracts from the Sangam Era', and on the third day, she spoke on 'Five Great Epics'. During each of her speeches, Poorani transported the audience back in time to the Tamil land of olden times.

While delivering the vote of thanks at the end of the final day of the conference, Rajanaickam said, 'We have not seen Avvaiyar. But long, long ago, Avvaiyar travelled to the Tamil regions, spreading the message of Tamil greatness and harmony. Today, this lady has taken on the mantle of an Avvaiyar and is a living example to remind us of those times.' As he said this, the audience responded with deafening applause. Poorani was presented a gold medal etched with the words 'Tamil Selvi', meaning 'the daughter of Mother Tamil'.

One of the famous poets in the audience was called up to the stage to present the medal to Poorani. As she accepted it with reverence and gratitude, thoughts of her father rose to her mind. In the presence of a large audience, on a brightly lit stage filled with the aroma of fresh flowers and incense sticks, the gold medal was placed in her hands. At that moment, in her mind, the medal transformed itself into a lamp with which she would walk amidst suffering humanity to dispel the darkness and liberate them.

That night, at the Rajanaickams' home, Mangaleswari performed a ritual to ward off the evil eye from Poorani. She asked Poorani to stand in a corner of a room; then she took fistfuls of salt and chillies and waved them in circles three times around Poorani's head before casting them into the kitchen fire.

'Why are you doing all this, Amma!' protested Poorani laughingly.

'The way you have been giving speeches over the past three days, I'm just making sure that any evil eye is kept away from you, my girl! I hope we will stay well and get back home safely. I threw so many chillies into the fire, but there is no odour, right? That means many have cast jealous eyes on you.' Mangaleswari spoke with an air of great conviction and came over to stroke Poorani's head affectionately.

The next day, Poorani gave a speech at the local Rotary Club meeting. The topic was 'Ancient Ethical Treatises and Modern Rules of Conduct'. She won great appreciation from the sophisticated and knowledgeable audience. Those who had listened to her over the past three days at the Tamil conference had witnessed her eloquence and the beauty she imparted to the Tamil language. Today, when they saw those same qualities on display again, when she spoke in English, they were lavish in their praise.

She said, 'Like trying to fit the wrong size of a pen cap, either too big or too small, onto a pen, the prescriptions in our ancient treatises do not fit into modern ways of life. We who live in Eastern lands have found purity in simplicity. Yet, with limited resources, we have got into the habit of craving the grand facilities that are available in the West. The ancient treatises tell us, "Ethics and righteousness are the tools for a good life." But money, power and dishonesty have become the tools for getting ahead in today's world.' Commencing thus, she expanded upon the theme. Mangaleswari had been bringing a tape recorder along to record Poorani's speeches, and she recorded this one as well. She planned to take them back home to Madurai and share them with the Women's Sangam members.

The next events on the agenda were a speech to the students at a women's college in Jaffna, followed by another at Vaideeswarar Vidyalaya on behalf of the Ramakrishna Mutt. They all travelled for *darshan* to the Thiru Ketheeswaram

Temple in Mannar and also to the temple at Nallur. Three days went by in visiting small towns and islands around Jaffna.

The Rajanaickams had made excellent arrangements for their sightseeing trips. They took a trip by motorboat from the port at Oorkaavalthurai to Nainativu Island. Rajanaickam had told them that, according to research scholars, the island had been historically known as Manipallavam. The unique surroundings of the island and its picturesque beaches captivated Poorani's senses. She imagined herself, in some previous birth, as an ascetic holding the *amudha surabhi* and walking, like Manimegalai, along these beach sands with the saintly image of Lord Buddha in her heart. When she thought of Manimegalai, she was momentarily gripped by an insane urge to be free of everyone else around her. She wanted to sit by herself on the sand, contemplate the calm sea and immerse herself in her own thoughts completely. She felt the intense aura of the glorious past in these surroundings, immeasurable and valuable beyond price.

After returning to Jaffna in the evening, they took leave of all their friends and acquaintances there and set out to visit Trincomallee, Anuradhapuram, Mattakalappu and other important tourist places of Lanka. This part of the trip took another five to six days, after which they returned to Colombo. In most of these places, Poorani had to speak at unscheduled events at just a moment's notice. She obliged every time by accepting each such request. Wherever she went, Poorani had never been able to refuse any request made with affection.

In Colombo, Mangaleswari had several friends. One of her friends had put a car at their disposal to go around and see places. On one of the days, they went to worship at the Kataragama

Buddhist Temple. As she stood in prayer at the temple, after a holy dip in the Manikka Gangai River nearby, Poorani was overcome with deep emotion and tears sprang to her eyes.

During the remaining days of their stay, Poorani delivered speeches at the Vivekananda Sabha and also at the Saiva Women's Sangam at Vellavattai, on the outskirts of Colombo. Poorani and Mangaleswari spent the next few days visiting the hill towns of Kandy, Nuwara Eliya, Navalapatti and Rathinapuram. Navalapatti was where Mangaleswari's husband had owned tea gardens. Poorani also spoke to some groups of tea garden workers in the area who belonged to poor Tamil families.

The Tamil-speaking students at the University of Kandy had made special arrangements to organize a speech by Poorani. Poorani was enchanted by the sight of the Navali Gangai River winding like a silver thread through the landscape and the spectacular hillside views. In Kandy, she had the opportunity to admire ancient Buddhist relics. Everywhere she went, Poorani felt overwhelmed by the spontaneous affection of the Tamil people. The local papers carried detailed reports of her speeches, along with photographs. When they returned to Colombo after their visit to the hill resorts, the Lanka radio station invited her and recorded two speeches.

Poorani reminded Mangaleswari that it was time to go back home to Madurai. 'We've been here for many days now, Amma. Aravindan and your son-in-law will be going around here and there trying to make the election campaign arrangements all by themselves. If we get back quickly, we can help them. Later, I also have to travel to Calcutta to participate in the Asian Women's Conference.'

'Oh, why did you ever take on this nuisance of an election? Aravindan is such a good man, but in this one matter he is so obstinate. I can't understand it. I had thought that after Meenakshisundaram passed away, this plan to involve you in the government would be abandoned. But now you say Aravindan has been forcing you to do this?'

'No, no, Amma! He does not like it either. When Meenakshisundaram told him about the plan and asked him to persuade me, Aravindan protested very firmly. But circumstances have changed now. It so happens that now he himself cannot abandon the plan and is committed to it.' Poorani went on to narrate the entire sequence of events leading up to the present point, including the roles of Burma Man and the Pudu Mandapam publisher.

They decided to take a flight back to India the following day. On the eve of their departure, they went shopping in Colombo. Mangaleswari bought a large selection of clothes for Poorani and her brothers and sister, as well as for her own daughters. When they emerged from one of the top Chettiar clothes shops in Colombo, Poorani paused at a watch shop nearby.

'Amma, I've heard that you can get excellent watches here in Lanka,' she said.

'Sure, if you would like something, we can get it. It would look pretty on your wrist. Come, I will get you a good one.'

'The watch is not for me…'

'Then for whom?' asked Mangaleswari in surprise, turning to look at Poorani's face. She noticed the shy expression and smile. Poorani said, 'Even though he is old enough, has a need for it and can afford to buy one, he goes about without a watch…'

'Oh! So, you want to buy a watch for Aravindan! Why do you feel shy to come right out and say so, Poorani? I will buy one for him and one for you as well! Please wear it.'

They stepped into the watch shop. Poorani tried her best to insist that they should buy a watch only for Aravindan and not for her. She said she did not need one. But Mangaleswari was determined. She not only bought a watch for Aravindan but also a smaller 'ladies' watch' for Poorani. She fastened it on Poorani's wrist right there and admired how it looked on her arm. Only then was the lady satisfied.

On the eve of their departure, the Tamil community of Colombo organized a lavish send-off dinner for them. The Rajanaickam couple also attended the event. The next day, a large crowd turned up at Colombo's Ratmalana International Airport to see them off. Poorani and Mangaleswari reluctantly took leave of their affectionate hosts and started their journey back. They were flying back to the Tamil motherland after a wonderful visit to her daughter, Lanka.

On the plane, Mangaleswari borrowed a newspaper from a Tamil gentleman. It was a four-day-old paper, published in Madurai. It had taken probably four days for the paper to get from Madurai to Lanka. But since neither of them had read any news from back home ever since they had arrived in Lanka, she knew that the contents of the paper would be news to her. She started reading the items under the title 'Madurai City News'. She was stunned when she read, 'Due to election campaign-related enmity, a young man has been kidnapped, and his whereabouts are not known. His friend has lodged a complaint with the police.' Mangaleswari's eyes widened in shock. 'Poorani, look at this! How can such a terrible thing happen?' She folded the paper in that section and handed it over to Poorani. As Poorani read it, her face darkened with fear, and the blood rushed to her head.

CHAPTER 30

Why does the dishonest man prosper and the honest one languish in poverty?
On this point let us ponder.
Amassing wealth by wrong means is like
Trying to store water in an unbaked mud pot.

– *Thirukkural*

The whole of Madurai city seemed to have taken on some extra energy. It was as if the people were preparing for a great battle. In the olden days, battles used to crop up now and then. There were wars like the Vellaatru War and the Thalayalanganam War, among others. But in recent times, there had been neither the opportunity nor the requisite valour for the government to engage in a war. In today's government, the 'civilized' battle of the ballot, without mud and blood, was the norm. The ancient wars featured leaders of the nation fighting at the battle front on behalf of their people. But now, a few people stood for election and the general population fought battles to determine who would win. There is no doubt that the modern version of election warfare involves plotting, deception and bribing of a kind far different in nature and greater in magnitude than conventional warfare ever did.

Just as close-up shots on a movie screen reveal every tiny

imperfection on the actor's face, the imperfections of those associated with the government became more and more clear to Aravindan's eye as the election date approached. The more he saw at close hand the petty thinking and worthless desires of these people, the more he grew disillusioned with the world. It seemed to him that humanity itself was turning into a laughing stock. At the same time, his upright nature and his belief in the innate goodness of people attempted to reassert itself, and his mind rejected his fears. If one cannot accept the reality of dishonesty and pettiness with a philosophical smile, and manage to work around these obstacles, even the brightness of day begins to seem dark.

As Aravindan embarked on the election campaign preparations with Muruganandam's help, he underwent several novel experiences. They had to work tirelessly day and night. Burma Man had set up several campaign offices for the Pudu Mandapam publisher, with bright lights and grand publicity. Poorani's election symbol was a lotus, whereas their opponent's symbol was a vulture.

The first clash between the two campaigns was about publicity posters on the city walls. In big cities like Madurai, it is generally inconvenient to stick wall posters during the busy daytime hours. So Aravindan had arranged a horse cart to leave at three in the morning to carry a load of posters and paste with Thirunavukkarasu and a few other helpers. The plan was to get as much of the city covered as possible and resume again the following night. Thirunavukkarasu was given the task of ensuring that the workmen did not slack off or disappear with the posters to sell them as wastepaper.

Except on the occasions when he stayed awake late into the

night, Aravindan was always up in the morning before dawn. He would finish his bath and morning ablutions and get into a fresh set of clothes. Then he would go into the front office and light a couple of incense sticks. In that calm, aromatic setting he would take out the pocket *Thirukkural*, which he always kept close at hand, and delve into it for a while. Inspired by the ideals in the *Kural*, he would take out his diary and his poetry notebook and proceed to write down any quotes, ideas or verses that occurred to him.

This early hour of the day gave him special joy. He was convinced that the hours between four thirty and seven in the morning were the ones that sowed happiness, pure thoughts and compassion in one's heart. Those were the hours when flowers spread out their petals and bloomed, when the sounds of temple bells and drums filled the air. A gentle cool breeze, with no hint of heat, wafts everywhere, as though to remind the world that it needs peace and harmony. Aravindan realized that the practice of waking up at dawn to start the day was an integral part of the self-discipline that had helped him to find a good path in life.

Although it was not yet close to dawn, Aravindan decided to start his day. He brushed his teeth, had a bath and read the *Kural* in the office room. When he raised his head and looked out through the window, he could see Poorani's election poster on the wall across the road in the early morning light. As he gazed at the lotus symbol on the poster, he thought to himself, 'I wonder which part of Lanka Poorani is visiting at this moment.' As he continued to gaze at the colourful image of the lotus on the poster, it transformed gradually in front of his eyes into the face of Poorani. She was smiling her beautiful smile. When he pictured her face, set with dark eyes like black jamun fruits, a line of verse sprang to his mind. He wrote it down at once: 'Jamun fruits set on whitening paste finely ground and spread, embedded on the face of the moon.' When this line jumped, fully formed, into his consciousness, Aravindan focused his mind on his poetic creativity in order to complete the poem. His mind was totally absorbed in other-worldly thoughts.

Just then, the horse cartman who had transported the posters entered the room in a state of total agitation. '*Ayya*, those rascals beat him up and ran away!' Aravindan's attention was restored to reality, far away from the realm of poetry. Aravindan rushed out into the street and looked into the back of the cart that stood there. Thirunavukkarasu lay curled up inside, injured and only half-conscious. No posters, no ladder, no paste. All the contents of the cart were gone.

The cartman continued to talk, and his words came out in a rush.

'*Ayya*, we had halted at a place near the Vaigai Bridge, and our workers stuck a poster on the wall. Just then, a group of fellows carrying the vulture posters arrived, pretending it was just a coincidence. They stuck their poster exactly on top of ours, hiding it totally. So Thirunavukkarasu and our fellows protested. "If you want to stick a poster here, stick it next to ours and not on top of it. It is unfair to hide our poster like this." Those fellows threatened us. They said, "Don't try to talk about justice with us. Just shut up and run away if you want to escape a beating." They started beating up our workers. Unable to stand that torture, they ran away. Thirunavukkarasu *thambi* stayed and confronted them.

'But they were a band of hooligans. They thrashed him

mercilessly and took away all the materials from the cart. When I got in their way, I also received a few blows. The whole city has gone to the dogs, *Ayya*. There is no hope for honest people.' Despite his gentle nature and his policy of not hurting anyone, Aravindan's blood boiled when he heard the cartman's story. His nerves were twitching with the instinct to go out at once and take some action. But he cautioned himself that a lack of self-control would only lead to a failure of all his plans.

He pulled himself together and, with the help of the cartman, lifted Thirunavukkarasu out of the cart, moved him into the office room and laid him down. The process of giving first aid to Thirunavukkarasu, arousing him to full consciousness and dressing his multiple wounds took a whole hour. By then, the day had set in, and the street was beginning to buzz with activity. Aravindan had requested the cartman to wait. He asked him, 'Can you identify any of those who attacked you?' The cartman could describe one of them accurately. From his description, it was clear that the rowdy man was none other than the one at Burma Man's home who had been ordered to thrash Aravindan. Aravindan seethed with fury.

He thought to himself, 'Who does this Burma Man think he is? Does evil have no limit? How much can a person be expected to tolerate? How long can his evil plots help him to flourish in his arrogance and pride? Is it not like trying to store water in an unbaked mud pot? I shall confront him courageously. I shall ask him, "What do you hope to accomplish by doing all this? Do you think that if you set your thugs upon us or browbeat us, we will cringe away in fear? Do you think we will cancel Poorani's candidature and allow your candidate to run unopposed in the election? Don't even dream of such a thing. Even without all the gaudy advertising you are doing, we can win on the strength of truth alone. At least, from now on, stop these criminal acts and play fair." While righteous people are falling deeper into poverty, why is it that this evil man's wealth continues to grow and his wicked plans continue to prosper?'

Aravindan's expression altered suddenly, as though he had arrived at an important decision. He asked one of the workmen to look after the printing shop and set out. 'Will you take me to the Burma Man's estate?' he asked the cartman.

'It will take a long time to go all that way and get back...' the cartman pointed out reluctantly. 'Never mind! Let's get started,' urged Aravindan, climbing into the cart. They set off for Burma Man's house.

That day happened to be the birthday of Mangaleswari's younger daughter, Chellam. Vasantha and Muruganandam came to the printing shop, hoping to take Aravindan to Mangaleswari's home for a special lunch that had been arranged. It was already past eleven o'clock, but Aravindan had not yet returned. The previous night, Muruganandam had been with Aravindan at the printing press till midnight and had told him about the lunch plan the next day. Now he wondered to himself, 'Where could Aravindan have gone when he knew this plan? Surely, he could not have forgotten about it?' The workman who had been left in charge of the shop told Muruganandam that Thirunavukkarasu was lying wounded in an inside room. The moment Muruganandam saw Thirunavukkarasu's condition, his body covered with plaster and bandages, he had a very good idea of what must have happened. His suspicion was confirmed by Thirunavukkarasu himself.

Muruganandam turned to his wife and said, 'Vasantha,

go home. There has been some kind of incident here. When Aravindan returns, I will bring him along for lunch.' Vasantha left, and Muruganandam sat down to wait. He recalled their conversation from the previous night and how he had told Aravindan, 'I will stay here tonight, supervise the poster-sticking operations and then leave in the morning.' Aravindan had bluntly refused. 'That kind of thing would have been all right before you got married. There have been times when you would finish a public speech late at night and then, when the crowd had dispersed, you would just spread a cloth on that very same stage, go to sleep and emerge the next morning rubbing your eyes. Forget all that now! Get home like a good husband. Don't make Vasantha angry.' How he regretted having obeyed his friend last night!

'Because those young lads were sent to do the job, the rowdy fellows were able to beat them up and take away the ladder, paste and posters. If I'd been there, those "vulture poster" fellows would have learnt the lesson they deserve. I'd have twisted off their arms and sent them packing.'

The clock struck noon. There was still no sign of Aravindan. Vasantha sent Sambandan, Mangaiyarkarasi and Chellam to find out what was happening. 'Akka told us to come and call you and Aravindan mama for lunch,' they said. 'After Aravindan gets back, we will come. Go home now. Don't wait for us. Eat earlier if you are hungry.'

Around one o'clock, the horse cart arrived at the front door of the printing shop. It was their usual horse cart and the same familiar cartman. Muruganandam rushed out excitedly to meet Aravindan.

What a disappointment! The cart was empty. The cartman

looked as if he had experienced a frightening nightmare. '*Ayya*! He got down from the cart at nine o'clock. He asked me to wait. He said he would be back in ten minutes. I waited till eleven thirty, but he didn't return. I got a bit suspicious because, when he got down from the cart and went into the house, he was in a very angry mood. I was very uneasy about that large garden and that huge house standing in the middle, like a haunted mansion. I was nervous when I went in and asked a person there, "The gentleman who came in the cart has not come back yet. He told me to wait for him. I want to know if I should wait longer or go away." That man said, "No one came. Go away now." At the door, I saw a bulky fellow. He looked like the one who came with the other fellows and beat up Thirunavukkarasu and our poster stickers last night.'

As the cartman related what had happened, Muruganandam's face darkened with fury. The muscles on his arm bulged, the tendons on his wrist grew rigid and his fists clenched, as though he would like to land a couple of hefty blows on someone. 'Oho! Is that so? That Burma Man fellow has dared to do this, has he? I will see to that!' exclaimed Muruganandam, accompanying the declaration by punching his own left arm forcefully with his right fist. Just then, Vasantha arrived at the printing press in a car. Her expression was like thunder. 'Are you two ever going to come for lunch or not?' she demanded, assuming that Aravindan was there.

Muruganandam's foul mood spilled over onto Vasantha. He spoke to her harshly. 'There are more important things to think about now than lunch. Just go back home!' She turned and left without a word. Muruganandam hurried to his tailoring shop. He knew many of those who went to the wrestling training schools in Ponnagaram, Azhagaradi and neighbouring areas. These fighters were always ready to help Muruganandam whenever he asked them.

Muruganandam sent one of his trusted shop assistants on an errand to recruit a bunch of them. He knew, of course, that Aravindan was opposed to physical violence of any kind, but when that philosopher of peace had himself been trapped in the snare of those deceitful villains, what other alternative was left? At that moment, Muruganandam's own preferred philosophy was topmost in his mind, namely, 'It is not possible to exercise mercy and non-violence always; where one is shown mercy, one must also show mercy, but where there is none, only a slap on the face will work.' He was convinced that Aravindan was caught in the clutches of Burma Man. He also knew that Burma Man would not hesitate to hide Aravindan in a cage somewhere until after the election was over. After all, the history of the government was full of examples of such evil plots.

By about three in the afternoon, a group of five or six fellows, all built like mud wrestlers, had assembled at Muruganandam's tailoring shop. 'Who has dared to lay a finger on our man? Tell us, and we will make a "bone tooth powder" out of them!' declared the burliest of the group, flexing his muscular arm. Muruganandam gathered them around and told them the details of what had happened.

As he was talking to them, an elderly man walked up the steps of the shop. He was wearing a loose jibba and had a cloth bag slung on his shoulder. On the centre of the bag, displayed behind clear plastic, was an identity tag – 'R.S. Pandian, Reporter, Dinachudar'. Spotting Muruganandam, the man started speaking, his diction somewhat slurred by the betel nut juice in his mouth. He said, 'What's the matter, Muruganandam? It's more than a week since I left some material here to stitch a new jibba, but your men have not yet got around to getting the job done. After you got married, seeing you is as rare as seeing a fig tree in flower!'

Muruganandam welcomed him. 'Please come in, sir. Your jibba will be ready by six o'clock this evening.'

'I'm rather scared to enter, Appa! You seem to have assembled a group of wrestlers to conduct some kind of wrestling conference!'

'No, no, there is nothing for you to be afraid of, sir. Please come in and sit down. We are talking about something that you should also hear about.' Reporter Pandian delved into his bag, extracted a wad of betel leaves and stuffed them into his mouth before seating himself next to Muruganandam. He listened to the whole story.

Muruganandam ended with a passionate declaration. 'I'm not going to let them get away with it, sir. I'm going to teach them a lesson that they will never forget.' Reporter Pandian laughed. 'Come, Muruganandam, let us have a couple of words in private.' The reporter took Muruganandam's hand and led him to a far corner of the shop.

'Don't be silly, Muruganandam! Your plan is like grabbing the animal's tail instead of holding the leash. What do you hope to accomplish? Whatever violent act has made Burma Man the criminal and the accused in this case is the very same one you want to inflict upon him in retaliation! How can justice be on your side if you also indulge in that same criminal activity?

When big and powerful people do deceitful things, they manage to do them away from the eyes of the police. But you will get caught if you just go in blindly and try to beat them up. Then the reputations of Aravindan and Poorani will also be damaged. Those who habitually indulge in harmful deeds will get away with their vengeful actions without any publicity. You and others like you stay away from such activities as a rule. If you suddenly do something violent, it will become a big story everywhere. It will be reported in newspapers, and Burma Man will use that to spread negative publicity about you all. Don't do anything that will cause even a whisper of suspicion about the uprightness of Aravindan and the pure reputation of Poorani. At this stage, even the smallest blot can affect Poorani's election chances. I will suggest a plan for getting Aravindan released. Do it my way.'

'What do you suggest?'

'You know that I am in charge of collecting news for the "Madurai News" section of my newspaper. A quarter of the space in that section is yet to be filled. Go to the police and lodge a 'Missing Person' complaint. Then send me a write-up about having filed a complaint. People like Burma Man will always try to avoid any negative news about themselves in the media. They are more worried about that than about any threats of physical violence. Beating and punching are things they can tackle well, without any problems. So, Burma Man will do anything to avoid getting mentioned in the news in such a manner. The very next day after the 'Missing Person' news appears in my paper, Aravindan will return as a free man. Take my word for it. Even in that quarter space available in my column, I will make a prominent announcement out of it.'

Muruganandam saw merit in the older man's suggestion, and he decided to go along with it. But that night, the old problem surfaced again.

CHAPTER 31

The world is my town and its people my kinsmen
Good and evil comes not from others.
Pain and respite emanate from within;
Neither death is new nor life.
We rejoice in the balmy breeze of felicity
and patiently bear adversity.

– *Purananooru*

It was three in the morning, and the streets of Madurai were deserted. Except for the occasional lorry or other vehicle going by, the roads were silent. However, the lights were still on at Meenakshi Printing House. Two horse carts waited outside the front door. Posters, paste and a ladder were loaded into one of the carts; Muruganandam also got into that cart. His wrestler friends climbed into the other cart. Muruganandam had given instructions that the carts should go to the same spot where Thirunavukkarasu and his helpers had been set upon and assaulted by Burma Man's henchmen. Muruganandam's first instinct had been to collect his burly wrestler friends, confront Burma Man and somehow get Aravindan released – through argument, threats or physical violence. But his close friend, Pandian the reporter, had made him abandon that course of action. Yet he needed to know if the enemy was going to continue opposing the sticking of posters. And that was why he was setting out that early in the morning towards the same spot that had witnessed a violent incident the previous night.

When they approached the spot, Muruganandam ordered that the cart with the wrestler gang in it should park in a side street, close at hand but out of sight. He proceeded on his own in the other cart towards the wall where the posters were to be stuck. This was the street on which Burma Man's burly bodyguard and the other hired thugs lived. The street was silent. Muruganandam asked the cartman to stop near a pool of light from a street lamp. He took down the ladder and propped it against the wall. He gave the cartman the job of applying paste to the back of a poster and handing it up to him.

Without any hindrance, Muruganandam put up five of the posters with Poorani's symbol of the lotus. As he was about to stick the sixth poster, there came a shout, '*Dei*, who is there on the ladder? Go and push him off the ladder and break his leg!' A gang of ruffians had arrived in force. Muruganandam replied calmly, 'Hold on while I finish sticking this poster. After that, you can break my leg.' He proceeded to finish the job and then pursed his lips and sent out a shrill whistle. Hardly had the sound of that whistle died out in the still night air than a horse cart rushed around the bend of the road.

What happened thereafter need not be chronicled here. The vulture symbol band of thugs were given a thorough beating, and they fled for their lives. One of them was caught in Muruganandam's clasp. At that crucial moment, Muruganandam forgot the advice given by his mentor Pandian, the reporter, that any aggressive act by him would reflect poorly on Aravindan and Poorani. Muruganandam proceeded to thrash and torture the remaining gang member for a whole hour, from four o'clock up to five. In the course of that ordeal, the fellow revealed a secret.

Pandian's strategy had been to publicize Aravindan's abduction in his newspaper, thereby forcing Burma Man's hand and making him release Aravindan. But now, with the secret revealed by the captured thug, it appeared that Aravindan could be released even before the newspaper hit the stands in the morning.

On the bank of the Vaigai at Chellur, on Thiruvaipudayar Temple Street, there was a building that the Pudu Mandapam publisher was using as a warehouse to stock his materials. It was a large two-storeyed building that belonged to him. Since the premises of his publishing shop in the city were small, he was using this building to store a large quantity of old and new books. It was situated in a location far removed from the bustle of human activity. It served not only as a warehouse for the books he published, but also as a 'stock house' of evidence of the various criminal deeds he had indulged in. The thugs whom Muruganandam had captured and thrashed had revealed that the Pudu Mandapam publisher had brought Aravindan away in the same car in which he had visited Burma Man and had locked the prisoner in a room in the building.

Muruganandam did not take the man's story at face value. He told him, 'You come along with me and show me the place where they have hidden him. If you are cheating me, I will flay you alive!'

Along with their captive, the two horse carts set off directly for Chellur. Since the spot where the fist fight had taken place was not far from their destination, they arrived fairly soon. The captured thug pointed out the house. It was like a haunted mansion looming out of the surrounding darkness. There was neither sight nor sound of anyone. A large padlock hung on the front door.

'*Enda*, have you been telling us the truth? Or is this a hoax?' Muruganandam asked his prisoner threateningly. The man swore that this was where Aravindan was locked up. So they got the door open by smashing the hasp of the lock. The man led the way into the dark house. Many electric light fittings were around, but none of the switches worked. It seemed that someone had disconnected the main electric supply. They could walk only single file because books and typeset blocks for the books were piled on either side from floor to ceiling. Rats scampered around as if they were welcome visitors in a childless house.

It was an old-style house with a central courtyard surrounded by rooms. The company walked along in silence with the prisoner leading the way. Muruganandam borrowed a flashlight from one of his men. At the foot of a flight of wooden steps leading to an upper floor, their guide stopped and pointed to a door, which was also locked with a padlock on the outside as the front door had been. This door too received the same treatment and was forced open.

The man had been telling the truth. Inside that room, on a couple of old newspapers on the floor, Aravindan lay sprawled, his head resting on a folded arm. They were all shocked at the pathetic sight that met their eyes in the glow of the flashlight. Muruganandam hurried over and tried to rouse him gently. One of his men remarked, 'They seem to have starved him, those rascals! He didn't wake up even at the sound of the lock being smashed.'

Aravindan opened his eyes and sat up. He was dazed. He could not comprehend what was happening and why so many people had suddenly turned up there. Muruganandam gave him a hurried summary of what had led them there. 'We must get out of here immediately. It will soon be dawn, and daylight will set in. Let us get back to the printing shop fast. If we don't move this minute, we will be in danger.'

Aravindan still had the energy to make a joke. He said with a smile, 'What you are doing is very unfair, Muruganandam. Some people have brought me here carefully and hidden me away. Now you are taking me away without even giving them due notice!' His handsome face, which habitually wore a pleasant expression and glowed with life, was now tired and faded. Although he tried to make some light conversation with the men, his fatigue was very evident.

The two carts arrived back at the printing shop in the early morning light. At the front of the betel shop nearby, the headline of that day's newspaper had been hung as an advertising poster: 'Young man abducted due to election rivalry'. Muruganandam bought a copy of the *Dinachudar* newspaper. Pandian, the reporter, had kept his promise. Under 'Madurai News', he had prominently carried the news of Aravindan's kidnapping. Muruganandam read it out to Aravindan.

Aravindan continued to tease his friend. 'Well, you could call Reporter Pandian and ask him to carry a fresh announcement in tomorrow's paper: "Young man rescued".' Muruganandam took his wrestler friends from Azhagaradi and Ponnagaram to a hotel for tiffin and coffee before sending them home with warm thanks.

Muruganandam was aware, to some extent, of what

Aravindan had been subjected to after he had been kidnapped. The thug he had caught and thrashed the previous night had revealed some of the happenings. Burma Man and the Pudu Mandapam publisher had inflicted pain on Aravindan for several hours before driving him in their car to the warehouse from which Muruganandam had later rescued him. Yet Aravindan, being someone who did not talk about himself much, had said very little about the details of his experience at the hands of these enemies. Muruganandam understood his friend's nature well. He also realized that Aravindan's present light-hearted banter was a cover for his deeper emotions. He was trying to deny his recent memories and forget them.

Aravindan had always been like this. When it came to helping others with their problems, he would keep questioning them for details to figure out ways in which he could ease their worries. He would empathize with them and devise ways to help them. But his own worries and problems, he preferred to keep to himself. Even probing questions would elicit only casual, smiling responses. Muruganandam had often told Aravindan, 'You know, you're such a tough-hearted fellow!' Like a miser who hoards money but does not like to spend it, Aravindan hoarded all his misery, problems and worries, without being able to share them with anyone. On the other hand, he would invite everyone to participate in his joys and successes. This had been his nature from childhood.

Muruganandam told Aravindan to stay at the printing shop while he finished an errand and returned. Aravindan's mind was brimming with recent memories. He had gone to Burma Man's home calmly and peacefully to argue for justice after Thirunavukkarasu and the poster stickers had been beaten up. But those two had subjected him to all kinds of torture. 'Is there no justice or decency left in this world?' he mourned inwardly. Those fellows had imprisoned him and called in their henchmen to inflict more pain on him. He could not bring himself to describe those details to anyone, but they smouldered within him like hot embers. He relived those memories in agony. He despaired at the general lack of morality in present-day society.

'The operations of government organizations are no different from those of criminal gangs. Is this the same Tamil land, where a poet once wrote, "The world is my town and its people my kinsmen. Good and evil come not from others; pain and respite emanate from within. Neither death is new nor life. We rejoice in the balmy breeze of felicity and patiently bear adversity."

'In a land, that once nourished such noble thoughts, is this what we have come to now? How much jealousy, how much hatred, how much pleasure people get in ruining others! Instead of governing in such a manner as to promote tradition, culture and ethics, governments are leading people down crooked paths. If it is at all possible, we must ensure that Poorani wins the election even without elaborate advertisements and passionate speeches. We need to teach evil-doers a lesson. More important than speaking and writing is to demonstrate one's values through living them. That is the only way to reform others and bring them to a righteous path. In fact, even the idea of printing posters to advertise her candidature was an incorrect decision. If she too had to go the same way as others, that is, boast about herself and her achievements publicly on the walls in order to be elected, then where is the satisfaction in that? How is she different? Those who will not offer even a single meal of *kanji* to a poor person or part with the smallest amount of money to help out a school suddenly find they can spend several lakhs, without a second thought on trying to win an election. Have the noble sentiments of finding fulfilment even in a condition of poverty, and of taking pride in following the path of honesty, disappeared from this land when Gandhi died?'

Having arrived at this point in his train of thought, Aravindan rose with an air of determination. He collected all the wall posters that had been printed for Poorani's campaign, took them to the backyard and threw them into the open.

About fifteen minutes later, Muruganandam returned to the printing shop. Aravindan was not in the front office. Smoke was billowing from somewhere in the rear of the building. When Muruganandam reached the backyard and saw Aravindan in the act of setting fire to the whole heap of advertising posters, he received the shock of his life!

'What is this, Aravindan! Have you gone mad? Just think how much we have spent to make these. Why are you burning them now?'

'Poorani's special quality is not in these posters. She needs to win on the strength of truth and righteousness alone. Through Poorani's approach to this election, we must show the people the true meaning of good character and righteousness. We don't need advertisement posters for that.'

'What utter stupidity!'

'Maybe so. But after the Mahatma, there is no one in this land who has ventured to think this way. That is why society is going to the dogs.'

'Whatever may be one's ideals, one has to conform to practical reality, Aravindan. The fact is that an election cannot be won without publicity and advertisements. There is no point in even standing as a candidate without that.'

'The very fact that we are living our lives honestly, truthfully, righteously – that is enough of an advertisement for us, Muruganandam!'

'It's all very well to talk. But without understanding what works in the real world, all the talk is of no use.'

'Go to the front office, Muruganandam. I will take a bath and then join you,' said Aravindan. He took off his jibba. Muruganandam got a glimpse of his friend's back. He was aghast! Across that attractive back, with its healthy golden colour, were two ugly, deep red welts that were beginning to darken.

'What… what are these?' asked Muruganandam, touching the injuries gently. His voice trembled with rage.

Aravindan replied calmly. 'Oh, nothing much, my friend. They are whiplashes. These are the prizes I got for seeking justice from an important man.'

Muruganandam's eyes reddened, his blood boiled in his veins. His lips twitched as though struggling to find words to express his outrage.

At that moment, Reporter Pandian stepped into the room looking very worried.

CHAPTER 32

When boundless wealth is afflicted with a disease
It collapses into an unrecognisable form;
When one goes searching for a treatment in the medical books, one finds
That misery is the only medicine available.

The reporter, Pandian, had tension written all over his face. When he caught sight of Aravindan, he summoned up a forced smile. He greeted Aravindan and made kind enquiries. After a brief chat, Aravindan excused himself to go and take a bath, leaving the other two men together in the front office. Muruganandam had not yet recovered from the sight of the painful, ugly scars that now marred Aravindan's back, as if someone had put two deep black scratches on a golden plate. He was seething with fury.

Pandian opened the conversation by saying, 'Despite all the advice I gave you about avoiding violence, you went ahead and did something very wrong, Appa!'

'What do you mean, Pandian?'

'Just read this news and you will understand. A little while ago, Burma Man and the Pudu Mandapam publisher arrived in a car at our newspaper office and gave this to our editor for publication. Our editor has doubts about whether this news is true or not, but he is hesitating to defy the wealthy Burma Man.'

Pandian handed over four or five closely typewritten pages to Muruganandam. The latter started reading with concentration. The complaint was from the Pudu Mandapam publisher. The story was that Poorani's poster crew had torn up the rival's posters on the walls and had stuck their own lotus symbol posters over them, totally hiding them. When the Pudu Mandapam man's crew had gone there to protest, Poorani's people had thrashed them mercilessly. Among the culprits named in the complaint, Muruganandam's name was typed in bold letters. It went on to say that Aravindan had come storming into Burma Man's house and ranted and raved and behaved very insultingly. The following day, it claimed, Poorani's gang had gone to a warehouse where the Pudu Mandapam publisher stocked precious books and other valuable items. The gang had broken open the locks of the warehouse by force and stolen many of the materials from there.

When Muruganandam finished reading this story and handed it back to Pandian, the expression on his face revealed his inner fury.

'Are you going to publish this word for word?' he asked Pandian.

'What can I do in this matter, Appa? Yesterday, did I not publish the news "Young man abducted due to election rivalry", relying entirely on your word for it? I knew you were telling the truth, and I myself suggested that method of solving the problem. Now, I know that what I am holding in my hand is an utter lie. Yet I am helpless to do anything about it. We are newspaper people. We belong to all the people. I have to obey my editor. My editor has to please all the big people in the city. All those big people are doing their best to please Burma Man out of fear. The daily newspaper is like the local pond. There is no guarantee that the water in the pond will be clean and pure. It is precisely because of this kind of danger that I warned you yesterday to restrain yourself and not to indulge in any violent acts of revenge.'

'Yes, you told me to stay calm, Pandian. But those fellows did not allow me to stay calm!' He described the entire series of events of the previous night to the reporter, starting from the poster sticking and up to the rescue of Aravindan. He also described the severe whip scars he had seen on Aravindan's back.

'We are well aware of all the dishonest and violent actions they are indulging in! But till the general public can be made to realize what is happening, we have to proceed very cautiously. Right now, Poorani is out of the country visiting Lanka. If this gets published, her reputation will also be tarnished. Those who had thought of Aravindan as a peaceful, non-violent man will begin to have doubts. And as for you...'

'Yes, I suppose everyone already knows that I am a violent ruffian! Why do you hesitate to say it, Pandian? Go ahead. After all, I would also like to know what kind of reputation I have in the eyes of people! I am supporting Poorani and Aravindan in this election campaign. It is Burma Man's calculation that if he can throw me into jail on some pretext for six months or so till the election is over, he will be free of my interference. Otherwise, why would he have made up this story that I went there with a gang and robbed his warehouse, when in reality, all I did was rescue my friend whom he had locked up there?'

'Calm down, Muruganandam! There is a way to ensure that this evil plot by Burma Man does not succeed. It is not as if they are the only ones who can send items to the newspaper. You also have an equal right to do it. You are a trade union leader and have earned the respect of the working class. You should write a detailed account of what happened – how they abducted Aravindan and how you had to rescue him from that Chellur warehouse. I will take your version of the events to them and suggest that I intend to run it in the paper along with the other one. Then they will probably telephone my editor and say there is no need to run either of the pieces and that they are willing to let the matter drop.'

'What if things don't turn out the way you expect? What if your editor is so keen on being in Burma Man's good books that he runs their version alone?'

'He will not. Leave that part to me. I will convince him.'

Aravindan's footsteps could be heard approaching from inside the building. Muruganandam hurriedly told Pandian in a low voice to avoid the subject altogether in Aravindan's presence, since he was already traumatized by it.

Aravindan came into the front office looking refreshed after his bath and sat down with the others.

'When is Poorani expected back from Lanka?' Pandian asked Aravindan.

'Very soon. In another two or three days, she will return.'

'Whatever happens, you both should not be worried or disheartened, Aravindan,' advised Pandian. 'These kinds of incidents are quite common during the time leading up to an election. If Poorani makes just three or four public speeches after she gets back, her victory is assured.'

'If the people believe in truth and justice, let them elect Poorani. But she will not go around clamouring from public platforms, "Elect me" or "Vote for me" like a child begging for sweets. Within a few days of her return from Lanka, she will have to travel to Calcutta for the East Asian Women's Conference. After her return from Calcutta, she has to visit Malaya for a few weeks. She does not have the time and money to spend on this election campaign as if it is some kind of commercial trade. I also do not wish to conduct the campaign like that.'

'What you say is very idealistic, but the rival candidate has money, men and a willingness to play dirty,' Pandian pointed out.

But this argument made no impact on Aravindan. Instead, he said vehemently, 'In a society that strives for the development of good human values and ethics, there should be absolutely no role for wealth. Just as the poverty of millions is a curse on the country, so too is the concentration of wealth in a few hands. If a person's body is equally well nourished all over, we say he is healthy. But if most parts of the body are starved of flesh, while there are lumps of excess flesh here and there, it is a case of tumours, a disease. These pockets of great wealth that we see here and there are like tumours on the poor body of our nation. Bodily diseases can be cured with medicines. But there is no treatment prescribed in any medical book for these tumours of wealth. Poverty, though it is also a disease in itself, is the only cure for the ugly tumours in society. Till a cure is found for these serious ills of society, political scheming will rule unchecked.'

After a while, Pandian left along with Muruganandam, and Aravindan settled down to work. Pandian took Muruganandam to the *Dinachudar* newspaper office. He asked Muruganandam to write a detailed report about how Aravindan had been abducted, harassed, tortured and imprisoned in the warehouse. Pandian took this handwritten report to his editor.

The editor was at a loss to decide which of the two totally contradictory reports on his table was the truthful one. Pandian told his boss, 'Sir, the report given by Burma Man and the Pudu Mandapam man seems to be a web of lies. The report stating that they abducted Aravindan, ill-treated him and locked him up is the truthful description of what happened. By now, the whole town is aware of it. If we publish the report of those two fellows, we will lose our credibility with the public. It is best to avoid this matter altogether. Let us not print either of the reports. Please call those men on the telephone and tell them about this other report you have just received from Muruganandam. They themselves will tell you not to publish either of them.'

That is exactly what happened! Pandian turned out to be right in his estimate. When the editor called Burma Man and told him about having received a contradictory report, Burma Man said, 'Our report, their report… don't print either of them. Don't breathe a word about this whole incident.'

Muruganandam thanked the editor and Pandian and set off for home.

Poorani and Mangaleswari, meanwhile, were on a plane from Colombo to Madras. Their plan was to take an overnight train from Madras to Madurai, arriving in the city the following morning. When they happened to see the news of Aravindan's abduction in a four-day-old newspaper on the plane, both were agitated and very fearful of what this could mean. Poorani's anguished face displayed her state of mind. She looked as if she would burst into tears at any moment.

Mangaleswari said, 'Politics is becoming murkier by the day, Poorani. If one disagrees with another person's ideas, one should oppose them only with one's own ideas. But here, we are seeing an instance of someone countering ideas with sheer brute force.'

'The fault is entirely mine, Amma. I should have said a firm no to the idea of this election. It was due to the tensions associated with the election that Meenakshisundaram sir died. It was due to this rivalry that the competing printing press sprang up next door to Meenakshi Press. And it is because of the elections that Aravindan has now been kidnapped. Who knows what other miseries await us!'

'Don't worry, Poorani. Aravindan will not come to any harm. God will watch over such a noble soul and guard him. When we land in Madras, we will place a long-distance call to Madurai and ask for the details. The news in this paper is four days old. It is possible that Aravindan has already been rescued. My son-in-law would not have taken even a second's rest in trying to get his friend freed. By now, he would have somehow found a way to rescue Aravindan.'

Before they left Colombo, Mangaleswari had sent a message to her relatives about their travel plans. When the plane landed at Meenambakkam Airport in Madras, Mangaleswari's relatives were waiting for them with a car. After completing the arrival formalities at the airport, they headed towards the house of the relatives. They had a telephone in their house, and Mangaleswari tried to place an urgent call from that phone to the one in her Madurai home.

Poorani stood nearby in a state of great tension, waiting to hear the news. The telephone connection with Madurai was established after about fifteen minutes. Vasantha picked up the phone at the other end. Mangaleswari told her about what she and Poorani had read on the plane and asked about the latest developments. Vasantha's reply brought a relieved smile to Mangaleswari's face. Poorani's hopes soared when she saw Mangaleswari smiling.

After a short while, Vasantha told her mother, 'Amma, your son-in-law is right here. Why don't you talk to him directly and get the whole picture?' She handed the phone to Muruganandam. The latter gave his mother-in-law a brief outline of the events. 'You will be here in Madurai tomorrow morning. We will have a detailed discussion then. Aravindan and I will be at the station to receive you when your train, the Thiruvananthapuram Express, arrives. So shall I put down the phone now?'

'Wait, wait! Poorani is standing beside me, and she has been very worried. If I tell her Aravindan has been released and is safe, she may not believe me! Please just tell her yourself.'

Poorani took the phone receiver from Mangaleswari's hand. She heard Muruganandam's voice. 'Greetings, Akka! I hope you had a good and comfortable time in Lanka. Here, Vasantha is becoming a tyrant. After we got married, she is controlling me all the time. I have lost all my freedom.' Hardly had Muruganandam finished saying this with a laugh, when Vasantha grabbed the phone and assured Poorani in a voice full of shy embarrassment, 'Don't believe him, Akka. That is a lie. He is just teasing me.' Muruganandam signed off the conversation by reiterating, 'Aravindan is well. There is no need for you to worry. We will both meet you at the station in the morning.' For the first time in hours, Poorani felt as if a burden had been lifted from her chest.

Mangaleswari's relatives in Madras lived in the Mylapore area. After being reassured that Aravindan had returned home safe, Poorani went to the Kapaleeswarar Temple nearby and offered a prayer of gratitude at the shrine of Karpagambal. That evening, they boarded the Thiruvanathapuram Express heading towards Madurai. During the journey, Mangaleswari gave Poorani many examples of the state of matters in politics and government and the kinds of dishonest dealings that had become common.

'Today, in our country, there is no human progress. Arts such as poetry and painting are not flourishing. There is no attempt to discard outdated ideas and traditions and awaken society. Like a person who has been stung by a scorpion and is therefore incapable of thinking of anything other than the pain, in today's society, everyone, from the smallest child at school to the toothless grandfather, cares only about politics, politics, politics! It is like a disease – like filariasis that makes the lower leg swell like an elephant's leg. People just accept it as fate and go along with it.'

Poorani listened closely to the older woman's description of the state of affairs in society. They went to sleep only after the train had crossed Villupuram.

The next morning, the train arrived at Madurai station on time. The platform was crowded with members of the Women's Sangam, who had assembled to welcome Poorani home from her travels. Vasantha had arranged for this warm reception after she had heard about their plans the previous day over the telephone. The platform, teeming with women, looked like a garden with multicoloured flowers. Aravindan, Muruganandam and the reporter, Pandian, were also there.

The moment she alighted from the train, Poorani's eyes looked for Aravindan – his face, his smile, that was like nectar to her soul. Her eyes and heart opened to soak in that heart-warming vision. But Vasantha and the crowd of women rushed forward with garlands in their hands and hid Aravindan from her view. However, Aravindan had already seen Poorani as she stepped out of the train. It seemed to him that her face now reflected a new nobility, a deeper beauty. A person who has gone through the experience of being honoured by hundreds of people is bound to develop a special glow. 'This explains Poorani's new beauty,' thought Aravindan. The sight of her pure, glowing face, framed by the halo of hair in disarray around her head and ears after the overnight journey, brought a feeling of joy to Aravindan's heart.

Poorani and Mangaleswari excused themselves from the welcoming party and came over to where Aravindan and the others stood waiting. Mangaleswari told Aravindan, 'When we read the news on the plane about your abduction, we were so agitated. Our minds were in turmoil…'

Poorani just stood and gazed at Aravindan's face. She could think of nothing to say. Muruganandam cut in to say, 'Why talk about all that here at the station? Let's go home.' Mangaleswari's car was waiting outside, and they all got in and set off for her house. At her house on Thanappa Mudali Street, they chatted for a while and caught up on news from one another. Later, Poorani and Mangaleswari went to Meenakshi Press to meet Thirunavukkarasu, who was still bedridden, recuperating from the injuries he had received at the hands of Burma Man's thugs.

Vasantha had arranged for a grand celebratory feast at her mother's home. After lunch, Chellam set up a tape recorder in the central courtyard of the house and started playing the recordings of Poorani's speeches in Lanka. Aravindan, Muruganandam and Vasantha sat and listened closely. Poorani was upstairs at that time. In a short while, Mangaiyarkarasi came up to Aravindan and told him, 'Akka sent me to bring you. She wants to talk to you privately.' She led Aravindan upstairs. Poorani was in the front veranda. She was hiding something in her hands, behind her back.

'You sent for me?' asked Aravindan, smiling. She smiled in response and said, 'Please hold out your hand'.

'Why?'

'Just do it. I will tell you,' said Poorani.

He held out his hand. On the wrist of his gold-complexioned arm, she fastened the watch that Mangaleswari had bought for Aravindan in Lanka on her request. 'I have tied Time to your hand and made it run!' she remarked jokingly.

'Wrong, Poorani! We are mere humans. We are the ones who run according to what Time dictates,' he said gently as he gazed into her glowing face.

CHAPTER 33

It is unworthy to be in awe of those who live in pomp and wealth
And even more unworthy to show contempt towards the lesser ones.
This world is full of suffering and woe;
But those who understand it can find its beauty.

– *Puranaanooru*

For a whole week after her return to Madurai, Poorani had no leisure time at all. Felicitation functions and parties filled the days. She spoke a few times at the Women's Sangam about her experiences in Lanka. On a Monday evening, she went along with Mangaleswari and the others to Thirupparankundram Temple. After offering prayers at the *sannadhi* of the deity, they visited Odhuvar *thatha*'s home and chatted with the family for a while. The old *patti* asked the same question she had been asking Poorani, again and again, but this time, she put the question to Mangaleswari.

'I've been telling this girl, but she doesn't listen to me. Shouldn't you at least remind her that it is wise to get married at the appropriate time? It's not as if she is very young now. I wonder what secret thoughts she is hiding from the world. Even if she is silent about it, surely, the rest of you should bring it up and talk about it.'

'Everything will happen as it is meant to, *Patti*. The right time will come,' responded Mangaleswari tactfully, without entering into further conversation on the subject. From there, they went to the home of Poorani's friend, Kamala, and stayed talking there for some time. Kamala had given birth to a daughter just a few days earlier. Kamala's mother, brimming with joy and pride at the birth of her granddaughter, welcomed the visitors with flowers and a silver platter piled with sugar.

The women went into the inner room, where Kamala had given birth to her baby. She lay in bed, radiant in her new motherhood. Alongside lay the child, like a small pile of soft golden *champak* flowers. Poorani felt an aura of great purity and beauty in that room, unmatched by anything else in the world. With hair in disarray, dark circles under her eyes and that indescribable essence of motherhood, Kamala lay exhausted on the bed like a divine idol that has come alive and is resting.

'Come, Poorani! Sit down. I heard that you have been touring Lanka. Did you have a comfortable trip?' asked Kamala affectionately. Poorani chatted with her for a while.

'I'll have to leave now, Kamala. Next week, I am going to Calcutta. After I get back, I will visit you again. Look after yourself.'

As Poorani got up to leave, Kamala remarked in a light-hearted manner, 'Good for you! You will go to Calcutta; you will go to America. After all, you are not like the rest of us. I heard you are even going to stand for election. May you win and become a minister in the government! When all those things happen, don't forget us, Amma!'

Kamala spoke the words in a casual manner. Yet somehow, to Poorani's ears, they did not sound like a joke. Those remarks agitated her mind and settled deep in her consciousness. For a moment, the thought crossed her mind, 'By doing the things I am doing these days, which are different from what "ordinary women" do, I know I am stirring pride in many hearts. But perhaps I am stirring some jealousy too?'

People who rise in life and attain high levels, even if they are totally pure in character and purpose, are invariably viewed with a kind of suspicion by those below, merely because of the differences in status. Poorani became acutely aware of this truth now. The whole of society seemed to be geared towards the single purpose of two lives uniting to create a new life. Getting married and having children was the cardinal goal, and society expected it and pushed people towards it.

She had to reluctantly admit to herself that at Odhuvar *thatha*'s house, and again here at Kamala's home, everyone who saw her, spoke to her or thought about her had this single thought in their minds. She had been yearning to live an exalted life of service, but an inner voice cautioned her on many occasions, 'Don't have such lofty dreams. You must live the way others do. That is the right thing to do. That is the tradition.' Yet Aravindan had told Mangaleswari, 'There is no hurry now for us to enter into a relationship of bodies. Let us live a little longer with a relationship of our minds.'

But what about her own thoughts? Her mind dwelt upon all the Tamil people, men and women, young and old, who were lost in poverty and darkness and were seeking a way towards the light. She would be that light, leading them to a better life. When this image blossomed in the highest levels of her mind, like the rare *kurinji* flower, her eyes welled with emotion. There was a touch of divinity in that mission. It was something she could experience only within herself but could not convey to others. What could one call such an emotion?

That day, at Thirupparankundram, in the minutes following Kamala's parting words, all these intense thoughts and feelings tumbled through Poorani's mind.

When she had left her rented home to travel to Lanka, she had left the key with Kamala's mother. She opened her house, which had been locked up for quite a long while. Mangaleswari had been urging Poorani to give up the rented house and move in with her. 'What's the point of locking up a house and paying rent for it? Just pack up all your things and move in with me. My house is large enough, and I can let you and your family have the whole of the upstairs.' Poorani had told her, 'We'll decide later. There's no hurry to take that decision right now.'

Her brother, Sambandan, and sister, Mangaiyarkarasi, had been living in Mangaleswari amma's house and going to school from there along with Chellam and had become a part of Mangaleswari's family. The other brother, Thirunavukkarasu, was staying at the press with Aravindan. It was only after considering all these facts that Mangaleswari had made the suggestion. 'What's the point of staying here all by yourself, my child? Our two families have grown close and have become like a single family. Why not live together in the same house? What's wrong with my wishing for that?' the older lady had suggested more than once. Yet Poorani had not given her a positive response.

That evening it was past eight o'clock when they started their trip back to Madurai from Thirupparankundram. As they were leaving, Poorani cast a yearning backward glance at the town through the rear window of the car. The large blue sign, of 'OM' shimmered and smiled up on the hill. At the sight of the familiar town, with its hill and its lighted sign, Poorani was filled with nostalgia. After all, wasn't this beautiful setting the one that had brought joy and fulfilment to her father and nurtured his scholarly thoughts and writings? Wasn't this where he had raised and educated her, his eldest daughter? Thoughts of the past and present came and went rapidly. She heaved a sigh. That night, Poorani tossed and turned sleeplessly for hours as conflicting thoughts racked her mind.

Whether in Thirupparankundram, with its narrow roads, or in Madurai, with its broad streets, whether with people she had long known or with new acquaintances, she had noticed that in recent times, people had started treating her with a kind of awe. She also realized that the more her reputation and adulation grew, with her public speeches, growing popularity, foreign travel and aspiring for elected office, the more she herself had subconsciously started withdrawing from common people because of her own self-image of her stature in society.

The more wealth, fame or popularity a person acquires, the more others view him with awe. But they hesitate to bestow their love on such a person. Attracting respect born out of awe, rather than one born out of love, seemed unworthy to her. Whoever she met these days talked to her only about the election and government. She had begun to wish that someone, sometime, would abandon these topics and talk to her about matters that were closer to their hearts.

The talk around her was either about elections and politics or about her marriage. If at least sleep would come, she could bury all these thoughts for a while. But it was not sleep that came to her eyes but the images of people and more people.

Aravindan's philosophy was, 'The life lived in the mind is eternal. Let us live a little longer within the relationship of our minds.' But Odhuvar *thatha*'s wife, Kamala's mother and Mangaleswari herself held a completely different view. 'This talk of a relationship of minds is impractical in the real world. You should conform to what is expected by society and accept it.' Her sleepless eyes were seeing two different images with two different messages. At long last, in sheer exhaustion, she fell asleep. And in that sleep of exhaustion, she had a dream.

She was standing on the peak of a massive mountain, so tall that it touched the clouds that clustered like bundles of cotton wool. She herself was clad in a fine, white muslin cloth, as though spun out of that same cloudy cotton wool. All around, as far as the eye could see, the mountain was covered with a carpet of fresh blue blossoms and the scent of nectar. There was a teasing memory at the back of her mind. She had seen flowers like these somewhere before. Looking down from that height, the earth below was just a tiny ball, devoid of all life forms. She longed to gather bundles of light in her hands and strew them on that lifeless earth below, as one would strew flowers. She quickly gathered flowers made of light. As she straightened up and prepared to strew those flowers of light downwards, golden rays of light emerged from the tips of her ten fingers. More such miraculous events occurred on that mountaintop. Some were connected and some were not.

When she woke up, Poorani found her pillow wet with tears. Tears had dried on her face but were still glistening in her eyes. She realized that she had wept as she dreamt.

The next few days were taken up with preparations for her forthcoming trip to Calcutta, and her mind found some relief from the earlier emotional turmoil. As for the election, Aravindan had completely given up all campaigning activity, except to inform people that 'Poorani is also a candidate'. He had extracted a promise from Muruganandam that no promotional activity of any kind would be undertaken. While keeping his promise to Aravindan, Muruganandam had nevertheless arranged for meetings to be held here and there on Poorani's behalf, as though sponsored by members of the public themselves. These meetings, to endorse Poorani's candidature, were held without any pomp or show. On the other hand, Burma Man and the Pudu Mandapam publisher were spending money lavishly on all kinds of publicity.

It was decided that Mangaleswari would accompany Poorani on the Calcutta trip. On the morning before they were due to depart, an earth-shaking event occurred in Aravindan's life. It was a new plot by Burma Man. True to his calm nature, Aravindan decided to take it in his stride cheerfully. Yet, he was deeply wounded by the event. It agitated his mind and dampened his spirits.

That morning, as usual, the press had started its operations. Out of the money Aravindan had brought back from his village after his uncle's funeral, he had spent only a small portion on early preparations for the election. The rest of it had been used to close outstanding debts and buy new printing machines. If he had not taken those steps, the business would have slid into bankruptcy. Aravindan was tallying the accounts in the front office.

A messenger arrived from Meenakshisundaram's house to say the lady of the house wanted to meet Aravindan. 'Amma asked me to come and bring you back with me,' he said.

Aravindan assumed that the lady would probably want to consult him about her daughter's marriage plans or the son's further education. If not either of these topics, then it could be to advise him to get married quickly! But he was confronted with something totally different when he arrived at her house.

Her two sons-in-law, one from Tiruchirappalli and the other from Tirunelveli, were there. This was the first time he was meeting the two men after Meenakshisundaram's funeral.

'Oh, how are you? It looks like both *mappillai*s have jointly decided to visit!' remarked Aravindan in a light tone. He was taken aback to find that their response was not cordial. The old lady hovered near the inner doorway. Aravindan turned towards her and asked, 'What is it, Amma? You sent for me?' Her face was lacking its usual cheerfulness, and she fumbled for a response.

'It seems to me that you are all troubled in your minds about something. I will go and come back some other time,' offered Aravindan, turning around and preparing to leave.

'No, no! Sit down, *Thambi*. I need to talk to you. That is why I sent for you.'

Aravindan sat. The lady started speaking hesitantly. 'My sons-in-law have given up their jobs and come here. They want to take over the press. They have plans to bring in a lot of improvements and grow the business. They have found some investors who are willing to put up the money to buy new equipment.'

The sons-in-law had been silent up to that point. Now the older one remarked harshly, 'Is that a press you are running? It's more like a hostel, where you and your friends are living and meeting and chatting. You printed posters for the election campaign of some Tamil pundit's daughter. You are doing whatever takes your fancy. Is this the kind of managing that our father-in-law had in mind for the press?' The younger son-in-law added his own insult. 'It isn't some property that is lying unclaimed that you can just take away.'

The old lady stood silent in the doorway with her head bowed. A fierce rage flared in Aravindan's mind. Bitter words rushed to the tip of his tongue. As a last resort, he turned towards the old lady and addressed her directly. 'Amma…'

She cut him short. 'There's nothing you can say, and there is nothing I can say.' She turned abruptly and disappeared into the house.

Aravindan realized that someone had deliberately planted this idea in the minds of the two sons-in-law. He had a very good idea of who that culprit was. But what could be done? What could have happened to make that generous, large-hearted lady change her attitude so completely that she would not even listen to him? He could have repaid rudeness with rudeness and spoken harshly to the two sons-in-law, but he did not. Being a person who, by nature, neither held the wealthy in awe nor the poor in contempt, he was incapable of ranting and raving. He had no desire to ignite violence by stoking the fire. The poet who wrote thousands of years ago, 'Evil is this world, Amma,' was so right, thought Aravindan. If he came across him now, he would reward his wisdom by offering him a mouthful of sugar!

What Aravindan did was this. He went inside, laid the keys of the printing press at the feet of Meenakshisundaram's widow, took leave of her and left quietly. His mind went back to that time in his life when he had left his uncle's home as a young boy, a homeless orphan wandering on the railway track. He had told no one about his ordeal.

Now too, he did not reveal this momentous downturn in his fortunes to anyone. He went about as usual, putting on a cheerful face for the outside world. That evening, he accompanied Poorani and Mangaleswari to Madras, and the next evening, he saw them off on the Howrah Mail from Central Station. He returned to Madurai. He had not breathed a word about this momentous happening even to Poorani and Muruganandam.

CHAPTER 34

My stubbornly stony heart melted
My thoughts churned and quickened
My mind was in suspended animation
As true love bubbled and brimmed over

– Ramalinga Adigal

When Aravindan returned to Madurai after seeing Poorani and Mangaleswari off to Calcutta, he experienced deep distress and a feeling of abandonment that he had never encountered in his life earlier. Not even in his wildest dreams had he imagined that his life would be somewhere other than in that press, nor could he have imagined that he would be forcefully separated from it. But what difference would it have made whether he had imagined such a situation or not? It had happened out of the blue. Could it ever have been possible if Meenakshisundaram had been alive?

How quickly people change their opinions based on rumours. How swiftly they become ungrateful and distant. Aravindan thought of all the personal sacrifices he had made to keep the press running and profitable, how he had worked tirelessly, even forgoing sleep on many nights. His heart ached at the injustice of it all. He had worked for Meenakshisundaram even more sincerely and tirelessly than his own son would have done. Did all the goodwill, gratitude and appreciation earned by his actions die when the old man died? Had they all been forgotten?

If Poorani and Mangaleswari had known about this bombshell on the eve of their departure for Calcutta, they would have cancelled their journey. Such was the enormity of this tragedy. He took some satisfaction from having successfully hidden his misery from them so that they could undertake their journey as planned. It was only after he had laid the keys to the printing house at Meenakshisundaram's widow's feet and taken leave of her, only after he had stepped out of the house with no home to go to except the sky overhead and the ground beneath his feet, that he had travelled to Madras with the two ladies and seen them off at the station.

He had tried his utmost to appear normal, but Poorani had been quick to detect that something was wrong. She had remarked, 'Your face seems rather drawn and tired. You look ill. You shouldn't have troubled yourself to come with us all the way to Madras. We would have managed on our own.' Aravindan had been striving to emulate that ideal being, Lord Rama. In the Ramayana written by Kamban in Tamil, Rama is described as one who 'whether asked to be an upholder of truth and justice or to abandon all royal comforts and go to the forest, always retained the serene countenance of a lotus in bloom'. Aravindan remembered reading the verse as a child. But despite his best efforts to hide his pain, Poorani had noticed. He had somehow managed to keep the truth from her till she was safely on her way to Calcutta.

On the morning of his return to Madurai, he went to the printing shop to collect his belongings. As Aravindan was leaving with his bedding and clothes, Thirunavukkarasu took some of the luggage from him and decided to accompany him. When Aravindan tried to dissuade him, the boy explained, 'They settled my dues up to yesterday and asked me to leave. So, there's nothing more for me here either.' Aravindan had hoped to leave the printing shop with his possessions quietly and discreetly without attracting any attention.

But that was not to be. Why did Vasantha and Muruganandam choose that exact moment to arrive at the entrance in a car? Muruganandam greeted him cheerfully. 'What's all this, Aravindan? Planning a trip out of town? We thought we would come and meet you here today because we knew you had gone to see Poorani off at Madras. But now it looks as if you yourself are setting off somewhere?'

'Muruganandam, this is not a journey to another town. This is my journey to a new life!' responded Aravindan with a smile. After all, his favourite book, *Thirukkural*, contained this exact advice, 'Meet adversity with a smile.' Yet he himself doubted that the smile he attempted would seem genuine.

'I don't understand, Aravindan. Explain what you mean.'

Aravindan could no longer hide the truth from his friend after this direct question. 'How should I explain what happened? Should I describe it chapter and verse? It is like this – I have handed over Meenakshi Printing House to Meenakshisundaram sir's two sons-in-law. I have nothing further to do with this place. I am on my way to find lodging for this boy Thirunavukkarasu and myself. I thought we could stay for a few days at Mangammal Chathram or some other similar shelter and then look for a house.'

'What an ungrateful and unjust world this is!' fumed

Muruganandam. Never had he imagined that Aravindan would have to face such a situation.

Vasantha stepped forward and said firmly. 'There is no need for you to go to any *chathram*. What about our home? All the rooms upstairs are empty. You both should come and stay with us. As it is, Amma has been urging Poorani to give up her rented house in Thirupparankundram and move in with us. If we let you go and stay elsewhere after knowing what has happened, Amma will be very upset. She will be angry. You should definitely not go anywhere but our home.'

Vasantha took some of the bags and boxes from Aravindan and Thirunavukkarasu and started loading them into the car. Muruganandam spoke frankly to his friend. 'Whatever it may be, Aravindan, your instinct to forgive everyone for everything should not extend this far! By being so gentle and forgiving, you have actually encouraged people to do you harm. "If one has the capacity to sting, he is a scorpion. If not, he is just a grasshopper." That is how the world views people. At least once in a while, you should sting like a scorpion.'

'But what is it that I should take revenge for? Is there some great enmity that has suddenly come about? The lady sent for me. She told me her sons-in-law wished to take over the printing business, and that they had investments lined up to make it large and successful. I said I was happy to hear it and that I wished them well. I handed over the keys to the place at once and left. That was the end of the story.'

'No, Aravindan, you must not take this at face value and dismiss it so lightly. I tell you, someone has been scheming to ruin you. You are hiding something from me. But I will ferret out the truth somehow and identify the person behind this plot.

By this evening, I will have the culprit's name for you. I am declaring this very confidently. If I fail, you can take me to task. Despite all your efforts to behave as usual, your face cannot hide the torment you are experiencing in your mind.'

Aravindan spoke calmly in an effort to soothe his friend's anger. 'Nothing of the kind, Muruganandam! It is best that you let this matter rest, right here and now. Let it go.' Despite his protests about staying at their home, Vasantha and Muruganandam would not give in. They took him and Thirunavukkarasu in their car to Mangaleswari's house on Thanappa Mudali Street.

Once they were home, Muruganandam continued his conversation where he had left off. 'Aravindan, I must say you were remarkably successful in hiding such a great calamity from me, as well as from Poorani, for such a long time. You even went with them to Madras to see them off, and yet you never breathed a single word about this matter to any of us!'

Turning to Thirunavukkarasu, he patted the boy on the back and encouraged him. 'Don't worry. I will see to it that you get a job in another printing shop. If that doesn't work out, you can join me at my tailoring shop. There is no shortage of work that needs to be done. I will train you in tailoring and also pay you ten rupees more than you were getting at Meenakshi Press.' Muruganandam could never bear to see someone close to him going through any kind of hardship.

Vasantha made arrangements in one of the rooms upstairs for Aravindan to stay in comfort. It was a bedroom with an attached bathroom. 'Please feel free to think of this as your home, *Anna*,' she told Aravindan affectionately. 'After all, you are familiar with the house already. There are books on the shelves.' Respectfully and kindly, Vasantha settled him in, making sure he had everything he might need.

'You are both taking so much trouble for my sake. How can I ever return this favour? I was thinking of going to my village and spending some time there.'

Vasantha and Muruganandam shot down his suggestion. 'No, you are not to go anywhere. You need rest right now. You have gone through a lot of mental agony. Till Akka gets back from Calcutta, you must not stir out!' With coffee, snacks and tasty meals, Vasantha lavished attention on Aravindan.

That night, when Muruganandam returned home after locking up his tailoring shop, he had news for Aravindan.

'I made enquiries and found out the truth. It was all the doing of Burma Man. It seems he knows the owners of the companies in Tiruchirappalli and Thirunelveli, where the sons-in-law were working. He arranged with them to dismiss the sons-in-law from their jobs. At the same time, he asked another friend of his to approach the two of them and offer to invest a lot of money if they would take over the printing press. He is pure evil, Aravindan. I heard that his men have been keeping tabs on all your movements. They know about your trip to Madras to see the ladies off to Calcutta, and they know about everything that happened after you returned, right up to the fact that you are here now. This is the kind of evil scheming that ensures victory in elections these days! You expect to be victorious by sticking to your high principles of ethics and righteousness. It doesn't work any longer. Nowadays, you have to scheme to survive.'

To Aravindan, his friend's news was only proof of what he had suspected all along – that Burma Man must have been a part of the plot. All doubts were put to rest by what occurred that night in that house after ten o'clock.

Aravindan was in the room upstairs that Vasantha had arranged for his stay. He was feverishly scribbling in his diary his thoughts and feelings about recent events. The time was fifteen minutes past ten, and the rest of the household was asleep downstairs. The night light glowed blue. The telephone started ringing downstairs. Aravindan let it ring for a while, thinking someone downstairs would wake up and answer it. But everyone there was fast asleep.

The telephone continued to ring. Aravindan walked downstairs and picked up the telephone receiver. His intention was to find out whom the caller wished to speak to and then go and wake that person. He was startled when the voice at the other end asked, 'May I talk to Mr Aravindan?' 'Why? I am Aravindan, who are you?' he replied. 'Just a moment,' said the voice and handed the phone to someone else. The next moment, Burma Man's gravelly voice came over the line. 'It is me, *Thambi*. I think you can recognize my voice. Even now, I have not lost trust in you. It isn't the end of the road for you. There is still a week left to withdraw your candidate's election application. If you are able to persuade that young woman to withdraw from the elections, Meenakshisundaram's sons-in-law will hand back the printing shop to you and go away. In addition, I will give you whatever else you want. I will arrange a special plane at my own cost for your candidate to fly back from Calcutta to withdraw her application. Please—'

'There is no question of a "please". My answer is a no,' said Aravindan curtly and put down the receiver. As he went back upstairs, he pictured in his mind how Burma Man's face must look at this moment. It would be fierce and dark with rage. Aravindan wondered, 'I had stopped all kinds of advertisements for Poorani's campaign. There have been no speeches and no promotional events. Meanwhile, he has spent a fortune on publicity of all kinds. So, why is he pleading with me? Why is he afraid of me? Why is he threatening me? Could it be that his lies are a sign of panic in the light of my truth?'

Aravindan was unaware that Muruganandam had arranged informal public meetings and events through well-wishers throughout the constituency to support Poorani. For the next two or three days, Aravindan did not stir out of Mangaleswari's house. He stayed in his room, reading and writing. He listened repeatedly on the tape recorder, to Poorani's speeches in Lanka. Her voice had a soothing effect on his troubled mind. He read and re-read Professor Azhagiya Sittrambalam's books with the utmost concentration. Whenever he felt low, he reminded himself of Poorani's face and smile. He revelled in her attractive voice as it spoke deep truths.

One speech particularly, the one Poorani had delivered at the Saiva Women's Organization, touched him deeply. Every time he listened to Poorani narrating the story in that speech, Aravindan would find himself moved to tears. It was the story from the Puranas about how, at Thiruvarur Temple, the *Paravai Naachiyar* looked at Sundaramurthy Nayanar and fell in love with him. Poorani was describing the divine nature of the love that *Paravai Naachiyar* felt towards the Lord. In describing this 'divine love', her honeyed voice sang a verse written by Ramalinga Vallalar, 'My stubbornly stony heart melted…' and ended with the line, 'As true love bubbled and brimmed over.' As he listened to the recording again and again, he thought he could detect Poorani's own heart brimming with a similar emotion as she sang that verse. He suspected that maybe at that moment during the speech, her thoughts had been about him, Aravindan. He never grew tired of listening to it repeatedly. As her melodious voice hit a high note on the last line, it was as if she had distilled her deepest feelings for him in that line and was calling out to him; and every time, his eyes brimmed with tears.

Because he had listened to those recordings so many times, Aravindan had almost memorized Poorani's Lanka speeches. The more he appreciated the power of her speeches, the more he felt that he himself had been consigned to the depths, while she had risen to heights he could never hope to aspire to. When he listened to her voice, 'true love brimmed over' in his own heart. He found himself reaching for his diary and writing his thoughts.

> *Poorani, you are like the* kurinji *flower. You have bloomed at such a great height that you cannot be plucked; so lofty, that your aroma cannot be savoured. Unlike other flowers that bloom at ground level in all seasons, you bloom on mountain slopes where human hands cannot reach, and that too, only very rarely. A* kurinji *flower is meant to be admired, to be worshipped. How can one pluck and take it? Is it right for someone so far below, like me, to reach up to where you are and try to pluck you? Is that even possible?'*

When Poorani and Mangaleswari reached Calcutta, they called to inform the family that they had arrived safely. When the telephone rang, Aravindan happened to be nearby. Vasantha took the call. 'Shall I tell them your news, *Anna*?' she asked quietly. 'Why don't you talk to them yourself?' Aravindan refused. 'Don't tell them all these things and worry them when they are so far away and have important things to do,' he told Vasantha. 'Just tell them all are well and end the conversation. There's no need for me to talk to them.'

No other suitable job could be found for Poorani's brother, Thirunavukkarasu, so Muruganandam took him into his tailoring shop as an apprentice. After four or five days of staying confined to his room, Aravindan started venturing out. He plunged into social service activities, which had always been his passion. The burden on his mind eased as he tried to ease the burden of others. Many families were too poor to get their daughters married. In Maninagar, the Poor Girls Marriage Aid Sangam was helping such families with money and resources. Aravindan helped to raise money for that good cause. Along with some friends, he explored the possibility of helping the orphaned pavement dwellers near the bus stand and the rail station. He persuaded his friend, a municipal councillor, to get a resolution passed in the council that steps should be taken urgently to help poor women, children and penniless families. He was also keen to arrange evening classes on *Thirukkural* for the children of the factory workers in Ponnagaram.

All the while, Muruganandam had been arranging unofficial meetings to promote Poorani as a candidate in the forthcoming election. This activity was taking up so much of his spare time that he was spending very little time with Aravindan during those days. When Aravindan asked, 'What are you busy with, Muruganandam? I hardly see you these days,' Muruganandam told him he was extra busy trying to improve business for his tailoring shop. Indeed, he was working feverishly, doing everything he could to ensure the defeat of Burma Man's candidate and Poorani's victory. He had vowed to discredit all of Burma Man's lies, to smear tar on his evil face.

Within three or four days of her arrival in Calcutta, Poorani had written an airmail letter to Aravindan. It was delivered at Meenakshi Printing House, and one of the workmen brought it over and gave it to Muruganandam. Since Aravindan was away in his native village that day, Muruganandam was able to give Poorani's letter to him only after he returned the following evening.

The moment he opened the envelope, the scent of *champak* flowers wafted out and filled the air. Within the folds of the letter of six or seven pages lay two *champak* flowers, pressed and dried, with their petals crumbling. Aravindan felt a thrill, as if Poorni herself had appeared before him in person with fragrant *champak* flowers tucked in her hair. He picked up the pieces of the flattened, crumbling flowers, pressed them lovingly to his eyes and put them carefully into his pocket. He then unfolded the letter and started reading.

To my dear one,

Greetings from Poorani. I had wanted to write a long letter like this to you even from Lanka, but never found the leisure to do so. Now, I have the time. I want to share all my new and wonderful experiences with you.

When you opened the envelope, you would have enjoyed the aroma of your beloved champak *flowers. Yesterday, at a meeting here, they honoured me with a garland of* champak *flowers.* Appappa*! What a fragrance! I wished I could just pick it up and run straight up to your table to lay it in front of you. I wished I could watch your face as you looked at it and smelt its aroma. I have taken just two flowers out* *of the garland and placed them in this letter, accepting with regret that I could not put in the whole garland!*

I am now sitting and writing this on the grassy bank of the Hooghly River, just north of the Ramakrishna Mutt in Belur. Nearby, Mangaleswari amma is sitting and writing a letter to her daughter. In the far distance, across the river, I can see the Dakshineswar Kali Temple, and beyond it the sprawling city of Calcutta, looking like a faded photograph from this distance. I've never seen a city as large as Calcutta. And what a beautiful city it is!

Just when Aravindan had reached this part of the letter, he heard Vasantha calling him from downstairs.

'*Anna*, someone is asking for you on the telephone.'

Aravindan folded the letter, put it into his pocket and went downstairs. He picked up the receiver that Vasantha had laid on the table.

'This is my last warning,' came the hated gravelly voice of Burma Man. 'Tomorrow is the deadline for withdrawing that young woman's candidature. Just get it done. Don't push me to do my worst. I am warning you. I have a very short temper.'

Aravindan slammed down the telephone receiver and cut off the call abruptly. His face reddened with fury. Vasantha asked, 'What is it, *Anna*? Who was that? Was it a nuisance call?'

'No, just some other bit of bother,' mumbled Aravindan vaguely, trying to cover it up.

At that moment, Muruganandam entered the house. The moment he spotted Aravindan, he said, 'Come upstairs. I want to share something with you in private.'

This abrupt statement from his friend made Aravindan uneasy.

CHAPTER 35

You spurned my body but entered my soul
And became one with my senses.

– Manikkavachagar

Muruganandam took Aravindan upstairs to talk to him in private. He told him earnestly, 'Look, Aravindan, I know that what I am about to say will not seem very important to you. But I feel it is my duty to talk to you and caution you. If not for your own sake, please pay attention to this matter for the sake of Poorani and the rest of us.'

'Tell me what this is about, *pa*. You make it sound very serious.'

'It's just this, Aravindan. Till the election is over, don't go wandering around outside at all hours by yourself. It is not safe. Our rivals in the election are not decent people. They are going around with all kinds of evil plots.'

Aravindan looked calmly into his friend's face and smiled.

Muruganandam told him sternly, 'This is no laughing matter, Aravindan. I hear all kinds of disturbing rumours. It is only after proper investigation that I am now asking you to be careful. Don't treat this matter lightly.'

Aravindan did not respond. He toyed with the idea of telling Muruganandam about the two times that Burma Man had telephoned him and warned him to withdraw Poorani from the election. But he decided not to do so. His friend was hot-headed and might stir up trouble if he heard about those calls.

When Muruganandam left the room, Aravindan pulled Poorani's letter out of his pocket and started reading again where he had paused earlier. Like taking a dip in a cool mountain spring after sweltering in the heat, Poorani's letter soothed Aravindan's senses after the discomfort caused by Muruganandam's words of caution and the distaste aroused by memories of those phone calls from Burma Man. Poorani had drawn word images of the sights and sounds of Calcutta. It wasn't only the scent of *champak* that rose from the pages; there was also the aroma of fresh ideas and warm emotions.

Aravindan, when I realize that I am writing this letter to you while seated on the soil of the great land of Bengal, I am filled with indescribable joy. This is the land that has produced great poets, writers, philosophers and warriors. I have travelled often to Bengal in my imagination. Whenever I read Tagore's poetry in all its melancholy beauty, or revelled in Saratchandra's novels, so full of noble sentiments and settings, I have travelled here. Whenever I steeped myself in the luminous wisdom of the teachings of Ramakrishna and Vivekananda, or when I read of the fearless valour of Subhash Chandra Bose, I have felt a thrill at the thought of the proud legacy of Bengal. But all travels in the mind through the world of books are merely dreams. It is only now when I am actually here that I can fully take in its beauty and grandeur.

Aravindan, spending these past few days here, at the serene setting of the Ramakrishna Mutt, and interacting with the representatives of many countries has brought an immense feeling of fulfilment to my mind. You always said that you wanted a share in any great experience of mine. It is only to give you a generous share of it that I am writing this long letter. If you had accompanied us here to Calcutta, I would have been so happy. But then, you are tied up all the time with the printing shop, my election campaign, your social work for the poor girls' wedding fund organization and so on. You are not able to stir from there because you have so much pending work piled up.

In the villages of Bengal, one can sense the all-enveloping silence that encompasses everything and everyone; it spells profound peace. Pools filled with water lilies, fertile green fields, thick groves of trees and tiled-roof huts built on stilts, these are the sights of Bengal's villages. I could sense the throbbing pulse of Bengali life in its villages. I notice that Bengalis too have ancient traditions, just like we in the Tamil land do. I am able to see for myself what our Bharatiyar meant when he wrote, 'From the excess water from the rivers of Bengal, we shall farm the deserts.' The Bengali men, with their majestic gait, clad in their traditional-style dhotis and full-sleeved jibbas; and the women with golden earrings swinging from their ears, bright vermilion marks in their hair partings and elegantly clad in attractive saris display the typical local customs and culture. I feel great pride in my Bengali sisters.

Yesterday evening, Mangaleswari amma and I went around Calcutta city along with a few other visitors from other countries. Even though you were not with me in person, Aravindan, you were in my mind and in my eyes wherever we went in this large city. Along with me, you too saw those same sights, felt those same feelings and marvelled at them as I did.

The Hooghly divides Calcutta into two parts. On one side are Howrah and Belur, where the Ramakrishna Mutt is situated. The massive bridge that links Howrah to Calcutta makes me gasp with amazement each time. We visited the Dakshineshwar Kali Temple. Inside the temple, they have preserved the room in which Ramakrishna Paramahamsa stayed when he was a pujari at the temple. All his personal items and artefacts from that time are still kept in that room for display. There is a large banyan tree on the banks of the Hooghly, just in front of the temple. It is said that Ramakrishna used to spend all his spare hours under this tree in deep meditation. When I stood inside his room and then under that tree, I felt deep within me an intense longing that cannot be described in words. It was an immense thirst, something noble, urging me to do meaningful service for my nation. Great ideas awoke rapidly in my mind like fresh, newly blossomed flowers. When we were in Kodaikanal, I remember telling you about the recurring dream that I have often experienced from early childhood. This inner urge is surfacing more and more often in recent times in my mind.

Soon after we arrived here, on the very first day of the conference, something remarkable occurred. As soon as I had finished my speech on the stage and returned to my seat, the special representative from China, a lady, came and stood in front of me. She said to me in English, 'Look straight at me for a while without blinking.' I was taken aback! I hesitated in confusion.

Mangaleswari amma was nearby. She asked the lady, 'Why? Why are you asking her to do that?' The Chinese lady's voice was full of emotion as she replied, 'When I look at her face and those wide eyes, I feel some kind of divine bliss within my mind. It is an indescribable sensation. As she was speaking, I was simply watching her face. And yet, I am still longing to gaze upon it even more.' I was so embarrassed! She made me sit still and took a photograph of me. She said she planned to publish my photo in the newspapers in her home country under the title 'The Divine Beauty of South India'. I spoke for forty-five minutes in English at the conference. Mangaleswari amma and many others told me that it was unique and excellent.

My speech was about the meaning of women's lives. Men live only in the present. We women are not like that. The life that a woman leads in this generation has to be one that will bring grace and goodness to the generations that are to follow. Rice plants that will later grow and flourish in the fields start as seedlings in plant nurseries. Like the manoranjan *flower whose aroma reaches places far from where it blooms, the woman of the family has the gift of being able to manage her home while also propagating the essence of righteousness across generations.*

The next morning, in their reports about the ongoing conference, the well-known newspapers in the city, like Amrita Bazaar Patrika *and the* Statesman*, had picked out my speech for special mention. Mangaleswari amma was overflowing with pride! 'With your speeches and your eyes, you are going to conquer the world and be triumphant, my daughter!' she declared. Do you know whom I thought about at that moment, Aravindan? I thought about my father. It gave me goosebumps. And I thought about your words, Aravindan. 'The message of traditional culture and good values must spread through all the streets of the world.'*

In Calcutta, many Tamil people live in the Rashbehari Avenue area and in Howrah. This evening, some of the Tamil organizations have asked me to give a speech. We have planned to leave tomorrow morning by car to visit Santiniketan village, where Tagore set up a university. Some other delegates from various countries will also be coming on the trip.

Now it is getting late, and I have to go and deliver the speech to the Tamil Sangams, so I will stop this letter here and get it to the post office. When we get back from Santiniketan tomorrow, we are supposed to return home to Madurai. But now, Mangaleswari amma is saying, having travelled this far, we should also visit Kasi before heading back home. If that is what is decided, I will write to you again when we get back from Santiniketan.

It doesn't matter which way the election goes. Please don't spoil your health by running around on that account. Please convey my affection to Vasantha, Muruganandam and the others. To Chellam and my brothers and sister, my warmest greetings.

Your loving Poorani.

With intense enthusiasm and an upsurge of love vying for space in his mind, Aravindan read and re-read that letter. The more he read it, the more insights and nuggets of wisdom it revealed.

That night at dinner, Vasantha asked Aravindan about Poorani's letter. He told her, 'It looks as if Poorani and your mother will visit Kasi before returning home.'

'Amma has also written to me about that plan. She says everyone who listened to Poorani's speeches is all praise for her and that news about her speeches formed headlines in the newspapers.'

Just as Aravindan was rising from the dinner table after finishing the habitual snack that comprised his dinner, Vasantha revealed another piece of good news. '*Anna*, I completely forgot to tell you earlier! The day before yesterday, a letter arrived from Radio Ceylon. It said that they would be broadcasting the recording of one of Poorani Akka's speeches in Lanka. The topic is 'Sensing the Divine'. Don't go out anywhere. The time is eight o'clock now. Let us all listen to Akka's speech together.'

Aravindan went up to his room, read for a while, and came downstairs again when it was almost eight thirty. Everyone was there, except Muruganandam. They all sat around the radio set.

The more deeply one senses the divine, the more one grows weary of the life of the flesh. A sense of the divine is not necessary for the mere growth of the body; a taste for food is enough for that. Ours is a religious tradition, which, for thousands of years, has witnessed those who built temples in their minds and filled their thoughts with a sense of the divine. Our great poet Manikkavachagar has written, 'You spurned my body and entered my soul to become one with my senses.' It is through purity of thought and feeling that we can lead righteous lives. Our bodies do not belong to us. We are merely temporary tenants, who have taken these mortal forms on rent. From a philosophical perspective, we can think of our body as a large sore. Every day, when we take a bath, we clean this sore. Our sweat is only pus from the sore. The foul smell of the cactus or the smell of rotting things, that is the smell of this sore. Rice, meat, water – all these are medicines we offer to the sore. Just as we apply ointments and bandage a sore, so too we feed our body and dress it in clothes. Those words of Manikkavachagar, 'You spurned my body but entered my soul,' contain such a wealth of meaning. Eastern religious traditions have always believed that the mind is the seat of prayer. But in modern times, with poverty and the demands of life becoming more and more difficult, it is only the concern for food, for material things, that has become dominant. The sense of the divine has vanished. The only way to preserve righteousness, honesty and culture as strong values in society, the only fence that can protect them from slipping away, is by developing a sense of the divine. That is also the prescription for developing the mind.

Many kinds of thoughts arose that night in Aravindan's mind after listening to Poorani's radio speech. 'She has voiced the very same philosophy that I used that day in Kodaikanal to turn down Mangaleswari amma's idea that Poorani and I should get married right away. But when she quoted Manikkavachagar's verse about ignoring the body and entering the mind, was she echoing my subtle thoughts, or was she criticizing my approach? Maybe she used this verse purely in the context of the topic she had chosen.'

That night, he wrote some more of his thoughts about Poorani in his diary.

> *Poorani, whenever I think I am standing right next to you, looking into your golden, smiling face and lotus eyes, even at that moment, my status is no match for yours. You ascend higher and even higher with each of your speeches. I have told you so often that you will always be the winner in any contest between us to climb upwards in life. At this moment, I am even more convinced about the truth of that. The man standing at the foot of the mountain can't reach to attain the flower that blooms atop the mountain slopes.*

It was only after he had put down these thoughts in his diary that Aravindan was finally able to go to sleep that night. The next morning, he was up before five o'clock. He felt achy and heavy-headed. He thought he would feel better if he had a hot water bath, so he went downstairs to see if Vasantha was up and about. No one had woken up yet. He was just turning to go back upstairs and wait for a while when he heard a bicycle bell and the sound of the newspaper being tossed through the window bars and landing on the floor. He picked up the paper and took it upstairs with him. He turned on the light in the veranda and settled down to read the paper. It was full of election-related news, as well as about fights and quarrels here and there.

He did not find any kind of news that would bring happiness or peace. On the centre page, he came across two news items that distressed him. There was an advertisement announcing that Meenakshi Press would soon come out with a magazine titled *Cinema Surangam*, based on the popular movies of famous film stars. The moment he laid eyes on that advertisement, Aravindan felt a deep sense of betrayal. From the same press that had brought out the scholarly writings of Professor Azhagiya Sittrambalam, this kind of magazine was now going to be released! What a great person Meenakshisundaram had been. What a terrible fate had befallen the press after his death! He told himself sadly, 'Those people plotted to get me out of there because they knew I would never agree to such things. *Che, che*! What low, mean specimens of humanity they are!'

But the next moment he thought, 'But what is the use of my regret at this point? In fact, do I even have the right to feel sad about this?'

Trying to put that unpleasant but unavoidable news behind him, he moved on to the next page. A headline read, 'Many Villagers Die of a Deadly Disease'. The report revealed that in an area to the west of Madurai District, a new deadly disease was continuing to snatch away the lives of many poor people. He felt an overwhelming urge to go to that place at once and do whatever he could to help the suffering people there. He did not want to wait for Muruganandam or Vasantha to wake up to tell them about his plan because they would try to stop him from going.

Muruganandam had already cautioned him against venturing outside the house before the election. 'There is no way Muruganandam will agree to let me go to the disease-infested village to do service,' he told himself. He hesitated for a moment and considered his options. The hesitation did not last long. His natural compassion and his Gandhian instinct to serve the needy won out. He outlined the news report in red on the newspaper so that the household would know where he was headed.

Next, he stuffed two or three changes of clothing in a bag, took out some money from his box and set off. At five forty-five in the morning, a bus was due to leave from Madurai bus stand towards the village where the epidemic was spreading. He hurried along, hoping to catch that bus. He made it well in time and got a seat. There were still a few minutes available before the departure time. Just in case Muruganandam missed seeing the outlined news item he had left behind as a cue, or having seen it did not understand what Aravindan meant, he drew out an old postcard from his pocket, hurriedly scribbled the details and posted it to Muruganandam from the post box at the bus stand.

That postcard addressed to Muruganandam, was delivered at Mangaleswari's house at eleven o'clock that morning. But even before that, he and Vasantha had seen the newspaper with its red marking and had understood Aravindan's plan.

Vasantha urged Muruganandam, 'Please leave at once on the next bus and bring him back home. Or as soon as the driver comes, take the car and go and fetch him. Otherwise, he could catch the deadly disease. And then, what would happen?'

'It's no use, Vasantha. Aravindan is very stubborn when

it comes to matters of social service. He will not listen to anyone.' In a way, it was a relief that Aravindan was away somewhere safe at a time when Burma Man and his henchmen were constantly plotting their next moves. It would also give him, Muruganandam, freedom to pursue Poorani's election campaign more vigorously, without being restrained by Aravindan. For these reasons, Muruganandam was not particularly upset by Aravindan's decision.

In the whirl of election campaign activities and other work, the days rushed by. Muruganandam had a packed schedule every day. He would leave home at six in the morning and come back only past midnight. The competition with Burma Man was heating up. It was a fifty-fifty situation.

On the third day after Aravindan had left for the village to offer social service, Poorani and Mangaleswari returned from Calcutta. Mangaleswari was unwell, and so they had decided to drop their plan to visit Kasi, and instead returned home immediately. They came to know about how Aravindan had been evicted from Meenakshi Press. The news came as a massive blow to Poorani. Although it had happened even before they had left for Calcutta, Aravindan had not breathed a single word about it to her. She was astounded by the strength of will that he must have exercised to keep that news from her. She recalled that on the train journey from Madurai to Madras, she had noticed that Aravindan looked rather preoccupied. She wanted to meet him right away. She got ready to go to the village to which he had headed.

'Don't do that, Akka,' said Muruganandam. 'He will return in two or three days. If he doesn't, I will go and fetch him.'

But for a whole week thereafter, Aravindan did not return, nor was there any news of him. Poorani became more and more worried about him.

CHAPTER 36

Thinking… feeling… melting with tenderness
Filling up with love… tears spring forth
To drench this bodily frame.

While Poorani, Mangaleswari, Vasantha and all the others were frantic with worry about the fact that Aravindan had not returned from the village, nor had he communicated with them, Muruganandam went about seemingly unconcerned, busy with election campaign matters. One morning, as he was about to set out early as usual, Vasantha came and stood in front of him, blocking his way. She was fuming.

'Do you really think what you are doing is right? Are you happy with it? You are not sparing a thought for your family. Akka has stopped eating since yesterday evening. She is crying in her room. Please go to that village immediately, track down Aravindan, wherever he may be, and bring him back here before setting your mind to any other task. Akka wanted to go there, and you stopped her, but you didn't go either. What were you thinking? The whole household is full of gloom. I feel terrible when I look at Akka's face; she is in such agony of mind. Take the car, go to that village at once and bring Aravindan back.'

When Vasantha confronted him with these heartfelt words, Muruganandam went upstairs to Poorani's room. Poorani was lying in bed, worn out, her eyes puffy from weeping. Mangaleswari was seated next to her, trying to talk to her. The children were huddled around, unsmiling and sad. When Muruganandam entered the room, Mangaleswari got up and went towards him. '*Mappillai*, other things can wait, however important they may be. Please go to that village at once and bring Aravindan back. Poorani has been refusing to eat since last evening. She keeps saying, "Leave me alone. Let me go back to my Thirupparankundram house." Aravindan's absence and silence have made her fear all kinds of dreadful things. If Poorani is unhappy, this whole household also descends into gloom. Please, for my sake, go at once. She says she does not want to stand for the elections; she does not want victory or a position of any kind. All she wants is to be assured that Aravindan is safe and well.'

Muruganandam responded to Mangaleswari's plea in a voice loud enough to be heard by Poorani. 'I never imagined that Akka would be so childish. Aravindan has gone there to do social service. There is no one there who would want to harm him. He will return safely.'

Poorani, in turn, addressed Mangaleswari, but what she said was meant for Muruganandam's ears as well.

'I somehow feel very anxious, Amma. Even if I try to calm myself, my mind continues to fester with a feeling of dread. Can I not also go to that village and help him with his work?'

'How can you go now, Poorani? You have to leave for Malaya in a few days,' Mangaleswari reminded her. 'If you go to that village, where there is an epidemic going on, you may fall ill and be unable to travel. Listen to my plan. I will ask my son-in-law Muruganandam to go in our car today and fetch

Aravindan back here. If he refuses to return, you can go and try to persuade him.'

Muruganandam had to put aside a few important tasks that he had planned for the day in connection with the election. Instead, he got into the car and set off for the village.

Ever since her return from Calcutta, Poorani's mind had been uneasy. There was some unspoken feeling of dread lurking in the depths. A sensation of impending tragedy gripped her, like the smell of damp earth just before a storm unleashes its fury. It was like walking alone in darkness, in a hostile environment, expecting every moment to feel a blow descending on one's head from behind. Poorani's mind was walking such a walk all the time, day and night, without respite, dealing with an unseen enemy. Like a frightened child abandoned alone in a dark room, she wanted to wail and weep aloud whenever she was alone. The tears she shed constantly within her mind wanted to come out and be shed in the open. Perhaps it was the chain of distressing events that she had experienced since her return from Calcutta that had precipitated this state of mind.

The day she returned, she had come to know about Meenakshi Press having been snatched away from Aravindan by the scheming Burma Man. She realized how cruel people could be, even when there was no great publicity campaign being conducted on her behalf. She had also come to know that Aravindan had gone to offer his services in a village where a deadly disease was raging. She now better understood the attitude of small-minded people, those whose sole intention was to spread enough lies to blot out the sunlight of truth. She and Aravindan had been trying to rise above this low filth, to ascend to a higher plane. But the quicksand continued to try and pull them down.

'Oh, god, why did you give us minds that yearn to soar high above the common earth? Why did you give us thoughts that bloom like the *kurinji* flower, only on mountain heights? Could you not, at least, have given me the desire to lead the kind of life that my friends Kamala and Kamu are leading now?' When she was in Aravindan's company, she had no thought for her physical self. But now that she was alone with her own thoughts, she asked herself despairingly, 'Why is my mind torturing me and my body this way?' Dark thoughts that she herself could not fully understand caused continuous agony in her mind. She wanted nothing more than to go off by herself somewhere and weep long and hard.

That night, it was past eleven o'clock when Muruganandam returned along with Aravindan. Poorani had been lying awake and was the first to hear the sound of the car driving up to the door. She ran downstairs and opened the door eagerly. The very next moment, her eagerness turned into alarm and distress. This Aravindan was not the one who had left for the village. In his zeal to ease the burdens of others in the world, he had taken those upon himself like a Buddha. The very disease that had brought him to that village in a spirit of service had invaded his body severely. His sturdy frame was reduced to skin and bone, his golden complexion darkened. His eyes, which had always held a smile, were now just deep hollows in his gaunt face. The driver and Muruganandam had to help him out of the car and to the doorway. He swayed and staggered as he walked.

Muruganandam said in a voice choked with emotion, 'Akka, it was a good thing that I followed your advice and went to the village. He has been toiling for all hours under the harsh sun, without proper food and water. In his eagerness to serve, he himself caught this severe disease. Could he not have written a letter, at least a couple of lines, to one of us? Instead, he was just lying in this state in some farmer's hut. There is not even a single doctor in that village. Once in two days, a licensed medical practitioner from a village ten miles away visits the village. But Aravindan has not been regularly taking the medicines that the physician prescribed for him. The man even sought him out to ask about his health, but each time, Aravindan sent him away, saying, "I'm all right. I will survive. Just save the others in the village who are suffering from this disease." When I saw him lying on the damp mud floor of that hut on a thin layer of prickly straw, running a temperature of a hundred and three degrees, I started crying, Akka. Without listening to any further arguments, I just took him straight to the car and brought him home.'

Poorani felt like howling aloud in shock and grief when she saw Aravindan in such a condition. They took him to a room upstairs and laid him on a bed. Poorani went up to him but could not think of what to say or ask in that extremely emotional state of mind. Her gaze was fixed on Aravindan's face, her eyes swimming in tears. Tears appeared in his eyes as a response. In a weak, hollow voice he told her, 'I received your letter. I enjoyed reading it, and I also enjoyed the fragrance of the *champak* flowers you had enclosed. I listened to your Lanka speech on the radio.'

'All that doesn't matter now. Who is going to praise me now? Isn't it because of me that the press which you managed so loyally all these years has sent you out? Wasn't I the cause of all those hardships you had to endure during my election campaign? What good has come to you because of me? You have brought me fame throughout the world. What have you got from me? What can you ever get from me?'

For the first time in her life, Poorani wept openly in Aravindan's presence. At that moment, she wept like an ordinary woman with ordinary emotions.

'Don't cry, Poorani. Don't be so foolish. I hate to see you cry. Why are you weeping like this now? What terrible thing has happened?'

'When I see you in this condition, half the person you were, how can I not weep? Was anyone going to find fault with you if you did not go to that village? How thin and sick you have become!'

'Poorani, in your Lanka speech, you yourself described the body as a big sore! If I have only half my body, doesn't it mean that half the sore is healed?' Even in that weak condition, Aravindan proved that he had not lost his wit or sense of humour.

Meanwhile, Muruganandam had rushed to fetch the doctor. Hearing voices, Mangaleswari and Vasantha woke and came into the room where Aravindan was resting. Poorani burst out in a voice verging on sobs, 'Amma, look at him! See how he has become!' Mangaleswari and Vasantha were shocked at the change in Aravindan. Vasantha hurried away to fetch a thermometer. He had a fever of more than a hundred and two degrees.

Muruganandam arrived with the doctor. After examining Aravindan, the doctor prescribed a course of chloromycin tablets. As he was leaving, he took Muruganandam aside and told him in private, 'It looks like typhoid. He has gone five to six days without treatment. There is no need to panic, but it is best to watch his condition closely. He could get over it in another ten or eleven days, or it could even go on like this for forty days. Anyway, don't say anything to alarm anybody now. I will come and see him again tomorrow.'

Muruganandam's normally strong check on his emotions was now challenged. He felt apprehensive after hearing the doctor's words. Tears came to his eyes. It was a very unsettling feeling to see his close friend reduced to such a condition.

Meanwhile, Mangaleswari also spoke frankly to Aravindan. 'Aravindan, you should never have been so foolish. It was foolish of you, in the first place, to go into a village that is infested with such a serious disease. Having gone there to do service, should you not have been responsible enough to look after your own health as well? The moment you became ill, you should have come back here. What's the point of staying there stubbornly and saying that fate should take its course?'

Nobody slept a wink the rest of the night in that household. Except Aravindan. He alone slipped into a deep sleep of exhaustion. The next morning, his temperature was lower. But by evening, it had climbed again to a hundred and two degrees. The doctor made regular visits. Every morning, the temperature would be lower, but it would rise again towards the evening.

No one had any peace of mind. They all went around looking gloomy. Their anxiety would dip when his temperature dipped and rise again when his temperature rose. Poorani sat near his bedside to be of help to him. There was not a moment when her eyes were free of tears or her mind free of dread.

Poorani cancelled her travel plans to Malaya. Meanwhile, the election date was approaching, but that was not a subject on anyone's mind in the house at that time. Even Muruganandam stopped going out for campaign-related work. All he cared about was that Aravindan recover from his illness. Although he did not himself spend any time on the campaign, he allowed his friends, who had been working with him, to continue doing their work. 'Why interfere with something which was proceeding on its own? he thought. Mangaleswari had arranged for pujas to be conducted every day for Aravindan's health at the Murugan Temple at Thirupparankundram and at the Meenakshi Temple and Sokkanadhar Temple in Madurai.

Many doctors came and went – junior ones as well as senior ones. Aravindan received all the latest treatments available for bringing down his fever and curing the disease. But the pattern continued. Every morning it would seem that the fever was subsiding, but after three in the afternoon, it would rise again rapidly. Poorani sat near the head of his bed constantly, weeping. This became a daily feature. When high fever made him delirious, Aravindan would often mutter her name, 'Poorani… Poorani,' and she would feel a fleeting thrill.

Watching Aravindan lying in bed like a broken reed day after day, Poorani was in constant inner agony. His face, his smile, which she could always picture clearly in her mind, had given her the enthusiasm to go out and make a mark in the world. They had given her the confidence to believe that her efforts would always bear fruit. But that face had now become unrecognizable. Gone were the vigour and glow. The smile was absent. The man who used to stride energetically, like a strong bullock, was now lying weakly in bed, a mere shadow of his former self. That golden, sturdy form was now all skin and bone.

In the mornings, when his fever dipped, Poorani would sometimes talk to him, eyes filled with tears and a quiver in her voice. 'Oh, why did this happen to you? Why have you become like this?' she would moan.

'Why do you cry, Poorani? Don't cry. I will recover and get up from this bed. I will get back to the way I was earlier. From now on, I can also accompany you to Burma, Malaya and other places. I no longer have the press to run, so all my time will be free from now on.' In those moments, there would be a hint of the old spark in Aravindan's eyes.

He would try to encourage her and give her hope. 'Just wait and watch, Poorani! The doctor himself said that when this kind of disease leaves the body, a newer, healthier body emerges. Did you not describe the body as a "big sore"? So, that sore of mine is now healing. I will be up and about soon and take a head bath. Mark my words, Poorani! Next Monday, I will compete with you to climb Thirupparankundram Hill. You were always annoyed if I lingered behind on our climbs. You insisted that we should both climb at the same rate together.'

Poorani sat constantly by his bedside, her face drooping with grief, her gaze never leaving his face. He did what he could to lift her spirits, trying to talk and smile like his old self. When he came to know that she had cancelled her trip to Malaya, he was angry with her.

'Why should you cancel your trip on my account? Aren't there enough people in this house? Won't Vasantha and Muruganandam look after me? You should have travelled with Mangaleswari amma as you had planned.'

Poorani, in turn, was upset with his argument. 'What a silly idea! I don't want to go anywhere. All I want is for you to recover and get back on your feet. Nothing is more important to me than you.' Her lips twitched with emotion as she spoke.

For four whole weeks, Aravindan continued in the same condition, with his fever dipping in the mornings and rising in the evenings. The doctor had said that a complete cure could take as long as forty days. Meanwhile, election day arrived. None of them had looked forward to it, and now none of them welcomed it either. Because some of Muruganandam's friends came and insisted that he should go with them, he went to the polling booth and roamed around there for a while. It appeared that the number of votes for Poorani might actually exceed what Muruganandam had hoped for.

Many of the cars and horse carts in the city had been hired by Burma Man to go around and bring the supporters of the Pudu Mandapam publisher to the polling booth. But the interesting thing was that in many of those vehicles, Muruganandam's friends themselves were bringing Poorani's supporters to the polling station! The Pudu Mandapam candidate seemed to have no doubt that he would win thanks to Burma Man's elaborate plans. In fact, that was the rumour going around the town as well. Muruganandam, however, remained confident and did not give up hope. When the long-awaited election day was over, the town took a respite from all the excitement till it was time to count the votes.

That night, after the polls closed, Muruganandam told Aravindan that he was confident of Poorani's victory. Aravindan smiled. 'Let us see. If what you say comes true, if Poorani really wins this, it is truly a victory for righteousness.'

That day and the next, Aravindan's fever did not rise as before. The disease seemed to be under control. He asked

Poorani to sit near him and tell him details of her trips. He enjoyed her descriptions of various places and events. He made her play recordings of her speeches and praised her for them.

'Poorani, you know… that song that ends "True love brimmed and spilt over" by Ramalinga Adigal? Please sing that song for me once. I want to hear it directly from you. I want my eyes to be looking at you while my ears enjoy listening to you,' he pleaded like a little child asking for a favour. She sang as he had requested. When she finished singing and looked at his face, she saw tears brimming in his eyes.

'Why are you crying?' she asked him. 'You're not a child!'

'These are tears of joy, Poorani. Your speeches and your song have made me a little child again.'

'You're always saying something like that to tease me!' she protested.

Aravindan looked steadily into her eyes and smiled. She bent her head shyly. 'Here, read these,' he told her, holding out his diaries. 'You will understand for yourself the kind of sweet perfume your speeches have spread in my mind.' Momentarily, his face glowed with all its old intensity and energy. The next moment, he heaved a sigh. An expression of yearning passed over his face and eyes. Uneasily, he turned over in bed.

That same evening, after two days of respite, his fever mounted rapidly. The doctor visited and prescribed a fresh medicine. That evening was also when the results of the election were to be announced for Poorani's constituency. Muruganandam had gone to the counting centre along with Vasantha, Chellam and the children, Sambandan and Mangaiyarkarasi. Mangaleswari, meanwhile, had gone to the Meenakshi Temple. Poorani was alone in the house with Aravindan.

Aravindan's fever continued to rise steadily. His temperature crossed a hundred and three degrees, and he became delirious. He started losing consciousness. Poorani was terrified.

Just then, she heard Mangaleswari's voice from downstairs. 'Poorani, you have won the election. They say the vote difference was five thousand.' Her voice was full of joy. She came into the room, her face mirroring the joy in her voice.

She was confronted by the sight of Poorani in a terrible state of tension. Poorani burst out in a voice trembling with fear amidst her deep sobs. 'Amma, let the result go to hell. Please call the doctor at once. Aravindan is very ill. He is having a seizure. He is unconscious.'

CHAPTER 37

Where countless people languished in distress
In the great land of Tamil Nadu,
There arose from this soil a young man who strove
to usher in a gradual transformation in their lives.
He stepped forward on a mission
to destroy outdated, mouldy ideas.
Such a one, who brought us a thrill of hope
Is going... is no more... is gone.

By the time the election result was announced in the Madurai District official's office, it was very late in the evening. Darkness was beginning to set in, but it was a full moon night. The moon had appeared in the sky, shedding its milky light below. In celebration of the election results, Muruganandam and his group, who had gathered at the entrance of the counting centre, were filled with joy when the assembled crowd broke out into full-throated shouts of 'Long live Poorani Devi'. Every face glowed with the acknowledgement that righteousness had won that day. Many of the people held garlands in their hands, ready to felicitate Poorani on her victory. It was a great disappointment to the crowd that Poorani did not appear. Muruganandam turned to his wife and said, 'Vasantha, take the car and go home. Give the good news about the victory to

Akka, Aravindan and Amma. Tell Akka that a lot of people have come here, hoping to greet and congratulate her in person. I am going to bring them all home. Ask Akka to be ready. Make plans for a grand feast this evening. When we left the house earlier in the day, Aravindan's fever had come down and he was feeling better. Help him downstairs and make him sit in the hall. We will be there soon.'

So Vasantha, Chellam and the children returned in the car to Mangaleswari's house. Meanwhile, the well-wishers with their garlands thronged around Muruganandam. Every ward and every zone in the constituency had sent its representative, each carrying a garland. An elderly man came up to Muruganandam and told him earnestly, 'This is indeed a remarkable victory. Even with no grandiose promotions or expensive advertisements, she has won convincingly on the strength of the belief and trust the people have placed in her. This is truly an example of the victory of truth and righteousness. It must be celebrated appropriately. The full moon has come out in all its glory. Let us hire a horse chariot, adorn it with flowers and take her on a procession around the four streets adjoining the temple. We must have a marching band, drummers and fireworks.'

Muruganandam was in such an elated mood that he could not turn down anyone's wishes. Although he knew that such celebrations would not be to the liking of either Poorani or Aravindan, it was not possible to ignore the flood tide of affection that was pouring out from the supporters. Each of them felt that her victory was also their personal victory. They started making all kinds of elaborate plans and arrangements to celebrate. In that situation, Muruganandam felt he had no choice but to go along with their plans and participate in them.

The arrangements proceeded at lightning speed. It was decided that the grand victory procession by chariot would commence near the *mandapam* close to the shrine of Amman, go to Thanappa Mudali Street to pick up Poorani and then go on a procession around the four streets abutting the temple.

In hardly any time at all, a chariot drawn by a pair of white horses, decorated with jasmine flowers as if for a wedding procession, was brought to the starting point. The band started playing, and the drummers joined in. The crowds gathered as for a temple festival. Muruganandam stood at the head of the procession holding a large tuberose garland. Others stood nearby holding various garlands. Slogans praising Poorani and hailing her victory rose loudly from the assembled crowd. The procession started on its way slowly, elegantly, through a sea of sound. It went past the south *gopuram* into West Gopuram Street and turned into Thanappa Mudali Street.

The two white horses strode majestically along the street, drawing the elegantly decorated grand chariot. Fireworks burst in multicoloured showers in the sky. It was as if happiness itself had found expression through light and sound. The music from the band set hearts and feet dancing, such was the magic of the moment. The air resonated with melody and swirled with the sweet aroma of flowers. From the houses on both sides of the street, onlookers gazed at the spectacle and participated in the joy. The procession was nearing Mangaleswari's house. There was very little distance left to cover.

'*Ayyo*! What is happening? Why is someone shouting in agitation? Why are the words "Stop! Stop!" being heard above the joyful sounds of the procession?'

Vasantha was running towards them like a woman possessed

as she continued to scream 'Stop!' She was dishevelled, her loose hair flew in disarray around her head. The garland slipped from Muruganandam's hands. He trembled in shock. The music ceased as though it had been choked off, plunging the street into a sudden silence. Everybody stood still as though frozen in that moment of time. Muruganandam wailed and rushed towards the house. The doctor emerged with head bowed and a solemn expression on his face. In the hall downstairs, Chellam, Sambandan and Mangaiyarkarasi were sobbing and weeping aloud. Upstairs, Mangaleswari and Poorani were wailing as grief tore their hearts.

Muruganandam felt that heaven and earth and all other things in the universe had shattered into bits and were falling on his head, battering him. As he entered Aravindan's room, he choked back the despairing cry, 'Aravinda!' that rose to his lips from the depths of his tortured soul. Deep sobs racked his body. Poorani lay on the floor like an uprooted plant, unable to do anything but weep.

On the bed, Aravindan had attained his salvation. Released from his hitherto tiny existence, wherein he had been walking, talking and living on the soil of this Earth, he had transcended into another realm. That noble soul, the one who had always placed the welfare of others above his own, had been released from earthly bondage. He had insisted that Poorani's victory should be attained through the path of truth alone. His wish had come true. But he had gone before he could savour that victory of truth over evil!

'Oh, my dear one! You have gone and left us all bereft!' wailed Mangaleswari.

As memories crowded into her mind, Poorani's tears welled

forth as though a dam had burst within her. She wailed in utter helplessness and despair like an abandoned soul. She recalled his words from a few days ago. 'I will be up and about soon and take a head bath. Mark my words, Poorani! Next Monday, I will compete with you to climb Thirupparankundram Hill.'

'Oh, why could my breath not be stilled with his,' she moaned inwardly in despair. 'In the classic *Silappathigaram*, the poet Ilango has described how when Pandian died his wife sent her own soul in search of his. Can I send my own life in search of Aravindan's life? How? How?' The tears flowed endlessly.

Those on the street outside, who had been holding garlands, now started coming into the house one by one, like silent shadows. They stood outside Aravindan's room with heads bowed, eyes wet and hearts heavy with grief.

One of the older men came slowly into the room, still holding a garland. In a faltering, trembling voice, he said, 'Young man, your life has not ended today. You will not die. In this Tamil land that is beset with poverty and misery, you will be born again and again, in every generation. You must do that to serve our suffering people.'

Having spoken these heartfelt words haltingly and painfully, he came forward and placed the garland gently on Aravindan's body. His words and his deed moved everyone greatly. Poorani looked up briefly from the floor where she lay weeping. The old man's words had made a deep impression on her mind. Now, as she looked at Aravindan lying in bed adorned with a garland, he appeared in her eyes to be alive, with his familiar teasing smile. This was what he had looked like when he had promised to climb Thirupparankundram Hill with her. Even when he was lying lifeless, how beautiful that garland looked on him!

Although she had fallen to the floor in grief earlier, unable to stay on her feet, a sudden urge gripped her at that moment. She rose slowly and wiped her eyes. She walked up to the doorway, where many were waiting with their garlands. She took the garlands one by one from them and placed them on Aravindan. She stood back and admired his beauty. As she saw him lying there with the pile of garlands on his body, the thought went through her like a stabbing pain, 'I should have placed a garland like one of these around his neck when he was alive.' The thought brought her tears pouring out again.

She had once given a talk at the Women's Sangam on the topic of Thilakavathy. Little did she know at the time that she herself was destined to experience only a relationship of minds, just as Thilakavathy had had to do. Poorani thought to herself, 'Thilakavathy's loved one perished in the Chozha war. My Aravindan's life was claimed in the war of life itself.' The thought deepened her distress even further. Poorani remembered what her father had once said about Thilakavathy: 'Thilakavathy died in her body but lived on inwardly, in her mind. Such a noble woman can be born only in this Tamil soil.' She shuddered.

A small voice spoke up from the depths of her numbing grief. 'I have a brother called Thirunavukkarasu. I have to live to bring up and support my young brothers and sister.' Thilakavathy's life story had captivated her ever since she was a mere child of five years. She now relived it in her mind and grieved afresh. Jumbled thoughts raged through her mind, stinging painfully like a nest of scorpions.

After a while, she stopped weeping. Her eyes were no longer dull and lifeless. She touched Aravindan's feet reverentially and pressed her palms against her closed eyelids. With her head bowed, she made her way past the group in the doorway. She went into the next room and shut the door. Sounds could be heard from the closed room as if something was being broken.

In a short while, Poorani re-emerged. The *pottu* on her forehead had been wiped away. Her bangles were gone. Her ears, nose and neck were bare of ornaments. Like a sea that turned calm after its waves had died down, the young woman walked slowly up to where Muruganandam was standing. She told him, 'Please proceed with what needs to be done.' Her face reflected an unearthly serenity.

What needed to be done was done.

The procession that had arrived as a joyful victory procession departed towards the cremation ground as a mourning procession. That night, under the light of the full moon, Aravindan's mortal remains were consigned to the flames on the north bank of the Vaigai River. A noble life was reduced to ashes and became one with the earth. The one whose face had been like 'the full moon with smudges wiped clean and a teasing smile drawn upon it, had departed without adding a tilak to that face. Those lips, twin corals set against the milky glow of pearls, would never smile again. Poorani had lost her support, her companion in her quest to climb ever upwards.

It was past two in the morning by the time the household returned. In the room where Aravindan had lain, his diaries stood in mute testimony. Upon the pile of diaries lay the watch that Poorani had lovingly bought for him from Lanka. When she put the watch on his wrist, she had told him smilingly, 'I hereby attach Time to you and let it run.' To which he had replied, 'We are mere humans. It is we who are tied to the hands of Time and have been asked to run.'

She recalled his smile and his voice as he had uttered those words. When she read his diary entries in which he had compared her to a *kurinji* flower, she was moved beyond words. From that day onwards, it was as if her mind was a cemetery for buried thoughts. She was steeped in contemplation of long-buried memories.

A few weeks later, the newspapers announced that Poorani had voluntarily given up her elected post. She said she did not want it. Before she made that decision, many had tried to talk her out of it, but she insisted that she did not want a role in government but would instead like to spend her life in social service and the upliftment of the people. Her decision amazed and perplexed most people.

Like a raw wound, grief overwhelmed her for some time. Out of grief was born a new wisdom. The inner eye opened. She became aware of the true meaning of life. With her gender aiding her journey, she ascended to the level of a modern-day Manimekalai in her understanding of the philosophy of life. She realized, 'Each person experiences whatever life has destined for him. It is no use clamouring for favours from life's grasp like little children clamouring for sweets from their mother's hands.'

She tried to comfort herself with this reality. She delivered lectures both locally and at international events. In many foreign countries, she won renown for her enlightening speeches. She immersed herself in a variety of social service projects. She was at last living the dream that had visited her many times as she was growing up. At last, she was going into the darkness among the poor and needy, holding up her lamp to light their way and her own. Hers was a noble life of deep knowledge and wholesome service. She watched her brothers and little sister grow and prosper under her care and tried not to regret what she herself had missed in her life. One could even say she covered up any regret that she may have felt.

Although she propagated philosophical truths and high ethics through her orations, she continued to be beset by a nagging inner pain that refused to subside. Whenever she walked up Thirupparankundram Hill along the path that led to the temple, there on one side, carved for eternity into a rock like a testament, were their names: Poorani – Aravindan. Tears would fill her eyes.

Wherever she came across young, handsome men of honest character with noble ideas, she pictured Aravindan. She yearned for him to be born again to grace the Earth, just as the old man with the garland had prayed on the day Aravindan died. Neither wisdom nor philosophical arguments could quench the embers of her sorrow.

The years rolled by. She was now past fifty. Yet her body was robust, her hair still dark with no hint of grey and her beautiful teeth still white and attractive. Her brother's young daughter smiled sweetly and remarked in her childish voice in all innocence, 'My Amma *patti* (mother's mother) is the same age as you, but she has grey hair and no teeth. How is it that you are not like that?' Poorani had no idea how to respond to the child's question. She sat down stunned.

Grief gripped her, and tears sprang to her eyes. Suddenly, the lurking sorrow that had made her mourn inwardly for years leapt into the open. She wept aloud. Her little niece was startled and stunned into silence by such an unexpected reaction. She did not understand why her remark would bring this kind of response from her aunt.

Another twelve years pass by.

Poorani is in Kodaikanal to attend a conference. It is once again a year that sees the flowering of the *kurinji* plants. The hillsides are covered with a carpet of *kurinji* flowers. After the conference concluded that morning, Poorani has accompanied some of her colleagues to the lakeside in the evening. The younger women decide to go boating. Poorani sets off alone for a stroll. Along the way, she comes to a photo studio. She stops abruptly and stares fixedly through the window of the photo studio.

There, on display, is the photograph that she and Aravindan had taken together all those years ago. It is as if someone has scratched an old wound and revived a powerful yearning. The dam she had been trying to construct in her mind against the tide of grief gives way. That picture, those garlands, the *kurinji* flowers blooming everywhere remind her of the one who had first brought all the beauty of those flower-draped hills to life for her and helped her to refine her senses to celebrate Nature's magnificence. He is no more, and her grief is fresh and agonizing again.

'We are together in a picture. But we were never together in life.' A sense of enormous loss fills her mind. She feels like running away somewhere to weep and wail aloud, to cry till death mercifully takes her away. At this moment, she is not a middle-aged woman of more than fifty years, a much-respected speaker famous for her mastery of philosophy and noble ideals. She is once again a young woman who has lost her true love forever. How can knowledge and philosophy offer antidotes to grief?

She is seized with a strong urge to go to the Kurinji Andavar

Temple, sit at the spot where she and Aravindan had sat and talked all those years earlier, open the floodgates of her accumulated grief and try to dissolve it in tears. She, who has been leading a life of service, advising and exhorting people everywhere, inspiring them through her words and deeds, that paragon of virtue that the world has come to know, acknowledges that her heart aches for what might have been. A sense of abandonment, of being orphaned, numbs her.

She sits on the hillock near the temple. In a lonely spot, away from watching eyes, Poorani lets down her emotional defences and sobs aloud. She is alone in the universe. All hint of other human life has been extinguished. Only the mountains, spreading mutely on all sides, cradle her among them. All the sorrow left in the world, all the pain, anguish and longing have come to live in her heart. It is a raw agony that no words can describe.

The temple bell tolls. Is it a message from Kurinji Andavan himself? Is he calling her to set aside her burden of sorrow and come to him?

Poorani rises unsteadily to her feet. Like a sleepwalker, she stumbles towards the shrine and stands before Lord Murugan. The priest holds the camphor flame high to illuminate the face of the Lord. A sharp tremor runs through Poorani.

Is this true? Are her eyes deceiving her? She opens her eyes wider and looks again. Lord Murugan's face is Aravindan's face. The small camphor flame expands into a large halo of light. In the centre of it appears Aravindan's face. He is smiling his familiar teasing smile. Is he trying to call out to her? Is he telling her, 'Leave your burden of sorrow behind and come here?'

She starts muttering to herself like one possessed. 'Aravindan! There is nectar in your smile. Nectar has the power to nourish lives.' Aravindan's smile enters deep into all the dark crevices of her heart and spreads its light where sorrow had burrowed in and grown.

Poorani sings softly under her breath.

Give me release from rebirth!

But if I am to be born again

May the memory of you live forever in me.

She wipes the tears from her eyes. She erases the sorrow from her heart. When she looks once more at the Lord's face, it is Aravindan's face, and he is smiling. She folds her hands in prayer, turns and walks away. She walks slowly along a path, somewhere in those endless mountains. On both sides, *kurinji* flowers in their hundreds crowd the hills and sway in the breeze. The evening hours give way to dusk. Poorani walks on.

In the garden of the universe, yet again, another flower wilts and dies.

AFTERWORD

A DREAM IS FULFILLED

On the flowering plant called Time
The flower of a dream has bloomed
While the sorrows caused by cruel Fate
Have withered and died away.

I sense that, before they reach this part of the book, my readers would have become very angry with me. 'A virtuous young man like Aravindan should not have died,' they would protest. They would take me to task, even condemn me severely, for letting him die. To all of them, I have only this to say – Aravindan is not dead! In today's headlines or tomorrow's, or whenever you come across any young man born on this Tamil soil who embodies all the noble qualities of Aravindan, it means Aravindan has been reborn. Respect and honour him.

Wherever you come across a young woman of virtue and honour, of knowledge and culture, who works selflessly among the poor, homeless and sick, who carries the lamp of wisdom into the darkness of deprivation like a guiding star, a Thilakavathy, think of her as Poorani reborn. Respect her and honour her.

Aravindan and Poorani are not mere characters in a novel. They are embodiments of the Tamil philosophy. They exemplify the ideals of Tamil manhood and womanhood. Only flesh and blood can perish; the highest ideals can never die. They are matters that transcend the mortal frame and exist on a higher plane. In this story, Poorani does not die. Death can never touch her.

For more than a hundred years now, Poorani has been spreading knowledge about the Tamil language and culture like Avvaiyar. She is Mother Goddess. Just as the *kurinji* flower graces the slopes of the mountains only once in many years, a woman like Poorani flowers only rarely. She is one who deserves to be celebrated in poetry and song like the *kurinji* is in literature. I was able to write Poorani's story only in the medium of prose. Alas, I do not possess the poetic talent of Aravindan!

I want my Poorani to keep walking forward always, with a lamp in hand, shedding light in the darkness of poverty, ignorance, disease and death. Let me end by wishing her well on your behalf and my own.

Long live Poorani! Long live Aravindan!

CASTE AWAY: PERSPECTIVES ON CASTE-EQUALITY STRUGGLES IN TAMIL NADU

NA. VANAMAMALAI

Translated and with an introduction by JOSHUA GNANASELVAN

NATIONALIZED TAMIL BOOKS IN TRANSLATION SERIES

A pithy and momentous collection of essays on caste-equality struggles in Tamil Nadu by scholar and social activist Na. Vanamamalai

Offering a meticulous exploration of Tamil Nadu's intricate caste dynamics, Na. Vanamamalai's pivotal work unveils the endeavours of 'lower-caste' communities in challenging established hierarchies. It spans the Chola dynasty to the early part of the twentieth century. Through extensive research and insightful analysis, the renowned scholar elucidates how certain communities strategically appropriated the *varna* system, elevating their social status. Drawing on various source texts – historical documents, verses by socially committed ascetics, court judgments – the work demonstrates how the Chola kings tactically offered concessions to different caste clusters, thereby navigating a delicate balance between benefits and exploitation.

Caste Away compellingly argues that caste-based conflicts were fundamentally manifestations of class antagonisms, and challenges conventional interpretations, showing how the pursuit of caste equality was aimed not at creating an egalitarian society but at elevating the social standing of specific castes.

ALSO AVAILABLE BY HACHETTE INDIA

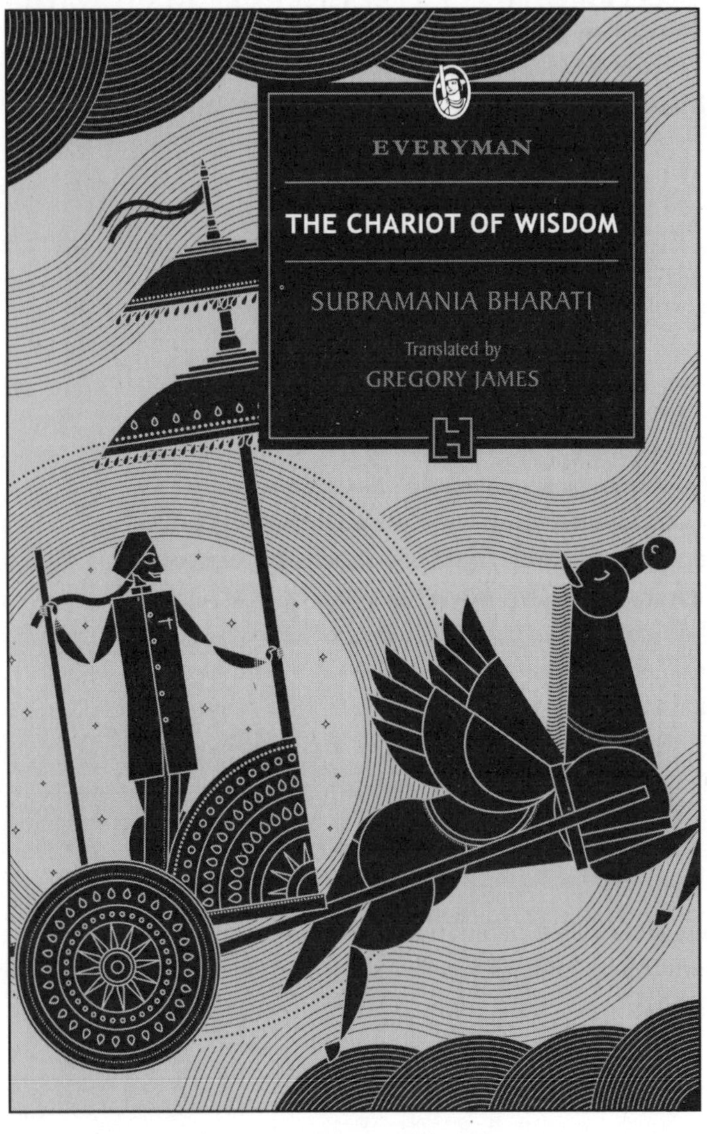

THE CHARIOT OF WISDOM

SUBRAMANIA BHARATI

Translated and with an introduction by GREGORY JAMES

SPECIAL BILINGUAL EDITION

NATIONALIZED TAMIL BOOKS IN TRANSLATION SERIES

Breaking the constraints of style and imagery central to classical Tamil literature, Mahakavi C. Subramania Bharati (1882–1921) heralded a new era for the language by making it simpler, thereby encouraging a wider readership. His prodigious contribution to the writings of his homeland – done while in exile during a tumultuous time in the nation's freedom movement – has since propelled his stature to that of a revered literary figure in the subcontinent.

In *The Chariot of Wisdom*, his only novella, a vexed journalist, plagued by material worries and the daily attrition of twentieth-century, British-occupied India, escapes into a daydream to realms mystical and unexplored. He navigates an imaginary chariot through The World of Tranquillity, The World of Pleasure, The World of Truth and The World of Dharma, and finds his values and ideals informing, competing and often contradicting one another. As his self-doubts deepen, he battles the notion that peace and happiness come at a price.

A critical examination of a colonized, afflicted civilization marred by corruption and greed, Bharati's pioneering work speaks to a morally wounded country through astute observations and lively humour. Translated with refined intellectual acuity by Gregory James, this modern classic – as timely today as it was a century ago – is a cleverly masked plea to the people of a distracted nation to rally together in pursuit of a just society.

ALSO AVAILABLE BY HACHETTE INDIA

THE SOUND OF WAVES

'KALKI' R. KRISHNAMURTHY
Translated by GOWRI RAMNARAYAN

NATIONALIZED TAMIL BOOKS IN TRANSLATION SERIES

WINNER OF THE FICCI BOOK OF THE YEAR (2023) – BEST TRANSLATION SPECIAL JURY AWARD

A fractured country on the verge of freedom finds its people navigating the slippery crevices of love, morality and nationalism.

To escape the despair of his all-consuming, failed relationship with Dharini, Raghavan agrees to meet Lalita in an arranged match. Finding Lalita's cousin, the vivacious and captivating Sita, a far more amenable fit, he marries her instead. With a charming wife and a powerful government job in pre-Partition Delhi adding to his smug contentment, Raghavan turns a blind eye to the evils of the British Raj. Along comes Sita's cousin Surya, a dauntless revolutionary burning to right all wrongs. His commitment to the socialist credo leads him to Dharini, a young and spirited party member, the woman Raghavan continues to long for. Cracks appear in the brittle foundations of their lives as the characters move across rural Thanjavur, Madras, Bombay, Karachi, New Delhi, Agra, Calcutta and Lahore.

With poignant detail and lyrical prose, Kalki's tour de force lays bare the emotions of ordinary people grappling with extraordinary changes, their circumstances riven with misfortunes, disasters and the carnage of Partition. *The Sound of Waves* is an impassioned tribute to everyday citizens and their woes, and an acute commentary on the aspirations of an emerging nation.

This book by Gowri Ramnarayan is the English translation of the bestselling Tamil novel *Alai Osai* by freedom fighter and novelist 'Kalki' R. Krishnamurthy (1899–1954).

ALSO AVAILABLE BY HACHETTE INDIA

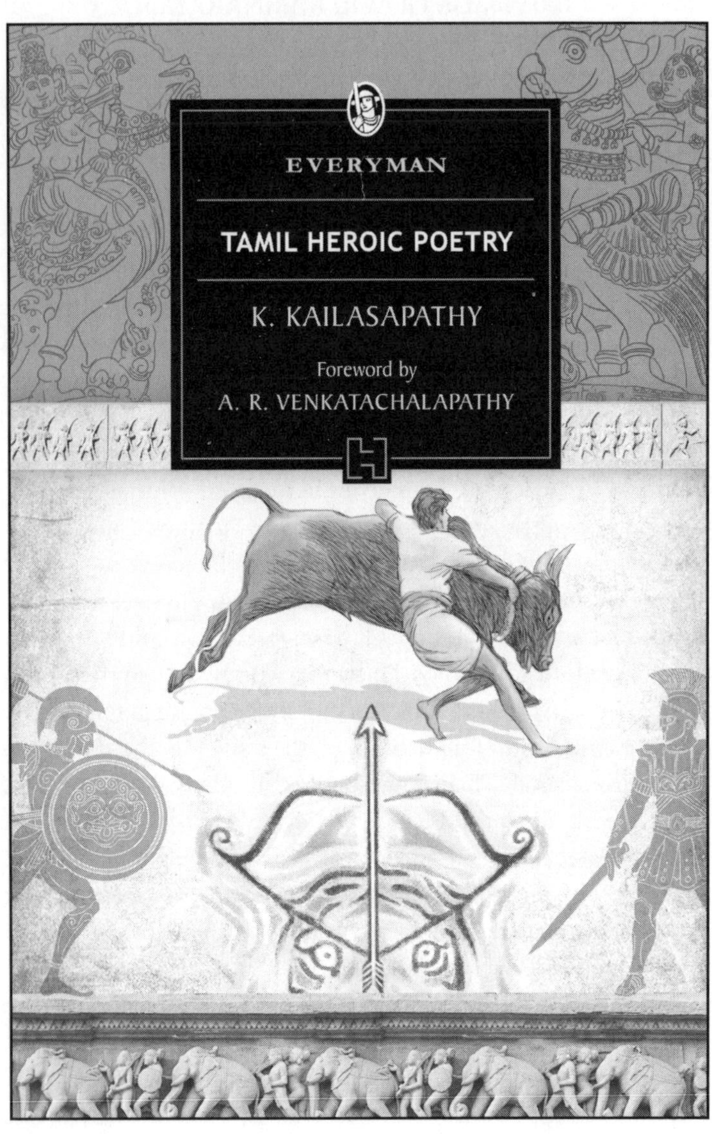

TAMIL HEROIC POETRY

K. KAILASAPATHY

Foreword by A.R. VENKATACHALAPATHY

An elegant and thorough examination of the riches of Sangam poetry

In this acclaimed comparative study, K. Kailasapathy, the celebrated Sri Lankan academic and critic, introduces and interprets ancient Tamil poems and examines the stylistic heritage, themes and motifs pervading Sangam poetry while building the literary corpus's bridge to heroic poetry in other languages – most notably Greek. He identifies the formulaic expression, stock phrases and overarching sensibilities pervasive in the poems and, going much against the popular grain, expands on the notion that oral verse-making is central to Sangam poetry.

A nod to Milman Parry, this deeply necessary exploration of our neglected past is an engaging and accessible discourse on one of our most fertile literary ages and, with much agility, connects the dots in studying early Tamil poetry for a modern reader.